Eduardo smelled nic[illegible]ably doused himself in this [illegible]table level. She leaned into him, seeking some leve[illegible].

'Darling, I'm freezing,' Harriet said then. 'Shall we go back to my lovely warm club and talk about this some more?' Sliding off the bench, she held out her hand to Chiara and hauled her to her feet. 'Come on, baby.'

'I'm not going to Italy, Harriet,' she said almost aggressively. 'Not now, not ever.'

Harriet's voice was soothing. 'You don't have to go if you don't want to.'

'That's right, I don't have to do anything I don't want to do.' She dropped Harriet's hand and, without a backward glance at Eduardo, stalked off, tears stinging at her eyes.

Nicky Pellegrino grew up on Merseyside but spent childhood summers in southern Italy. There she learned to live to eat, instead of eating to live. Nicky now lives in Auckland, New Zealand, where she is the editor of a weekly women's magazine. She hoards her annual leave so she can return to Italy regularly to eat the best mozzarella. *Delicious* is her first novel.

Delicious

Nicky Pellegrino

ORION

An Orion paperback

First published in Great Britain in 2005
by Orion
This paperback edition published in 2005
by Orion Books Ltd,
Orion House, 5 Upper St Martin's Lane,
London, WC2H 9EA

All characters in this book are fictitious, and any resemblance to actual persons living or dead is purely coincidental.

A CIP catalogue record for this book is available from the British Library.

Typeset by The Spartan Press Ltd,
Lymington, Hants

Printed and bound in the UK by
CPI Mackays, Chatham ME5 8TD

www.orionbooks.co.uk

For Sylvia and Dino
who met on the Via Veneto

Part One

San Giulio, Italy, 1964

I

Sunday evenings were the time for romance in the little village of San Giulio. Romance Italian style.

And that is why Maria Domenica Carrozza was strolling down the main street, arm in arm with her mother, Pepina. Her younger sister Rosaria hung reluctantly off Mamma's other arm.

The evening was pleasantly warm and Pepina in no hurry. She took time to show off her daughters, walking them at a leisurely pace past tall, narrow buildings the colour of washed sand and down the worn stone steps in front of the church onto the cobbled piazza below.

'Mamma,' Rosaria whimpered, prodding her mother with slightly grubby fingers. 'I'm tired. Can we go home now? Please?'

'*Basta*, Rosaria,' hissed Pepina, without changing the even rhythm of her very best shoes clip-clopping over the cobbles. 'It's still so early. We'll take a little drink at the *caffe, bellisima figlia*.'

Broad beam swinging, she steered her two dark-eyed, dark-haired daughters towards the bright lights of Il Caffe dei Fratelli Angeli where the pastries were rich and creamy, the coffee strong and the tables always overflowing with friends, neighbours and, who knew, maybe a suitable husband for one of her pretty girls?

For as long as anyone could remember, Caffe Angeli had stood guard over the far corner of the main piazza of San Giulio, a dusty, old village that rose boldly from the empty plains of Campania. There were no hills or valleys for San

Giulio to nestle in, no high stone walls to hide behind. The wide, flat tract of land upon which it lay stretched out all the way to the Mediterranean Sea.

But although San Giulio stood open and defenceless, the villagers had somehow managed to hold the outside world at bay. Like most people born in the fertile lands surrounding Naples, here they still clung tightly to the old ways. Young women married early; old women dressed in black from the day they lost their first loved one; Rita Pavone crooned soothingly from the village's one and only jukebox; and Mamma still knew what was best for her daughters.

For sixteen-year-old Maria Domenica, that meant a life spent between the four walls of her mother's kitchen, except for Sunday evenings when she escaped for a few short hours to make *la passeggiata* through the streets of San Giulio.

Maria Domenica had never questioned being made to leave school at thirteen. After all, she was the eldest of six. There was bread to be baked, chickens to be fed, children to be bathed, and Pepina couldn't do it all alone.

As for her father Erminio, he was busy driving his truck laden with peaches and plums across the country. Looking after babies? That was women's work and best that Maria Domenica learn about it early so she'd be ready to bring up her own children when they came along in a couple of years.

It fell to Pepina to find men good enough to marry her daughters. Sunday after Sunday she strolled determinedly through the dusty main street and around the plain little fountain in the piazza, showing the village what she had to offer: nice girls in their finest dresses, good girls who'd have pretty babies and keep the pans in the kitchen bubbling with delicious things.

'Mamma,' repeated Rosaria, nudging at her insistently with her shoulder, 'can I have a Coca-Cola? Mamma, please? I'm thirsty.'

At fourteen, Rosaria was too young to be paraded through

the town on a Sunday night, Pepina knew that, but better to show off two daughters than one, especially when there were three more at home growing up fast. Six children and only one of them a son – *porca miseria*. Where had she gone wrong?

'Mamma, Coca-Cola.'

'OK, OK, Rosaria.'

Across the busy *caffe*, Pepina glimpsed Elena Manzoni and waved. Elena had a nice son, Marco, who was around Maria Domenica's age. A good boy, he'd inherit their farm one day and both she and Erminio had agreed their eldest daughter could do worse.

Obediently, Maria Domenica let her mother weave her through the crowded tables of Caffe Angeli. She wasn't a truly beautiful girl. Her legs were too gangly, her skin too freckled, her eyes too deep-set and her nose too long for real prettiness. And yet she had long, black hair that fell down her back like water and a smile that made old men smile back in reply.

A quick kiss on both cheeks for Elena and her son. Marco wouldn't meet her eyes. His gaze was fixed over her shoulder at apple-cheeked, soft-bellied Rosaria, already sucking up her Coca-Cola greedily through a straw.

Pepina nudged her.

'Marco, come and help me choose a song on the juke-box,' Maria Domenica stammered, jingling the change in her pocket. 'Who do you like? Rita Pavone? Little Tony? Maybe they'll have some new songs on it this week.'

As she moved him reluctantly away from her little sister's orbit, Maria Domenica wished she could say what was really in her mind: 'I don't want you, Marco. You're welcome to Rosaria. Have her, take her now. I'm tired of listening to her whine, I'm sick of watching her eat. She'll be old and fat in a heartbeat and she'll nag you for the next forty years but, if you want her, then take her, Marco, *per favore*, take her.'

Instead she stood quietly next to the boy her mother had picked out for her, uncertain how she was expected to behave.

Marco's full, soft mouth drooped as he ran his eye over the jukebox. '*Merda.* No one listens to this stuff in the city. In Rome, in Naples, they wouldn't put good money in this useless heap of junk.'

'So what if they don't listen to it in the city?' she countered with some spirit. 'That doesn't mean we can't like it here in San Giulio.'

'San Giulio,' he spat bitterly. 'I'm not wasting any more of my life in this place. Don't look for me here next week drinking Coca-Cola with the old women and the children.'

'You have plans?'

'Maybe.'

'Tell me, Marco. Where will you go?'

'To the city, of course, where do you think?'

'What will you do there?'

Frowning at the jukebox, Marco stayed silent.

'Marco, what will you do in the city?' she repeated, her voice growing louder.

'Shut up,' he hissed. 'Do you want everyone to know? I'll tell you if you'll just shut up for a minute.'

It turned out Marco had a cousin living in Rome. A cousin who had a job in a butcher's shop, a rented room in Trastevere and a good line in following the pretty female tourists looking for *la dolce vita* on the Via Veneto. All Marco needed was his train fare.

'I could come with you, maybe? To Rome?' Maria Domenica's black eyes widened, as the possibility of escape occurred to her for the first time.

'Come on, you're a girl,' said Marco, his sulky lips now stretched into an amused grin. 'You're just a girl. And you're not going anywhere.'

Around the room many pairs of eyes were watching Maria Domenica and Marco exchange their few words. Their mothers gazed at them hopefully, keen for any sign of romance. As for Rosaria, her eyes were resentful and dull. Banging her now empty Coca-Cola bottle repetitively on the side of the table, she frowned. What was Mamma doing trying to matchmake those two anyway? Wasn't it obvious who Marco wanted? And if she had anything to do with it, Marco was going to get his wish before the year was out.

From behind the fine Gaggia coffee machine that he worked like a musical instrument, Franco Angeli watched the young couple too. How long before he heard this pair's complaints? he wondered. *There are no Beatles songs on the jukebox. There's no pop music.* Bah! He slammed down a frothing jug of milk on the shining stainless steel counter in disgust.

From the high walls many more Franco Angelis were staring down on the couple just as disapprovingly. When Franco and his brother Gennaro had started Il Caffe dei Fratelli Angeli many years ago they'd indulged their passion for Italian art. They'd hired a talented young painter who had spent many, many months balanced precariously on a scaffold, slowly covering the walls and ceiling with reproductions of the brothers' favourite paintings. In the finest Renaissance tradition, the patrons' faces appeared somewhere in every picture.

So here on the ceiling was a surprised Franco Angeli almost touching the finger of a bearded God in Michelangelo's *Creation of Adam*, and there on the wall an admiring Gennaro Angeli watching Botticelli's Venus step out from her half-shell. And behind the counter were a couple of cheeky Raphael cherubs with more than a passing resemblance to photos of the young Franco and Gennaro.

The locals barely raised their eyes to all this beauty any more. Most of the young ones had hardly ever registered it was there at all. In the quietest way, as he served people coffee all day, this broke Franco Angeli's heart.

'Hey, Marco.' Maria Domenica laughed now and raised her eyes to the ceiling. 'If you go to Rome you can go see the real Sistine Chapel. See how it compares to Caffe Angeli.'

Marco rolled his eyes. Beauty was what he saw in the mirror every morning, not a bit of old paint on a wall. 'When I get to Rome I won't be wasting any of my time,' he promised her. 'I'll find a job and once I've started earning I'll buy myself a Vespa like my cousin Antonio's. And then we'll have some fun.'

'Will you ever come back?'

'Maybe, in ten years' time. You'll be married with kids by then, I expect. I'll come by and see you though. You and your sister Rosaria. And I'll take you both for a ride in my Ferrari.' He laughed, turning away from her and the jukebox that had so disappointed him. 'See you in ten years, eh, Maria Domenica? I'll be looking forward to it.'

If anyone had been watching Maria Domenica at that moment they'd have seen an expression settling on her face that she'd never worn in all her sixteen years of being an obedient and conscientious eldest daughter. An expression that spelled trouble.

2

Pepina had a fear of running out of bread. The shelves of her big wooden dresser were always groaning with hard, coarse loaves that would break the teeth of anyone not brought up on their tough crusts. And still every morning Maria Domenica was expected to rise early with her mother and bake more.

'So long as there is bread on those shelves our stomachs will never be empty,' Pepina said without fail each day as they pulled out the big sack of flour and lit the oven. And if her eldest daughter breathed a sigh or cast an eye at the row of loaves they'd baked the day before, she never noticed.

Side by side, they worked at the long kitchen table as the sun rose, chickens clucking around their feet. Backs bent, they kneaded the stiff yellow dough with strong fingers. And as they worked, they talked. Well, this morning Pepina talked and Maria Domenica daydreamed of a different life outside these familiar flaking walls.

The kitchen was where mother and daughter spent most of their days. It was dominated by a pine table worn smooth from decades of use by Carrozza women, and its windows looked out on the vegetable patch where they dug and weeded in the cool of the morning and the late afternoon and at the orchard of peach trees that stretched beyond and behind them.

This was the original part of the single-storey house: its walls had been built to last and its floor flagged in stone. But open the door that led to the bedrooms and things became crooked and haphazard. Here was a doorframe scrounged from a demolition site up the road and there a window ledge that Erminio's father had tacked together from a few old pieces of wood. Walls leaned inwards, ceilings sloped and Pepina lived in fear of what would happen if there were an earthquake. On the wall above each bed there was a picture of Our Lady and an effigy of Christ on the cross and, whenever she remembered, Pepina prayed to them both to keep her creaking walls standing.

The bedrooms, tacked on to the building whenever a new child was born, were really only for sleeping in. During waking hours family life revolved around the kitchen where the day always began with baking.

It was Maria Domenica's job to mix the sugar and yeast with warm water and let it stand until it grew foamy. And then, once the round, flat loaves her mother had shaped were in the hot oven, she was in charge of spraying them with water so the crusts would be hard enough for them to last for days. It wasn't work that could be rushed and often half a morning had passed before mother and daughter had the satisfaction of seeing their warm bread cooling on the wire rack above the stove.

Pepina's hands were tough and callused from years of toil, her shoulders stooped from the hours bent over the kitchen table, yet she didn't seem unhappy with her lot. Every morning she greeted her daughter with a smile and gossiped and laughed through the day's long work.

'Don't get me wrong, I'd miss you around here,' she was saying now as she kneaded the dough. 'You're a good helper, Maria Domenica. You've always been a good girl. But Rosaria could take over your work when you go. It's time that girl had a little more discipline.'

Her mother's words jolted Maria Domenica back to

reality. 'Go, Mamma? Where am I going? I never said I was going anywhere.'

'*Scema*! Have you been listening to a word I've said?' Pepina slapped down her dough in a warm sunny spot and, covering it with a damp cloth, left it to rise. 'You're sixteen now. I was betrothed to your father by then. And Marco Manzoni is a nice boy. Perhaps a little vain, but then all these young people seem obsessed with their clothes and hair these days. Elena and I think you will do well together. You and Marco.'

'But Mamma, I don't want to be with Marco Manzoni.' Maria Domenica's fingers stilled and sank into the floury dough. 'And he doesn't want to be with me. I think he has other plans.'

'Oh, plans. I'm sure he has lots of plans. He's a clever boy, that Marco. And no one's saying that you have to rush into anything. Just take some time to get to know each other. Elena has asked that you go and eat with the family one day soon. Mind, I hear she's not much of a cook so you may have to have a bit of bread and cheese before you go. You know what, Maria Domenica, I really think we should bake an extra loaf. I'd hate to run out.'

With a despairing glance at the already full shelves, Maria Domenica poured another mound of coarse flour onto the table, made a well in the middle and filled it with yeasty water. As she began to mix, a sleepy-eyed Rosaria pushed open the kitchen door. Her dark hair was tousled and her skin so sticky with sweat that her nightdress was clinging to the curves of her generous young body.

'Oh, it's so hot today,' she yawned. 'Mamma, can I go to the beach this afternoon?'

Each summer Pepina's sister, Lucia, rented a small cabin on the nearest stretch of beach, known as La Sabbia D'Oro, and most stifling July and August days she and her two daughters would rush through their chores in the morning and spend the afternoons cooling off in the sea and working on their tans.

But Lucia's family lived in a little apartment in the centre of town. Cleaning and shopping took no time at all for them. Here in Pepina's sprawling farmhouse in the dusty countryside outside San Giulio there was a long list of chores to be done and it was a rare day when her girls got to the bottom of it in time to join their cousins on the sand.

'The beach? Not today, Rosaria. You can help your sister finish the bread. And then I want you to make some gnocchi for your father, in case he's home tonight.'

'Yes, but—'

'And there's a pile of dirty washing once you've finished that.'

'But Mamma, the Manzonis have rented a cabin on La Sabbia D'Oro this year. They'll be there today.' Rosaria cast a sly look towards her sister. 'I told Marco me and Maria Domenica would make a big tray of cannelloni and take it over for his lunch. I promised him.'

'Well, if you're going to make a decent cannelloni you should have been up an hour ago, lazy girl.' Pepina was already crashing about trying to unearth a tray worthy of bearing Marco's cannelloni. 'Hurry. You get dressed and we'll start.'

Triumph shone briefly in Rosaria's small black eyes. She didn't usually get her own way quite so quickly and easily. But these days her mother would agree to just about anything if it meant throwing her big sister together with Marco. Today was going to be a good day after all – an afternoon at the beach and a big plate of Mamma's cannelloni for lunch. And who knew? Maybe Marco really would be there.

While she loved the sea, Maria Domenica dreaded beach life. Her cousins knew everyone on La Sabbia D'Oro. They'd been going there since they were children. Now they were teenagers, bronzed and confident. As they laughed, exchanging gossip and morsels of food with their friends, Maria Domenica would stretch her skinny, sun-starved body stiffly on the sand, trying not to look as much of an outsider as she felt.

Rosaria was right. It was hot, boiling hot. And for a second Maria Domenica was tempted to dig out her faded old swimming costume and brave the beach. But other, bigger plans were forming in her mind and, if she played her cards right, this could be the day she put them into action. First she had to get Mamma and the rest of them out of the way for a few hours.

She'd watched Rosaria often enough over the years to have learned how best to manipulate her mother.

'Mamma, why don't you come to the beach too?' she called in a voice big enough to reach the vegetable patch where Pepina was picking ripe tomatoes for the cannelloni sauce, and loud enough to echo down the corridor and through the bedrooms where her brother and sisters were waking up. 'We could take all the kids and make a day of it. What do you think?'

It had the desired effect. Within seconds a swarm of noisy kids surrounded her mother. Dogs were barking, Rosaria was laughing and little voices were chanting insistently, 'Beach, beach, beach.'

Maria Domenica waited until her mother was busy trying to cram trays of food and wriggling children into her car to tell the first real lie of her life.

Rubbing her stomach, she began, 'Mamma, I've got cramps. I think maybe I'm getting my monthly. Do you mind if I don't come to the beach?'

'But Maria Domenica, the whole point . . . you do look pale, I suppose.'

'I don't feel good, I really don't.'

Minutes later, watching the cloud of dust raised by her

mother's car as it headed towards the beach, Maria Domenica did feel something. But it wasn't cramp. It was a little flutter of excitement.

3

Franco Angeli was having a quiet day. It seemed as though the heat had driven the whole town down to the beach. Franco could have shut up shop and followed them down there, he supposed, but sometimes the quiet times were the best times in his little *caffe*. He hummed contentedly as he polished up his Gaggia coffee machine, with its sturdy stainless steel body and varnished wooden handles, until it was so clean it gleamed.

He was so deep in thought he didn't notice Pepina Carrozza's eldest girl sidle in. When Franco finally looked up she was standing quietly, staring at the three Botticelli muses dancing across his wall.

'Have you been to Rome and seen the real one?' Maria Domenica asked him finally.

'That one's not in Rome, it's in Florence. But, yes, I've seen it. It's called *Primavera* and it's a very beautiful painting.'

She nodded up at the ceiling. 'What about that? Isn't that in Rome, in the Sistine Chapel? I remember learning about that one at school. Have you seen it?'

'Yes, I've seen them all. And they are all incredible. Maybe you'll get to see them one day too.'

Maria Domenica stared steadily at him. She was about to tell the second lie of her life. 'That's sort of what I came to talk to you about,' she began, climbing onto a stool and resting her elbows on his gleaming counter. 'My father Erminio – you know him, he drives the fruit truck – he gets to travel all over Italy and see everything. But my mother, on the other hand, she has never been beyond Naples. So I have a secret plan. I want to save up and take her on a trip to Rome to see the Sistine Chapel.'

'Well, that's wonderful, but why are you telling me?'

'Because I need to find a job to earn the money. And I wondered if I could help you in the *caffe*. I'm a hard worker and a good cook. I can clean, serve customers. Whatever you want really.'

It wasn't a bad idea now Franco thought about it. Things had been a bit stretched in Caffe Angeli since his wife had died and his brother Gennaro had left him and moved up north. He had just one son, Giovanni, but he was busy with his schooling and too young to be much help around the *caffe*.

'You'd be here to work, not hang about the tables talking to your friends,' Franco warned.

'Yes.'

'I'd expect you to work as hard as Gennaro did before he moved to Milan.'

'That's OK.'

'And I might need you in the evenings sometimes – how will your parents be about that?'

'They'll be fine . . . only you mustn't tell them why I need the money,' she reminded him. 'That's a secret surprise.'

'A secret surprise?' Franco's elfin features creased into a smile and his eyes danced behind his round, silver-framed spectacles. 'OK, OK, you've got yourself a job, I guess.'

'Oh, *grazie*, Franco, *grazie*, *grazie*.' Maria Domenica was tripping over her words in her hurry to thank him adequately.

'*Prego*,' he replied and, with a hiss of his Gaggia, produced two steaming cups of coffee. 'Since we have a deal, we'd better drink on it,' he told her.

As Maria Domenica's coffee cup clinked against his, Franco grew more serious. 'You know you'll be the first person to work here who isn't part of the Angeli family. The first outsider. I hope you won't give me cause to regret it.'

A worm of guilt joined the butterfly of excitement deep in Maria Domenica's stomach. Two lies told already today and still one more to go.

The third lie was the most difficult. That came later back home, as her family tumbled out of Mamma's little car, all sunburned, sandy limbs and satisfied smiles.

'You missed a great day at the beach,' her little brother Salvatore told her, jumping up and down with the sheer excitement of it all. 'We had ice cream.'

'The sea was so warm, it was gorgeous,' smiled Rosaria lazily. 'The only strange thing was that Marco wasn't there.'

'Oh. Where was he then?'

'Nobody knew,' shrugged Pepina, pulling the licked-clean cannelloni trays out of the boot of the car. 'Still, there were plenty of takers for the pasta. It didn't get wasted, eh, Rosaria?'

Catching a whiff of onions sweating gently in olive oil, Pepina ducked through the vine-covered doorway and into her kitchen. 'Oh, you're a good girl, Maria Domenica. You've started the dinner. How are you feeling, eh, those cramps gone away, *figlia*?'

'Oh not so bad.' She realized with some shock that she was almost a practised liar by now.

'Before Papa gets home I have something I wanted to ask you, Mamma,' she continued quickly. 'I was talking to Franco Angeli last night when we were at the *caffe* and he asked if I'd go and help out there some evenings. Since his brother Gennaro moved to Milan with his wife the poor man has been exhausted. He needs an extra pair of hands.'

Pepina frowned. 'So it would be like a job then? I don't know what your father will say about that.'

'Well, more like a favour than a job. But he will pay me a little. And I thought I could save the money. You know, for the future, for when I'm . . . when I'm . . . married.'

If she could get her mother to agree, she didn't think her father would put up much of a fight.

'The thing is, Mamma, I'll just be in the *caffe*. You and Rosaria can come in and see me whenever you like.' She stirred a smooth swirl of sieved tomatoes into the gluey mass of onions. 'And I'll still be here at home in the morning to help you with the baking.'

'Well, I don't know.' Pepina had been taken by surprise.

Rosaria, too, hadn't expected anything like this to come from her usually so dull older sister, but already she could see the possibilities. 'Imagine the gossip Maria Domenica will hear in that place every day,' she cackled. 'Everybody goes there. She won't miss a thing.'

'She'll be working, not gossiping.' Pepina flicked a tea towel at her second eldest daughter. 'And work will be something you'll be doing a lot more of too, *figlia*, with your sister busy at the *caffe* every day. Here, take this.' She tossed the tea towel at her. 'You may as well start now.'

And so Maria Domenica found herself on the other side of the stainless steel counter at Caffe Angeli, dressed in a starched white apron and learning, from an ever patient Franco Angeli, the secrets of his sometimes temperamental Gaggia.

Soon she could pull the wooden handles like an expert and put a perfect *crema* on the top of every cup of espresso she made. And each night, as she fell into bed exhausted, her long black hair still smelling of the roasted beans, she thought of the growing pile of money stuffed inside her mattress. Her savings, for *her* future.

4

Rosaria had been right about one thing: from her little spot behind the Gaggia, Maria Domenica heard all the town's gossip. People talked and she listened.

'Did you hear the news?' Gina Rossi eased herself onto one of the red leather stools lined up beside the stainless steel counter. 'Marco Manzoni has disappeared. He went out early on Monday morning and he hasn't been seen since.'

Later from Aunt Lucia: 'I heard his clothes were gone. And his records. His mother Elena hasn't heard a word from him in days.'

Next day: 'Poor Elena – she's been robbed,' confided Gloria Ferrero, the butcher's wife. 'The golden holy medals she used to carry around in her bag everywhere with her for safekeeping? Gone! She refuses to believe it was Marco. But really, who else?'

And then a week later: 'Did you hear that Elena Manzoni got a letter from that no-good son of hers at last? In Rome apparently. Living with one of his cousins and getting into no end of trouble, I bet.'

Finally Elena herself, jowls quivering as she announced loudly to all those gathered on the stools and round the tables: 'My Marco, such a hard-working boy. Only been in Rome a week or two and already has a job in the butcher's shop with his cousin. He'll go far that boy of mine.' Then, patting Maria Domenica on the hand, 'Never mind, *cara*. I know you had hopes of him. But you'll find another nice boy in town to be your sweetheart.'

As she served tiny white cups of strong, black espresso to the regulars at the counter, Maria Domenica was aware of sympathetic glances aimed in her direction. She supposed that Elena – or her mother – had been talking. Well, let them all think she was heartbroken over Marco. It made no odds to her. The only person she couldn't bear to believe in the lie of her love for Marco was Franco Angeli.

'So your boyfriend skipped town,' he teased one busy afternoon during a lull in the endless stream of customers.

'He's not my boyfriend. Our mammas kept trying to matchmake us. But I promise you that I never showed the slightest bit of interest in him. I don't want a boyfriend. I'm happy as I am.'

'All young girls want a boyfriend.' Franco was laughing at her now. 'You want to get married and have babies, don't you?'

'Would you like to tell me exactly where it's written that all girls have to marry and have babies and then spend the rest of their lives slaving in the kitchen like my mamma does?'

A couple of regulars in the corner looked up from their glasses of Campari and soda, surprised at her vehemence.

'It's not written anywhere,' Franco said reasonably. 'Most just do want to marry, that's all. And so do the boys, although often they pretend they'd rather not. My wedding day was the happiest of my life. And the day my Giovanni was born the proudest.'

Maria Domenica felt irritated with Franco and then immediately guilty. It wasn't his fault he didn't understand her – she only half understood herself. She stared at the painted Venus hovering behind the jukebox.

'Well, not everyone's the same, are they?' she replied. 'There are people who want different things from their lives.'

Franco stopped wiping the Gaggia and gave her his full attention. 'So what is it you want from your life, Maria Domenica, if it's not marriage and babies?'

She frowned. How best to explain it? She'd known for a long time that the farmhouse she'd grown up in was too small a fit for her. Even as a child, at the end of the day's chores, she liked to throw off her apron and lie beneath the peach trees, staring at the patches of blue sky between the branches and pretending she was somewhere else.

The longing to escape was growing stronger, especially as Marco seemed to have managed it so easily. For just a short while she'd like to live some place where not a soul knew who she was, where nobody knew her family or remembered her as a baby, no one had sat next to her at school or played with her on La Sabbia D'Oro. Then she could be whoever she wanted to be. She could be someone totally different. But how to explain that to Franco?

'It's not that I don't want a husband and family,' she managed at last. 'Just not quite yet. I want to be someone first.'

'You're someone already!' Franco was laughing again. He threw the cloth over to her. 'Here, you can be the someone who finishes this. I'm running across the road to buy a newspaper and then I'd like five minutes' peace and quiet to read it before we get busy again.'

Some days Franco's son Giovanni abandoned his schoolwork and came to lend a hand for an hour or two. He was a skinny, serious boy who followed her round the *caffe* like a faithful puppy and blushed to the very roots of his close-cropped, dark hair whenever she said a word to him. Although he was only trying to be helpful, he always seemed to be standing in the very spot where Maria Domenica wanted to be. He dropped things and he mixed up orders. But he was Franco's only child and she was kind to him.

Some days Rosaria came in and sat on a high stool by the counter. She never said very much – just seemed happy to eat and watch them work. Her appetite for sweet fizzy drinks and creamy cakes amazed even Franco.

'I love a girl who knows how to empty a plate,' he'd say, pushing a crisp, shell-shaped pastry filled with ricotta, vanilla and sugared orange peel towards the calmly chewing Rosaria. 'Try one of these *sfolgliatelle* next, they're delicious. *Buon appetito.*'

Franco was so soft-hearted that half the time he didn't charge Rosaria for her sweet treats. But she always seemed to have a few coins rolling round in her pocket to offer in payment. Once or twice Maria Domenica had tried giving her sister a quizzical look as she handed over her small change and she'd received a hard, sullen stare in reply. Perhaps Rosaria was rattling round in Pepina's chest of drawers when her back was turned or sweeping the odd stray coin off the tabletop whenever she got the chance. Maria Domenica knew she ought to say or do something about it but she dreaded the drama that would ensue. It seemed easier to stay silent and watch Rosaria chew.

She was convinced her sister had gone up an entire dress size, maybe two, since Marco left. If you watched her carefully it seemed she was growing fatter by the hour.

'Another Coca-Cola, *per favore*?' Rosaria's voice was muffled by the large pastry she was stuffing into her mouth.

'My God, Franco, take the plate off her, she'll eat that next.'

'Don't be so revolting, Maria Domenica. I'm just hungry. Hardly a thing has passed my lips all day. Just some of Mamma's bread and a hot chocolate this morning. It's been work, work, work all day. I haven't stopped for weeks. Do you know, I haven't even been near the beach since that day when you wanted to go to look for Marco and then changed your mind.'

'*You* wanted to go look for Marco, not me.'

'Didn't find him though, did I?' Rosaria polished off her pastry and took a long swig of Coca-Cola. 'Wonder what he's doing now?'

'Who knows?'

'Maybe I'll go to Rome and find him.'

'Yeah, right. You're fourteen, Rosaria. Maybe you'll be picked up by the police and brought straight back home again to a big slap from Mamma.'

Slyly now: 'You're just jealous. He always liked me more than you.'

'No, he liked himself more than he liked any of us!'

Franco broke in. 'Girls, girls, no fighting. Maria Domenica, there are some tables over there that need a wipe. And Rosaria, can I get you anything else?'

As she wiped and her little sister ate, Maria Domenica felt oddly content. It seemed these days as if some of her happiest moments were spent in this steamy little *caffe*. She loved her view from behind the counter – the red leather banquettes that stretched down the length of one wall, the wooden tables and chairs she wiped down each day, the jukebox glowing in the corner and the vast gold-framed mirror on the far wall that reflected the whole scene. There were times when she felt she never wanted to leave the place. But she only had to raise her eyes to the paintings that covered the rest of the walls and ceiling to remember there was a whole big world out there. Surely it wasn't so wrong for her to want to go and see just a little bit of it?

5

Maria Domenica's father was home at last. His big truck blocked the dusty driveway that led to the farmhouse and his enormous body loomed over the kitchen table.

Anyone wondering where Rosaria had got her love of food need look no further than Erminio, who had returned home with half a dozen rotisserie chickens cooked up at a roadside stall. Rapture lit his face as he sliced into fresh, milky buffalo mozzarella or cleaved a juicy red watermelon in two. He pinched the cheeks of his children with delight and caused Pepina serious alarm as he made inroads into her bread stocks.

'Ah, it's so good to be home,' he sighed and inhaled the steam from a vast bowl of *spaghetti con le vongole*.

The farm was a different place when Erminio was home. Dogs barked less, children played quietly and even Rosaria rose early each morning to bake bread with her sister without a word of complaint falling from her lips.

Salvatore, his only son, was the favourite naturally. Still young enough to curl up on his father's knee and rest his dark head on the soft, rounded belly that shook and trembled whenever he found something funny. But for Maria Domenica, his first-born, there was also a special place in Erminio's heart. And when he learned she'd found herself a job, the smile dropped right off his big, laughing face.

'A job? Why do you want a job? Do I not provide for you?' He was angry and hurt. 'Am I not doing a good enough job for you all?'

'It's not like that, Papa.'

'No? What is it like then?'

'I'm helping Franco Angeli out.'

'If Franco Angeli wants help, let him look to his own family and leave mine alone.'

'But that's just it. He doesn't have any family.' Maria Domenica felt quite desperate. 'His wife is dead, his brother has moved to Milan and his only son is still at school.'

All afternoon, as they ate around the long wooden table, Maria Domenica pleaded. Through the pasta course, the meat and the vegetables; as her father despatched a plate of fried eel and picked the most delicious bits out of a salad. Finally, when her mother placed the pecorino cheese and some of her precious rough, golden bread on the table, Erminio relented.

'OK, OK, you win, Maria Domenica. Just this one time you win. You can have your job. But no woman in my family has ever worked before.' He chewed the hard bread thoughtfully. 'None of your aunties and certainly not your grandmother.'

Matching her father mouthful for mouthful had kept Rosaria quiet so far but now she spoke up. 'What about me? Can I get a job as well, Papa?'

Laughing again, he pushed a pile of dirty plates towards her. 'You already have a job, *cara*. And you'd better get started on it right now.'

Rosaria washed, Maria Domenica dried. It seemed as though the pile of oily pans and tomato-smeared plates would never shrink.

Maria Domenica took the soapy dishes from her sister's hands and watched her family. Her father fiddling with the radio dial trying to find something to listen to; her mother with eyes half closed and belly full, struggling to stay awake; her younger sisters and brother playing quietly in the hope that no one would remember they were there and send them for a nap; and Rosaria, glowering over the sink filled with dishes and scrubbing only half the dirt away. She loved them all but sometimes Maria Domenica felt like an outsider.

She spoke her thoughts out loud. 'Isn't there more to life than this?'

Rosaria half caught her words and gave her a sidelong glance. 'What's that you're saying?'

She hesitated and then plunged on. 'Don't you ever want to travel, Rosaria? See the world? Get away from here?'

Rosaria shrugged. 'Francesca Maggio's daughter went to Capri for two nights on her honeymoon. She said it was beautiful. I wouldn't mind going there when I get married.'

'Yes, but I mean further than Capri. Further than Italy maybe.'

Rosaria shrugged. 'Why would I want to do that?'

Maria Domenica didn't have an easy answer for her and so she said no more. Instead, taking the pasta pot, she rinsed it clean of suds and wiped it dry carefully.

'Oh, I'm so full,' Rosaria groaned. 'That was a feast. But why does Mamma have to make this terrible mess? Everything anyone does in this house seems to leave a mess behind and I'm the one who has to clean it up.'

6

When rumours spread through the town of San Giulio, sooner or later they seeped into Caffe Angeli. And, although she rarely joined in with the gossips, Maria Domenica would have had to take her hands off the wooden handles of the Gaggia and place them firmly over her ears to avoid hearing it all.

'You'll never guess what! You'll never guess what!' Aunt Lucia was excited and quite breathless. She'd clearly run from somewhere, gold jewellery clanking and peroxide blonde hair stiffening in the warm breeze, in her haste to be the first to pass on the news. 'Marco Manzoni has got some girl in Rome pregnant.'

'What?'

Coffee cups hit saucers and the Caffe Angeli regulars stilled as they waited to hear everything.

'Well . . .' Lucia slid onto one of the red leather banquettes that lined the far wall of the *caffe*, her face glowing with the pleasure of a secret known and about to be told. 'It's an English girl apparently, living in Rome, teaching or nannying or whatever. Of course,' Lucia hurried on to the most important and dramatic part, 'Marco will have to marry her now or she'll be ruined!'

Girls in San Giulio didn't fall pregnant unless they were married. And if somehow they did manage to fill their bellies with baby, they could be sure they'd find themselves standing in front of a priest before they got too big to look respectable in a wedding dress.

All week long the *caffe* hummed with the scandal.

'Elena is going up to Rome to meet the girl,' confided one regular.

'I heard they'll be married in Rome and she won't come to San Giulio until after the baby is born,' revealed another.

'Apparently Marco's just lucky there aren't a dozen girls carrying his babies the way he's been behaving in Rome,' hissed a scandalized Lucia.

And finally Elena herself: 'My Marco, he's such a good boy. He did want to marry the girl, make an honest woman of her. But her English father said he didn't want a daughter of his marrying a greasy Italian.' Her voice grew shrill with indignation. 'Greasy, he said, greasy!' Then it fell to a whisper. 'To be honest, she was a fast piece. She seduced my Marco. I can only thank God that he wasn't trapped into marriage with her for the rest of his life. It was a lucky escape.'

Maria Domenica broke her silence at last. 'What about the baby? It'll be your grandchild,' she pointed out reasonably. 'Won't you want to see it at least?'

'Oh no, no, no.' Elena's head shook with small, rapid, nervous movements. 'Best not, I think. There'll be other grandchildren, I'm sure, when my son settles down with a nice girl. This one, it will be far away in England – like it didn't exist. It's no grandchild of mine. No, no.'

Like priests in the confessional, Franco and Maria Domenica listened to the stories that unfolded each day in the little *caffe*, murmuring the odd comment where and if it seemed appropriate. They couldn't afford to take sides when an argument broke out. An offended customer might not return and Franco needed the business.

But sometimes, when the closed sign was up on the big glass door, as Franco stacked wooden chairs on tables and Maria Domenica mopped the tiled floor, they swapped stories.

'I can't believe Elena doesn't want to see that baby of

Marco's. In fact, I don't believe it. She's just putting on a brave face,' declared Maria Domenica that evening.

'I think you're right.' Franco wasn't surprised at her insight. Over the weeks of working side by side he'd come to realize she very often picked out the truth. 'It's sad for Elena to lose a member of her family like that. If it were my son's baby I wouldn't let it go so easily.'

'Would you make him marry the girl though?'

Franco looked thoughtful. 'That depends.'

'On what?'

'On the situation. Marriage isn't an easy thing, you know. You need to have real love there before you make those vows. Otherwise you're condemning yourself to a lifetime of unhappiness.'

'What about the disgrace of having a baby and no husband?'

'Unhappiness or disgrace?' Franco shrugged. 'I know which I'd rather live with. But then I'm a man. I suppose it's different for us.'

Maria Domenica flicked the mop beneath the small round tables to dislodge the day's grime. 'Yes, I suppose it is different. It shouldn't be but it is. If it were me I don't know what I'd want. Although,' she added with a laugh, 'I'm pretty sure I wouldn't want to marry Marco. That man was right – he is kind of greasy!'

By the time she got home that night the news had reached her family. Her father was as horrified as her sister Rosaria was jubilant.

'That *cretino*,' Erminio rumbled like Vesuvius about to explode. 'That *disgraziato*. He should be forced to marry the poor girl. Her life is ruined. Who will marry her now? She has brought disgrace on her whole family. It's a tragedy.'

To his children Erminio sounded angry. Only he and his wife knew that what he really felt was fear. Girls get into trouble, they get pregnant. They need a close eye, an iron fist and to be married off as soon as possible. And he had five of them.

'I'm only thankful I never let you get involved with that Marco.' Pepina shook her head at her eldest daughter dramatically. 'I never liked him. Elena Manzoni she was so insistent – Marco and Maria Domenica, they'd make such a fine pair, she'd say. But I knew there was something about that boy that was bad to the core.'

Erminio roared, 'No daughter of mine is to go near him, do you hear?' His eyes swept the room, moving from Maria Domenica to Rosaria, settling on Sandra for a moment, then Giovanna and finishing with little Claudia who, at four, had no idea what anyone was on about but strongly suspected her chances of a decent bedtime story were growing smaller by the minute.

'No daughter of mine is ever to speak to him again.' Erminio was quite red in the face and his jowls trembled with indignation. 'Never, ever!'

'But Papa . . .' Rosaria couldn't believe her ears. 'He offered to marry her, didn't he? What else could he do? It's not his fault. It's not fair to blame him.'

'No!'

'But—'

'No!'

As Rosaria turned to the already full sink with another stack of dirty dishes she muttered audibly, 'It's not fair.'

The answer she'd expected came thundering back at her from her father. 'Life's not fair, Rosaria, life's not fair.'

7

As the weeks sped by, Franco came to realize that he couldn't imagine Caffe Angeli without Maria Domenica. She'd become part of the very fabric of the place. In fact, a thought had occurred to him once or twice . . . but no, he wasn't quite ready for that yet; it was perhaps a little premature. A nice idea but . . .

The place was quiet today. Franco quickly pushed a few coins into the jukebox and Gianni Morandi's voice rang out. '*Ho chuiso le finestre*,' Gianni sang passionately.

Maria Domenica giggled.

'What are you laughing at?' Franco enquired politely.

'Oh, you know.'

'No, I don't know.'

'The music, Franco. Why won't you have some English music on the jukebox? Or some American songs?'

'Not you too. I'd thought better of you than that.' Franco's eyes rolled in an exaggerated fashion, but Maria Domenica could tell he was genuinely a little exasperated with her.

Nevertheless she pushed it. 'Just one or two songs, Franco. It wouldn't kill you.'

'Oh no,' he replied. 'Not while I'm in charge of things at Caffe Angeli.'

'But all the young people laugh at this music, Franco.'

'Let them laugh. This is Italy and we listen to Italian music,' he replied steadfastly.

Maria Domenica had never loved anyone outside her family before but suddenly she realized she loved Franco.

She loved his serious little pixie face and the twinkle in his eyes. The way he carefully wiped his Gaggia clean, then wiped it again and again. She loved the deep laughter lines around his eyes and most of all she loved the times when the closed sign went up on the big glass door and she talked to him like she talked to nobody else.

Impulsively she touched his shoulder and pressed her lips quickly against his cheek.

'What was that for?' Franco looked a bit pink.

'It was a kiss for you.' She grinned at him foolishly.

'And what did I do to deserve such a beautiful kiss from a pretty young girl like you?'

'You gave me this job, Franco, and I love working here, I really do.'

'I love having you work here.' She could tell he meant it. 'You must have lots of money saved by now to take your mother to the Sistine Chapel.'

'Yes.' She paused and looked at him. For a moment Franco was sure she was about to confide something important. Then her eyes left his face. 'Yes, I have almost enough money now, that's for sure.'

'Well, you've worked hard for it. I only hope your mother appreciates both you and Michelangelo,' he laughed.

Maria Domenica watched him as he turned away to busy himself with some little task. It would be so easy just to stay here and relax into the rhythm of life at Caffe Angeli. Why had she ever started with this crazy plan of hers to escape from San Giulio? Was the longing really so strong as it had been all those months ago when she started working here, all fingers and thumbs as she tried to coax the Gaggia to perform for her?

'My son Giovanni wants to start helping out a little more in the *caffe*,' Franco remarked conversationally, his quick hands tidying plates into neat piles.

'He does?' Maria Domenica frowned.

'Don't look so sad. It's a good thing,' Franco assured her.

Giovanni was still only twelve but he was growing up fast. He'd soon want a job behind the counter at Caffe Angeli. It was time for Maria Domenica to make her move. She could see that now. It was time to extract her savings from her mattress, pack her few belongings and run away from San Giulio before it suffocated her. She could do it tonight if she liked. There was nothing to stop her. The thought was intoxicating . . . and frightening too. She touched Franco's shoulder again and then pulled her hand away and chewed the skin around her fingernail.

'Don't worry, *cara.*' Sometimes it seemed like Franco could read her mind. 'Giovanni won't take your place. There'll always be a job here for you at Caffe Angeli – for as long as you want it.'

8

Rosaria opened her eyes and squinted in the daylight. Oh God, was it morning already? She was exhausted. Slowly her mind calculated how many hours she had to get through before she could crawl back under the sheets again.

Next to her, Maria Domenica's bed was empty. The covers were pulled tight and smooth and the hospital corners were efficiently neat. It didn't look as though she'd even slept there.

Her crazy sister had been up with the birds again, thought Rosaria as she opened the window, leaned out and lit her first cigarette of the day.

She was careful to blow the smoke well clear of the room. Mamma would kill her if she knew she'd started with this, especially since she'd only given up herself a month or so ago. But really, she had to have some pleasures in life, didn't she?

The mirror had finally told Rosaria what her sister had been trying to tell her for months – she'd grown too fat. Determined to get her generous curves under some sort of control, she'd cut out the sweets and pastries she loved so much and stopped hacking off a slice of hard, golden bread every time she passed the shelf full of loaves in the kitchen.

She didn't enjoy the smoking all that much, but at least it kept her mouth busy during the times it would normally be chewing. And what harm could the odd sly cigarette do anyway? What Mamma didn't see, couldn't hurt her.

Rosaria wafted her hand around to expel any stray swirls of smoke and poked her head out of her bedroom door.

Strange. Where was the smell of warm yeast that usually hit her nostrils first thing each morning? She wandered barefoot down the dark, narrow corridor and, with a creak, pushed open the kitchen door. The room was empty, the table clean of flour, the oven unlit.

'Maria Domenica,' she called out. 'Where are you?'

From beneath the table a chicken squawked loudly in reply.

'Get out of there. Go on, shoo, shoo.' Opening the door, Rosaria chased the still screeching creature outside. The dogs let loose a volley of barks in reply.

Where the hell was Maria Domenica? She couldn't have gone to work this early, could she? She'd kill her if she had. There was all that bread to bake, the children would be up in a minute demanding breakfast and what if Salvatore had wet the bed again?

'Great, just great.' Rosaria hefted a sack of flour onto the table and made a reluctant start on the day's work.

It was fifteen minutes before she heard her mother shuffling down the corridor.

'Mamma,' she called indignantly, 'Maria Domenica has gone to Caffe Angeli already and left me to do everything. It's not fair.'

Pepina's weary face was as grey as the morning sky. 'Gone to work? At this time? She can't have.' She yawned and sat down heavily on one of the big, red vinyl chairs. 'Make me a coffee, Rosaria, that's what I need.'

Slapping the coffee pot down on the stovetop, Rosaria turned and yelled down the corridor, 'Sandra, Sandra, get out of bed right now, do you hear? I need an extra pair of hands in here.'

If Maria Domenica thought she was going to get away with this trick again she was wrong. And Rosaria was going to march straight into Caffe Angeli and tell her so.

Four hours of solid work later a belligerent Rosaria put on

her headscarf and strode alone past the dusty fields and all the way down the long, straight road that led to the main piazza of San Giulio. As she burst through the door of Caffe Angeli, Franco looked up from the newspaper he was scanning.

'Where is she then?' Rosaria blurted.

'Your sister? Haven't seen her. I'm not expecting her in for another couple of hours.'

'Well, if she's not here, where is she?' Rosaria demanded bossily.

'Well, I don't know, do I? Shopping maybe?'

Rosaria looked distracted all of a sudden. Her hard, little black eyes had been drawn to a platter piled high with the most glorious selection of cakes and pastries.

'Can I interest you in a little something this morning?' Franco smiled. 'I've got your favourites here, look.'

Rosaria sighed. 'Maybe just one little pastry.' She squeezed her generous buttocks onto a chair. 'I've had a terrible morning. I think I deserve it.'

By the time Rosaria looked at the clock again it was lunchtime, an extravagant spray of crumbs decorated her table and there was still no sign of her sister.

'I can't sit around here all day,' she decided finally. 'When you see Maria Domenica, tell her she's in trouble . . . with Mamma and with me.'

But Franco didn't see Maria Domenica. He worked the whole day alone. As he silently shut up shop after the last customer had left he felt uneasy. This wasn't like her. She hadn't missed a day at work since he'd first agreed to hire her. What was going on?

In Pepina's farmhouse they were getting anxious too. It had grown dark outside and no one had seen Maria Domenica all day.

'I wish your father was here.' Pepina paced around her kitchen nervously. 'I just don't know what to do.'

Even Rosaria was looking worried. 'Oh, for goodness'

sake, Mamma, sit down!' She pulled the packet of cigarettes out of her apron pocket. 'Here, have one of these with me. We need them . . . it's an emergency.'

They sat together in a fug of tension and smoke until streaks of grey light began to spread across the night sky.

'Look at the time.' Rosaria hoisted a bag of flour onto the table and made a reluctant start on the day's chores. 'The kids will be up soon wanting their breakfast.'

They didn't find the note until three days later. It was tucked beneath a monstrously large loaf of bread on the very top shelf of the wooden dresser. It read:

> I'm sorry if you've been worrying about me. There's no need. I've just gone to Rome like Marco did. I promise I'll be in touch when I've found myself a job and a place to live.
>
> Maria Domenica

Pepina screamed, 'She's gone to find that Marco Manzoni in Rome. She never gave up her hopes of him all this time. I don't believe it. She'll be ruined.'

White-faced and angry, Rosaria only half listened to her mother's wailing. She'd always assumed that Marco would come home once he'd had his fill of what Rome had to offer and then she'd make her move. Had her sister beaten her to it? She'd never forgive her if she had.

Meanwhile, over in the centre of town, behind the heavy red velvet curtain that separated the public part of Caffe Angeli from his private world, Franco bent his head over another letter and read it one last time:

> Dear Franco,
>
> I am so sorry to leave you without any notice. But Giovanni will be old enough soon to help you run the *caffe* and I hope you can manage alone until then.

I am very sorry about something else too – I lied to you about why I wanted the job. I never planned to take my mother on a trip to the city like I told you.

By the time you read this I'll be on the train alone, on my way to Rome. I'm so excited. I promise I'll go to the Sistine Chapel one day very soon and I'll give your love to Michelangelo.

Please don't be too angry with me. I'll miss you and the *caffe* very, very much. But I know I'm doing the right thing. I'm sure of it.

Your friend

Maria Domenica Carrozza

9

Life went on in the little town of San Giulio. Bread was baked and coffee was served. Weddings were held and babies were born. The peach trees behind Pepina's farmhouse sprouted their buds, blossomed and bore their fruit. But, aside from a couple of hastily scrawled postcards assuring everyone she was quite all right, nothing was seen or heard of Maria Domenica Carrozza.

A heartbroken Erminio had squeezed his big truck through the streets of Rome, scanning the faces of strangers and hoping and praying to see his eldest daughter's familiar features. But there was no sign of her. When he'd been told that she'd run away Erminio had lost himself in bluster. 'She's no daughter of mine now,' he'd boomed. But no one had believed him and later Pepina had seen the tears in his eyes. Erminio still hadn't given up his search and continued to add a couple of hours to his journey whenever his truck passed by Rome so he could make a wide sweep through the city that hid his Maria Domenica.

While her husband searched, Pepina cried and her children, infected by the sadness, cried too. Only Rosaria's eyes and cheeks stayed dry. Silently she cursed her big sister. Not only had Maria Domenica run away to steal the man who rightfully belonged to her, but since she'd left, Rosaria's parents had cracked down on all the little freedoms she'd once enjoyed. There was no more going into town alone for a start. No more taking off to the beach to join her cousins, and now they'd even taken her out of school. 'I can't do everything around here on my own any more,' Pepina had told her. 'Your sister isn't coming back so you'll have to take over the things she used to do.' And then she had cried again.

Life went on in Caffe Angeli too. Franco's son Giovanni cut down the hours he spent on schoolwork and took some of the work off his father's shoulders. That left Franco free to daydream and hatch a plan for another painting to cover one of the few bare patches on his beautiful walls.

Sometimes customers would idly ask if he'd heard any news of Maria Domenica. Usually he grunted and pretended to be too busy to talk. But if pressed he might produce the postcard he kept behind the counter. On the front a picture of Michelangelo's Sistine Chapel ceiling. On the back just a brief message: '*It's fabulous – better than I imagined in my wildest dreams. Now I just have to get to Florence to see Botticelli!*'

It was quite tricky for him to explain to Giovanni just why he'd become so attached to the girl. He was a gruff man who didn't like to talk about feelings. All his soul, his passion and colour was expressed on the walls of his *caffe*. The words that left his mouth came out in black and white.

'She was like a daughter to me,' he managed finally. 'We talked a lot – I could really talk to her.'

'What do you think she's doing now?' his son asked.

Franco frowned. 'I don't know – I worry about her. And I don't understand why she had to run away. Her parents aren't ogres. If she'd talked to them, explained that marriage and babies weren't what she wanted, I'm sure they wouldn't have tried to force her into anything. Running away wasn't sensible . . . and yet she always seemed like such a sensible girl.'

'Sensible people don't get into trouble,' Giovanni replied gravely.

Scrubbing vigorously at the same spot on the counter, Franco spoke his thoughts out loud: 'Oh, but there's so much trouble she could get into all alone in a city like Rome.

I only hope she's found herself a nice job in a little *caffe* somewhere with people who are good to her.'

The gossipers finally grew tired of discussing what may or may not have happened to the Carrozza girl. There was never any decent news to feed their fire. Even Elena wouldn't tell them a thing – she swore her son Marco had seen nothing of Maria Domenica in Rome. Soon there were fresh scandals and she was all but forgotten.

So when the bus rolled with a screech of brakes into San Giulio's little piazza one year later, no one looked twice at the dark girl struggling clumsily out of the doors with her small battered suitcase.

Franco could easily have glimpsed her from his spot behind the counter but he was busy with customers in his bustling *caffe*.

Giovanni, who'd run across the road to fetch a newspaper, did notice her and paused for a second. She looked so beaten and exhausted as she lifted her bag that he almost offered to help her with it. But there was something in her eyes that didn't invite an approach and in the end he let her walk off without saying a word, her big belly sticking out in front of her as she made her way uncomfortably down the street.

Maria Domenica Carrozza had come home at last.

10

Trudging heavily through the dusty streets, Maria Domenica took care not to look either left or right. She walked slowly past San Giulio's only church without lifting her eyes to its peeling white façade and onwards past the little lemonade stand on the corner of the piazza without a glance at Gina Rossi's shocked face peering out from behind her garlands of lemons. She picked up her pace, as the sweet smell of baking from the *pasticceria* hit her nostrils and then the metal tang of the butcher's shop. Her gaze fixed firmly on the cracked flagstones beneath her feet, her long dark hair falling over her face, her bony shoulders slumped, she slipped through the dirty old town.

The same whispered word chased her down every narrow street: '*Pregnant, pregnant, pregnant.*'

Then, more loudly, a familiar voice called out, 'Maria Domenica!'

She lengthened her stride.

'Maria Domenica. Slow down. It's only me, Aunt Lucia. Stop and let me catch up.'

Her aunt's stiletto heels clattered insistently over the pavement. Reluctantly Maria Domenica swung round to face her.

'*Ciao*, Lucia,' she said steadily. And '*Ciao*, Gabriella,' to her saucer-eyed cousin three short steps behind.

'Well . . .' Lucia made a big show of looking her up and down, her tight blonde curls wobbling with excitement. 'Well, look at you.'

'I'm over eight months gone,' Maria Domenica offered.

'So I see.' Lucia raised her eyebrows.

'Eh, but it's good to see you home again in San Giulio, isn't it, Mamma?' Gabriella's smile was a sly one. 'Where's your husband, though? Hasn't he come home with you?'

'There's no husband, Gabriella. Just me.' She patted her swollen belly. 'And this.'

'Where are you going now?' Lucia asked. 'You can't go home like that. Your father will go crazy. You'll break your mother's heart. Maria Domenica, what are you going to do?'

The town was buzzing now. Black-clad women, shopping baskets over their sturdy arms, were trickling towards them, anxious not to miss a thing. Old Luciano, the village idiot, wobbled past crazily on his rusty bicycle, steering badly with one hand and in the other clutching the cob of corn he'd been gnawing on.

'*Puttana*,' he cried lustily, showering Maria Domenica with a hail of kernels and saliva.

Lucia grasped her shoulder. 'This is ridiculous. Let's get you out of the street. Come up to the apartment and we'll sit down and think about this properly. Gabriella, grab her suitcase. Come on, hurry up.'

Maria Domenica tried to argue but a picture of her father's sad face had been fixed in her mind for months now and it was growing clearer by the second. So she allowed her aunt to propel her off the street, across the smooth floor of the lobby, into the stuffy little lift and up to her fourth-floor apartment. Inside everything gleamed. Her mother had always joked that Lucia followed visitors around with a duster and wiped their fingerprints off the brass door handles, and it wasn't too far from the truth.

Her place was a palace with shining marble on the floors and pretty glass chandeliers glinting from the high ceilings. It smelled of mothballs and of the furniture polish Lucia rubbed lovingly into her carved oak furniture every day. She had married well, to a man who worked for the council and wanted only the best things to surround him.

With a shove from her manicured hand, Lucia steered Maria Domenica into the kitchen, narrower than the one at the farmhouse and full of the latest appliances. She pushed her down into a chair and crouched on the floor in front of her. Taking her niece's face in both her smooth hands, she asked softly, 'Who's the father?'

Silence.

'You have to tell me, *cara*. Who is he?' Her voice was rising. 'Was it Marco?'

Harsh laughter.

'Well?'

'No, not Marco. Of course not Marco. I saw him twice when I was in Rome and he barely had a word for me either time. It was just a boy I met, Lucia. No one you know. He's gone now. I don't know where he is.'

'Anyone can be found,' Lucia told her. 'Do you want to find him?'

'It wouldn't do any good.'

'Did you love him?'

'Yes, of course.'

'Did he love you?'

'Obviously not.'

A rapping on the front door interrupted them. Tearing herself away reluctantly, Gabriella ran to answer it. She returned clutching a tall glass of cloudy homemade lemonade.

'Gina Rossi sent this. She thought you looked tired when you passed her stall.'

Maria Domenica accepted it gratefully and sipped the bitter drink. 'That's good,' she told Gabriella. 'Thank you.'

But there was more knocking at the big, polished wood door and Gabriella was on the move again.

This time she returned with a small paper bag of *biscotti*. 'Stefano at the bakery thought you might need to nibble on something,' she explained. 'Everyone is worried about you.'

The third knock on the door didn't bring concern. It brought Rosaria. A thinner, cleaner, smarter Rosaria than the one she'd left twelve months ago. An angrier Rosaria.

'If it's a boy, will you call it Marco?' she spat.

'How did you know I was here?' Maria Domenica asked.

'The phone. It hasn't stopped ringing since you got off the bus.'

'You've got a phone now?'

'Life hasn't stood still since you left us, Maria Domenica. We've moved on and things have changed.'

'Does Mamma know about . . .' Her eyes fell to her bulging belly.

'Mamma sent me.' Rosaria looked contemptuous. 'She said you shouldn't bother going home. Not until you've got your husband with you.'

'I can't go home?'

'No, you can't.'

'What about Papa?'

'He's not there.'

'Does he know?'

'Everybody knows, Maria Domenica. The whole town knows.'

Rosaria turned on her heel smoothly and walked away. Maria Domenica heard the front door slam but didn't try to call her back. What was the point?

Lucia's words were kinder. For all her brassy bleached curls, the gobbets of gold that hung from her arms and her ears, the layers of mascara that blackened her eyelashes, she had a good heart and a generous nature. Maria Domenica could stay with her temporarily. She'd have to share a bed with her cousins, which would be fine for a week or two, but then she'd need to make alternative arrangements.

'Have you got any money?' Lucia asked.

'No, not really. I was working as a waitress in a restaurant near the Spanish Steps. But they fired me when my pregnancy started to show. I've been living off my savings ever since. There's not much left. That's why I came home. I had nowhere else to go. I didn't know what else to do.'

Lucia stroked her hair. 'You only really have one choice then,' she said quietly.

'What?' There was hope in Maria Domenica's voice.

'You'll have to go to the nuns. They'll look after you until you have the baby and then they'll find a home for it.'

'No.'

'There are nice couples who can't have babies of their own. You'll be bringing them joy. And then you'll be free to carry on with your life. Not here. You can't stay here, the gossip will kill you. But maybe in Naples or back in Rome.'

'I'm not giving away my baby.'

'You don't have any choice, Maria Domenica. I really can't see that you have any other option at all.'

The front door slammed again and Rosaria appeared back in the kitchen doorway. Her face was spiteful now.

'You asked about Papa,' she said, lighting a cigarette with a certain defiance. 'Well, he's not in San Giulio. When he heard the news he didn't say a thing, he just got in his truck and drove away. Mamma says he's gone to Rome. He'll bring Marco back with him and then there'll be a wedding.'

Round and round in circles they went as they talked late into the night. Now, with Marco on his way back, Maria Domenica realized that she did have a choice. She could give up her baby and keep her freedom. Or give up her freedom and keep her baby.

'I can't do either of those things,' she told her aunt desperately. 'I can't marry Marco. I don't like him. And he'll hate me for trapping him into marriage when he knows perfectly well that this isn't his baby.'

Lucia sighed. Her own daughters and husband had gone to

bed hours ago. Her head ached and she longed to lay it on her pillow. This could go on all night and she was running out of patience.

'Just stop for a moment and think,' she told her niece. 'No one will believe Marco when he says he's not the father. He's had at least one girl pregnant, hasn't he? He's a wild boy. You'll be doing him a favour if you marry him. He'll have to settle then, won't he? His mother will be pleased too. She won't admit it but she's been worried sick about him all this time and she'd have him back home under her nose once you were married. Plus she'd have a little grandchild to dote on.'

'I don't love him.'

'You loved the other one, didn't you, and that hasn't done you any good. If you want to keep your baby you need to find it a father. Sleep on it, Maria Domenica. Things may seem clearer in the morning.'

Maria Domenica couldn't sleep. She sat in Lucia's tidy kitchen, resting her head on the cool tabletop and feeling her baby kick hard inside her. By the time the sun rose again she had made her decision. Rosaria had been right. There was going to be a wedding.

11

'It's not my baby. The bitch. Is that what she told you? I haven't laid a finger on her. I'm not bloody marrying her.'

No one believed Marco's denials. The more vehement he grew, the guiltier he sounded.

And while his mother tried to win him over with soft entreaties – 'Do the right thing Marco' – his father stuck to home truths. Marco had an inheritance to think about, a thriving farm and good land that would be his some day. Did he want to risk losing it all?

Then Maria Domenica's father pulled out the final weapon – his cheque book. Slowly he wrote down a number. If Marco got married he'd need cash to set up home. The money was in the bank. Did he want it or not?

Marco was a stubborn boy and it took a while for the threats and the bribes to grind him down. But finally he held out his hand and accepted Erminio's cheque. 'When is the wedding?' he asked wearily.

'Soon, soon.' Erminio smiled for the first time in days. 'Your little bambino is due any minute. There's not a moment to waste.'

There was no white dress and no flowers. No celebration, not even the traditional family photographs on the stone steps in front of the church. Instead, her ankles swollen from the heat, Maria Domenica was hustled into the side door of the chapel where the priest and Marco stood waiting for her and the smell of incense hung heavy and sweet in the suddenly chill air.

She saw that Marco had been unable to resist a few small touches. A bud of a flower was tucked into the lapel of his best jacket, a silk handkerchief poked out of his top pocket and his hair, which he'd been growing into wispy tendrils, was neatly slicked back.

'Let's get on with it, shall we?' he told the priest. 'Before we change our minds.'

Tonelessly Maria Domenica repeated the vows. This didn't feel real. Even when the thin, cold wedding ring was slipped on her finger and the priest's voice declared they were man and wife, it was still difficult to believe. She thought she was probably in shock.

Behind her she could hear the sound of soft sobbing but couldn't tell if it was coming from her mother or Rosaria. The church was dim: they hadn't even bothered to turn on all the lights.

She half turned and looked over her shoulder to where her father sat, head hanging in disappointment and shame. Beside him Lucia's blonde curls shone out of the darkness. Her aunt twitched her fingers in a subdued greeting and gave an encouraging smile.

Afterwards Maria Domenica lay on her old bed in the farmhouse while the others ate lunch together. She heard the dull sound of their voices through the thick stone walls. Rosaria had plastered the walls of the room they'd once shared with photos of movie stars. Her clothes lay jumbled with shoes and magazines on the floor. She'd made it into her own space now, but that didn't matter for Maria Domenica wouldn't be sleeping here tonight anyway.

There was a cottage all set up for her and Marco on the Manzoni land. The farmhands had carried in big, old mismatched pieces of furniture that no one else wanted: a chipped formica table for the kitchen, a pine dresser that had been gathering cobwebs in the barn, a couple of sagging, musty armchairs and a double bed covered in crisp white linen waiting for the newly-weds' first night together.

Maria Domenica couldn't imagine lying next to Marco's slender body or picture his pretty, soft face next to hers on the pillow. Perhaps they'd let her stay here instead, she thought. She listened to the voices next door growing louder as the wine bottles grew empty. She'd taken Marco's name now so surely that was enough to buy her some respectability? He could move into the cottage alone and she could stay here in the narrow, single bed she'd slept in safely since she was a little girl. If she cleared some of Rosaria's junk away there would even be space beside it for the baby's crib. Comforted by the familiarity of home, she closed her eyes and drifted off to sleep.

In the kitchen Marco drained his glass with gusto, his face growing ruddy from the alcohol. He was feeling more cheerful by the minute. Perhaps this marriage wasn't such a bad thing after all. To be honest he'd been getting sick of Rome. The hours in the butcher's shop were long and his boss was a real slave-driver. He'd grown to hate the stink of the meat carcasses. It seemed to cling to him no matter how long he scrubbed at his skin in the shower. No wonder the girls never bothered with him for long. Silly little tourist bitches.

Maria Domenica wasn't what he'd have chosen as a wife. He liked girls with soft, sexy bodies and plenty of spirit, girls like Rosaria whose full buttocks were right at this moment presenting themselves to him invitingly as she bent over to rummage for sugared almonds in the cupboard. Very nice, very nice indeed. And why should he give up girls like that just because he had a wife at home and a bastard baby? He could still have his fun. Even his father had said as much. 'Just be discreet, Marco. Stay away from the village girls or there'll be trouble,' he'd warned.

Maria Domenica would be OK for the other things – the cooking and cleaning, the bringing up children. As soon as she'd given birth to the bastard he'd do his very best to fill her belly with a Manzoni baby. He held out his glass to be topped up again with Pepina's strong, nearly black wine and took another gulp. Life wasn't so bad after all. Maybe things were turning out for the best.

As Marco drank himself silly, Erminio looked him over. He wasn't pleased with his new son-in-law. Marco wasn't the man he would have chosen for his eldest daughter. He wasn't a man really, he was a boy. He was almost twenty now, yet his cheeks were so soft they didn't look like they'd ever seen a razor. He carried a comb around in his back pocket. His eyelashes were too long.

And the boy had no guts. When he'd opened the door of his bedsit in Rome and found Erminio and his father looming on the doorstep he'd almost fainted. He'd put up no resistance when they'd bundled him into the cab of the truck. Erminio hadn't even had to pull out the rifle that he'd slipped beneath the seat in case he'd needed to illustrate his threats.

Maria Domenica could have done so much better for herself than this. But what choice did he have? The girl had got herself into trouble. Better a husband like Marco than no husband at all. A tear trickled slowly down Erminio's left cheek and he brushed it away impatiently with his big, rough hand. No one had noticed. Not even his wife who was busy clearing the empty dishes off the table and replacing them with platters piled high with cheese, bread and fruit. He looked fondly at the woman who had shared his life for all these years. Her dark hair was peppered with grey now and pulled back harshly from her round, still barely wrinkled face. Her body grew stockier by the season and strained at the seams of her Sunday best dress. She was a wonderful woman.

Perhaps, in time, his daughter and Marco could find the sort of peaceful happiness he had with Pepina. He couldn't ask for any more than that.

12

Franco Angeli sat in his private place, the cool, dim spot behind the thick red curtain that separated him from his busy *caffe*. He'd slept badly last night and was tired. His son Giovanni had told him to have a rest before the lunchtime rush. 'I'll look after things out here. You go and close your eyes for an hour or so,' the boy had ordered, suddenly sounding very grown up. And now Franco's eyes were obediently closed but still sleep didn't come.

He listened to the whoosh of the Gaggia as it frothed milk for another tray of cappuccinos, to the clinking of cups and to Gloria Ferrero laughing loudly at the corner table. Then suddenly the chatter died and there was silence.

'Papa!' Giovanni called out and Franco heard excitement in the boy's voice. 'You have a visitor. No, don't come out – she'll come in to you.'

The red curtain was pushed aside and Maria Domenica's belly appeared, encased in something large and floral. But Franco didn't stare at that, he studied her face. She looked the same, perhaps a little older and a little more tired, but essentially the same.

'I was never allowed in here before,' she said, looking round curiously at the small, gloomy space she almost filled with her bulk.

'No,' Franco agreed, 'you weren't. But now you are here you should sit down.'

Maria Domenica settled herself in the armchair opposite him and gave a little sigh. 'That's better, my feet were killing me. This pregnancy business is hard work, I can tell you.' She smiled at Franco. 'I don't need to tell you anything, do I? You've heard it all by now?'

'You've certainly caused a stir. People are still talking and you've been back for nearly three weeks.'

'Three weeks tomorrow.'

'Why did you leave it so long before coming to see me, *cara*? I've been waiting for you.' Franco looked hurt.

'I was ashamed, guilty for lying to you,' she admitted. 'I felt stupid for getting myself into this mess. I thought you'd be so disappointed in me.'

'You made a mistake,' Franco told her. 'Everyone makes mistakes.'

'Actually I think I made a whole series of mistakes, starting with leaving this place. I should have just stayed here. I was happy.'

'Ah, but then you'd never have seen the things you saw, done the things you did. Would you have given all that up just to stay here and live the same old life? I don't think so.'

'I'm living the same old life now though, aren't I?' Maria Domenica pointed out bitterly. 'Just a worse version of it.'

'Is Marco cruel to you?' There was a note of worry in Franco's voice.

'No, no, he's not cruel at all,' she replied hastily. 'For a boy who has been forced into marriage with a girl who is carrying someone else's child, he's been fine. He mostly ignores me. He works with his father all day, comes home, I feed him and then he goes out drinking with his friends. Because I'm like this,' she stroked her belly, 'we haven't had to, well, you know . . .'

'And after the baby's born. What then?' he asked.

Maria Domenica frowned and Franco saw the beginnings of a wrinkle that would one day form a deep crease between her eyebrows. 'We'll just carry on the same, I suppose – more or less,' she said. 'I don't have any other choice.'

'How long before you think you'll be ready to come back to work?' he asked casually.

'Back to work? Here at Caffe Angeli?' She couldn't keep the hope out of her voice. 'That would be impossible. What would I do with the baby?'

Franco shrugged and looked around the cramped space behind the red curtain that he'd filled up over the years with odd bits of furniture and old family photographs. 'I'll shift things about a bit and there will be enough space for a crib back here,' he decided. 'I can maybe get rid of that armchair you're sitting in. This is a family business, Maria Domenica. There's always room for a baby. The only question is, will your husband allow it?'

She thought about it for a moment. 'I don't think he'd care,' she said hesitantly. 'It doesn't seem to matter what I do so long as the house is clean and he gets fed. He might even be pleased that I'm earning my own money since he keeps telling me how expensive it's going to be keeping me and the baby. No, I don't think he'd mind at all. Oh, Franco, thank you. You can't even begin to imagine how happy you've made me.'

'Don't thank me yet,' Franco cautioned. 'You have to check with Marco. He's your husband and it would be wrong to make a decision like this without him.'

Even that didn't wipe the smile off Maria Domenica's face. She looked so pretty when she smiled, thought Franco. He only hoped her baby wasn't a screamer, otherwise the noise might drive the customers away.

Giovanni smiled too, a grin that almost reached his ears, when he heard the news that Maria Domenica was coming back to work. Any fears she'd had that the boy might feel displaced by her return melted away as he seized her arms, kissed her on both cheeks and held her for a heartbeat or two longer than was strictly necessary.

Giovanni had changed in this past year. She watched him as he turned to serve another customer. He'd grown taller and filled out and he moved about the *caffe* with an air of confidence that he'd lacked before.

The boy felt her eyes on him, looked up and smiled again. 'Hurry up and have that baby,' he told her. 'Papa and I need you here. See how busy we are.'

Maria Domenica walked beneath the shade of the palm trees in the piazza and towards the ugly old church. She felt different. Not happy exactly, but calm. She felt she could cope with anything now. Quite soon she'd give birth to her baby and even though it might be painful, she was sure she could handle it. In a month she'd have no excuse not to sleep with Marco as a wife should, but it might not be too awful. Eventually she would have to bear his children and even the thought of that didn't worry her so much now. So long as she could slot into the rhythm of life at Caffe Angeli she'd deal with anything else that came along.

She heard her name being called. From behind her stall, Gina Rossi was waving and trying to attract her attention. '*Cara*, come over here. Don't you want to buy a nice, cool glass of lemonade from me? It'll be good for you and your *bambino*.'

Maria Domenica smiled and handed over a handful of coins to the nosy old street vendor. Sipping the bitter liquid, she asked the question Gina was happy to answer all day, every day: 'So, what's happening?'

'Well.' Gina leaned forward conspiratorially. 'Did you not hear? Gloria Ferrero had the most enormous fight with her husband. She chased him down the street with a carving knife. The poor man was still in his pyjamas and they had a huge hole in them right here.' She slapped her rump and cackled. 'We all saw his big, old bottom. It looked like a side of ham!'

Maria Domenica joined in the laughter. At last there was something new for people to gossip about. Soon they wouldn't stare so hard when she walked down the street or whisper so fiercely. She was almost old news. She was just a wife, nearly a mother. People wouldn't forget, they never forgot anything around here. But daily reports of her condition wouldn't be bartered in the bakery and traded in the butcher's shop.

Draining her glass, she smiled at Gina. 'Did she catch her husband?' she asked.

'No.' The old lady was still wheezing with laughter. 'I don't think she did. Who'd have thought the old bugger could still run so fast. I didn't think he had it in him!'

13

Rosaria clattered pans angrily in her sister's ramshackle kitchen. Maria Domenica's waters had broken this morning and since then she had been closeted in the room next door with her mother and the midwife. Every now and then a cry escaped her but she didn't seem any closer to giving birth.

So she, Rosaria, had come to get things organized. Marco would need a meal when he came in from the fields and there was no one else to cook it. Dried beans were soaking in a bowl and there was a bunch of leafy celery on the kitchen table, so clearly her sister had been planning a *pasta e fagioli*. That was fine by Rosaria. There would be plenty of time for a few cigarettes and a glossy magazine while she let the beans boil.

She looked round the little cottage with disdain. Maria Domenica really hadn't made much effort. It was clean, she'd give her that, but there were no curtains at the windows and she'd made no attempt to cover up the battered old armchairs with a rug or a throw, or put pictures on the plain white walls.

'If this were my place I'd have it looking really nice, like a real home,' she muttered as she threw some parsley and garlic in with the boiling beans. 'Marco deserves better than this dump.'

Next door she heard her sister yell out again. Her cries were becoming more frequent now, which meant the baby couldn't be too far away.

Rosaria eyed the celery. There was a little soil clinging to the bottom of the stems but did it really need washing? A bit of dirt never did anyone any harm, she decided, and chopped it roughly. Sighing, she fried a finely chopped onion in some green olive oil with fatty pancetta. Then she added the celery, leaves and all, as well as a little chopped carrot to the heavy-bottomed pan. She found a cup or two of chicken stock in the fridge and poured it into the fragrant sizzling mixture along with the inevitable sieved tomatoes. A pinch of sugar, a little salt, a grind or two of black pepper and then the lid went on and she could relax until the beans were tender and it was time to add them to the pot.

By the time Marco came through the door, Maria Domenica was screaming far more than seemed necessary and Rosaria was sitting smugly with her nice little sauce bubbling on the stove.

'Mmm, that smells good.' Marco grinned, lifting the lid and breathing the steam. He slapped Rosaria on the bottom as she hurried to break up the spaghetti and chuck it in a pan of foaming salted water. 'You know how to please a man, eh?'

Just then Maria Domenica gave another huge shriek, followed by a string of words that nice girls didn't say. Mamma will let her have it now, thought Rosaria cheerily. But instead she heard Pepina's voice encouraging her sister: 'You're nearly there, you're nearly there!'

All the colour drained out of Marco's face and he looked distinctly queasy. 'Has this noise been going on all day?' he asked Rosaria.

'Not really. But I think this is the worst bit and she'll be quiet in a minute.' Calmly Rosaria stirred the spaghetti to stop it sticking and popped the lid on to bring it back to the boil.

The pasta was still only half cooked when Rosaria realized her sister's screams had stopped and been replaced by the sound of a newborn baby's weak wailing. 'It's over,' she told

Marco. 'And I should grate some *parmigiano* because you're nearly ready to eat.'

In the room next door Maria Domenica lay exhausted but happy, her daughter cradled in her arms. She didn't think she'd ever seen anything so tiny, so helpless or so beautiful. 'Her name is Chiara,' she told her mother.

'Don't you think you should wait to see what Marco wants to call her?' Pepina asked. 'I think I heard him come home a few minutes ago. I'll call him.'

'Call him if you like.' Maria Domenica's black eyes held her mother's in a calm, steady gaze. 'But my baby's name is Chiara.'

To give Marco his due, he tried. He held the baby and pronounced her very pretty before escaping back to the kitchen to finish his bowl of *pasta e fagioli*. Rosaria was less affable. She simply gave Chiara a look worthy of an evil fairy godmother and said, 'Ugh, they're so creased when they're first born, aren't they?'

Maria Domenica didn't bother to reply. Her baby's face had filled her whole world and everything else had diminished almost to nothing.

The next days were lost in a milky haze of happiness. For the whole nine months she'd carried her, Maria Domenica hadn't been sure how she'd be with this baby she was never meant to have. So she was astonished by the intensity of the love she felt and couldn't bear to let the child out of her arms. Even her own mother had to plead to be allowed a cuddle.

As for Marco, he stayed out of her way. At night he slept on the two old armchairs that he'd pushed together and during the day he'd sometimes poke his head round the door or bring her a plate of bread, chopped fruit and slices of cheese. But after that first time he hadn't asked to hold the baby again or shown the slightest interest in her name, her clothes, her sleeping and feeding habits, or any of the thousand tiny things Maria Domenica found so fascinating.

For four strange and magical days she stayed shut in her bedroom, waking when Chiara cried for a feed, sleeping when she slept. It felt how life was supposed to be. On the fifth day Pepina began to scold her.

'Get up, get dressed. You have a husband out there to cook for. You can leave that baby alone for five minutes, you know. It won't do it any harm.'

Maria Domenica did as she was told. She spent the days closeted with her baby, but by the time Marco came home she'd be in the kitchen shelling peas or baking bread to her mother's recipe.

Chiara was a month old before Maria Domenica dared to ask her husband the question that had been playing on her mind. 'Marco, would you mind if I went back to my old job at Caffe Angeli?' She used the humblest voice she could manage. 'I wouldn't have to do long hours and Franco says I can take the baby with me. I thought the money I earned would help with some of the extra expenses.'

Marco looked down at his bowl of minestrone. 'What about me? Who will cook for me if you're cooking for strangers in the *caffe*?' he asked sulkily.

'Oh, I'll leave lunch all prepared for you and I'll always be back in time to make your evening meal,' Maria Domenica reassured him, hating the sound of her own pleading voice. 'You'll always come first, don't worry.'

Marco smiled slyly. 'Well, if you're ready to go to work, you must be feeling strong?'

'Yes, yes, I am.'

He cast a glance at the two armchairs, still pushed together. 'I won't need to sleep there tonight then, will I? You are ready to be a real wife at last.'

That night her husband's naked body slipped into bed beside her. Even the heavy work on the farm hadn't given him much in the way of muscles. His chest was hairless and his body as delicate as a girl's. This would be so different from the last time. The last time, in Rome.

Marco's slight frame seemed almost weightless as he lay on top of her. As his thin, white penis drove into her and his pretty face crumpled with the pleasure of his orgasm, she kept her eyes tightly shut. 'Don't wake the baby,' she hissed, as he grunted and groaned.

He rolled off her and wiped his penis clean with a corner of the white monogrammed Manzoni sheet. 'A little bit of that every night and we'll soon have you pregnant again,' he told her. 'Only this time you'll have a baby that really does deserve my name.' He glanced at the crib in the corner where her daughter thankfully still slept peacefully. 'Not like little Chiara Manzoni over there. Tell me, what should her surname really be?'

Maria Domenica stayed silent.

'Who's Chiara's real daddy? Who's the man who should have married you?'

'Does that really matter? I'm married to you now,' she said, fighting to keep the edge of irritation out of her voice.

'That's right, you're married to me now.' His hand reached round to the back of her head and pushed her down his body with a firm pressure. 'So why don't you get on with behaving as a wife should?'

Her heart sank and for a moment Maria Domenica considered fighting him. But it wasn't worth the risk. If she did what Marco wanted tonight, then tomorrow she would be behind the shining stainless steel counter in Caffe Angeli where she belonged. She'd put on her starched white apron and produce perfect coffee all day. Shutting her eyes tightly, she took his softness into her mouth and began to suck obediently.

14

Maria Domenica pushed Chiara in her second-hand pram through the dusty streets of San Giulio, past the wealthier people's houses built around their own private courtyards and the modern apartment block where Lucia lived. She dawdled down the main street, gazing into the shop windows, then quickened her step to hurry past the church where she'd been forced to marry and across the piazza with its dumpy little fountain and graceful palm trees. As she walked, Maria Domenica felt as though every pair of eyes in town was following her progress. Franco was going to do good business today, she realized. Once they'd all worked out where she was heading, no one was going to be able to resist popping into Caffe Angeli to take a good look at her and the baby.

Franco had pulled Giovanni's old wooden crib out of the attic and spruced it up. Maria Domenica found it tucked behind the red curtain, dressed prettily with clean, white bedding, just waiting for a baby.

'Oh, you didn't need to do that. She could have stayed in her pram,' she told Franco.

'Just say thank you, Maria Domenica.'

'Thank you, thank you and thank you again.' She kissed him quickly on both cheeks and then gave him one more kiss for good luck.

Not that Chiara spent much of the day in the little crib; she was far too popular. As Maria Domenica had expected, half the village passed through the *caffe* over the course of the day and nearly everyone clamoured for a glimpse of the new baby.

'Bring her out, bring her out, let me have a cuddle,' begged Lucia.

'Me next, me next,' giggled Gabriella.

'Put that cigarette out first,' ordered Elena Manzoni. 'You don't want to be blowing smoke all over a new baby. It's not healthy. Here, give her to me, she'll be safe with her grandma. Oh, smell the top of her head – isn't it divine? She's so like her father was at this age. So like my Marco.'

Maria Domenica rolled her eyes at Franco. She thought her mother-in-law really had to be one of the stupidest women in the world.

Lunchtime brought Rosaria with Pepina in tow. 'We just came for a slice or two of pizza,' her sister declared. 'And maybe a little piece of pastry.'

'And to see if the rumour was true that you were working here,' Pepina admitted to her eldest daughter. 'That damn phone has been ringing all morning. I wish we'd never bothered with it.'

'It's the sixties, not the dark ages, Mamma,' Rosaria snapped. 'Only the peasants don't have their own phone nowadays.'

But Pepina wasn't listening. She'd noticed that Gloria Ferrero at the corner table was smoking and drinking coffee with one hand and cuddling her very own granddaughter with the other. 'Here, give her to me,' she hissed, scooping Chiara up into her arms.

Sighing, she plopped the baby onto one of the café tables and calmly proceeded to strip off her soiled nappy. Franco paled visibly.

'Not here, Mamma.' Maria Domenica was alarmed. 'This is no place to do that. Come with me.'

'Well, this is no place for a baby at all,' Pepina complained, as her daughter pushed her through the red velvet curtain. 'If babies were meant to be in a *caffe*, God would have given them a taste for coffee. You should be at home with her, not back working in this place surrounded by all these heathen pictures on the walls.'

'Shush, Mamma,' Maria Domenica begged. She lay the baby in the crib and deftly wrapped her in a clean nappy. 'I'm glad of the job and glad of the money. And so is Marco.'

'Oh, well, if Marco's happy . . .' Pepina began, then the sheer cuteness of Chiara overwhelmed her and she pinched a fat little cheek gently. 'She's such a gorgeous little thing. She's just like you were as a baby.'

Maria Domenica couldn't believe she had ever looked quite this beautiful. Her daughter had a shiny helmet of dark hair, dusky purple eyelids and the funniest stern expression on her face. Chiara seemed to know she had to be good, to understand that her mamma wasn't strong enough to cope with sleepless nights and a red-faced screaming baby. She cried when she was hungry and the rest of the time she gurgled happily to herself or she slept.

'She's a little angel,' breathed Pepina.

'And was I an angel too at that age?' Maria Domenica teased.

'Oh, yes, yes you were.' Pepina sank back into the softness of Franco's one remaining armchair. 'Your father made me pregnant with you so soon after we were married. He said he didn't want me getting bored. I'll never forget the look on his face the first time he saw you – his daughter, his little girl. You were such a happy little thing, hardly ever cried. Not like that Rosaria, she didn't stop screaming for at least the first three years. I used to have to pay Francesca Maggio's daughter to take her for a walk every day. I'd hear her screams growing quieter as the child wheeled her away in her pram and then louder again about half an hour later as she wheeled her back home again. But not you.' She leaned over and stroked Chiara's shiny slick of hair. 'You were like this little one, no trouble at all. Even when you started crawling and walking I never had to worry about you too much.'

'I'm sorry, Mamma.'

'Sorry for what, *cara*?' Pepina looked up.

'For causing you so much worry in the past year. For running away to Rome and coming home pregnant and having the whole village gossiping about me.' Tears pressed hard behind Maria Domenica's black eyes. 'Every day I regret what I did to you and Papa. I must have been mad.'

Her mother shrugged. 'I won't pretend we weren't upset. You broke your father's heart and still I don't think it's truly mended. We worry so much – if this is what our good girl did to us, God only knows what the others have in store. But look at you now: a beautiful baby, a handsome husband, good prospects. It's all come out right in the end.' Pepina heaved herself up onto her generous haunches. 'Anyway I can't sit around here all day. There's work to be done at home. I'll expect you and Marco for lunch on Sunday, shall I? I've been making pasta all week and Fabrizio Maggio brought me a pan of live eels yesterday, so we'll have a real feast. Your father loves having all his family around the table again.'

She took Maria Domenica's face in her hands and for a moment it seemed as if she was going to kiss her. 'Don't leave us again, just promise me that,' she said quietly. 'Stay here. This is where you belong.'

15

Maria Domenica shovelled well-rotted manure onto the raised patch of earth and spread it with her spade. It was hard, hot work. She handled her spade carefully, trying not to damage too many of the fat, pink worms squirming beneath it.

'Good to have plenty of worms in your garden,' Elena called approvingly from the old canvas deckchair she'd positioned under the shade of a tree. 'They fill the soil full of air and help your vegetables breathe so they will be all the more delicious.'

Not for the first time Maria Domenica wondered how she was going to stomach a lifetime of this woman's inane comments. She smiled but said nothing in reply.

Picking up her hoe, she began to work the hard slabs of red earth. It was Marco who had decided he wanted a kitchen garden like the one his mother had at the big house. 'I want tomatoes and basil and parsley,' he'd told her. 'Maybe some beans, perhaps some rocket leaves. All here outside the kitchen door so you can pick them fresh as you're preparing my meals.'

Seized by the sudden enthusiasm, he'd spent a rare industrious hour digging up a rectangle of flat earth into huge, rough slabs. 'There, I've given you a head start,' he'd said finally, standing back to admire his handiwork.

So now, as the cool of an early Sunday morning built up to the midday heat, Maria Domenica finished the job, hoeing the earth patiently section by section and mixing it carefully with the black rotten manure. When she'd finished she'd plant the beans at the back with bamboo poles to support them, then the tomatoes in the middle and the herbs and salad leaves here at the very front.

'Of course, it's really far too late to be planting,' called out Elena knowledgeably, her fat round face sweating gently as the heat grew more intense. 'You should have done it weeks ago. Next year you'll have to remember to get going a lot earlier.'

Maria Domenica paused for a second and gazed at the buffalo grazing peacefully in the paddocks beyond her cottage. 'Next year?' she asked.

'Yes, yes, you want to get your manure spread at least a month before you start planting and then sow your seeds when the earth is warm but the rain is still falling. That way you'll see the most growth.'

'I see.'

'And you should plant your basil in amongst the tomatoes, not all to one side in a patch of its own. It's better for the insects.'

'Yes.'

'I've been growing vegetables since I was a child, Maria Domenica, I know what I'm talking about. You young people don't care to listen to advice from your elders, I understand that, but sometimes it pays to open your ears. I remember when I was your age . . .'

She ran on and on. It was like having the radio on in the background – one of those annoying stations that was too much talk and not enough music.

'Anyway, my dear,' she was still banging on, her round cheeks flapping, her short fingers waving imperiously in the air, 'I'm glad you're making a vegetable patch here. Keep piling on the manure and compost and the soil will be beautiful by the time Marco's father and I move into the cottage.'

'What?' Maria Domenica was confused. 'Why would you want to move into the cottage?'

'Oh, I'm talking years from now. You and Marco will have had more babies by then and your family will be too squashed in this little place.' Elena leaned back in the deckchair and stretched out her hairy, brown legs complacently. 'That's the plan – we'll swap houses. And then when we're dead and gone and your children have grown up and had families of their own, you'll move back to the cottage and let them have the big house. That's the way it works in the Manzoni family, that's the tradition. And I think it's nice to have the future all mapped out. That way there's no surprises.'

'Are surprises bad?'

'Well, we've certainly had enough of them in this family recently, haven't we?' Elena glanced at Chiara sleeping peacefully in the pram beside her. 'I think we can do without any more for the next fifty years or so.'

For a moment, as she hoed the hard red earth into submission, Maria Domenica knew exactly what it would feel like to be buried up to her neck in it. To be unable to move, the idea of a life all mapped out, no changes, no surprises . . .

'What if you're forced to change?' she said to her mother-in-law breathlessly. 'Forced by circumstances.'

'What circumstances?' Elena's wide forehead wrinkled in confusion. 'Nothing needs to change here – not ever. People will always want to eat good mozzarella cheese so we'll always keep buffalo. No, nothing about our lives needs to change. We can stay here on this farm doing what we do until they carry us out in a box and then our children will take over from us. That's the way it is. That's the way it's always been.'

'You can't see into the future.' Maria Domenica was sweating profusely now she was stabbing at the earth so fiercely.

Elena squinted at the sun. 'Well, I can see into the immediate future,' she replied smugly. 'And if you don't get yourself into the house and clean up pretty smartly I can see that you're going to make us all late for your mother's Sunday lunch.'

For once Maria Domenica couldn't argue. Stacking her tools away in the corrugated iron lean-to by the side of the ugly old cottage, she tried to feel more kindly towards her mother-in-law. It wasn't easy. The woman was so irritating. And she'd ruined Marco, really she had. It was plain to see why he had turned into the vain, lazy, ineffectual little man he was today. Elena hadn't only cooked and cleaned for him all his life, she'd also washed his hair and cut his fingernails and toenails. And now he expected the same service from his wife. The first time he'd handed her the nail scissors and thrust his foot in her lap Maria Domenica hadn't been able to believe it.

'Cut them straight across,' Marco had instructed. 'And then get the nail file and smooth down the edges.'

How a man who did physical work on a farm each day could be so particular about his appearance, she didn't know. As she hunched over the handbasin in her little bathroom, soaping away the soil and sweat, Maria Domenica smiled. She hoped the buffalo and the pigs appreciated his lovely pedicure.

She heard Elena's voice echoing down the hallway, urging her to hurry. Quickly she tidied her hair and slipped on the shapeless red flowery garment that passed for her best dress these days. 'Just a minute,' she called back.

Lucia had told her she should start wearing a little make-up. Just a slick of lipstick and a lick of mascara, she'd urged. Give yourself some colour. But it looked foreign on her face. Licking her fingers and wetting down her hair to make it smooth, she decided that she'd do.

The drive to her parents' place was short, thank God. Being crammed beside Elena in the little Fiat made her flesh crawl. Every time her mother-in-law changed gear, a fat brown hand brushed her knee, and when she turned the steering wheel, a surprisingly sharp elbow jabbed her in the ribs. She couldn't stand it. Marco came from inside this woman's body, she thought with revulsion, pressing herself close to the passenger door. He touches me . . . she touches me . . . it's as though they own me.

She held Chiara close as her mother-in-law skidded in the dust, taking a corner too quickly. Not far now. Just down the dirt track past Francesca Maggio's place and over the busy main road and they'd be home.

As they pulled into the driveway, she could see the family already gathering round the long wooden table they'd pulled out and set down beneath the lemon tree. Erminio was at the head of the table, gazing rapturously at the tray of lasagne in front of him. Beside him were Marco and his father Gino who'd come directly from an illicit morning card game in town. Marco's glass was already half empty, she noted, and his face growing pink.

Her younger sisters were squashed on the high bench at the far end of the table, Salvatore propped between them. Giggling into each other's long hair, they talked quietly of the things that concern little girls.

Rosaria was nowhere to be seen but an angry clanging of pans from the kitchen signalled clearly where she might be found.

Erminio glanced over at his eldest daughter with love in his soft eyes. Patting the chair beside him, he called, 'Come here and sit down. Show me that baby of yours. Let me see how she's grown.'

Maria Domenica hesitated. 'Perhaps I should go and see if I can be of any help in there,' she told him, nodding towards the kitchen.

'No, no. Your sister has everything under control. Today you don't work, you rest. Now bring the *bambina* here and let me give her a kiss.'

Gratefully Maria Domenica moved away from her mother-in-law's side and sank down into the old, ripped vinyl chair beside her father. 'It's good to be home,' she told him.

'It's good to have you home,' he replied, reaching over and pinching Chiara's soft cheek gently between his thumb and forefinger. 'Isn't she beautiful? My little granddaughter, the prettiest baby in the world.'

His words were almost drowned out by an extra loud crash echoing from the kitchen, followed by a shriek of '*merda*'. Rosaria had broken something this time.

Elena half jumped out of her seat in fright; no one else seemed to register there was anything wrong. Perhaps the little girls giggled a little harder and Pepina, hot and sweaty as she barbecued the peppers over the woodfire, might have rolled her eyes a couple of times.

Finally Rosaria tottered out of the kitchen under the weight of a stack of bowls. 'About time,' Erminio told her mildly. 'The lasagne is growing cold and we're all starving out here.' He forced a thumb into his too-tight waistband. 'See, my clothes are growing looser by the second.'

Rosaria's round face looked pinched and grim as she dealt the plates out like a pack of cards. Erminio took no notice. He was too busy smiling at the huge tray of pasta, tomatoes, mozzarella and creamy bechamel sauce that lay before him. 'Who's hungry?' he asked and sliced carefully into the lasagne. 'Remember this is just the first course. We have artichokes, we have *melanzane alla parmigiana*, we have *pollo alla cacciatora* and barbecued eel, we have the best salty *pecorino* and *prosciutto* from our very own pigs and, of course, plenty of my wife's beautiful bread. And then, to finish it all off, I myself have prepared fresh white peaches soaked in red wine, which will be delicious.'

He kissed the tips of his fingers and sent an expansive smile down the length of the table.

As Rosaria carted full platters and empty platters in and out of the kitchen, Erminio ate steadily. He cleared his own plate then helped Maria Domenica finish her leftovers. Between mouthfuls he subjected her to a gentle interrogation.

'Are you happy?'

'I'm not unhappy.'

'Is Marco good to you?'

'He's not bad.'

'Is working at Caffe Angeli too much for you?'

'No, Franco doesn't work me hard.'

'Do you miss Rome?'

'Yes, a little bit.'

'What do you miss?'

'Oh, places . . . people.'

'What did you do there all day for all that time?'

How strange. This was the first time anybody had shown much interest in anything that had happened in Rome other than who had fathered her baby. That was all most people cared about – except Franco, of course, but he was far too private a person himself to pry too much into someone else's business.

But now her father had thought to ask the question. And what would she tell him? How much could she tell him?

'Well,' she began, 'the first thing I did was find a job. I ended up in a little *caffe* near the Spanish Steps. It was very different to Caffe Angeli – full of tourists, different faces every day and people babbling away in all sorts of strange languages. There were lots of English people . . .'

'Yes?'

'The owners of the *caffe* were OK at first. They rented me a room right at the very top of the building . . . so many stairs. Some days, if the *caffe* had been busy, I hardly had the strength to climb them.'

'Did they give you days off?' Erminio forked a hunk of chicken off her plate and swallowed it down.

'Oh, yes. I had two days off each week and they were wonderful. Mostly I walked around the city looking at the buildings. It seems that every corner you turn in Rome, there's a beautiful fountain or piazza right there in front of you. I didn't have a map, I just walked and explored. Sometimes I tried to see if I could find the paintings I remembered from the walls of Caffe Angeli. Whenever I saw one I felt a little closer to home.'

'And did you find many?'

'A few. But lots of them aren't in Rome at all, they're in Florence. And I never managed to make it there. Maybe one day I will, you never know . . .' Maria Domenica tailed off. She realized Marco was staring at her and wondered how long he'd been listening.

Erminio flicked his eyes up from the dish of chicken, tomatoes, onions and rosemary, and focused briefly on his son-in-law. 'Marco,' he instructed, 'go into the kitchen and find out what Rosaria is doing to that *prosciutto*. Tell her I want it sliced thinly. She may need some help.'

Marco slid off obediently and Erminio turned back to his eldest daughter. 'Maybe some day you'll go to Florence for a little visit,' he agreed. 'There's no reason why not. But only for a short time and then you'll come back to San Giulio. This is where you belong.'

Maria Domenica nodded.

'This is your home, *figlia*.'

'Yes, this is my home, Papa. Not that cottage on the Manzoni farm. Please let me come back. Marco won't care. He won't miss me. And I'm needed here.' She looked pointedly towards the kitchen. 'Rosaria isn't coping, Mamma looks tired. Let me come home and help out. Please?'

'Rosaria will cope,' her father said sternly. 'It's time she pulled her weight around here. Don't worry about Rosaria. And your mother? Maybe she is a little tired. But she wouldn't want you to come back here. She knows your place is with your husband now. We all know it.'

'I would be happier here.'

Erminio sighed. 'Just give it some time. I know it may seem strange now but they're not so bad.' He shot a glance at Elena fussily trimming imaginary fat from her meat and at Gino's shining bald head bent low over his plate as he crammed food into his mouth. 'They want the best for you. They may not do things the same way we do but . . . you'll get used to it.'

Then he heaved himself up out of his chair and patted his hard, swollen belly. 'Too full,' he told her. 'Better go and empty something out or I won't be able to fit the next course in.'

16

Maria Domenica couldn't stand it any longer. She had visions of Rosaria alone in the kitchen surrounded by swaying piles of dirty plates, washing and drying late into the night. So she slipped a sleeping Chiara into Pepina's grateful arms, found one of her old aprons and offered to help.

'I'm fine,' Rosaria told her sulkily.

'You wash and I'll dry,' Maria Domenica replied, glancing round at the familiar kitchen with the strange empty space where the table should have been.

'I said I'm fine, didn't I?'

'I want to help.'

'And you get everything you want, don't you?' Rosaria's voice was as bitter as Gina Rossi's lemonade.

'What do you mean?' asked Maria Domenica, although she knew exactly what Rosaria meant.

'Well, you've got it all, haven't you?' Rosaria spat out. She'd finished washing the glasses now and was letting the dirty water out so she could refill the sink and start on the plates. 'You've got the man, the house, the job, the baby and still you walk around all day looking as miserable as sin.'

'Maybe things aren't as perfect for me as they might seem to you,' Maria Domenica offered.

Rosaria laughed. 'I could kill you,' she said in a low voice as she scrubbed a crust of melted mozzarella and tomato off the pasta plates. 'I hate you. Why did you have to take Marco? Couldn't you have found a man of your own?'

'Rosaria, believe me, I—' Maria Domenica stopped. How

could she tell her sister that she didn't want Marco, that she'd never wanted him? There was no point in reminding her of his many faults because she wouldn't see them. Rosaria had the most enormous crush on her husband for reasons she would never understand. She'd get over it, Maria Domenica shrugged, but until she did she was going to be hell to have around.

'I don't want to talk to you, I just want to help you with the dishes,' she told Rosaria finally. 'So move over and give me that tea towel or this could take you hours.'

To the music of the chatter down the long wooden table outside, the two sisters washed, dried and put away in silence. Maria Domenica stacked the leftovers in the fridge for her father to raid in an hour or two. Rosaria scrubbed the top of the stove and all the kitchen surfaces.

The sunny afternoon burnt out to a warm evening and eventually the little girls trooped in tiredly to bed and the adult voices grew louder. Maria Domenica could hear Marco, his voice an octave or two higher than her father's, sounding boastful about something. The farm, probably, or his masterful handling of the buffalo. She tried not to listen.

Then she heard another sound – Chiara crying. Tossing down her apron, she hurried outside. 'She needs a feed, Mamma. Give her here.'

Pepina didn't move. 'Let her cry. You can't be feeding every time she demands it. You have to get her into a decent routine.'

'Mamma, she's my baby and I'll decide when she needs a feed. Give her to me.'

Pepina narrowed her eyes. 'Five daughters I've raised and one son. I think I know what I'm doing. Leave her alone.'

To Maria Domenica's surprise it was her mother-in-law Elena who spoke up. 'Eh no, Pepina. It's getting late. Let her feed the baby and then we should be getting home. I hate driving down those lanes in the dark. And anyway, I want these two young married people to come and have a *digestivo* with me before bedtime. Just one little drink before we go to sleep.'

The trip back in Elena's rattling Fiat was hair-raising. The car crabbed sideways round corners and more than once Maria Domenica thought they were heading for the ditch.

'What a lovely lunch. A real success,' Elena was babbling. 'Such wonderful cooks your family. And what a charming little cottage they have. I can't believe how they've brought you all up in that tiny place. Your poor mamma, where did she put you all? It makes me realize how Gino and I have been quite spoilt with our two-storey farmhouse and all our lovely huge rooms.'

Elena braked suddenly and the car swung halfway round a bend and skidded through the dust. 'Oops,' she giggled.

Maria Domenica glanced over at her mother-in-law. Her cheeks were quite red. How much of Mamma's wine had she drunk? 'Perhaps you should slow down,' she suggested nervously. 'It's getting quite dark.'

'Never had an accident in my life,' Elena hiccupped as she crabbed round another corner.

By the time they drew up at a rakish angle on the driveway of the farmhouse Maria Domenica felt quite shaky. She didn't have the strength to argue as Elena hustled her inside for a *digestivo*. 'One last drink before bedtime. It'll help you sleep,' she was told.

In the stuffy, dark kitchen, Maria Domenica watched Elena slop sticky liqueur into two red wine glasses and begin to drink determinedly.

'Mmm, that's good.' She smiled. 'The boys won't bother with this stuff. They say it's too sweet. I'd better pop the cork off a wine bottle for them. They'll be back in a minute.'

'We never drank much at home,' Maria Domenica offered. She gazed round at the furniture that cluttered the kitchen.

Looming down from one wall was a huge dark wooden dresser, an intricately carved ottoman lined another and a sort of wooden chest on legs was pushed up near the back door.

Elena followed her gaze. 'It's a radiogram,' she explained, lifting the lid of the chest to show her daughter-in-law the record player concealed beneath it. 'Gino bought it for me last year. Isn't it smart?' Taking another mouthful from her glass, she proceeded to give Maria Domenica the provenance of all her shiny pieces of furniture. 'The dresser, a wedding present,' she explained, brushing her fingers over the dustless surface. 'The ottoman, handed down from my grandmother. The old oak kitchen table, been in the Manzoni family for generations. The china,' Elena waved a hand at the glass-fronted cabinets full of plates and cups, 'collected by all the Manzoni wives. Some of it is very valuable, I'm sure.'

Shuddering, Maria Domenica imagined herself growing old surrounded by this museum of giant furniture, dusting it until she drew her last breath. As if she'd read her thoughts Elena smiled generously. 'All yours and Marco's one day, *cara*, of course.'

Outside a car door slammed and Gino's voice was heard urging, 'Get up, *cretino*, get up.' There was the sound of scuffling, a high-pitched giggle then Gino poked his fat, bald head around the doorway. 'You'll have to come and help me get him home,' he smirked. 'Don't know what's wrong with the boy. He must have had a glass of bad wine.'

Between them they managed to half carry, half drag Marco back to the cottage and manhandle him onto the bed. Maria Domenica said goodnight to her in-laws and then stripped the clothes from her husband's slender body and pulled one of the monogrammed linen sheets up over him.

'Water. I need a glass of water,' Marco told her, as she moved to leave the room.

'OK, I'll just be a minute. I need to see to the baby.'

'Hurry up. I'm thirsty.'

When she returned with the full glass and held it out towards him, Maria Domenica felt Marco's arm snake out around her legs. His grip was surprisingly strong.

'Come to bed,' he ordered.

'Yes, I will in a little while.'

'No, come to bed now.'

He pulled her down on top of him and the full glass of water went spinning out of her hand and smashed against the bedside table.

'No, get off me.' She tried to fight him, her fists pummelling his bony shoulder, but he flipped her over onto her back with ease and pressed down on top of her.

'Shut up,' he told her.

'Marco, not now. I don't want to do this now.'

'Trust me to marry the frigid Carrozza sister,' he said bitterly, taking a handful of her long black hair and tugging at it sharply. 'I bet you little Rosaria wouldn't be whining, "Not now" to her husband if he wanted to make love to her.'

A half-sob escaped Maria Domenica's lips. 'This isn't making love, Marco,' she told him.

But he wasn't listening. He lifted the skirt of her flowery dress and tore at her sensible underwear. Grabbing her arm roughly with one hand, he thrust himself into her and began to pump away. His warm breath, acrid with the vinegar smell of stale wine, panted into her face and sweat dripped from his hot forehead onto her skin.

Maria Domenica kept her eyes wide open and waited for Marco's flushed face to twist with the pleasure of his orgasm. It seemed to take for ever tonight. But finally his eyes popped slightly, then he screwed them up, pursed his mouth and groaned. It was over. He rolled back onto the sheets and rubbed himself clean with the corner of her dress.

'Shit, I'm going to have a hangover tomorrow,' he told her. 'That wine your mother makes is bloody strong.'

'I'll get you another glass of water,' she replied. 'The last one got spilled.'

17

There was a stranger waiting outside Caffe Angeli the next morning when Maria Domenica arrived early to open up, a tall man with tangled black hair and paint-splattered clothes clutching a step ladder. 'Franco is expecting me,' he told her in a voice heavy with an unfamiliar accent. 'He knows I'm coming.'

'You're here to do some decorating?' she asked with a nod towards the ladder and the paint pots.

'Some painting,' he replied shortly.

Maria Domenica balanced Chiara in one arm and with her free hand unlocked the big glass door. Beside her the stranger was lazily rolling a cigarette. He seemed in no hurry to start work. Savouring his cigarette, he slouched around the *caffe*, gazing at Franco's frescos, choosing a ballad on the jukebox and making it clear with a tilt of his head and a raised eyebrow that he really could do with a cup of coffee. As she coaxed the Gaggia into action Maria Domenica watched the stranger smoke. There was no filter in the cigarette he'd rolled himself, so each time it touched his lips it left behind clinging curls of brown-gold tobacco. It should have looked unattractive but somehow it didn't.

'Do you have a name?' she asked him finally.

'Vincenzo.' He lingered over the jukebox, sipping his coffee.

'Well, Vincenzo, I'm Maria Domenica and if there's anything you need to get you started with your painting let me know. I'll just be through there in the kitchen getting today's food organized.'

He nodded, pushed his empty espresso cup across the counter and smiled slowly at her.

'Another?' she asked him.

He nodded again.

Maria Domenica shrugged and reached for the coffee beans. She hoped whatever Franco had asked him to do in the *caffe* wasn't a big job or the man would be with them for months – smoking, drinking coffee and making her feel slightly uneasy with his black curls, strong body and quiet ways.

As she busied herself behind the counter she kept a curious eye on him. One hour passed and then another and still he did nothing. Instead he sat squarely in one of the spindly wooden chairs, staring at a blank space on the wall. It was quite a big space between the copy of Botticelli's *Birth of Venus* and another by the same artist, his Mars and Venus reclining languorously surrounded by naughty satyrs. Vincenzo clearly found it fascinating.

It was a quiet morning with few customers, but Vincenzo had fed the jukebox well with his coins and the *caffe* was filled with the sound of the love songs he'd chosen. Not that he seemed to be really listening to them. He was in a world of his own. Even when Old Luciano the village idiot stumbled in and gleefully shrieked, '*Cretino, puttana*,' Vincenzo didn't look away from the blank space on the wall.

Finally he stood up and stretched his legs. Gathering his paint pots and stepladder, he began to stack them behind the red velvet curtain in Franco's private area.

'You can't leave those there,' she told him.

He just smiled again. 'I'll be back in a couple of days,' was all he said and he slipped out the door.

The cheek of it, Maria Domenica thought as she clattered cutlery and china. Perhaps he expected her to move all his dirty painting gear to a more suitable place. Well, she didn't see why she should.

When Franco caught sight of the ladder and the clutter of

paint pots he simply grinned. 'So Vincenzo's been here,' he remarked. He tied the strings of his crisp white apron behind his back.

'He didn't achieve much,' she complained. 'What exactly is he supposed to be doing anyway?'

'Oh, just a few improvements,' Franco replied. 'Tarting the old place up a bit.'

He didn't have time to say more. The morning rush had finally started and thirsty customers clogged the little *caffe*. It wasn't until she heard a thin, polite wail that Maria Domenica realized she'd been neglecting her daughter. She pushed aside the red velvet curtain and half stumbled over a paint pot in her rush to get to the baby's crib. Chiara was hungry and she'd dirtied herself. Food first, thought Maria Domenica. She unbuttoned her blouse. As Chiara sucked hungrily at her swollen nipple, her mother rooted in her bag. Damn, no nappies. She was sure she'd packed some of the clean towelling squares but in her rush to get to work early this morning she must have left them neatly folded on the old armchair in the kitchen. Damn, damn.

Maria Domenica considered her options. She could probably buy some in one of the shops on the other side of the piazza but that was extravagant – she had plenty at home. Or she could borrow a couple from someone nearby, but really, she grimaced, did she want her daughter in a strange child's nappies? Who knew how well they'd been washed? There was only one thing for it, she'd just have to walk home to get some of Chiara's own beautifully laundered, cloth nappies. It would take an hour to get there and back again. She cursed her stupidity at rushing out of the house without the nappies this morning.

'What's wrong?' Franco poked his head around the red curtain.

'Oh, I've just left the baby's nappies at home and she's all dirty so I've got to change her.'

'Well, get off home now then,' he told her. 'You may as well take the rest of the day for yourself. Everything's so well organized here this morning there's hardly anything left for me to do.'

'No, no, you've still got the lunchtime rush. I can't leave you on your own for that. I'll walk home as fast as I can and then come straight back.'

'You don't have to walk,' Franco pointed out. 'I'll get Giovanni to come by in the car to give you a lift home. It'll take no time at all.'

'But isn't he studying?' Franco's son had decided he wanted to go to university one day and had been buried in books ever since. 'I don't want to interrupt him.'

'Nonsense. Since I taught him to drive he's barely got out of that old car of mine. Anyway I'm sure he can spare a few moments.'

Maria Domenica smiled gratefully. Her pretty little daughter was crying quietly but fretfully and an unmistakable smell was coming from her full pants.

Rosaria too had woken early that morning. She was filled with a new sense of purpose and determination. Today was the day, her day. There would be no more pussyfooting around.

Slipping quietly out of her bedroom on stockinged feet, she felt around the dim kitchen for the keys to her mother's Fiat Cinquecento. Above her head the shelves of the dresser groaned with round loaves of coarse bread dusted with flour. There would be none baked fresh this morning though. Rosaria had better things to do than knead dough and boost her crazy mother's supplies.

Starting the little car was easy. She'd seen Pepina turn the key in the ignition a thousand times. That business with the foot pedals wasn't so straightforward though, as she quickly discovered. Rosaria bunny-hopped out of the driveway with a graunching of gears loud enough to wake the entire neighbourhood.

She breathed a sigh of relief as she made it safely across the main highway and began weaving down the quiet, dusty tracks that led to the Manzoni farm. Driving wasn't so difficult after all. Third was her favourite gear, decided Rosaria. In third gear the car almost felt as though it was driving itself. It shuddered a bit if she slowed down so she just kept her foot pressed firmly on the accelerator for the entire trip.

She was thankful as her sister's cottage came into view and she could pull over to the side of the road. Owing to a small confusion between the brake and the clutch she didn't stop the little car as quickly as she meant to. Still, it wasn't so bad being parked in the middle of the leafy bush. At least it kept her well hidden.

She watched for signs of life in the cottage. Maria Domenica appeared first, pushing Chiara's pram, a large bag swinging from her shoulder. Turning, she called a few curt words back through the doorway as she left. From her position in the bush Rosaria couldn't hear what her sister was saying but the important message got through to her: Marco was still at home. He hadn't left for the fields yet.

Rosaria waited until her sister's straight back had disappeared briskly from view. Then, pushing her way through the branches, she manoeuvred her wide, soft body out into the open. She took a deep breath and brushed the bits of leaf and twig from her dark hair and her best lapis lazuli blue dress. Her time had finally come.

The door of the cottage was unlocked and Rosaria walked straight in. Marco was leaning against the kitchen sink, looking glum and drinking milky coffee. He looked up in surprise.

'Rosaria. What are you doing here?'

She stared at him but said nothing.

'Your sister just left,' he continued. 'You missed her by seconds.'

Rosaria took quick, determined steps across the kitchen until she was standing face to face with Marco. She seized his shoulders in her strong, brown hands and pushed him back against the kitchen sink. Pressing her lips bossily down on his, she kissed him hard. It felt good. Thrusting out her tongue she explored the warm, milky wetness of his mouth. For a moment he did nothing and then he started to kiss her back. Rosaria felt desire washing over her entire body.

'Take me to the bedroom.' Her voice was gruff and insistent. 'Take me to bed.'

'I can't.' Marco sounded all wobbly. 'I can't, Rosaria.'

But his body was saying he could. Rosaria could feel how hard he was as she rubbed herself rhythmically up and down against him.

'Shut up, you know you want to.'

Marco screwed his eyes tight together and let his hands explore Rosaria's body. She felt so yielding, so juicy. But his father's words ran through his mind. *Do what you like, but stay away from the village girls or there'll be trouble.* It was good advice. Marco knew it.

'I can't, Rosaria, I can't,' he repeated.

She had a strong grip on his hand and pulled him towards the open bedroom door. Ignoring his weak protestations, she forced him down on the bed and stretched herself out on top of him.

'I can't, I can't,' Marco groaned. Yet his hands tore at her dress, touched her breasts and pinched her nipples hard. She rolled over onto her back and opened her legs, offering him everything.

'No, no, we mustn't,' he moaned. But now he was on top of her and he couldn't stop himself. With one wild thrust he took her virginity and there was no going back. 'No, no,' he muttered weakly as he sank into her fleshy, warm body.

'Oh, that feels good, so good,' she moaned. 'Don't stop, Marco, don't stop.'

Marco couldn't have stopped now even if he'd wanted to. Bucking like an excited horse, his skinny hips disappeared between the soft mounds of her inner thighs over and over again. He was lost.

Beneath him Rosaria arched her back and threw her head back on the pillow so her hair spread out prettily. She tried one or two experimental thrusts of her hips but Marco was pumping so wildly it was impossible to match his rhythm. So she gave up and simply lay like a starfish, enjoying the strange new sensations that had taken hold of her body. If this was sex then she liked the taste of it and she wanted more, much more.

'I'm coming, I'm coming,' Marco gasped and it was over. Afterwards they lay tangled together, the sheet half pulled over them, the sweat drying on their bodies.

Rosaria brushed her lips over the thin down of fair hair that covered Marco's chest. He closed his eyes and she admired the way his long eyelashes swept down towards his peach-soft cheeks. With one finger she reached out and touched the blue beauty spot beneath the right-hand corner of his lips.

'Jesus, my father's going to kill me,' he groaned. 'I'm going to be so late for work.'

'Don't go, stay here with me. The buffalo won't miss you for one day. You can tell your father you were ill.'

Marco remembered his hangover – the throbbing in his head and how bitter and unpalatable his sips of milky coffee had tasted as he stood propped against the kitchen sink. That seemed a long time ago. He felt much better now.

'Rosario, my father won't care. This is a farm, he'll say, there's work to be done.'

'Wouldn't you rather stay here with me?' she wheedled.

'Yes but . . .' She stopped him with a kiss. Then she began to stroke his body, feeling the tautness of his skin, the hard ridges of his ribs and letting her short, strong fingers teasingly dip into the wiry hairs between his legs before running them over his neat buttocks and his lean back. Soon his eyelashes sank towards his cheeks again and he began to snore gently. Rosaria leaned her head against him so she could breathe the perfume of his body and she slept too.

When Giovanni's car pulled up outside, they hadn't moved. They didn't hear the rumble of the engine, the whine of the brakes or Maria Domenica calling out to the boy behind the steering wheel, 'I won't be a minute.' The front door of the cottage opened and still they slept on, oblivious.

Maria Domenica had snatched up the pile of nappies and was about to pull the front door shut behind her when she heard the unmistakable sound of her husband snoring. He couldn't still be in bed, she didn't believe it. Astonished, she peered into the bedroom. It was semi-dark, the curtains drawn, but she could make out that there were two shapes in the bed. One was most certainly Marco. The other? She moved closer. A big girl, full-breasted, with long black hair thrown over the white cotton pillows. Her sister Rosaria.

Maria Domenica stood stock-still for a moment, taking shallow, silent breaths through her mouth. She said nothing. Slowly she backed out of the bedroom, clutching the little pile of nappies to her chest. Within seconds she was out of the cottage and back inside Giovanni's car.

'OK?' he asked.

She nodded and waved the nappies at him. She still didn't trust herself to speak.

As Giovanni steered them back to the village, Maria Domenica tried to decide how she felt. Not angry and not jealous. Not even disappointed.

They'd reached the outskirts of San Giulio and the tumble-down cottages where the poor people lived, before the numbness wore off and Maria Domenica realized that, beyond shock, what she mostly felt was sadness and maybe pity for her sister Rosaria. How could this bring her anything but unhappiness? Unhappiness and disgrace.

*

Pepina was furious. No sign of Rosaria, the kitchen empty, the day's work not started. She cast a weary eye around the kitchen she so rarely left. That daughter of hers was useless. Things had been so much easier when Maria Domenica was still at home.

She thought about the tasks that lay before her for the day. The house was filthy and she couldn't afford to let more time pass before she cleaned it properly. The weeds were springing up in her garden and there was so much food to prepare. By the look of the kitchen table, the younger children had helped themselves to milk and biscuits for breakfast but there were still two more meals to organize before she could lay her weary body down again.

'I'm so tired even my teeth ache,' she muttered to herself. Perhaps she was getting ill.

She heard Erminio stumbling down the hallway and into the kitchen. A big white bath towel was slung around his swollen belly and his greying hair was standing up on end. 'I'm starving,' he rumbled and poked about in the fridge. 'What's for breakfast?'

'Whatever,' Pepina replied tersely.

Erminio looked up in surprise. 'What's the matter with my beautiful wife then?' he asked, cupping her sleep-creased face in his huge hands.

'Oh, I don't know. I just don't feel right today, that's all.'

'You wait there,' he told her. 'I know how to make you feel better. I'll just put some clothes on, I'll be two seconds.'

Sure enough he was back in a minute in a mismatched shirt and trousers. 'Come with me, quickly,' he urged.

As he pulled her out of the door and around the corner of the house, she heard the sound of the younger children teasing the pigs. She tried to pull away from her husband and rescue the poor squealing beasts, but his grip was gentle and firm.

'Where are we going?' she asked, resisting him with all the weight of her body.

'To pick peaches, fresh peaches for breakfast,' he replied, pulling her onwards.

When they reached the strand of fruit trees, he made her sit on the hard earth, baked to a burnt sienna by the sun, and plopped down beside her. He kissed her – at first like an old friend and then more passionately. As he heaved himself on top of her, she tried to bat him away. 'Not now, get off, I've too much to do. What about the peaches?'

'Mmm.' He kissed her once more and loosened his trousers.

'Erminio Carrozza, if you get me pregnant again I swear this time I'll leave you and go to live with the nuns,' she hissed. 'I don't want any more daughters.'

'Mmm.' He ignored her.

'Someone will see us,' she warned, 'right out in the open like this.'

But her husband didn't care. The weight of his body pushed her into the unyielding earth and she felt the familiar touch of his hands caressing her. 'Pepina, *amore mio*,' he muttered.

She rolled her eyes and parted her legs. Surely it was only a week or so ago that she was bleeding? She couldn't get pregnant right now, could she? She tried to remember what the priest had told her last time she had fallen.

Erminio was inside her now and it was too late to worry. She'd just have to hope for the best. She rose to meet his desire and for a few happy moments she felt once again like the passionate girl she had been.

Afterwards Erminio hugged her tightly. 'You have dirt on your face,' he told her.

'Oh, just my face?' she asked, laughing now. 'My love, I have dirt everywhere. My whole life is dirt waiting to be cleaned.' She struggled to her feet. 'You pick your peaches for breakfast. I'll be in the kitchen. I'll see you there.'

18

Marco opened his eyes. He wondered what time it was. He felt the heat of the day wrapping itself around him like a warm, wet blanket and realized it must be lunchtime. Too late to worry about his father or the buffalo. Too late to regret sleeping with the young girl whose soft body still lolled against his. His head ached. What was he doing in bed with Rosaria? What had he been thinking? He couldn't let it happen again.

He reached out and touched the soft mounds that her body formed when it was lying down. The peaks of breasts, the mountains of buttocks, the little hillock of belly.

'*Cara,*' he muttered despite himself and her eyes opened.

'Marco,' she replied happily, burrowing her face in his chest.

'What are we doing?' he asked her.

'What do you mean, what are we doing?' she said, her voice muffled by his body.

'They'd kill us if they saw us. Your parents, my parents, Maria Domenica.'

'Well, they can't see us.' Rosaria was wide awake now and her eyes were blazing. 'All we are doing is taking the happiness we deserve, Marco. We'd be stupid not to. We belong together.'

'We can't do this again,' he argued.

'Oh, yes, we can.' She was fierce now. 'We can do it over and over again as many times as we like. No one can stop us.'

'What if they find out?' Marco sounded afraid.

'I won't tell them.' She tilted her chin at him. 'Will you?'

'No.'

'I love you,' she told him.

'You're so young,' he replied nervously.

'I know what I want,' she retaliated. And then she kissed him again. 'Do you know what you want?' she asked.

He was afraid to reply. But again his body spoke for him. He felt himself stiffen against her.

'Have you ever had an orgasm?' he asked tentatively.

She shook her head. 'I don't think so.'

'You didn't have one before?'

'No. It felt good. But no, I don't think so.'

Suddenly he felt powerful. 'Well, maybe this time.' His mouth twitched with a smile and he eased her up until she was straddling him. 'This will feel so good, Rosaria, so good,' he promised.

At Caffe Angeli Maria Domenica's cheeks grew flushed as she plonked platefuls of food down in front of hungry customers and whisked the empty ones away from those who were replete.

'How's that baby of yours?' asked some of them.

'How's that husband of yours?' asked others.

Maria Domenica just smiled and kept moving. Fortunately she was too busy to talk, but she couldn't forget what she had seen. She could wipe down the tables but she couldn't scrub her mind clean of the picture of her husband and sister entwined in her bed.

'So didn't you like Vincenzo?' Franco's teasing voice intruded on her thoughts.

'What?'

'My friend Vincenzo, the painter. Didn't you like him?' Franco repeated.

Maria Domenica wrinkled her nose. 'Well, he didn't do much, did he? Just made a big mess.'

'Ah, but he hasn't really started yet. He'll be back.'

'So he said.'

'And then I'm sure you'll be impressed by him.'

'Franco?' There was a no-nonsense tone to Maria Domenica's voice.

'Yes?'

'Gloria Ferrero wants an espresso and her husband says do you have a spare pack of cards behind the counter because he's forgotten his.'

The long day's work wore on. By the time Franco packed her off home, Maria Domenica was bone weary. As dusk fell, she pushed the pram through the clouds of mosquitoes that were settling over San Giulio's hot, dry streets. It felt like a long walk home.

Marco was sitting at the kitchen table waiting for her when she arrived home.

'You're late,' he complained. 'I'm starving.'

'I won't be a minute,' she assured him, hurrying to settle Chiara in her cot. 'Franco gave me some cold chicken. I just need to prepare a little salad to go with it.'

As she prepared his food she stole a few glances at her husband. He looked the same as ever and he smelled clean, as though he'd just stepped out of the bath. There was nothing to betray the fact that he'd spent the day tangled in the monogrammed Manzoni sheets in their tiny bedroom with her greedy little sister Rosaria.

One thing had changed. That night as they lay down in bed together, Marco didn't reach out to her. There was no arm snaking over her in the darkness, none of the usual frantic rubbing and pressing she dreaded. Instead Marco lay curled with his back towards her and said an exhausted goodnight.

'If that baby of yours doesn't scream herself hoarse for hours I may get a decent sleep,' he murmured. 'God knows I need it.'

19

For once Marco rose before the sun. Maria Domenica heard him struggling into his trousers and work-shirt in the darkness and muttering to himself under his breath.

'You're up early,' she remarked drowsily, hoping the noise he was making wouldn't rouse Chiara.

'Yes, well, I've got a lot to do, haven't I? Farming is no job for part-timers, as my father is always pointing out.'

Maria Domenica allowed herself a smile. Marco was well aware he'd be in trouble for missing a whole day's work yesterday. He wasn't going to give Gino any more reasons to complain.

'If you were any sort of wife you'd get up and make my breakfast,' Marco grumbled. But she feigned sleep and, slamming the cottage door hard behind him, he left without saying goodbye.

The crash of the door woke Chiara. Maria Domenica heard her crying softly. She eased herself out of bed and lifted her daughter from her crib. This was her favourite time of each day – that first moment of waking, remembering afresh that she was a mother now and holding her warm little bundle in her arms. No matter what happened to her, no matter how trapped she was in her life, the one thing she could never regret was Chiara.

She was feeding her baby in the kitchen when she heard footsteps outside and assumed it was Marco, driven home by hunger pangs, come to demand his missed breakfast. She was surprised to hear a light, polite knocking on the door.

'Hello. Who is it?' Maria Domenica called out.

A blonde head poked around the door.

'Aunt Lucia,' she said with some pleasure. 'How good to see you. What are you doing here so early? Come in, come in.'

Her aunt was carrying a tray of cakes wrapped in gold and white paper. 'They nearly died of shock when they saw me at the *pasticceria* at this hour,' she chuckled. 'But I wanted to bring you some *baba*. Mmm, they're so fresh, they're almost still warm.' She tore off the paper, plucked one of the rum-soaked, golden domes of cakes and bit into it with relish. 'I should make some coffee to go with these,' she mumbled, mouth still full. 'No, you stay there. I'll make it.'

Lucia liked her coffee strong. She ground extra beans and piled up a precarious pyramid before jamming on the top of the coffee pot and putting it on the stove.

Maria Domenica watched her, confused. 'It's lovely to see you, Aunt Lucia but—'

'Why am I here?'

'Well, yes.'

Lucia pursed her lips and looked round the small kitchen, at the poverty of the bare walls and the few sad sticks of furniture. 'This place is awful,' she said shortly.

'Oh, it's not so bad.'

Lucia nodded in the direction of Elena's farmhouse. 'She's got that big old place stuffed with furniture she never uses. You'd think she'd let you have a few bits and pieces. They're a stingy lot those Manzoni wives. Always have been.'

'I don't care,' Maria Domenica assured her. 'I don't want any of her things. We've got everything we need. And anyway, I'm not here all that much. I try to stay at Caffe Angeli as much as I can.'

'I know.' Her aunt nodded. 'That's why I'm here so early. It's my only chance to have a proper chat to you in private.'

'What about?'

'I've been worried about you. With everything that's

happened I . . . well, I just wanted to make sure that you're happy.'

Maria Domenica said nothing, just stared at her aunt dubiously.

'Or at least not too unhappy,' Lucia added quickly.

'And what if I was unhappy? What would you do?'

'Do? I'm not sure that I could do anything, Maria Domenica. The time for doing things is past. You are here. You are married. Nothing is going to change that. But I wanted you to know that you can talk to me – say the things that perhaps you wouldn't want to worry your mother with.'

Maria Domenica nodded, but stayed silent. Her aunt looked round the kitchen again and through the open door into the stark bedroom. 'The one thing I could do is help you cheer this place up. Bring some ornaments, a picture or two. Maybe run up some nice bright curtains. See if the little *contessa* over the way will deign to let you have some of her good china.'

Maria Domenica shook her head. 'Thank you, but I don't need any of that.'

'What do you need then?'

Maria Domenica paused, looked down at her now peaceful baby and blurted, 'If only he had seen her. I'm sure if he could have only seen Chiara then he'd have never left.'

'You mean her father?'

Maria Domenica nodded. The coffee pot was gurgling, filling the kitchen with the smell of bitter roasted beans.

'You still think of him?' Lucia asked gently.

'All the time. I think of him every minute of every day.'

'What was he like?'

Maria Domenica smiled. Much as she wanted to keep her secrets, talking about him brought him alive for her. 'He had blond hair and strong hands,' she began. 'He was so clever, an artist, and I loved being with him. We had so little time together. He ran away from me just like I ran away from San Giulio.'

'You loved him a lot?'

'I loved him and I was so sure he loved me. It was a wonderful feeling. I can't imagine living through every day for the rest of my life and never, ever feeling like that again.'

'Maybe you'll grow to love Marco?'

Maria Domenica clicked her tongue against the roof of her mouth derisively.

'You know that love you felt, that fierce love, it doesn't last for ever,' Lucia promised. She poured coffee into two tiny chipped cups and reached for another *baba*. 'The years pass by and they wear it out. Old married women like me, we take our real pleasure from our homes, our children and one day, hopefully, our grandchildren. Oh, we care for our husbands, of course, and we look after them, but we don't burn with passion.' Lucia laughed. 'No, no, we don't.'

Maria Domenica looked into her aunt's eyes, fully made up with eyeliner and mascara even at this hour of the morning, and said in a quiet but intense voice, 'That's not what I wanted. That's not how I wanted my life to be. I was going to be different.'

Lucia sighed. 'Ah, you're so like your grandmother.'

'No one's ever said that to me before.'

'I can't say I ever noticed it before but it's true, you are. She was so fey and fanciful, so beautiful and creative, sometimes I wonder how she ever gave birth to your mother and me.' Lucia sipped her coffee thoughtfully.

'In what way was she fanciful?'

'Oh, I don't know. I think she had too much love to give and my father . . . well, he never quite knew how to take it from her. In the end she poured all her energies into making things instead. You know those beautiful embroidered christening gowns your mother and I have? She stitched all those. In fact, she made so many I think she managed to fill a drawer for every mother in town before she died.'

'And you think that I'm like her? That I've got too much love to give?'

Lucia nodded. 'Yes, in some ways I do.'

Maria Domenica stood up and put Chiara in her pram. Carefully, she wrapped the paper round the tray of rum *babas* and pushed it over the table towards her aunt. 'Here, you take these back to your own family. We'll never eat them here,' she said.

'You're angry with me?'

'Not angry, no, but I don't agree with you. I don't think it's possible to love too much. Look at my mother and father – they still adore each other, don't they?' She tucked a light blanket around Chiara and brushed a kiss over her soft cheek. 'Anyway, you're right. This is my life now and I can't do anything to change that. It's not so bad really. I have my baby. I can give my love to her.'

She turned her pram towards the door. 'Thanks for your visit, Lucia. I appreciate it, really I do,' she said politely. 'But I have to get along to Caffe Angeli now. Franco and Giovanni will be waiting for me.'

20

Rosaria was deliciously sore. Her soft inner thighs were bruised from the pounding of Marco's hip bones and each time she sat down she felt the twinges that reminded her she was now a woman.

She wanted to smile all day long but she couldn't. She had to be careful not to give anything away. No one must know she and Marco were lovers.

But Rosaria was drawn to Caffe Angeli, she couldn't help it. She walked in, hips swaying, perched on a stool at the counter and lit a cigarette with a flourish.

'I need food,' she announced. 'I'll have one of those potato croquettes, some little fried ham and cheese sandwiches, and a delicious sweet thing to finish.'

'I'll be with you in a minute, I just have to finish making this coffee,' a harassed-looking Maria Domenica told her. 'And anyway, what are you doing here? Don't you have work to do at home?'

Rosaria shrugged and pretended to be engrossed in a magazine. But although her fingers flicked through the pages her eyes weren't really focusing on the glamorous shots of Sophia Loren and Gina Lollobrigida. Instead she peered up through her lashes and took a fresh look at her elder sister.

Beaky nose, Rosaria decided, piggy eyes and much too skinny everywhere. Her hair looked harsh pulled back from her face like that and the dusting of freckles over her nose was more pronounced than ever thanks to all those hours spent working in the sunny garden without a hat. She really was no competition at all. If she hadn't trapped Marco so cleverly, Rosaria was convinced she'd never have found a man to marry her.

'What's your problem?' Maria Domenica had noticed her staring.

'Hey?'

'What are you looking at me like that for? Is there something you want to tell me?'

Rosaria's round cheeks turned pink. 'No, no, nothing.' She grabbed her plate of treats from the counter, tucked the movie magazine under her arm and headed for a table in the far corner of the little *caffe*. 'I'll let you get on with your work,' she muttered.

Just as Maria Domenica had got rid of her sister she became aware of another pair of staring eyes. The painter Vincenzo had returned and today, instead of the blank wall, he seemed to think she was worthy of examination. He was sitting at the table next to Rosaria, a pile of books at his elbow. Maria Domenica looked up to meet his eyes but he didn't shift his gaze.

He was taking in her long graceful fingers, the way her glossy black hair fell down her back and the rich gold tones of her skin. He admired her deep-set, almond-shaped eyes and the fluid, calm way she moved between the tables.

His staring was quite off-putting and she began to fumble and mix up the orders.

'What's the matter with you today?' Franco's voice rang with amusement. 'It's not like you to get in such a muddle.'

'Well,' she blustered in reply, 'it's not easy, you know, being a mother and holding down a job. It's no wonder my head's in a whirl sometimes.'

'So that's it, your head's in a whirl.' He was still laughing.

'Franco, not now. I'm not in the mood,' she snapped. She cast a baleful glance towards Vincenzo, who was still watching her carefully. His rough, handsome face was blank and it was impossible to tell what he was thinking.

Finally curiosity overcame her. She was clearing empty cups and glasses from a nearby table and happened to glance over at one of the books at Vincenzo's elbow. It was the cover that caught her eye with its reproduction of Botticelli's *Birth of Venus*. She was far less crude than the Venus on the wall above Franco's jukebox, a beautiful fine-featured woman with a high forehead and wide-set eyes whose long tendrils of golden hair were escaping from her ribbons and blowing in the wind. In a bold typeface above the picture, the words *The Art of Renaissance Italy* were printed in English.

Reaching out, she touched the book reverently.

Vincenzo pushed it towards her. 'Help yourself,' he told her, his white teeth gleaming in a smile.

She didn't need a second invitation. Perching on the chair beside him, she lost herself in its thick, glossy pages. Franco brought her a glass of cold Coca-Cola but it lay untouched as she drank in page after page of beautiful pictures and fascinating stories about the artists and their work.

'Maria Domenica?' Franco's voice intruded.

'Hmm?'

'Are you actually reading that?'

'Oh.' She looked up guiltily. 'I'm sorry. I'll get back to work.'

'No, I didn't ask you that.' Franco looked quizzical. 'What I asked is are you actually reading that book?'

'What do you mean?'

'Well, it's all in English, isn't it?' He raised his eyebrows. 'And you don't speak English. You can't have learned it at school. After all, you left when you were thirteen.'

'Um . . .' Maria Domenica shifted in her seat uncomfortably. Out of the corner of her eye she could see her sister Rosaria at the far table, her magazine forgotten now as she eavesdropped furiously.

Franco and Vincenzo were still waiting for an answer. 'I was just looking at the pictures,' she began, then glanced down and realized the page she'd been staring at for several minutes was quite empty of pictures, just a solid bank of English words telling the story of the artist Masaccio and his creation of a painting about the expulsion of Adam and Eve from Paradise.

Franco raised his eyebrows again.

'Well, I suppose I was reading it a bit,' Maria Domenica admitted. 'I picked up a little English the year I was in Rome. The *caffe* I worked in was always full of tourists and lots of them were art students and I got talking to some of them and . . . well . . . you know . . . learned some of the language. But I don't really understand it very well. Just enough to get the gist of things.'

'Say something in English then.' Her sister Rosaria hadn't been able to resist sidling over.

'No.'

'Oh, go on,' Rosaria wheedled.

'I can't remember any of the words now.' Her face flushed, Maria Domenica dropped the book and bolted back to the safety of the bulky Gaggia, which she began to clean energetically. But Vincenzo had followed her.

'When were you in Rome?' he asked.

'Oh,' she shook her head in irritation, 'last year.'

'And which *caffe* did you work in?'

She sighed. Couldn't he see how much he was annoying her? But she was much too polite to deny him an answer. 'Just a little place by the Spanish Steps,' she began. 'Full of English tourists who liked to drink cups of tea with slices of lemon.'

'I think I know it,' he mused, then nodded his head and smiled with recognition. 'You know, you struck me as being familiar the first time I saw you here but I couldn't put my finger on why.'

'Well, I don't remember you.' Her voice was chillier than Franco's iced Coca-Cola.

'No, you wouldn't.' Vincenzo's white teeth flashed again.

'When you weren't delivering cups of tea with slices of lemon you always seemed engrossed in that tall, blond boy, the one who carried his sketchbook everywhere with him.'

'Oh, yes?' Rosaria was craning round now, desperate to be part of the conversation. 'What blond boy?'

Maria Domenica banged the coffee tin down on the counter and gave Vincenzo a hard look. Miraculously he seemed to understand.

'Well, can't hang around here all day,' he said quickly, turning away. 'I'll leave the books though. Feel free to read them.'

As the door slammed behind him, Rosaria slid over and poked her arm. 'Blond boy?' she asked insistently.

'Now,' Franco broke in, 'didn't you say you wanted a delicious sweet thing to finish, Rosaria? I have a special cornetto today you really must taste. It's quite divine.'

'A cornetto?' Rosaria looked up sharply. 'Does it have chocolate in it? Only I've had a terrible craving for chocolate all day.'

Distracted, her little sister filled her plate and Maria Domenica turned her face away in relief. Rosaria was welcome to steal her husband but she didn't want her near her memories of the blond boy in the *caffe* by the Spanish Steps.

21

Vincenzo made her laugh and he knew so much about the paintings she loved – lots more than Franco. On the days he didn't turn up at the little *caffe*, Maria Domenica was surprised how much she missed him.

He was more than just a decorator, as she had swiftly realized, and he seemed to have ambitious plans for Franco's bare stretch of wall.

He hadn't accomplished very much though. The wall still didn't have a lick of paint on it and his pots and brushes remained undisturbed behind the red curtain.

Day after day he sketched. Sheets and sheets of paper were scattered around the table that he had made his own, some crumpled angrily, some stacked neatly in a pile.

'Ah, it's a Madonna and child,' Maria Domenica exclaimed. She leaned over his table and squinted at the shape he was tracing so repetitively. 'That's what you're going to paint? A Madonna and child?'

'Well, that's the idea.' Vincenzo ran his big square hands through his untidy black curls. 'But I can't seem to get the shape of it right.'

'Are you copying that?' Maria Domenica nodded towards a picture that had been ripped out of one of his art books. It showed a rather solid, plain Madonna balancing a fat, healthy baby on one of her big knees.

'Yes, that's the Masaccio Madonna and child. That's the one Franco wants me to put on the wall.'

'But what you've drawn here isn't right,' Maria Domenica

told him. 'Masaccio's Madonna looks like she enjoys her pasta; your one is too thin.'

Vincenzo laughed. 'Well, my Madonna is on her feet all day. She hasn't had the chance to get fat.'

'So after you've finished sketching, what then? What's the next step to making a fresco?' Maria Domenica was fascinated.

'It's quite a long process,' Vincenzo began. 'It doesn't do to rush it so I may be hanging around here for some time.'

'Why doesn't that surprise me?' Maria Domenica teased.

'No, no, I'm serious. You have to get it right. In the old days it was even more complicated when they made a fresco. They used wet plaster and there would be several of them working away at once. It could get pretty messy.'

'Well, we don't want that.'

'No, we most certainly don't.' Vincenzo flipped over the page and ripped a clean sheet of paper from his sketchbook. He handed it over to her along with a thick, soft pencil. 'Draw something.'

'What?'

'I can tell that you're fascinated by art but I want to see if you've got any talent,' he told her. 'So draw something.'

'I can't, I'm working.'

'The place is half empty. Stop making excuses.'

'But what will I draw?'

'Whatever you want.' He waved his hand in the air. 'There are a hundred things in this place you could draw if you want. But draw me, if you can't think of anything better.'

Maria Domenica clutched the pencil in her hand and stared at the blank piece of paper. She felt self-conscious, clumsy, stupid. She didn't know where to begin.

'Well, if you're going to draw me, you'll have to look at me,' Vincenzo told her.

She flushed. All the same she lifted her eyes to his and held his gaze.

'I'm not sure I can bear to draw something so ugly,' she told him cheekily.

Vincenzo threw his head back and laughed. 'Steel yourself, that's my advice. Sometimes the ugly ones make the best subjects.'

As Rita Pavone crooned from the jukebox, Maria Domenica studied the man before her. His face was starting to wrinkle and when you looked closely there were grey hairs streaking through the black. His nose was straight and strong, his lips full and his brown eyes dangerous. He had the look of a man who might quite easily run to fat. There was the hint of an extra chin and a slightly pouchy look around the eyes that suggested a fondness for the good things in life. There was something about him she found compellingly attractive.

Vincenzo didn't seem to mind her staring. Head bent, he got on with the job of perfecting his Madonna. She noted that he wasn't afraid: he sketched freely and easily, his pencil flowing across the paper.

'Draw,' he urged without looking up from his sketchpad.

'I am, I am. I'm just studying my subject.'

'No you're not, you're procrastinating. Don't begin with a detail,' he instructed. 'You'll end up with the scale all wrong. Sketch a rough shape and then work in the details.'

So she began, nervously at first, tracing the shape of his head, his strong shoulders and his arms.

'Don't worry if you get it wrong. I have more paper,' Vincenzo told her.

His nose was difficult. It was so straight and chiselled in real life that it was almost impossible to make it look natural on paper. His hair too posed problems, not to mention his crazy eyebrows, so long and curly, which unashamedly dominated his face.

As she drew, Giovanni passed behind her chair and peered over her shoulder. 'That's fantastic. You're so clever,' he said admiringly. But she was concentrating too hard to spare even a few words for him and, after a few seconds of silence, he moved on, disappointed.

In the end she wasn't unhappy with what she had drawn. It wasn't at all bad for a first try, although there was definitely still something wrong about the nose and it was impossible to capture the laughter in his eyes. The man in her picture was raffishly sexy. He was likeable but not entirely to be trusted. And he really needed to do something about those crazy eyebrows.

Vincenzo took the sketch off her and appraised it. 'See, that wasn't so difficult, was it, once you got started?'

She waited for more. But he had gone back to his own work.

'But do you like it?' she asked. 'Do you think it looks like you? Do I have talent?'

He put down his pencil, leaned back and smiled. 'What do you think? Are you pleased with it?'

'Well,' she was hesitant, 'I don't think it looks like you exactly but I do think that somehow I've captured the essence of you – your spirit.'

He nodded.

'Aren't you going to tell me what you think of it?' she asked again.

He smiled and shook his head. Reaching down into his big, black canvas bag, he pulled out a fresh sketchpad and a bundle of pencils. 'Here, these are for you,' he said, pressing them into her hands.

'I can't accept these. They must have been so expensive.' She tried to give them back.

Vincenzo held up his hands. 'They're a gift. Accept them in the spirit in which they were given. All I ask is that you use them. Don't think about it too hard, just draw. Draw your mother, your baby, your fat little sister. Draw Franco serving coffee, Giovanni wiping down the counter and the old men playing cards. Fill up the pages.'

'But why? I'll never be a real artist like you. I'd need to go to classes or take a course at the university and there's no hope of that.'

'Lots of people take those courses. They come out with a certificate at the end of it and they call themselves artists. But they're still only as good as the work they do, it doesn't matter what that certificate says.'

'But how will I ever learn to paint?'

Vincenzo laughed. 'You've only just picked up a pencil and already you want to paint? One step at a time, Maria Domenica.' He waved her little sketch at her. 'In exchange for the paper and pencils I'm claiming your first work. I'll pin it up on a wall somewhere, I promise. That's if it truly is your first work. Did you do anything in Rome? Did that blond English boy of yours encourage you to do some sketching?'

'No.' She bit her lip. 'He loved to show me his work – lots of it was beautiful – but he never suggested that I have a go myself.'

'Probably worried you'd be too much like competition for him.'

Maria Domenica screwed up her face and laughed.

'Don't underestimate yourself,' Vincenzo told her seriously and began packing his mess of paper into the black canvas bag. 'You're capable of more than you think.'

Buoyed by his words, Maria Domenica moved about the *caffe* in a state of barely suppressed excitement for the rest of the day. Her head was full of the things she could draw and how she might draw them. She glanced outside at a bare-headed young boy whizzing past on a Vespa, his girlfriend riding side-saddle behind him, and she wondered how she might show the wind running through their hair. Five minutes later a farmer trundled past in a rickety wooden cart pulled by a couple of white oxen. It was a familiar scene, she must have seen that old man in his cart a thousand times, but now she itched to reach for her sketchpad and draw him. It was quite extraordinary, she thought, that something that had been so unimportant to her when she climbed out of bed this morning was now the only thing on her mind.

When Franco told her she should take herself off home she didn't linger to talk as usual or help clean up. Chiara was bundled into her pram, the sketchpad and pencils tucked in beside her, and she half walked, half ran down the dusty roads that led home.

Bursting through the front door of the ugly old cottage, she found Marco pottering in the kitchen looking for some food to pick at.

'Quick, quick, sit in the armchair,' she told him breathlessly.

'What?'

'In the armchair. Sit. Take the baby. Now, don't move.'

'What the hell are you doing?'

Maria Domenica had the sketchpad and pencils out and was pulling out a chair at the kitchen table.

'I'm going to make a picture of you and Chiara.'

Marco looked confused but not unwilling. 'How long will it take? Can I move at all or do I have to sit perfectly still? And what if the baby starts crying or fills her pants or something?'

But Maria Domenica wasn't listening, just staring at him intently. Her pencil began to fly over the sketchpad and it was as if she were in some sort of trance.

'My arms are starting to ache. This baby's getting heavy,' said Marco into the silence.

Five minutes later: 'Maria Domenica, do I have to sit here all night? What about my dinner?'

Twenty minutes further down the track: 'This is getting boring. I'm going to move now.'

'No, no, I'm nearly done,' Maria Domenica held up the picture. 'See, it's still a bit rough but I can add some more detail later.'

Marco put the baby down and came over for a closer look. He seemed entranced by what she'd drawn. 'It really does look very like me,' he told her, his voice laced with surprise. 'Perhaps my eyes are a little bigger in real life but that's all.'

He was peeling off his shirt now. 'Draw me again, *cara*,' he said, stretching out on the floor and wriggling out of his trousers. 'But this time draw me nude.'

As she began to sketch, Maria Domenica realized she'd never truly looked at her husband before, at the blackness of his lashes, the regular planes of his face and his skin smooth as an egg. He wore a wide-brimmed hat throughout the day so he wouldn't tan but during those long hours in the fields the sun's rays always found him at last and toasted him to a pale caramel. The wispy tendrils of hair he'd been trying to grow had made the back of his neck all sweaty so in the end he'd made her cut them off and now he kept his short, fine hair lightly slicked down with Brylcreem. As she struggled to capture his essence on paper, as she'd somehow managed to do with Vincenzo, she slowly came to understand what girls like her sister saw in Marco.

'Do I look better from this side?' he asked her seriously, tilting his chin one way and then the other. 'Or this?'

'Your features are very regular,' she promised. 'You look good from any direction.'

When Marco grew hungry, he didn't demand that his wife drop her pencil and put on an apron. Instead he wound one of the monogrammed Manzoni sheets around him like a toga and foraged in the refrigerator, piling a platter high with cheese, salami, olives, bread, tomatoes from her garden and salty anchovies. He put it on the floor, not the kitchen table, and curled up beside it, propped up on a couple of ancient cushions. Lying there, swathed in the sheet and eating with his fingers, he looked as decadent and pleased with himself as a Roman emperor. Maria Domenica turned the page and began to draw him once again.

Even when it grew late and Marco went to bed she couldn't separate herself from her sketchpad. In the hard light cast by a single bare bulb, Maria Domenica filled up the empty white pages her new friend Vincenzo had given her.

Finally she shifted tiredly to the armchair and slept for only an hour or two. When Chiara's thin wail woke her it seemed as though she'd just closed her eyes. And yet still she felt suffused with energy, light on her feet. She spread her sketches from the night before across the kitchen table so she could review them. That was a good one of Marco eating grapes, but the first one she'd tried, with him and Chiara sitting in the armchair, wasn't working at all. The little girl looked stiff and unreal, like a china doll. How do you capture a baby's essence? wondered Maria Domenica.

She left the pictures there scattered round the room for Marco. He was sure to want to see them but she couldn't wait until he woke up. There were still some empty pages in her sketchpad and, if she walked into town early enough, she knew how she could fill them: Giovanni, still a boy but so nearly a man, gazing at her adoringly; Gina Rossi looping garlands of lemons around her market stall; Franco opening up Caffe Angeli; the priest like an old black crow pecking and fussing outside the crumbling white church where she'd been forced to marry. She could see each picture clearly in her mind's eye and couldn't wait to start putting them down on paper. Once her sweet, uncomplaining baby was fed and changed, she bundled her back in her pram and ran down the long straight roads that led to San Giulio.

Rosaria was walking too, trudging angrily through the dust, kicking it into a cloud and coating her sturdy legs with a dirty layer of gold. She couldn't believe Mamma had done this to her. Once, just that one time, she'd borrowed the car and now Pepina thought it was necessary to hide the keys from her.

She had searched for them all over the dim kitchen this morning. She'd felt up on the high shelves, under the hard loaves of bread, she'd even checked inside the pots and pans. Nothing. So now she was reduced to walking to Marco's house. The track stretched out interminably in front of her. She was creeping up it, swimming through syrup. Marco would have left for the fields by the time she arrived.

She picked up a stick and clouted the dry little bushes and weeds with it as she passed, raising more dust. A secret love affair was all very well in theory, Rosaria thought. But in practice it meant long, dull hours of pretending everything was normal and a few, far too rare, snatched seconds of deliciousness. She wanted more.

Her sister lay next to Marco all night long, she thought bitterly. He touched her, he breathed on her, maybe some nights he even made love to her. She had never dared ask him. Jealousy rose like bile in her throat and her stomach heaved just like it had on that day she'd insisted on eating a piece of leftover fish that had been in the fridge for four days. She'd felt bad that time but now she felt even worse.

Anger made her bold. She didn't bother to pause outside the cottage and skulk in the bushes until she was sure Maria Domenica had gone to work. Who cared if her sister was there anyway? She could always make up some excuse for why she'd appeared on their doorstep so early in the morning.

But the house was quiet and the kitchen empty and untidy. What was all that paper strewn about the place? she wondered. Rosaria picked up a sheet and studied it more closely. The light of recognition shone in her eyes immediately. This was a drawing of Marco, stretched out languidly on the black-and-white kitchen floor tiles, and quite, quite naked. She threw it down and then picked up another, and another. A sob caught in her throat, tears spilled from her eyes and she sniffed furiously.

'Are you getting a cold, Rosaria?' Marco's voice was

sleepy, his body unclothed as he leaned in the doorway. 'I don't want your germs, you know. I don't want to get sick.'

She hid her tear-stained face behind a thick curtain of hair. 'No, I don't have germs. I'm fine. There's nothing to worry about,' she mumbled.

'Ah, you've found the pictures Maria Domenica made.' He came and stood beside her and gazed down at the little gallery of Marcos on the kitchen table. 'Not bad, huh?'

He was so close she could have reached out and touched him but she didn't. Instead she kept her arms folded stiffly in front of her and stayed safely behind her barrier of hair.

'I like this one the best, I think.' Marco picked up the Roman emperor picture. 'Who'd have thought little Maria Domenica would turn out to be an artist, hey?'

Rosaria let out a hiss of breath.

'Well, admit it, they're not at all bad,' he persisted. 'This one really looks like me. And I had no idea she could draw, you know.'

'Well, it's no surprise to me,' Rosaria was sulky.

'Did she draw at home when you were kids?'

'Never.'

'So how did you know she could do it?'

Rosaria shrugged. 'Well, it's the company she keeps, isn't it?'

Marco looked exasperated. 'Stop talking in riddles. Spit it out, whatever it is you want to say.' He'd never used that impatient tone with her before.

'That artist who's always hanging about Caffe Angeli. His name is Vincenzo something. The pair of them are so tight, their heads are always together. They whisper their secrets all day long. I think they know each other from Rome or something.'

'What are you saying, Rosaria?' Marco spoke carefully.

'I'm not saying anything.' She was defensive. 'I'm not accusing her of anything. All I know is he's always staring at her and he said he remembered her from Rome . . . that's all I know.'

Marco lifted a slender arm and swept the drawings off the table in one smooth movement. 'I won't be made a fool of,' he said unsteadily. 'I didn't want to marry the dirty little slut in the first place and now you say she's making a show of herself with another man in front of the whole village.'

'No, I didn't say that.' Rosaria was worried she'd gone too far. 'I only said—'

But it was too late. Marco was on his knees, in the drift of paper he'd swept from the table, ripping it into a fine confetti. 'Get out,' he screamed at her, his face red, his eyes bloodshot to match. 'I'm sick of your entire family. My life was fine before you all came along and ruined it. I said get out. Out of my house. Out!'

'Marco, please, you're over-reacting. All I said was—'

'*Out*!' He was up on his feet again and heading towards her, the palm of his hand held flat and looking for all the world like he was going to slap her. She backed out of the cottage hurriedly and, kicking up another cloud of yellow dust, ran for home.

She wanted to cry but the tears wouldn't come. As she ran, her body shuddered with hard, dry sobs. Marco hated her now. She'd ruined everything with her stupid jealousy. Then she imagined him lying there naked on the chequered floor while Maria Domenica drew him over and over again, and the envy that washed over her was so strong that she tasted it like metal in her mouth.

When Maria Domenica found Vincenzo outside Caffe Angeli she bubbled with excitement. He was lounging on a low wall, smoking one of his messy, home-rolled cigarettes, waiting for her to unlock the big glass door and let him in.

'You'll be happy to hear I plan to stop procrastinating today,' he told her, stray curls of tobacco falling from his lips as he spoke. 'I've done enough sketching. If my Madonna isn't right now she never will be. So I'm going to begin working on the wall. It may get a little untidy but I'll try not to get in your way.'

Maria Domenica didn't care about anything as trivial as mess. Gently pushing aside Chiara's chubby feet, she pulled the now depleted sketchpad out of the pram and rummaged around for the pencils. 'I've been drawing all night long,' she told him quickly. 'I couldn't stop. And if you've got time, I'd like to make one more picture before we start work. I want to draw you again, to see if I can capture you better than I did yesterday.'

'OK, OK.' Vincenzo let her push him backwards towards a chair. 'Just make me a coffee and you can do anything you like with me.'

Today it all seemed easier. His long straight nose, his wild eyebrows, the folds of flesh beneath his jawline, none of them proved too difficult for Maria Domenica's pencil. And as she drew, she tingled with sheer joy.

The *caffe*'s morning routine started without her. Franco knotted his starched white apron around his waist and stood behind his Gaggia. The regulars came in to drink an espresso at the counter before they got on with their day's work. Maria Domenica was so focused on her sketchpad she barely heard the click of the big glass door opening and closing.

But the sound of her husband's name being spoken snapped her back to reality.

'Ah, Marco, *buongiorno*,' Franco was saying. 'You're a stranger in here these days. What can I get you?'

'Espresso,' he replied shortly, his gaze not wavering from his wife at the corner table sketching the dark-haired stranger.

'Marco.' Maria Domenica looked up, still dazed with concentration. 'What are you doing here? Did you see the pictures I left for you on the kitchen table?'

He nodded and then issued another staccato instruction to Franco. 'And a whisky.'

Sipping his coffee and scotch, Marco hung over the jukebox. His finger stabbing at the buttons, his lips turned down in disdain, he made a few selections. Maria Domenica's pencil slowed on the sketchpad. She felt uneasy. Something was wrong but she couldn't quite work out what.

Marco drank another coffee, another whisky.

'A little early, isn't it?' Franco remarked mildly, but he only grunted in reply.

Leaning against the jukebox, Marco stared at his wife and the stranger she seemed so absorbed with. Through narrowed eyes he watched Vincenzo roll another cigarette and then finally he approached the table.

'You, what's your name?' Marco asked gruffly.

'I'm Vincenzo,' the artist replied and held out his hand, but it remained empty as Marco hung back, his arms held stiffly to his sides. 'How do you do,' he said nevertheless.

'Will you make me one of those?' Marco nodded towards the untidy cigarette.

'Sure, no problem.' Vincenzo pulled out another cigarette paper, laid a short cable of tobacco, licked and rolled and handed it over. 'Would you like a light?' he asked amiably.

Marco pulled out a chair, sat and leaned down to the lit match. 'Cheers,' was all he said.

'I've been drawing some more, see? I've made a picture of Vincenzo.' Maria Domenica felt unaccountably nervy, knew she was twittering.

Marco nodded, drank and smoked.

The silence between them was broken only by the half-hearted scratching of Maria Domenica's pencil. Finally she threw down the sketchpad and stood up. 'That's enough of that,' she declared. 'I have things to do.'

Her husband and Vincenzo watched as she disappeared behind the Gaggia. Still they said nothing. They smoked together and took turns to flick the spent ash into the small ashtray they shared.

Maria Domenica wished Marco would just get up and go. Normally he never came near the *caffe*. He preferred to avoid her during the daytime and so she couldn't imagine what he was doing here now.

Finally her prayers were answered. Marco stubbed out his cigarette, drained his glass of whisky, pushed back his chair and without a word he was gone.

'So what was that about?' Franco asked her.

'God knows.' Maria Domenica dismissed her husband with a shake of her head.

'Is everything all right with you two?' Franco's concern was at war with his natural inclination to mind his own business.

'As all right as it's ever been, I suppose.'

'If there's anything I can do,' he continued hesitantly. 'You know you only have to ask.'

'I know.' Maria Domenica touched his arm lightly. 'I do know.'

Vincenzo had turned his back on them. He was gazing again at his piece of blank wall. Whatever was going on, he didn't want to be involved, she realized. He was only passing through.

The rest of the day in Caffe Angeli was out of kilter. Maria Domenica boiled the milk over while she was making cappuccino. Marcello Bruni found a hair in his pastry. Chiara grizzled behind the red curtain. It was a relief when it was time to tuck her into her pram and wheel her home. Franco's face betrayed concern as she shut the door behind her. 'Take care,' he mouthed through the glass. Maria Domenica sketched a wave and began to walk.

She dreaded what she might find at home in the cottage. Marco angry? Or monosyllabic? Or worse still, wanting to take her to bed and work out his frustrations with her there. She slowed her step, in no hurry to know.

All seemed peaceful enough as she strolled up the track to the Manzoni farm. The buffalo in the fields were grazing on the sparse, yellow grass and casting fat shadows in the evening sun. There were ripe tomatoes that needed to be picked hanging heavily from the vines in her vegetable patch and the basil was threatening to run to seed.

The cottage was empty, the door shut tight.

'Marco?' she called hesitantly as she stepped into the stuffy, dim kitchen.

The place felt all wrong but at first she couldn't tell why. Then she spotted the drift of snowy white paper on the kitchen floor. Picking up the nearest fragment, she recognized the work of her pencil. Marco had destroyed everything, every last picture. Sinking to her knees amid the ruin of it all, she felt hopeless and empty, like stone. It should have been easy enough to cry but the tears didn't come. Maria Domenica knelt there for she didn't know how long, staring at what was left of her brief moments of happiness.

She felt Marco before she saw or heard him, felt his clenched fist slamming into the side of her head. She screamed at the pain and Chiara screamed back in reply.

'Marco, no.' She tried to slither back over the tiles and held her arms over her face for protection, but his fists found her again and again. 'Please, please, no,' she begged, as his curled hands, so feminine with their long tapered fingers, hit home with a wholly male strength.

There was a roaring in her ears and the tang of blood in her mouth and still she pleaded. 'Please stop, Marco. Don't do this, please.' But it seemed that her voice enraged him further. He picked up a handful of the shredded paper and, forcing open Maria Domenica's mouth, tried to stuff it in. She choked and spluttered and struggled to break free.

Chiara's cries were louder now, her body red and rigid.

'Shut up, shut up, shut up,' screamed Marco at the crying child.

Pure fear cut through the pain. *Don't hurt my baby. Please don't hurt my baby*, Maria Domenica thought. But she didn't dare speak the words out loud.

Enraged, Marco uncurled his fist and slapped her full across the face with his open hand. He'd wound the fingers of his other hand into her long black hair and it felt like he was pulling it out by the roots.

'Why? What have I done?' Maria Domenica spluttered, still choking on fragments of paper. 'Marco, please stop. Tell me what I've done wrong.'

'You know, you bitch.' His breath in her face smelled strongly of whisky. He must have been drinking all day.

'I don't know. I don't understand.' Her tears were flowing down her cheeks easily now, the salty water mixing with the warm blood that seeped from her lip. 'Marco, please stop and tell me what's gone wrong.'

He slumped to the floor beside her and held her face inches from his own. She tried to move away from the reach of his rank breath but he held her close and fast.

'See, this is how it's going to be from now on,' he said, and she could feel his heartbeat slowing as he struggled to calm himself. 'You are my wife and you'll stay here in my house, do you understand?'

She could only blink in reply.

'You can forget the *caffe*. I don't want you going back there. Not ever. I'll go to see Franco in the morning and tell him that you've given up your job. You won't speak to him again. And your artist friend? You won't speak to him either. There will be no more shaming me in front of the whole village. There's no reason for you to leave the farm alone. If you need to go into the village to shop my mother will go with you. Otherwise you'll stay right here, out of the way of trouble.'

She knew it was safer not to argue while he was in this mood. But this wasn't fair, surely he could see that? She tried to explain. 'Marco, I don't know what you think has been going on but you're wrong—'

Flushed magenta and spitting in fury, he took her shoulders in his hands and shook her hard. 'Don't try to tell me I'm wrong. What sort of fool do you think I am? Did you think you could make another baby with that *cretino* artist and bring it up under my roof?'

Then he stood and Maria Domenica watched, her heart in her mouth, as he grasped the handle of Chiara's pram. 'She looks like her father.' He leaned down and his acid breath washed over the baby. 'And no doubt she'll soon need a smack in the face like her mother.'

With that he slammed the cottage door behind him and she heard the roar of an engine as he drove off through the dust.

Finally the length and depth of the silence convinced her he wasn't coming back. Not for a while anyway. She heaved herself to her feet. Chiara's cries had subsided now and the wet warmth she felt on her own cheeks was blood not tears. Dabbing at her face with a dishcloth, she held her baby close.

Outside it grew dark but Maria Domenica didn't bother to turn on the lights. She curled up in the armchair, her body wrapped protectively around her baby, lost in thought. At last, her eyes closed and sleep blotted out everything.

22

Maria Domenica's body was stiff when she woke to Chiara's hungry cries. She unfolded herself awkwardly from the armchair and blinked in the early morning sunlight. Everything hurt. The events of last night came flooding back to her and she put her hand to her face. There was a scab forming on the corner of her mouth, the flesh around her left eye felt swollen, her cheek was tender to the touch. She knew that when she peered into the small, square mirror on the bathroom wall she'd see the bruises and cuts delivered by her husband's fists. She felt as empty and defeated as she felt sore.

Everything took longer this morning. Bathing, feeding and changing Chiara, making a pot of strong coffee to wake herself up, nibbling on a piece of hard twice-baked bread soaked in water then olive oil and covered in chopped tomatoes – it all seemed to take her hours. When she checked the alarm clock on the floor beside her bed it was already nearly lunchtime. Not that it mattered. She had nowhere to go and nothing much to do once she had cleared up the shreds of paper still scattered across the floor.

She sat at the scarred, formica kitchen table, chewing the skin around her fingernails and staring blankly at the plain white walls. Here and there they were splattered with browny red blobs where Marco had slapped the palm of his hand down on a blood-filled mosquito that had been feeding on his ankles. He was tormented by the insects during the summer months. They loved the flavour of him.

Maria Domenica wondered where Marco had spent the

night. At the big farmhouse with his parents, she supposed. Elena had probably fussed over her boy, bathed the knuckles that were bruised from the contact with his wife's cheeks and reassured him that he'd done the right thing. Marco would have filled their heads with nonsense and lies and they'd be ready to believe the worst of her. Eventually, when he calmed down, they'd send him back to her. But perhaps she could hope for a day or two's grace.

By mid-afternoon the heat of the day seemed to have sucked all the oxygen out of the drab little cottage. Maria Domenica put a sunhat on her baby daughter and gently laid her in her pram. She didn't dare go into town, but she had to walk the stiffness from her legs.

The thin wheels of the pram weren't designed to run over the hard, rutted farm tracks and Chiara was bumped and jiggled as they walked. Not that she seemed to mind. She gazed around with serious eyes and Maria Domenica was convinced that, young as she was, she was taking everything in. She seemed to be watching the little cottage and the bigger farmhouse behind it disappear into the distance as her mother pushed the pram through the dry fields. And her face definitely lit with a smile when she saw the black buffalo grazing quietly in the sunshine in the boggy ground by the lake. Chiara was growing so fast, soon she wouldn't be a baby any more, thought Maria Domenica sadly. She'd be a little girl and the Manzoni farm would be her whole world.

Breathlessly she pushed the pram to the top of a gentle slope and turned back to look at the view. The empty blue sky and flat, yellowing fields seemed to stretch for miles and miles, yet still Maria Domenica felt trapped. Beyond the fields she could see the road that led to San Giulio and then to Rome and Florence. Much further on lay other countries filled with foreign people. 'Switzerland, France, Germany, England.' Maria Domenica recited the words out loud, tasting them on her tongue. To her they were only names remembered from a schoolroom blackboard and languages that she'd heard in that little *caffe* by the Spanish Steps.

She stayed there, sitting quietly beside her daughter, until she felt the afternoon sun begin to scorch her skin. Sighing, she released the brake on the pram and held on tight as it juddered back down the bumpy track towards the cottage. Someone had been there, Elena probably, and left a small brown paper parcel in a shady spot beside the doorstep. The cottage door was always left unlocked so she could have gone inside with her package. Her mother-in-law didn't want to see her, Maria Domenica realized. She was to be left alone.

She found fresh mozzarella and thin slices of *prosciutto* in the parcel. And a note. '*Marco has gone to the city with his father for a few days*,' it read. '*You are to stay here. I will be keeping an eye on you.*' It was signed by Elena.

Maria Domenica chopped up the mozzarella and wound each milky chunk in a ribbon of *prosciutto crudo*. It wasn't what her husband or father would call a meal but it would do. Her teeth cut through the fatty raw ham and sank into the soft cheese. Eating comforted her. As she chewed the food, she tried to clear her mind. She had been feeling so depressed. She'd felt as if Marco had backed her into a corner. But now, swallowing hungrily and pushing another mozzarella ball into her mouth, she remembered she had people to turn to.

There was Lucia, although all she would have the power to give her was coffee and sympathy. And then there was Franco – he would surely help her. He would be worrying about her right now, wondering what was wrong. Yet perhaps it was best that she stay away from Caffe Angeli. She didn't want to make more trouble for Franco than she already had. No, she would go to her parents. And when he saw what Marco had done to her face, it would be all she could do to stop her father killing him.

It was tempting to flee straight away. Tempting but perhaps not so wise. From the window above her kitchen sink

Maria Domenica knew that Elena had a clear view of her cottage. She had stood there herself after Sunday lunch, washing dishes and looking out at the drab little building she was meant to call home. Elena might be there right now gazing down on her. She rarely used her formal living room with its hard couches and highly polished furniture. That was just for when important visitors came – which they hardly ever did.

No, Elena would be in the kitchen, listening to the radio, cleaning already spotless surfaces and every now and then staring out of the window, keeping an eye on her daughter-in-law, just as she'd promised to.

To be on the safe side Maria Domenica waited until it grew dark. Then, like a thief, she crept out of her cottage. The squeak of the pram's wheels sounded deafening to her ears. She was sure the noise would carry in the stillness of the night and prayed that if her mother-in-law heard anything she'd dismiss it as the call of a bird or the yelp of an animal.

As quickly as she could, Maria Domenica put some distance between herself and the Manzoni farm. With one hand she pushed the pram and in the other she carried a small bag packed with a few essentials. She didn't mean ever to come back to this place where she'd been so unhappy. She was going home for good.

'Maybe Papa will build another room for you and me to live in,' she told her sleeping daughter. Not that she really minded where they slept. She'd lie on the flagstones beneath the kitchen table if necessary, just so long as she didn't have to take her baby back to that miserable cottage.

It was a long walk by moonlight and, burdened with her bag and her baby, it seemed to take Maria Domenica for ever to reach the main road. She crossed it carefully, her eyes scanning back and forth for the headlights that would warn of oncoming cars. She didn't want to get caught. Not now that she was so close to home.

It was with relief that she recognized the low, dark shape of the farmhouse. She hoped they wouldn't all be in bed and fast asleep by now.

'Mamma, Papa,' she called out, but there was no reply.

Someone was still awake. Maria Domenica could see light escaping from the chinks in the window blinds. She pushed open the kitchen door and breathed in through her nose. There were layers of smells – baked bread, pans full of bubbling tomato sauces, grated Parmesan – the smells of a thousand delicious meals her mother had cooked as she raised her family. It was enough to make her feel hungry again.

'*Madonna mia*, look at you.' Her mother was at her side now, fussing and worrying.

Maria Domenica felt relief wash over her. She sank into the comfort of Pepina's familiar soft arms. 'Marco hit me,' she whispered, and then at last the tears began to run down her bruised cheeks. She couldn't stop crying. Her body shuddered with sobs and the stinging salty tears washed into the cuts on her face. She tried to talk but it was ages before she could get the words out. Then she could only repeat stupidly, 'Marco hit me.'

Pepina studied her face for a moment and then her eyes slid away into a corner. 'I know,' she replied heavily. 'I know all about it.'

'What did he tell you?'

Pepina stroked her daughter's hair and dabbed at her swollen face with one of Erminio's old handkerchiefs.

'Mamma?' Maria Domenica's sobs were subsiding and her eyes growing wide with indignation. 'What did Marco tell you I'd done? You can't believe him. It's not true, whatever he said is a lie.'

Pepina's shoulders slumped. She still couldn't meet her daughter's gaze. 'I must admit, I didn't expect you to look this bad. He said it was just a smack he gave you and that you'd deserved it.'

'What!'

'Calm down, Maria Domenica. You're not the first wife to get a smack or two from her husband,' said Pepina, her voice a low monotone.

'Papa never hit you. Not once.'

'No, but then I never gave him a reason to hit me. I wasn't trotting back and forth to the village on my own, working in some *caffe*, talking to men all day. I never shamed my husband with some long-haired artist.' Pepina's voice was rising now. 'What were you thinking? How did you expect your husband to react?'

The beginnings of an argument were on the tip of Maria Domenica's tongue but she bit the words back and instead asked more calmly, 'Where is Papa?'

'Gone.'

'Gone where?'

'Marco and his father came to pick him up. They went into the village to have a word with this Vincenzo fellow but he'd disappeared. Your sister Rosaria thought they might find him in Rome so they've followed him there.'

Maria Domenica couldn't quite take in what she was hearing. 'How could he believe Marco over me? Doesn't he trust me?'

'No, not really. He used to trust you but then you ran away, remember? And you came home pregnant and you lost his trust. I blame myself. I gave you too much freedom when you were growing up. But what could I do? I had so many daughters to watch over.' Hot tears began to course down Pepina's cheeks. She nodded at the bag that Maria Domenica had put down on the floor next to Chiara's pram. 'You brought your things with you? I'm sorry, *cara*, but you can't stay here. Your father said you're to stay at home and wait for your husband. That you're not to bring any more shame on this family.'

'No, Mamma, please let me stay here. Don't make me go

back. Please.' The two women clung to each other, both crying now. Maria Domenica felt her mother's stomach heaving with sobs and the wetness of her cheeks pressed against her neck.

'I'm sorry, *figlia*. I'm so sorry.' Pepina was pushing her out of the kitchen now and into the dusty yard. She pressed the bag back into her hands and turned Chiara's pram around so it pointed back in the direction of the Manzoni farm. 'I daren't disobey your father. You'll have to go home. But me or Rosaria will come and check on you every day. And we won't let him hit you again, I promise.'

Maria Domenica felt a last squeeze from her mother's hand and, as the door was closed in her face, she took a final lungful of the sweet-smelling air from the warm kitchen. Then she turned and slowly walked into the growing chill of the clear autumn night. She hadn't even said goodbye.

Part Two

New Brighton, England, 1968

I

New Brighton Baths stood beside the soupy grey waters where the River Mersey met the Irish Sea. It was a long, low-slung art deco place, built when this was a bustling seaside town filled with day-tripping factory workers and holiday-makers staying at the Bed and Breakfasts up the road. An open-air swimming pool was a huge attraction and families would flock there on hot summer days. The children would play in the wide, deep pool and fountains, hurtle down the slides and long for the day when they were old enough to climb the high diving board and plunge headfirst into the dark rectangle of water below.

But now the once grand seaside town was fading, long past its glory. There was still a funfair of sorts with a Ferris wheel, go-carts and merry-go-rounds, and, best of all, the waltzers where spotty adolescent boys would spin the prettiest girls around in the brightly coloured carts until they screamed and screamed or were sick – whichever came first.

New Brighton Baths still stood there beside the beach, perhaps a little more dilapidated than before. In the warmer months local families continued to come to spread their towels on the terrace of wooden benches, break their teeth on toffee apples and turn their fair English skins so red that they'd be peeling long strips of dead skin off each other's backs for days to come.

There was a little café there too and in the summer it did a roaring trade. The café had two entrances. One was on the street side, so fully dressed people who had been taking a stroll along the promenade could break their walk and come in for a cup of tea. The other door opened directly onto the pool area and all day dripping children would hurtle in and out, stocking up on fizzy drinks, wispy pink candy floss, ice cream and sandwiches filled with egg and cress. Across the centre of the room was a wooden rail to keep the two types of customer from cross-pollinating – and to prevent teenagers from sneaking into the pool through the café instead of handing over their entrance fee and going through the turnstile as they were supposed to.

The café smelled of wet swimming costumes and brewing tea. Behind the counter, buttering scones and slices of white bread, was a slender girl with black eyes and golden skin. Perhaps her nose was too beaky and her eyes too deep-set for true beauty, but her glossy hair fell down her back like water and she moved with a grace and fluidity which set her apart from the solid, sunburned girls in swimming costumes who thundered in and out of the café.

'Do you want some sugar with that, love?' the dark girl asked as she passed a tray of tea and scones to an old lady who had come in through the street entrance and who was bundled up in a coat and hat despite the heat of the day.

'What's that? What do you say?' The old lady turned an ear towards her and leaned closer. 'I can't understand a word she's saying,' she announced to the café.

Maria Domenica shrugged. Her English was good enough after three years working in this place, but what she didn't appreciate was that her strong accent had become infected with flat northern vowel sounds and sometimes it wasn't so easy to make out what she was saying. The little girl sitting half tucked under the counter at her feet never had any problems though. Fairer of skin and paler of hair than her mother, head bent over a picture book, Chiara played by herself, quietly and neatly, until she was told it was time to move.

They were outsiders here, she and her mother, 'Eye-talians', although most people were friendly enough. If they tried they could just about manage to say the word 'Chiara' in their strange singsong voices, but Maria Domenica had given up trying to teach them how to pronounce her own name. 'Maria de what, love? Bit of a mouthful, isn't it?' they'd complained so she ended up telling them, 'Just call me Maria, it's far simpler.'

It had taken her a while to get here but she'd never doubted that she'd make it. When her mother had turned her away that chilly night she'd gone directly to Franco for help – not to Caffe Angeli, which was all closed up for the night by then, but to his house, nearby. She'd never visited him there before.

It was one of the older houses, hidden behind high walls and built around its own small cobbled courtyard. Franco had left the gate hanging half open and, through a lighted window, Maria Domenica could clearly see his son Giovanni sitting at the kitchen table behind a stack of books, studying late into the night. He was growing up and on his face was the soft downy beginnings of a beard, yet he was still so young. Too young to hear the story Maria Domenica had brought with her.

She had hesitated then. Her steps had stilled on the threshold and she wondered what to do. All it took was a touch of her fingertips to her cheek, swollen and sore from the beating, and a glance at the face of her sleeping baby to propel her onwards through Franco's courtyard and his front door.

Shocked when he saw her ruined face, Giovanni had reached out and held her tight. 'What happened? What happened?' he crooned.

It was she who broke away from the embrace. Pushing Giovanni down into an armchair, she settled beside him and let him hold her hand. 'Marco hit me,' she said softly. 'He went completely crazy and I'm still not really sure why. I think maybe he's jealous of Vincenzo. He imagines there's something going on between us.'

Giovanni's eyes met hers. 'And is there?'

'Don't be ridiculous. I hardly know him.'

'I'm sorry, Maria Domenica, I'm sorry.' He grasped her hand tighter and listened in silence as she poured out the story of how her mother had turned her away, sent her home to Marco.

'I can't go back to that cottage. I'm scared he'll hurt me again. Or worse, he'll hit Chiara,' she told him.

'What are you going to do?'

She shook her head and her shoulders slumped in defeat.

'I know what.' Bravado made Giovanni's voice deeper and stronger. 'I'll go and find Marco. I'll tell him what I think of men who hit their wives. And, if I have to, I'll thump the bastard myself.'

'No, no, you can't do that.'

'I can,' Giovanni insisted. 'I'm just as strong as he is and nearly as tall.'

'But I don't want that. It's not going to help.'

'Well, what will help?'

'I'm not sure. But I do know that I don't want you to do anything that will bring trouble for you and Franco. You've got a business to run. You can't afford to get involved.'

'Don't worry about us. We can look after ourselves.'

'I can look after myself too, Giovanni. I managed it for a whole year in Rome. I can do it again if I have to.'

'Don't run away again, please, Maria Domenica.' He sounded distressed now.

'But I think I have to. Surely it would be better for everyone if I just wasn't here any more? If I didn't exist?'

'Don't leave us.'

'What other choice do I have?'

Giovanni looked at Chiara still sleeping peacefully in her pram. He said nothing for a moment. And then he stood and began to rummage in a big wicker basket full of envelopes, pens and coins. He pulled out a small bronze key and unlocked the top drawer of the polished wooden bureau.

She tried to pull back her hand as he pressed a thick roll of money into it. 'Yes, take it,' he urged. 'My father would want you to have it.'

He kissed her on the cheek, wrapped his arms around her shoulders and held her. 'Will I ever see you again?'

'Maybe not.'

'Where will you go?'

For a moment she hesitated. How could she leave her family behind a second time? Her mother and father loved her, they thought what they were doing was for the best. But this was her only chance. It was now or never.

'I'll go further than Rome this time, I think, Giovanni. Please tell my father not to try to find me. And tell Franco that I'm sorry.'

As soon as it grew light she'd taken the early morning bus to Naples, then boarded a train heading north. The carriages were crowded but a family from Salerno had made room for her, squeezing closer together until there was half a seat for her to wedge herself into. They'd shared their food with her: hard bread, salty *pecorino* cheese and pink, fatty *mortadella* sausage. In return she'd sung songs with the children and told them stories.

She'd changed trains in Rome and gradually the landscapes flowing past the window had grown unfamiliar, the fields were greener, the hills dotted with cypress trees and the air blowing through the open windows felt cooler on her face.

Then they got to the Alps and Maria Domenica felt the sadness loosen its grip on her as she pressed her nose to the window and drank in the beauty of the snow-capped mountains.

There had been a problem when she reached the border with Switzerland. Without the correct papers they wouldn't let her through.

'You need a passport,' the official had barked at her. 'Where's your passport?'

So Maria Domenica had to leave the train and queue for half a day outside an office in the nearest town hall. There was nowhere to sit in the corridor, which smelled of moth-balls and highly polished shoes, so when her legs grew tired she sank down in the dust on the marble floor beside Chiara's pram.

Finally it was her turn to sit across the desk from an officious little man with hard eyes and a neatly trimmed moustache. She'd tried tears at first, but he merely plucked a tissue from a box and busied himself with his files until she dried her eyes and stopped crying. Then she unpeeled a few notes from Franco's roll of cash and handed them over. He slipped them into the top pocket of his jacket and drummed his fingers on the desk until she passed over a couple more.

It was worth it. With the right papers she was allowed to board the next train and cross the border to Switzerland and then France. She unpeeled a few more notes from Franco's roll and paid the extra to travel in a couchette. At night the seats were folded away and six little bunks were pulled out from the walls of the carriage. It was hot and cramped, but there was something romantic about falling asleep in one place and waking up somewhere entirely different. The air in France smelled strange, she decided. It smelled foreign.

At Calais she'd taken the cross channel ferry. She'd never been on a boat before and, by the time she disembarked at Dover, she felt no desire to repeat the experience. The rolling motion left both her and Chiara feeling sick to their stomachs and, while she managed to choke back the bitter-tasting bile that rose in her throat, her baby girl understandably felt no such compunction. The glares of the other passengers as Chiara sobbed and puked long into the night had made her wriggle with discomfort.

From Dover there had been yet another train to London. She had thought to stay there a while, savouring the city, but it wasn't what she'd expected. Everything was too big, from the railway station concourse to the roads full of traffic. She wouldn't know where to begin exploring a city like this. So she pressed on and boarded another train heading north.

She'd ended up here, in New Brighton, and rented some rooms at the very top of a tall Victorian house on Egremont Promenade. The house faced the water, which Maria Domenica had thought would be nice, but the foamy, grey, fishless sludge of the River Mersey was a poor replacement for the sparkling blue Mediterranean. Still, at night, on the far side of the river, the lights of Liverpool sparkled with a certain gaiety and, once Chiara was asleep, she could happily spend hours sitting by the window looking out at them.

When it came to finding work she stuck to what she knew best. She asked around in the local cafés until at last she found one where they said, yes, they did need an extra pair of hands. Then, instead of tiny cups of espresso, she produced steaming pots of tea. Rather than slices of pizza and rich pastries there were fishpaste sandwiches and jam doughnuts.

Chiara came to work with her each day, just as she had at Caffe Angeli. The owners had been dubious about that at first. 'Can't you find a childminder or something, Maria love?' they'd asked. But when they saw what an angel she was and heard how strongly her mother felt about being separated from her, they left them well alone.

'Do you know, we're made up we hired you,' Mr and Mrs Leary often told her now. 'We've never had such a hard worker. Not ever.'

Mr Leary had a long face and crooked teeth like a horse; his wife was fleshy and covered in moles and freckles. The couple made a reasonable living from the café, except in the winter months when the door that led to the empty swimming pool stayed locked and there weren't many walkers brave enough to risk a trek down the windy promenade. On those cold days Maria Domenica was needed for fewer hours, leaving her free to wrap her daughter in woollen sweaters and mittens and to wander the streets. Together they walked for miles, exploring the roads, lanes and alleyways that ran between New Brighton and the nearby town of Wallasey. As they patrolled the grey stone pavements, Maria Domenica would carefully scan the faces of the people they passed, as if she was searching for something or someone. And when she spotted a blond head shining out from the unrelenting greyness she'd stop and stare for a moment before giving a half-sigh and trudging on.

'What are you up to, love?' Mrs Leary had asked her once when she'd passed them in the car and had insisted on giving them a ride home. 'It's cold enough to freeze the balls off a brass monkey out there. You'd be better off staying indoors.'

Thankfully it was snug inside. Her landlord, Mr Fox, had an Aga stove in his long, narrow kitchen that stayed warm all the time. Beside it were three big, plastic bins filled with some mysterious bubbling liquid.

'Beetroot wine, carrot wine, blackberry wine,' Mr Fox had told her, tapping each bin proudly.

Maria Domenica had grimaced. 'At home we make it from grapes,' she'd told him politely.

'Ah, but you wait till you taste this, love. You'll never want to drink that poxy grape juice again, I can tell you.'

Mr Fox had a son called Alex. He was unemployed but always busy. Most of the time all that Maria Domenica saw of him was a pair of legs sticking out from beneath whichever of his wrecked old cars he was working on.

When Alex wasn't tinkering with his cars he was shut in the front room playing records by the Beatles, the band that had lit up the city on the other side of the River Mersey. Often Maria Domenica heard the music echoing up through the floors and for a moment she'd let herself remember how Franco never had given into her entreaties to put a Beatles song or two on his jukebox. Mostly she tried not to think about what she'd left behind. It was kinder to focus on the future, to plan and dream for that.

In the summer there was less time for wandering, but the Learys offered to give her Mondays off and Maria Domenica used up her free day trying to cover as much ground as possible. Sometimes she'd peep into pubs and betting shops as she passed by – dark, masculine places where she never dared linger. Once she came across an art school in the middle of the park and sat outside for hours, watching the students come and go, until Chiara finally lost patience and dragged her off to the swings and the duck pond.

The summer was a good one. Maria Domenica had never imagined England could be so dry and warm. She tried not to let it remind her of home but sometimes she couldn't help tilting her face to the heat of the sun, squinting her eyes so all she could see was a patch of blue sky and imagining she was once again lying on her back beneath the peach trees in her parents' orchard.

One Monday Maria Domenica dressed Chiara in light clothes and a sunhat and got ready to leave for their regular excursion.

On her way out she found Alex lurking in the kitchen, blushing to the roots of his short brown hair and nervously trying to catch her eye.

'What you up to then? Off for a walk?' he asked.

'That's right,' she nodded. 'I thought I might take some stale bread and go to the park. Chiara wants to feed the ducks.'

He glanced out of the window at the cloudless sky. 'Too nice a day for the park. Why don't you go to the beach?' he suggested hesitantly. 'The kiddie can build sandcastles.'

This was the most Alex had ever said to her and Maria Domenica was completely thrown. 'The beach?' she replied stupidly. 'What beach?'

'You know, past New Brighton Baths, up Harrison Drive. It's dead nice and sandy there,' he told her. 'Hang on, I'll just dig out an old bucket and spade for the kiddie and then I'll give you a lift there myself.'

She tried to refuse but Alex was off rummaging in the shed for the promised bucket and spade. He emerged clutching something dirty and cobwebby, his slightly comical face flushed with pleasure. 'Just needs a bit of a clean-up in the sea,' he insisted. 'Come on then, love, jump in the car and we'll be off.'

'Which car?' Maria Domenica looked at the three rusting hulks clogging up the driveway. To her eyes none seemed a likely prospect. Even shiny, enthusiastic Alex seemed nonplussed for a moment. 'Er, now, let me see,' he mused. 'The brakes on the Austin need adjusting and I dunno about that Morris. What about the Triumph?'

The car door creaked alarmingly as he opened it for her and the front passenger seat was lumpy and torn. But Maria Domenica wedged herself in, clutching Chiara on her knee, and after a little bit of engine-revving and a few clouds of exhaust they were off.

'Lean back and you'll get a longer ride,' Alex cried and accelerated along the street. Maria Domenica looked at him quizzically. 'At least, that's what my nana always used to say,' he added hastily.

The beach, when they found it, was big and bleak. Instead of shading herself beneath a beach umbrella like she always had at home, Maria Domenica found she was expected to huddle behind a striped windbreak, which gave some shelter from the stiff breeze that raced off the muddy Irish Sea and whipped the sand up in their faces.

'Lovely day.' Alex nodded to a neighbouring family of sunbathers and spread their beach towels on the ground.

'Gorgeous,' they agreed, wriggling their long white limbs with pleasure.

Maria Domenica thought they were quite mad. She watched while Alex stripped the clothes quickly from his pale body. He was all ribs and stiff as an ironing board.

'I can hold a towel around you if you want to get changed,' he offered, his watery blue eyes widening.

'No, no, I'm fine,' she replied.

'Aren't you going to come in for a swim then?'

Maria Domenica eyed the scene dubiously. To her right she could see the cranes and sheds of the docks that lined the Mersey estuary. Ahead of her the brown sand stretched out to grey waves that finally met up with the washed-out sky. To her left, the long, flat beach was dotted with families playing cricket, building sandcastles and enjoying the day for all they were worth.

'Well, I'm going in for a dip,' Alex declared. 'And when I get out I'll buy the kiddie an ice cream.'

She watched him run into the sea awkwardly. She could tell the exact moment when the cold hit him. He gave a half halt, hopped about and his shoulders shot up to his ears.

'Chiara, do you want to go for a paddle?' she enquired.

Her daughter, bucket in one hand, spade in the other, stared at her with serious brown eyes.

Maria Domenica held out her hand. 'Come on then, pull me up and we'll go and play in the water.'

Chiara shook her head. 'Ice cream,' she said in a small, determined voice.

That's right, ice cream. *Gelato*. Say *gelato* for me, Chiara.'

At the sound of the foreign words Chiara stuffed her fingers in her ears, scrunched up her face and yelled, 'Ice cream, ice cream, ice cream.'

Curious faces peered around windbreaks. Maria Domenica gently removed her daughter's hands from her ears. 'OK, OK, ice cream,' she said soothingly in English. 'In a minute, when Alex gets back, we'll get you an ice cream.'

She turned away from her daughter for a moment. Despite

the breeze, the feeling of the sun warming her skin was good. Leaning back on her elbows, she soaked it up.

Alex ran out of the icy water far faster than he'd gone in and dried his pink, glowing body with a rough towel.

'Brr, that'll put hairs on your chest,' he declared to no one in particular and then, turning to Chiara, 'Right, love, ice cream first and then we'll build a proper English sandcastle, shall we?'

Chiara nodded and let him take her by the hand and lead her to the ice cream van. They returned with orange cornets, topped by yellow balls of milky ice, chocolate flakes sticking proudly out of the top. 'Here you are.' Alex thrust one in her hand. 'Have a 99.'

Licking, dribbling and giggling, Alex and Chiara raced to finish their ice creams first. Then they collapsed on the sand and began to dig and build. Some of Alex's stiffness seemed to seep away as he played with her daughter. First they dug out the shape of a boat, then surrounded it with sandcastles and finally Alex buried Chiara in the sand so just her head and her feet were sticking out. He seemed tireless.

'What a great day,' he said finally.

Maria Domenica noticed belatedly how he was growing pinker than usual. 'You're getting sunburned,' she warned.

Fumbling in his beach bag, he produced a sticky bottle of Ambre Solaire suntan oil and asked, 'Could you rub some of this on my back then?'

She wanted to say no, but realized she couldn't. So she slapped and patted the oil onto his skin rather than massaged it. Touching him felt strange. His skin was broken by freckles and tiny red pimples with white heads.

He smiled. 'That feels good,' he told her.

Embarrassed, she handed back the sun oil and rolled over on her towel to let the sun warm her shoulders. She must have fallen asleep because when she opened her eyes she realized what heat there was had gone and the breeze had picked up.

Alex was dismantling the windbreak. 'Come on,' he called, 'let's get this little lot in the car and then fish and chips for tea on the way home, hey?'

Chiara was staring up at him and smiling. Damp, brown sand coated her feet and knees and clung to her hair. Her swimming costume sagged down at the back comically. She was filthy, Maria Domenica realized, and she was happy.

Three-quarters of the way home the Triumph shuddered to a halt and, try as he might, Alex couldn't restart it. In the end they had to push it to the side of the road and walk the rest of the way back. Alex didn't let it ruin his good mood. Instead, he hoisted Chiara up onto his shoulders and took to galloping down the pavements yelling, 'Clip-clop, clip-clop, giddy-up, I'm a horse.'

The child laughed until she was half hysterical.

2

Maria Domenica liked to wake early. There was no bread to bake or chickens to feed these days, but she was used to rolling out of bed at first light and couldn't break the habit.

Usually she had the house to herself at that hour. Some mornings she'd potter round the kitchen making toast and jam for Chiara and cleaning up any mess Alex or his father had left the night before. Other times she'd fetch the newspaper from the letterbox and slowly make her way through an article or two in a bid to improve her English. Her grasp of the language was pretty good now although she still thought and dreamed in Italian.

This morning she was halfway down the stairs when she heard the sound of whistling. Alex was already awake and wandering around the kitchen in his dressing gown.

'Morning, love.' He gave her a sleepy grin. 'Fancy a cuppa?'

'You're up early. Couldn't you sleep?' she asked.

'No, no. Just thought I'd get a good start on the day.' He poured milk over a bowl of cereal and mashed it up with the back of his spoon. Leaning over the sink, he shovelled his breakfast into his mouth. 'I'll put the kettle on, shall I?' he asked between mouthfuls of the sloppy mixture.

She felt his eyes following her as she reached into the bread bin for the loaf. Self-consciously she put the bread beneath the grill and waited for it to brown. The silence between them felt uncomfortable so she racked her brain for something to say.

'What are your plans for the day then?' she said eventually.

'Actually, if you don't mind, I thought I'd come along with you to the swimming baths.' He'd finished eating now and was filling the kettle with water.

'But I'll be busy working.'

'Yes, I know. I thought I could play with the kiddie while you're working. Have a bit of fun in the pool. Keep her amused. Must be boring for her all day just sitting around the café with you.'

'She doesn't mind.' Maria Domenica was defensive.

Alex quickly picked up on the tone in her voice. 'No, of course she doesn't,' he said lightly. 'More fun to have a swim and a play on the slides though, eh?'

It seemed there was no arguing with him. He had his swimming trunks already rolled up inside the sausage he'd made of his towel, and his bag of suntan oil was waiting by the back door. Maria Domenica chewed on a corner of Chiara's toast absent-mindedly.

Normally Alex was an invisible presence in the house. She heard him behind doors and through walls, found his dirty dishes in the sink or his oily overalls crumpled on the bathroom floor. It was a big house, four storeys high, and Maria Domenica had a bedroom and sitting room on the very top floor. She was out most of the day anyway so it was hardly surprising she and Alex hardly ever met face to face. Now it was beginning to feel as though she'd seen more of him over the last day or so than the previous three years. She had her suspicions about what was going on, but hoped she was wrong.

As tea was drunk and breakfast was eaten, they danced around each other awkwardly in the narrow kitchen, Maria Domenica staying an arm's length away from him at all times.

'Right then,' Alex said finally and drained his mug, 'I'll put on some clothes and see if I can get that Morris going.'

'There's no need. We can walk. It only takes half an hour.'

'You'll walk your legs off if you're not careful, girl.' He grinned affably at her. 'Anyway, I think I know what the trouble is. Shouldn't take me too long to get it started. Easy-peasy.'

As it turned out it wasn't so easy-peasy after all. Maria Domenica heard the car's engine coughing unhealthily as she and Chiara were getting washed and dressed. But by the time they'd brushed their teeth and tracked down one of Chiara's sandals that had mysteriously gone missing, he had the thing running.

'Sandcastles?' Chiara asked hopefully, as Alex opened the car door for her with a flourish.

'Not today, love.' He pointed to an inflatable rubber ring waiting for her on the back seat. 'Today, we're going to learn to swim.'

'Lovely,' she declared and wriggled in beside it.

Maria Domenica smiled despite herself. 'It's really very kind of you,' she told Alex. The car lurched out of the driveway.

'Nah, no problem. I like your little kiddie. We have a laugh together. Anyway, I've got plenty of time on my hands.'

'I suppose you do,' she mused. 'Do you mind if I ask you a question?'

'Go ahead.'

'Why don't you get a job?'

He laughed. 'Now you sound like me dad.'

'No but really, don't you get bored all day?'

'Never been bored in me life, I promise you. Anyway I've got the cars to do up and I make a bit of cash whenever I flog one. Enough to get by. That answer your question?' He took his eyes off the road for a moment and glanced over at her.

'I guess so.'

'So can I ask you a question now?'

She nodded.

'What's a pretty Eye-talian girl like yourself doing in a place like this, all on her own except for a kiddie?'

'Well . . . I fancied a change, didn't want to stay in Italy all my life, I suppose.'

'Yes but why here? I mean it's bit of a hole, isn't it?'

'I had a friend who told me he lived here,' she began slowly. 'But I think he's gone now. I can't find him at any rate.'

'Boyfriend?'

'Sort of.'

'The kiddie's dad?' he asked in the same neutral tone.

Maria Domenica shook her head. 'That's more than one question,' she told him. 'It's my turn again now. Here's my next question. Is driving difficult?'

He laughed. 'Talk about changing the subject. The answer is no, it's dead easy once you get the hang of it. Would you like me to teach you?'

She hesitated. 'I might not be any good at it.'

'Look, if I can do it, anyone can. Tell you what, I'll get some L-plates for the car and on your next day off you can give it a try, OK?'

'OK,' she agreed.

For the rest of the short trip she watched carefully as he shifted gears, glanced into the mirror and indicated carefully whenever he turned left or right. She felt a tingle of excitement. She was going to learn to drive. For an instant she felt light and free. Her future was here, opening itself up for her. There were so many possibilities, anything could happen. She couldn't wait to see how her life turned out.

Alex drove slowly down the hill. The rows of shops and terraced houses stammered to a finish and they were faced with the wide expanse of waterfront. The sky was so blue this morning that even the sea didn't look as dense and bottomless as normal.

'Another lovely day. Bet it'll be a scorcher,' remarked Alex, as they passed the funfair and the crazy golf. New Brighton Baths was ahead of them, curving gracefully along the line of the sea wall, turning a blank face towards the murky waves. From here it might have looked like just another utilitarian council building were it not for the brightly coloured poles of the high-diving board sticking out above the roofline.

'Swim, swim, swim.' Chiara was bouncing up and down on the back seat in excitement.

'You will be careful with her, won't you?' Maria Domenica turned a suddenly anxious face to Alex.

'Course I'll be careful,' he promised. 'No need to worry. We're going to have a great time.'

The blue skies were like a call to prayer for the sun worshippers and they responded in their hordes, filling up the terraces of wooden benches that rose like an amphitheatre around the pool.

In the café, they were rushed off their feet all day but, busy as she was, Maria Domenica couldn't help glancing down every so often to the space beneath the counter that Chiara usually occupied and realizing with a jolt that she wasn't there.

She saw no sign of them until gone lunchtime. Then she spotted Alex heading towards the café and a tired but happy Chiara trailing behind him. Her wet hair was slick and dark and her skin turning golden brown. She looked like a proper little Italian girl and Maria Domenica was almost surprised when she opened her mouth and English words came out.

'Mummy, I'm hungry,' Chiara complained.

'Could do with a bite to eat myself,' added Alex.

As she buttered bread and sliced up cheese and tomato, Maria Domenica heard all about their day. They'd learned to swim in the shallows, played in the fountain, made friends with a naughty boy who'd been splashing them, and been on the little slide but not the big one.

'You must be exhausted,' she laughed, serving up a doorstep of a sandwich for Alex and a plate piled high with cheesy soldiers for her daughter.

Chiara wrinkled her nose in disapproval. 'Yuk,' she declared.

'What do you mean yuk? It looks delicious,' Alex told her.

'No! Yuk!' She pushed the plate away.

'Oh well, if you don't want any, I'll have some,' he shrugged and pretended to devour a slice of cheesy soldier. Maria Domenica tried to hide a smile. 'Mmm, yummy,' he sighed.

Chiara snatched her plate back and began nibbling on her food. By the time Maria Domenica returned a few minutes later with ice cream sodas for a treat, they were eating together companiably. They made a funny pair, she thought. No one would ever mistake them for father and daughter and yet they seemed to get on well enough.

Mrs Leary, the café owner, had been grinning broadly all day as she always did when the place was busy, but now her beam was several watts brighter and she was waving at them from behind the counter. As soon as she got the chance, she sidled over to Maria Domenica and hissed, 'You never told me you were courting, you naughty girl.'

'What?'

'You've got yourself a young man at last. And very nice he looks too.' She gave Alex another cheery wave.

'Oh no, we're not really courting.' Maria Domenica hurried to correct her. 'He's my landlord's son. We're just good friends.'

'Just good friends, hey?' Mrs Leary's moles and freckles sank into her wrinkles as her face wreathed itself in another huge smile. 'Get away with you, Maria. I can tell he fancies you just by looking at him.'

Maria Domenica didn't want to be fancied, especially not by Alex. She liked her two small rooms at the top of the tall, narrow house and feared an embarrassing situation with her landlord's son could lead to her being asked to move out. She would simply have to avoid him for a bit until he'd got over his little crush. It was a shame because Chiara liked him so much, but it couldn't be helped. Men were bad news, they'd wrecked everything in her life so far. Nice as he seemed, Alex wasn't going to be allowed to ruin what she had left.

3

Avoiding Alex wasn't just difficult, it was impossible. He developed an eerie habit of just happening to be wherever she went. He'd bang into her in the greengrocer's and help her carry her shopping home. Or she'd hear the familiar clanking of the Morris's engine as she walked home from work and he'd stop to give her a lift. There was always an amiable smile on his face and he never forgot to make a fuss of Chiara. Short of being rude, she couldn't get rid of him.

And, just as promised, come her next free day, he waggled a pair of L-plates at her and asked, 'Are you ready to learn to drive?'

'Oh,' she hesitated, 'I don't know.'

'Come on, you were dead keen last week.'

'Yes, but—'

'Give it a go, Maria. Get in the car.'

From force of habit she went to the passenger side. 'Oh no you don't,' Alex told her. 'Get over here.'

It felt strange having the steering wheel in front of her. She stared stupidly at the car's controls as if she'd never seen anything like them before. Chiara clambered into the back seat. 'Drive?' she asked hopefully.

Maria Domenica turned the key in the ignition and the engine coughed into life.

'OK, remember, mirror, signal, manoeuvre,' Alex instructed.

'Alex, I can't manoeuvre, I don't even know how to begin

to make the thing move.' Maria Domenica was laughing helplessly.

So the engine was turned off and Alex started again from the beginning, explaining the clutch, accelerator, brake and all the different gears. He was a remarkably patient teacher and when Chiara became bored and grizzly in the back seat he simply turned and said authoritatively, 'Quiet now, your mum is concentrating.'

By the end of the lesson Maria Domenica had only managed to drive once round the block and she lurched and bunny-hopped most of the way, but Alex seemed pleased with her progress. 'We'll go a bit further next week,' he promised.

'OK,' she replied.

'Now about my fee.'

'Oh, your fee!' She hadn't realized he'd want to be paid.

'That's right, in return for my taking time out from my busy schedule to give you a driving lesson, I think you should take time to come to the pictures with me.'

For a moment Maria Domenica thought he wanted her to go to an art gallery with him. 'You like pictures?' she asked surprised.

'Yeah, I do. I really love musicals and they've got a special season of them showing at the cinema round the corner,' he continued enthusiastically. 'This week it's *The Sound of Music*. I've seen it before but I'd love to see it again. So will you come with me tonight?'

Finally catching on, Maria Domenica searched her mind wildly for an excuse. 'What about Chiara?' she offered. 'Who will look after her if I'm at the, er, pictures?'

'No problem. My dad and his girlfriend Maureen would be happy to babysit.'

Maria Domenica had met Maureen once or twice. A funny little wispy-haired thing with thick-lensed glasses, she looked as though she was born to babysit.

'Come on,' Alex wheedled. 'You owe me. I gave you a driving lesson, remember. It's the least you can do.'

He'd backed her into a corner and she could see she had no choice. 'OK then.' She remembered her manners and added, 'That would be nice, thank you.'

Somehow Alex managed to herd her into the back row of the cinema. Spilling cellophane-wrapped chocolates into her lap, he sat down close beside her in the darkness. She heard his arm edging round her before she felt its weight and warmth. Rigidly, she let it rest across her shoulder. They were on a date, she realized, as the big screen in front of them lit up. All her plans to avoid Alex had ended in miserable failure.

The theatre curtain jerked upwards and there was a soaring of strings and a voice raised in song. 'The hills are alive . . .' Julie Andrews sang so lustily that her voice seemed to have been projected from her very boots as she skipped over the Swiss Alps.

By the time the Von Trapp children were dancing round a fountain in clothes made of old curtains, Alex's arm was fully extended around her shoulders and he was absent-mindedly playing with her hair. She didn't mind nearly as much as she'd imagined she might.

'That was lovely,' he told her later and swung the car into the driveway. She thought he might lean over and kiss her then but instead he just smiled. 'We should do that again some time,' he said lightly. 'They've got *My Fair Lady* showing next week, how do you fancy that?'

'Maybe.'

'Be good for your English, wouldn't it, going to the pictures? Help it along a bit.'

'Isn't my English good enough?' she asked, mildly offended.

'Maria love,' he smiled again, more shyly this time, 'everything about you is good enough.'

4

As always, Mrs Leary's smile faded with the summer. The heatwave ended, the crowds at New Brighton Baths thinned out and the queues in the café grew shorter and shorter.

'We'll be cutting down your hours soon, I reckon,' she told Maria Domenica in a depressed tone one day when the place was particularly empty.

'It's been a good summer though, hasn't it?'

'Oh aye, not bad. We've made enough to get us through the winter and that's the main thing.'

Spending less time in the café would be a relief. Maria Domenica was tired of looking at the plain white walls and red formica table tops. The place looked more rundown with each passing year but Mrs Leary was reluctant to spend good money doing it up. Nobody came here for the decor, she pointed out. Still, it was a stark place and it echoed when it was empty. Maria Domenica wouldn't be sorry to see the back of it for a couple of months.

What she wanted was to spend more time in her two snug rooms at the top of the tall, narrow house. There was plenty to look at there. Alex had finally taken her to see the real pictures, the ones that were hung in the Walker Art Gallery just a ferry ride away over the Mersey to Liverpool, and she'd come back with a huge bag of postcards and posters. He'd spent practically an entire day helping her pin them up all over her walls.

'Never had much time for art myself,' he'd admitted. 'But this stuff really jazzes up your room, doesn't it?'

Alex had become her constant companion. She'd long since stopped correcting Mrs Leary when she referred to him as 'your young man'. She now allowed him to hold her hand and once or twice he'd even dared to lean over in the car and kiss her. A quick, polite kiss it had been, more of a touch of the lips really. He seemed aware that if he tried too much, too soon, he'd be pushing his luck.

Now she was going to have more free time, Maria Domenica assumed she and Alex would see even more of each other. He'd promised to take her back to Liverpool to have another look at the gallery and said this time they'd walk through the back streets and take a look at the famous Cavern club where the Beatles were born. Chiara was looking forward to it. She liked being on the top deck of the ferry, watching the seagulls wheeling and shrieking overhead. Mind you, once the weather turned really cold, it wouldn't be much fun up there.

'Mrs Leary, do you think I could have tomorrow off?' Maria Domenica asked on the spur of the moment.

'I don't see why not. This place is hardly likely to fill up again. Take as much time as you like.'

But when she got home and hurried to share her plans with Alex there was no sign of him. Later that night she heard the front door slam and assumed it must be him but was much too tired to bother trekking downstairs. Never mind, she thought, she'd catch up with him tomorrow.

That night she dreamed of Alex and although when she woke, slightly later than usual, she couldn't remember the dream properly, she still held in her mind an image of him, mouth tilting and blue eyes creased with laughter, and it made her feel warmed right through.

When, yawning widely, she came downstairs, it was to find Mr Fox rushing out the door.

'Is Alex still in bed?' she asked.

'Um, no, you've missed him . . .'

'He's gone out? Well, do you know when he'll be back?'

'Oh, at the usual time, I think. He didn't mention that he'd be late again.'

With that her landlord was gone and Maria Domenica was left alone with an empty day stretching ahead of her.

She was confused. What on earth had he meant by 'the usual time'? There was never a usual time with Alex. Since he had no job to keep him chained to a routine, he lived life by his own internal clock.

She felt mildly put out. After all, Alex was always here when she wanted him. He was endlessly amenable. And now she'd taken today off work specially and he'd disappeared, leaving her at a loose end.

Her daughter had woken at last and was sliding downstairs on her bottom, one step at a time, clutching her teddy bear in one hand and a grubby pink blanket in the other. She was trying to suck the thumb of the hand that was holding her teddy bear, with limited success.

'Chiara, get your thumb out of your mouth and come and tell me what you want to do today,' she ordered. 'Would you like to go for a long walk like we always used to?'

She got sulkiness in reply. 'No. Don't want to walk, want to drive.'

'We can't drive, I haven't got my licence yet and Alex isn't here to take us out. It's just you and me, like the old days. So we'll have to walk.'

'Want Alex, want to drive.'

Lord, but her daughter was stubborn. Sometimes she even feared she saw flashes of her sister Rosaria in her. She could be the sweetest little girl but once she dug in her heels about something, Chiara would make life hell until she got her own way.

'We can't drive, but we can go on the ferry,' she offered. 'How about that?'

A smile lit up Chiara's little brown face and she happily

danced upstairs to put on warm clothes for the short boat trip.

They took the bus to the ferry terminal. There Maria Domenica discovered that if you bought one ticket you could cross and re-cross the River Mersey as many times as you liked so long as you didn't try to get off at the other side. It wasn't strictly allowed but the ferrymen were happy to turn a blind eye, especially when it was an exotic-looking dark-eyed girl and her pretty little daughter who seemed to be having such a good time on the top deck of the boat.

They had meat and potato pies for lunch, bought at the café in the snug down below. They were pretty revolting so she let Chiara feed most of them to the seagulls that chased the ferry back and forth.

It had taken her a while but Maria Domenica was beginning to see the beauty in the place she'd chosen to make her home. Matt black shadows hugged the shoreline on the Liverpool side of the river, monuments to an age when this was a thriving port. The once graceful buildings had been built in porous stone and for years they'd soaked up the smoke pumped out by a growing industrial town until their dove-grey façades had turned ebony with age. Now Maria Domenica saw how the muddy river met the black buildings beneath the granite skies and her artist's eye found the drama in it. She was almost tempted to buy some paper and pencils and see if she could draw what she saw. But the memory of what had happened to her last attempts at art was still fresh in her mind and she decided to resist the urge.

5

It was a proper autumn. The dull, grey pavements were buried in carpets of golden leaves that eddied and swirled when the wind grew blustery. The days became colder and shorter and Maria Domenica's sightings of the sun were almost as rare as her glimpses of Alex.

She was relieved when she finally solved the mystery of his disappearance – he had found a job. He was working at the garage down the road, helping the mechanic fix up cars. The place was busy and Alex was keen to take on as much overtime as possible. He said, with the pink of his skin deepening slightly, that he wanted to save some money. Then his head ducked down beneath the bonnet of one of his clapped-out cars and he set up a tuneless humming that discouraged further questions.

The job sucked up most of his time. There hadn't been a chance for their usual driving lessons and they'd only managed a couple of nights out at the pictures.

'It's great that you're working so hard,' she told Alex but she didn't really mean it. She'd discovered that she missed having him around. Even sunny-natured Chiara was feeling out of sorts and neglected.

So when Alex came and asked if he could take her out for dinner Maria Domenica felt almost excited. 'Oh, don't waste your hard-earned cash on a restaurant,' she told him though. 'It would be just as much fun getting fish and chips and eating them down on the promenade.'

'No, I want to take you somewhere nice to have a proper dinner,' he insisted.

'But we can't . . . I've got nothing to wear.'

'Don't be daft, you've got loads. You always look lovely,' he grinned.

Smart restaurants had never been part of Maria Domenica's life so she couldn't help feeling nervous as she dressed to go out. The few outfits she had in her wardrobe were soon flung about the room as she tried on and discarded skirts and blouses, trying to pick out the best combination. She settled on a cream belted dress with a hemline that hovered decently above her knee. Although she felt comfortable enough as she left the house, the very moment she stepped into the restaurant she knew she didn't belong. The room was plush and too brightly lit and the head waiter over-starched and supercilious. He realized instantly that they were once-in-a-blue-moon diners and there was no point in currying their favour. Things didn't improve when they were shown to their table. For Maria Domenica there was too much cutlery, too many plates and a long, long menu filled with unfamiliar French words to wade through.

She and Alex conversed in whispers, frightened to disturb the sanctity of the place. Maria Domenica almost felt that she should roll up her sleeves and help out in the kitchen, or at least wait on some tables. But to Alex all she said was, 'It's lovely here. This is such a treat.' He nodded and gulped. He seemed nervous and looked pinker than usual.

They'd eaten their first course and were just starting on their mains when Alex reached into his pocket and pulled out a small square box that he pushed across the table.

'Maria, will you marry me?' he asked in a tiny voice.

She stared back at him in absolute shock.

'I love you,' he continued. 'I want you to be my wife.'

Maria Domenica felt as though she were acting in a movie and someone had forgotten to tell her the next line. She searched her mind desperately for a response. 'Alex, I can't. I'm sorry but I just can't.'

To her horror, tears began to stream down his face. Everyone was staring, the waiters, the other customers, the man playing the piano in the corner. But still Alex cried silently. Maria Domenica felt tears pricking her own eyes in response.

'Alex, I really, really like you,' she managed. 'I think of you as my very best friend. But I can't marry you. It's just not possible.'

He looked at her across the plates piled with steak, chips and creamy sauce. 'Don't you want to look at the ring at least? It's an emerald.'

'No, put it away, Alex. Please put it away.'

They tried to eat but suddenly the food seemed lumpy and impossible to swallow. By the time the head waiter ushered them out, Alex had lighter pockets and an empty stomach. His body was ironing board stiff again and he was avoiding her eyes.

Maria Domenica wanted to explain to him that there was a good reason she couldn't say yes – she was already married. Back home in Italy there was a person called Marco who called himself her husband even though he'd never loved her. But although she could string the words together in her mind, somehow she couldn't get them out of her mouth.

They drove back in silence and the longer they were silent the more difficult it became to speak. It was a relief for Maria Domenica to bolt upstairs to the sanctuary of her rooms and escape his reproachful eyes and the now obvious bulge in his pocket where the engagement ring lay. But if she'd thought she'd be able to sleep she was wrong. She lay awake on her clean, white sheets, listening to the ticking of the clock and felt as though she'd forgotten how to sleep, that she'd never sleep again.

There didn't seem any point in lying there so she got up and went over to the armchair she'd positioned so it looked down over the dark river and the lights of the Liverpool skyline.

Curled up and hugging a cushion to her chest, she stared at the view and struggled to organize her thoughts.

Firstly, she was married. To marry again would be against the law. But even if she were free, if divorce had been an option for her, would she have accepted Alex's ring? She didn't love him. She felt no passion when she looked at him and no excitement when he touched her.

On the other hand, if she were married to Alex, she could live in this big, old house for ever. He was so nice, he'd never raise a hand to her, never leave her. His love would be so comfortable and warm, and she would take care of him. Perhaps, as Aunt Lucia had said, that was enough for a marriage.

Maria Domenica glanced at the clock. It was 1 a.m., he'd be in bed asleep by now. She crept out of the room quietly, careful not to wake Chiara, and eased herself down the stairs.

Alex's door was ajar and, although she couldn't see him in the darkness, she could hear him breathing. She stood there for a while, listening to the even rhythm. She was on the brink of something. If she stepped through this door it would be the most reckless thing she'd ever done, and at the same time the most sensible.

It wasn't the thought of breaking the law that worried her. Laws were made by corrupt men and surely there would always be one who would accept a handful of cash to make everything all right, just like that official at the Swiss border had. As for standing up before God and promising to be with Alex till death did them part – well, she wasn't afraid to do that. Surely no sane God could expect her to stay with a man who hurt her and threatened to hurt her baby?

Putting Marco out of her mind wasn't the problem. She was a different person from that frightened girl who had been forced to marry him, swollen with baby, empty of dreams. If it would buy some happiness for herself and Chiara, then surely she could bear the quiet shame of being a bigamist, reasoned Maria Domenica. She knew how to keep a secret. No one need ever find out.

What she feared was that she couldn't find any passion inside her for Alex. She tried to imagine lying next to him and letting him touch her with his rough-skinned hands. She imagined his long legs tangled with hers and his skin against her skin, but it didn't seem possible, never mind likely. She dithered at his doorway, her eyes now accustomed to the dark and able to make out his shape in the bed.

Her feet carried her forward before her brain had consented to what she was doing. She felt grit beneath her bare soles and her mind registered, of all things, that he hadn't vacuumed his carpet in a while. Then she was pulling back his limp, unwashed sheets and sliding into bed beside him. She pressed her cheek against his chest and felt it rise and fall with his breath.

Reflexively, his arms wrapped round her. Then, with a start, he woke and whispered incredulously, 'Maria?'

'Alex, the answer is yes.'

'What?'

'The answer is yes, I will marry you.'

'Really?'

'Yes, yes.'

'Then why did you say before that you couldn't. I thought that—'

She stopped his words with a kiss. Not a brush of the lips or a kiss between friends but a real kiss. Her tongue pushed between his lips and she arched and pressed into him. She felt his body reply to hers.

'God, you're so beautiful. I'm so lucky,' he moaned.

'No, I'm the lucky one.' She kissed him again. 'I can't believe how lucky I am.'

Tentatively, he ran his hands over her and she felt the roughness of his palms, coarsened by the endless contact with the engines of cars. As they rubbed against her they set her skin tingling.

He shifted his weight on top of her and she opened her legs to accommodate him. For a moment she thought she knew how a whore felt, although she was sleeping with Alex for kindness and security, not money. Then he kissed her and, surprised by the desire licking at her body, she forgot about everything else.

Alex was a gentle lover. He stroked and kissed her for what seemed like hours and then at last, he tentatively pressed into her. She heard a moan of pleasure and realized it was her own. Alex pushed more urgently now, their bodies grew slippery with sweat and their breath ragged. For the first time in her life Maria Domenica felt an orgasm rising within her. For one unbearably gorgeous moment her pleasure peaked and then she gasped and shuddered with the final release.

Afterwards Alex placed his hand over her belly and whispered in her ear, 'Wouldn't it be wonderful if a baby was being made in here right now.'

'Mmm,' she replied, her mind still distracted by the intensity of her body's response to him.

'We'll get married soon, won't we? I don't see the point in long engagements.'

'Yes.'

'Wait a minute.' He dived out of the bed and began rummaging among the clothes he'd left in a heap on the dirty carpet.

'Come back to bed, Alex,' she said, sleepy now.

'Just a minute, just a minute,' he hissed. 'Ah, here it is.'

He wriggled back under the covers and took her left hand in his. Carefully, he slipped the emerald engagement ring on her finger. 'It seems to fit all right,' he told her in the darkness. 'But we won't be able to see what it looks like until the morning.'

'You must have worked so hard to pay for this and for the dinner.'

He laughed. 'Well, the dinner's all paid for but there is a bit of money owing on the ring,' he admitted. 'Still, it won't take me too long to pay it off. I'm going to work really hard and I'm going to look after you and Chiara, I promise. And Maria Domenica?'

'Yes.'

'If there's stuff you don't want to tell me, you know, about Italy and Chiara's father, why you really came to New Brighton and all that, it's OK. I don't care about the past, only the future.'

She fell asleep with her head on his chest and his arms around her. His skin smelled soapy even if his sheets didn't. The window was open and she could hear the sound of the waves sloshing against the sea wall. She felt sheltered and secure. She promised herself that, whatever might happen, she'd never hurt this man who was lying beside her.

6

Each time her eye caught the flash of the emerald sitting on her finger, it made Maria Domenica start. People hugged and kissed her, and offered their congratulations. They seemed more excited than she was.

'I'm so pleased for you, my love,' Mrs Leary told her, pressing a hairy cheek against hers. 'It couldn't have happened to a nicer girl.'

And Maria Domenica obediently held out the third finger of her left hand so the few customers who happened to be in the café could admire it properly.

Plans for the wedding were being made almost despite her. To her relief Alex hadn't been fussed about a church wedding, so they'd booked their fifteen-minute slot at the registry office. Her landlord Mr Fox, who now wanted her to call him Dad, had been buying a bottle of champagne each week when he got his wages and the Learys had put their heads together and come up with a plan for the wedding supper.

'You can have it in the café, love,' Mrs Leary told her excitedly. 'Mr Leary's getting the painters in next week and they're going to freshen the whole place up. We'll have flowers and white linen tablecloths, the whole bit. You won't recognize the place.'

'That's really, really kind of you, Mrs Leary.' Maria Domenica felt embarrassed.

'Don't mention it. It's the least we could do. You've been a gem these past few years, a gem. Me and Mr Leary say so all the time. The girls we had working here before you, well, you wouldn't believe it. No, giving you a decent send-off on your wedding day would be our pleasure.'

As for Alex, at times he seemed lit up by the excitement of it all, but there were other moments when Maria Domenica could tell he was brooding over something. 'What's wrong?' she asked repeatedly, but he just shook his head and replied, 'Nothing's wrong. I've never been happier in my life.'

At last, one night as they lay curled up in the front room listening to records, he opened up to her.

'I'm really sorry, Maria. I've been saving like mad but I'm not going to be able to afford the honeymoon I had planned.'

'Alex, I never expected a honeymoon.'

'I know you didn't but this was something I was dying to do for you. I wanted to take you home to Italy. I wanted to meet your family.'

Maria Domenica froze. In her mind's eye she saw the little house she'd grown up in, surrounded by dust and peach trees, and she longed to see it again for real. But just the thought of rolling up there, Alex in tow, facing her parents and Franco, seeing the people of San Giulio and the family on the Manzoni farm, not to mention Marco, her husband, made her shudder. She grasped Alex by both arms. 'Promise me you'll never ask me to go back there.'

'But why?'

'You said you'd never ask me that. You said the past didn't matter, only the future.'

'I know what I said and I meant it, but are you certain, Maria? Surely you have family there? Don't you want to see them? Won't they need to know you're getting married?'

Maria Domenica was fighting not to cry. 'Promise me you'll never mention Italy to me again or I won't marry you. I'm English now. My name's going to be Maria Fox and I'll be English. As English as them,' she nodded at the record on the turntable, 'as the Beatles.'

'I just don't understand.'

'There's nothing for you to understand. Just accept things the way they are and we'll all be happy.'

Alex was silent for a moment. She sat beside him quietly and let him think. It was a friendly silence, she wasn't too worried. At long last he spoke. 'I want you to be happy, Maria,' he told her. 'Perhaps one day you'll trust me enough to tell me about Italy but until then I promise not to ask you about it. OK?'

'OK.'

'So no more talk about backing out of the wedding?'

She smiled. 'No, don't worry. I won't do that.'

He smiled in reply and edged off the sofa to flip the record over and play the B-side.

All the same, despite her promise, she felt unsettled. In her free time she couldn't help slipping on her comfortable walking shoes and taking to the streets again. She retraced her steps along the lacework of lanes that reached from the promenade and led past the big houses set back in well-groomed gardens and on to the shops beyond. She peered over shelves of buns and loaves in bakery windows and ducked into pubs and betting shops.

'Oops, sorry,' she'd say to anyone who stared. 'Just looking for someone.'

She pulled her coat sleeve down over her left hand so her ring was completely covered and kept walking.

Sometimes she found familiar faces. The woman from the wool shop where she'd bought yarn for Chiara's first winter sweater or the man from the greengrocer's who'd sold her rotten potatoes. But after a quick glance or a nod she kept on walking.

For Chiara she tried to make it fun, kicking through the piles of the last autumn leaves as they walked, or stopping off to feed stale bread to the ducks in the park. On rainy days they jumped in the puddles to see who could make the biggest splash and when the sun shone they dawdled on their way back along the promenade so Chiara could peer into rock pools in search of crabs.

Despite her efforts, the little girl quietly let it be known she'd rather be somewhere else. 'Ferry boat?' she enquired politely as they left the house each morning. 'Motor car?'

'No, sweetheart, we're just going for a walk today.'

The child looked downcast. 'OK, walk,' she said almost wearily.

As the day of the wedding approached, Maria Domenica threw her net wider and their walks covered more ground. She looked more carefully at the men they passed, imagining this one without a beard and that one with fairer hair. But each evening, as they rounded the final corner and walked the long stretch home, it was a struggle not to show her disappointment in the droop of her shoulders and the hang of her head.

'*Che sera, sera*,' she told herself. 'Whatever will be, will be.'

She reminded herself that Alex was a good man and she was lucky to have him. They had friendship, they'd found passion. Surely there would be one day, not too far away, when his ring would stop weighing so heavy on her finger and she'd feel that she was in love with him at last.

It was time to stop walking, she realized, and definitely time to stop running away. She could pause now in the old, tall house by the river. Her daughter would start school and she would take her driving test so she could drop her off at the gates each day in one of Alex's cars. She'd springclean her way to the dustiest corners of the house and she'd move the big bins of fermenting wine that cluttered the narrow kitchen and fill it with the smell of baking bread instead. In the summer she and Chiara would tan darker than everyone else but eventually that would be all to set them apart. Alex would fix cars, she'd serve tea and sandwiches, and the years would pass. They'd grow old and Chiara would grow up, but otherwise nothing much would change and suddenly that didn't seem such a bad thing.

7

Maria Domenica had never seen rain like this before. Huge droplets were pelting down from a stormy sky, overfilling the gutters and the storm water drains, spilling down the streets like a river. Looking out of the window, it was almost impossible to tell where the Mersey ended and the promenade began. Waves crashed over the sea wall and reached towards the house before falling back into the boiling mass. This was her wedding day, thought Maria Domenica, staring disconsolately out at the storm. Wasn't the sun supposed to be shining?

'Brrr, cats and dogs out there.' Mrs Leary was on the front doorstep, bright plastic mackintosh dripping. 'You might want to sandbag out the front. It's going to get worse before it gets better and if the river gets any higher you'll be in trouble.'

Maria Domenica looked out towards the estuary and the angry Irish Sea and realized she was right. The waves were getting bigger, the storm more fierce.

'Perhaps we should cancel the wedding?' she suggested.

'Don't be ridiculous. This will blow over. And we're not going to let it spoil your big day.' Mrs Leary grasped her by the arm and pulled her down the long hallway towards the kitchen. 'Come here, Maria love. I've got something for you.' From her pocket she pulled a small, white linen handkerchief embroidered with blue flowers. 'This is for you to carry somewhere about your person.'

'Oh, thank you.' Maria Domenica was confused but much too polite to refuse the strange little gift.

'It's a tradition,' Mrs Leary explained. 'Every bride should have something old, something new, something borrowed, something blue. Well the hanky is old, borrowed and blue, and I guess your dress will have to do as the new thing.'

Her dress was hanging upstairs in the wardrobe still encased in plastic. It was the most beautiful thing she'd ever owned. Sheer white silk, cut on the bias, with a corsage of pink silk rosebuds trailing over one shoulder. Hopelessly unfashionable, it had been tucked away in the back of the shop and the saleswoman had been so relieved to sell it she'd agreed to a huge discount. Maria Domenica might freeze to death in the flimsy thing on a day like today but she didn't care.

Chiara would be wearing a new dress as well. It had a huge skirt with layers and layers of net and when she'd tried it on she'd looked less like a bridesmaid and more like the fairy from the top of the Christmas tree. 'Mummy's marrying Alex and I'm going to help,' she'd been telling everyone who'd listen.

She was over-excited about the wedding and had hardly slept last night. Maria Domenica had tossed and turned too. Her dreams of home had been so vivid they'd startled her back to consciousness more than once and this morning she looked like she always did when she hadn't rested properly. Her olive skin had turned sallow and her deep-set eyes were swallowed by black circles. She rubbed at them fiercely with the back of her hand.

'Don't do that.' Mrs Leary tutted and slapped her hand away. 'You'll have them all red and swollen if you rub at them. I tell you what, go upstairs and lie down with a piece of cucumber over each eye for half an hour. Then you'll be right as rain.'

Maria Domenica might have tried it had she had half an hour to spare. But no sooner had she ushered Mrs Leary back out into the storm than Mr Fox appeared and beckoned her into the front room. He had the semi-furtive look of a man who wanted a quiet word.

'Have you got a minute, love?' he asked.

Mr Fox – or Dad as she was now meant to call him – looked how she imagined Alex might in twenty-five years' time. Office work had made him soft. His arms and legs were still skinny but his middle was rounding out. He tended to slouch when he stood, his stomach and breasts hanging slackly in the clinging nylon shirts he invariably wore. His face looked like Alex's would if his nose and ears grew and his pink skin began to hang in folds. He wasn't an attractive man, but he was blessed with a kind smile and quiet ways. Maria Domenica had always liked him.

'Yes, Mr Fox, I've got a minute,' she told him.

'Dad,' he corrected gently.

'Sorry, Dad.'

He rubbed his hands together nervously. 'That's what I wanted to talk to you about really. Alex explained to me how your own family can't make it over for the wedding so I wondered how you'd feel about me being the one to give you away. *In loco parentis* as it were.'

He spoke quickly and quietly and Maria Domenica sometimes missed the odd word or two. But today she had no problems understanding. For a moment she thought of her own father, so big and colourful that, if he were in the room, Mr Fox would disappear into the faded pattern on the wallpaper.

'It would be lovely if you'd give me away,' she managed. 'I'd really appreciate it.'

'No, I'm the one who appreciates you, Maria.' His words came out in a rush. 'You've done our Alex the world of good. Before you took him on he was a dead loss, he really was. Didn't want to work, happy to fritter his life away. I didn't know what to do with the lad.'

Maria Domenica murmured something unintelligible.

'Well, I'm bloody glad he met you, and that's all I'm going to say on the subject,' he continued. 'So welcome to the family.'

With that he folded her into his thin arms and pulled her against the striped nylon of his shirt. He smelled strongly of aftershave and cigarettes and it wasn't entirely pleasant being pressed against his soft chest. She held herself rigid until he let her go.

'Off you go then,' he told her. 'Go and make yourself beautiful for your wedding day.'

She escaped gratefully, but only managed to make it halfway up the first flight of stairs before she was waylaid again. This time it was Alex, all shaved and starched and blushing nervously. He looked at her as though she was the most precious thing he'd ever seen and for a moment she felt afraid.

'I know we're not supposed to see one another before the wedding,' he began, 'but I've got something for you and I really want to give it to you now.'

'Something for me to wear?'

'No. Why, would you like something new to wear?' He was so eager to please it was almost unbearable.

'You don't have to give me any more gifts, Alex,' she replied gently. 'You've given me so much.'

'Ah, but this is different.' With a mysterious smile he was gone, bounding up the next flight of stairs to his bedroom. Maria Domenica heard frantic rustling and then he reappeared clutching a brown paper bag with the words Liverpool Art Supplies stamped on it.

'This was a bit of a mad idea. You might not like it,' he told her, pushing the bag into her hands. There was no need to open it. Maria Domenica knew what it was the minute she touched it.

'A drawing pad and pencils.' She was stunned. 'Oh, and watercolour paints. Alex, what made you think I'd want something like this?'

'I dunno, you seemed to love those pictures in the Walker Art Gallery so much I thought you might like to have a go yourself. But if you don't like them I suppose they'll let me take them back. Or you could give them to Chiara to play with.'

'No, I like them, Alex. I love them.' She held the bag tightly against her. 'It's the best present you could ever have given me.' She stepped forward and touched his lips with hers. 'Thank you ever so much.'

His face looked like the sun had come out. 'I found out about art classes for you as well,' he continued enthusiastically. 'They've got them on Tuesday nights at the adult education centre down the road. Might even come along with you and have a go myself. I could be an undiscovered talent!'

Maria Domenica kissed him again very quickly as she darted past and headed upstairs to her room to get ready for her wedding ceremony. She felt light and happy. The hard-edged block of paper in her hand seemed a sign that, at last, she was taking the right path in life.

There was nothing about this wedding to remind her of the last. No church this time, just a plain registry office with orange plastic chairs and a big wooden desk with a smiling man behind it.

Alex was beside her, fidgety and uncomfortable in his suit, and Maria Domenica sensed that he couldn't wait to have this part of the day over with. On her other side, fairy girl Chiara clutched a bouquet of white silk flowers and smiled winningly at their guests like a child born for stardom.

They may not have come close to filling the long rows of orange chairs, but all the important people were there. Mr Fox and his mousy girlfriend Maureen were sitting beside a beaming Mr and Mrs Leary. Fred, the mechanic who'd employed Alex, had brought his girlfriend, the frighteningly fashionable Brenda. And at the back were Bob and Tony, old schoolmates that Alex sometimes drank a pint or two of Bass with at the Farmers' Arms pub round the corner.

Resplendent in her rosebud dress, Maria Domenica felt beautiful, loved and surrounded by friends. It was a glorious feeling and it grew stronger as the day went on.

The only music at their wedding supper was the sound of the rain lashing at the café windows. Outside the wind had whipped up the swimming pool into a mini-ocean but inside it was warm and there was Champagne to drink and crates of Mr Fox's beetroot and carrot wine for anyone still thirsty.

Mrs Leary had gone to extra effort to make the supper special. She'd produced the promised white linen table cloth, had cut the crusts off the sandwiches, sliced the sausage rolls on an angle and made liberal use of paper doilies. In the centre of the table was the cake she'd baked, iced and crowned with a plastic bride and groom. Beside them she'd placed with care a tiny Christmas tree fairy.

'That's me,' exclaimed Chiara, delighted. 'That's me on the cake. I'm a bridie-maid!'

Maria Domenica laughed and glanced from her daughter to her husband, who smiled back at her.

'Are you happy, Mrs Fox?' Alex asked shyly.

'Very happy,' she told him in her rich Italian accent and it was true. 'I feel . . . I feel . . . well, I suppose I feel like we're a family at last.'

Part Three

London, 2000

I

A generous dusting of flour covered every available surface. It lay like a blanket over the worktops, shrouded the stove and clogged up the toaster. Clouds of the stuff drifted to the floor and settled in a gritty film, but only until it got the chance to cling to the sole of a passing foot and be trekked out into the carpeted hallway.

The very air was full of flour. It filled Chiara's lungs, sank into her pores and powdered her hair. She looked like some demented French courtesan who'd staggered dustily straight out of history, she decided.

And what was worse, every time she picked up her rolling pin, she felt depression settle over her just as deeply as the flour had settled over her kitchen. She was nauseated by the sweet, cloying scent of baking bread that filled her small apartment day after day and it was a relief to heave open one of the sash windows and fill her nostrils with the smell of London streets. No country cob or ciabatta, no French stick or sun-dried tomato loaf could compete with the metallic tang of traffic fumes and the rank smell from the bins full of refuse that ought to have been collected yesterday.

When Chiara had suggested the book about baking to her publisher, Janey, it hadn't seemed such a terrible idea. They were at the Ivy restaurant at the time, eating salmon fishcakes and surreptitiously star-spotting over their menus. Despite the fact that bread probably hadn't passed her lips since carbohydrates were outlawed in the late 1990s, Janey had seized on the idea.

'Baking,' she'd breathed. 'You could make baking sexy

again. Baking could be the new gardening. This is the right time for it. People are retreating into their homes, they want tradition, they want solid values. Baking can give them that. Although obviously your recipes will make the whole process far less messy and time-consuming so that baking fits in with their busy lives.'

'Um, yes, obviously,' Chiara murmured in agreement as she wondered, with a rising sense of panic, quite how she was going to manage that.

Janey leaned forward, excited now. With one hand she pushed back her curtain of dead straight blonde hair. The other hand had drifted into the bread basket and was stroking a small walnut roll lovingly. 'I could get you a TV show or a slot on *Get Set Cook* off the back of this. There's masses of sponsorship potential as well. Maybe a tie-in with something like Light 'n' Lovely Flour. Or you could release your own range of non-stick bakingware. I need to go away and get the team to come up with a proper marketing strategy but I can see a lot of leveraging opportunities in this.'

Chiara had allowed herself a small sigh and a roll of her wide brown eyes. Food was what she loved. Shopping for it at market stalls piled with glossy, purple-coated aubergines, dirt-dusted field mushrooms, ripe red peppers and artichokes with their hard green leaves tightly clasping their hearts. She loved unpacking her bounty and imagining the extra life she could bring to it with a lashing of chilli sauce or a sizzle in oil over a high heat. But most of all she loved eating it, greedily tasting as she cooked, licking her fingers and the backs of spoons, piling it onto plates and bowls, or sometimes eating more than was good for her straight out of the pan. Marketing strategies and leveraging opportunities were all very well but she could hardly be blamed if they didn't fill her with the same passion as a tray of slow-roasted tomatoes bathed in balsamic vinegar or a slab of beef braised with red wine and onions until the meat fell softly from the bone.

'And what would you call the baking book?' Janey, ever the businesswoman, dragged her back to reality. '*Queen of the British Kitchen Uses Her Loaf*?'

'What?' Chiara pulled at her short brown tufts of hair, a nervous habit she'd sworn to give up.

'I'm joking, I'm joking,' Janey promised. The little walnut roll was sitting on her plate now but she still hadn't been tempted to nibble on it. Instead she squeezed it between her fingers like an executive stress toy. 'Bread is so real, isn't it? There's something genuine about it. You trust someone who bakes. Bread is honest.'

Chiara stopped listening and focused on what was left of her fishcake. She had only herself to blame for this, she knew that. All the years she'd worked in the steamy, stressful kitchens of London restaurants, she'd dreamed of publishing a recipe book. In her free time she'd pottered around her own kitchen coming up with ideas. She was clever with food, always had been. As a child she'd helped her mother, Maria, in the kitchen almost from the moment she could walk. First she'd been allowed to stand on a chair and stir the gravy for the Sunday roast to stop it sticking and then she'd graduated to rolling out the pastry when her mother made a pie, stealing the off-cuts for jam tarts and turnovers.

When she looked back on those years, it was the tastes and smells of the meals they'd made together that stoked Chiara's memory more than any particular event or moment. Still vivid in her mind were winter dishes of pork sausages wrinkled from simmering in thick brown onion gravy, huge comforting helpings of shepherd's pie with a crispy crust of Cheddar, or plates filled with oven-roasted cod and fat crinkle-cut chips that they could never resist wrapping in over-buttered soft white bread and devouring as the heat of the fried potato melted the butter which ran down their hands.

Then there were the stolen moments with her dad Alex,

sitting on the promenade in the evening as the sky blistered with pink and gold, listening to the waves slapping against the sea wall and eating fish and chips from newspaper and mushy peas out of a plastic pottle. Or spending all her bus fare on toffee apples at the amusement arcade and then having to walk home.

It was almost inevitable that Chiara would end up cooking for a living, although the food she produced under the eyes of top chefs in London's restaurants was different: pristine stacks of expensive ingredients on fine china produced amid heat, noise and sometimes fear. There was much she didn't enjoy about those cooking years. The hours were long, the chefs prone to shouting. But thanks to that childhood spent in her mother's narrow kitchen, she never lost her love of traditional British comfort food. Most people had been preparing it badly for so long they'd forgotten how satisfying it could be if you did it right. And that's what her book had set out to provide – failsafe recipes for people to produce wholesome, tasty British grub.

Unfortunately, nobody else seemed to think it was such a great idea for a book. In fact, she'd had so many rejections from agents and publishers she considered papering the wall of her bedroom with them. Janey alone had seen the potential and been confident that she could pull it off.

'Chiara, I think you've hit on something,' she told her at their first meeting. 'You've reinvented British food for the low-fat, low-on-time generation. This is going to be huge.'

Chiara had been so grateful she'd have agreed to anything. She'd allowed Janey to rechristen all her recipes with terrible names – 'Hot, Hot, Hot Lancashire Hotpot!' and 'Right Royal Rissoles' were two that sprang to mind – and she'd agreed to pose for the book's cover picture seated on a throne, wearing a crown on her head and clutching a large marrow in place of a sceptre. The book had been titled *Queen of the British Kitchen* and Janey had been right, it was huge.

Extracts were printed in newspapers, she appeared on TV and radio so much she achieved minor celebrity status and the books kept flying off the shelves. A rather bewildered Chiara had lost count of the number of reprints that had been ordered.

Janey began to push her for book number two. 'We've got to capitalize on your popularity,' she pointed out.

The trouble was Chiara felt she only had one book in her. It had taken her years to perfect the recipes that graced the pages of *Queen of the British Kitchen*. They were good, she was confident of that, but she didn't have a clue what she could do next.

'Haven't you got some recipes left over? Why don't you go back through your notes and see if you can come up with something?' Janey had suggested.

But Chiara's notes didn't yield any surprises and her mind was empty of ideas. She began to worry she had lost the ability to do something that had once come so naturally to her. It reached the stage where every time she tried to think about her second book her head was filled with a sort of white noise of panic and she felt simultaneously nauseous and tearful.

Janey told her it was normal, that second books were notoriously difficult, that she should just relax and let it come. But the well-meant advice didn't help. Time passed astonishingly quickly, Chiara filled her days with anything but food, and her second book was consigned to the same guiltily neglected zone of her brain occupied by dusty thoughts of things like pension funds and tax returns.

The lunch at the Ivy had been a bid to chivvy her along. Janey had brought her own list of ideas that Chiara struggled to read upside down. She saw something that looked like *Queen of the Inuit Kitchen*, although it may have been Indian. Whatever, her heart sank. Her eyes had drifted to the bread-basket filled with tiny walnut rolls as delicate as speckled birds' eggs in a nest and that's when she'd blurted, 'Bread, I want to do bread next. You know, simple country breads, flavoured loaves, filled breads, calzone, sweet breads. The possibilities are endless.'

And so she'd found herself locked away in her little kitchen, steeped in flour, yeast and sourdough starter, the oven belting out heat. Generations of women before her had done this, bent over a hunk of dough, kneading, shaping, rolling and stretching. Bras had been burnt, equal rights fought for and still here she was, feeding her oven with tray after tray of neat doughy mounds and then peering through the glass door anxiously as they rose into loaves.

'Now doesn't that make a pretty picture. All you need is a frilly pink apron and you'd look like the perfect wife.' Her best friend Harriet was leaning coolly in the doorway, martini glass in one hand, the leash of her Irish wolfhound Salty in the other.

'What's that you're drinking?' Chiara sniffed at the air. 'Could it be . . . alcohol?'

'Chocolate martini actually. Vodka, white crème de cacao, a snifter of vermouth and shavings of Milky Bar floated on top. It's delicious.'

'Can I have one? Or possibly two?'

'Darling, I drink for a living. You bake. You can have one when you've finished working.'

Harriet really did drink for a living. She ran a private drinking club, called The Office, where a few select members, generally of a literary bent, got fantastically drunk six nights a week. 'Not drunk, darling, a little tight,' Harriet liked to remind her.

She and Harriet had known each other since they were eighteen and at university. Her mother, Maria Domenica, anxious that she might not make friends, had instructed Chiara that she had to knock on the doors either side and opposite her room in her hall of residence and introduce herself to the occupants. Nervously Chiara had obeyed and she'd found Harriet behind the door opposite. She was a glamorous creature with bobbed black hair, dressed in a yellow silk twenties flapper dress. She had a case of decent red wine in the bottom of her wardrobe and split a bottle with Chiara, who had never met anyone quite this exotic growing up in Merseyside. She was hooked on Harriet from the very beginning and, even when they'd left university and moved to London, was unable to give her up.

They spent the following years in one of the more anonymous little streets that criss-crossed the area between Oxford Street and Shaftsbury Avenue and was famously known as Soho. What had been a colourful, slightly louche area filled with artists, writers and dissolute aristocrats had changed a lot since those early days. Now they kicked through junkies' syringes as they stepped into the gutter and had to push through hordes of trendy young things sipping Starbucks coffee out of paper cups if they wanted to shop for vegetables at Berwick Street Market.

They'd changed too, both she and Harriet. They'd left their twenties behind and grown wealthier and more successful as they'd grown older. There was no earthly reason why they should still live squashed together in their cramped attic flat, but they'd stayed there nevertheless, hanging on to what little was left of the old Soho and their old lives by the stubby ends of their well-bitten fingernails.

Harriet's drinking club occupied two floors of the crooked Georgian terraced house. The blinds were kept down and the lights low to hide layers of dust and paint peeling from the walls. Cellphones and music were banned, so the only sound was the popping of champagne corks and the steady hum of clever conversation. There was one big main room, furnished with mismatched chairs, tables and old leather sofas, where most of the eating and drinking took place. Bowls of lemons graced the tables and white votive candles sputtered in saucers. Next door was a tiny room that was almost entirely filled with an enormous bed mounded with cushions and it was there that members could retire for a while if they were feeling rather 'tight'.

With Salty, her mammoth wolfhound, always at her elbow, Harriet never had any problems with unruly members no matter how inebriated they might become. And at the end of the night, when the door had closed on the last drinker, she climbed the final flight of uneven wooden stairs to the tiny flat on the top floor she shared with Chiara.

By now their friendship had developed into a kind of marriage – better than a marriage, Chiara always thought. Arguments were rare and lovers, when they passed through, could never steal their intimacy, no matter how they tried. At the end of each day Chiara and Harriet told their secrets to each other. They couldn't imagine it any other way.

No one had been more excited at the success of *Queen of the British Kitchen* than Harriet. Dozens of bottles of champagne had been downed in The Office as toast after toast had been proposed to Chiara and her cleverness. And now her friend was taking a lively interest in book number two.

'What's this then?' She sniffed at the loaves Chiara had left to cool on the wire racks.

'White olive bread, wholemeal olive bread and granary olive bread,' Chiara replied wearily.

'And?'

'It's all revolting,' she wailed. 'You should take it down to the club and serve it up to the drunkest members with some strong goat's cheese.'

'Do you think?' Harriet said dubiously.

'Yes, just get the bloody stuff out of my sight.'

'Chiara?'

'Hmm?'

'Do you actually like bread?'

'Once I did, Harriet. I loved bread. I thought it was the stuff of life itself. But not now.'

Harriet sipped her martini and licked the shavings of Milky Bar from her full lips. 'So,' she began thoughtfully, 'have you considered that writing an entire recipe book about bread might possibly be a mistake?'

Chiara dropped the loaf she'd been prodding and her hands fell to her sides. 'It is a mistake, isn't it?' she said miserably. 'Oh God, what am I going to do? Janey will kill me.'

'Bugger Janey.'

'Well, yes, but it's not that simple, is it? I've signed contracts, made promises, put my name on the dotted line. She's probably legally entitled to kill me if I don't produce the damn bread book.'

Harriet pressed the martini glass into her hand. 'Drink,' she urged. 'It's all you have left.'

Chiara took a massive gulp and reeled back in shock. 'My God, that's strong.'

'It's pure alcohol, darling. It tends to be strong.'

'I don't know how you drink that stuff.'

'I drink it, my dear, because it's my job. And I'm dedicated to it, just as you are dedicated to providing the unwashed masses with some idea of what to put on their dinner plates every night.'

'Do you think the unwashed masses would prefer their olive bread to be white, wholemeal or granary then?'

Harriet held up her hand. 'Just give me a moment,' she said. Carefully she tore a crusty hunk of bread from each loaf. She popped the first hunk into her mouth and chewed carefully a neutral expression on her face. Then she held out her hand for the martini glass. 'I need to cleanse my palate,' she declared.

She repeated the procedure with the second and third hunks and then she smiled at Chiara. 'Look, it's not revolting, it's fine. I'd be perfectly happy to feed it to my members with or without strong goat's cheese. But I still reckon you should rethink the whole bread idea. You don't have a passion for it. And it was your absolute love of simple British grub that made the last book so successful, not Janey's recipe names and that mad front cover.'

Chiara looked glum. 'I know,' she agreed.

'So this is what I want you to do. You're to come downstairs to the club with me and Salty now and have a drink or two before we close. And tomorrow you're to have a bread-free day. That means no bread. None. Do you understand?'

'Yes, I'll avoid bread at all costs.'

'Good. And what you'll do instead of baking is think. You'll think about what you really want to do. What sort of food makes you feel passionate and curious and alive. And then you'll write a book about it.'

'You know what, Harriet?' Chiara smiled. 'For one so permanently soused, you're incredibly wise.'

2

Chiara's eyes opened as the first fingers of grey morning light reached through the grimy windowpane and touched the whitewashed walls of her bedroom. Try as she might, she couldn't sleep past dawn. Harriet would doze for half the day given a chance, but the minute Chiara woke up she had to swing her legs out of bed and stretch her cramped limbs.

There was no more space in her bedroom than anywhere else in the little flat. The kitchen was just a glorified corridor and Harriet slept in what should have been the living room, leaving Chiara with just enough space for a single bed, a rail for her clothes, a desk for her laptop and a few neat piles of recipe books and food magazines for inspiration. Luckily she'd never been a great lover of possessions. Stuff weighed you down, in her opinion. And even though she loved Soho, she found romance in the idea that she and Harriet could pack up in minutes and move on if they ever wanted to.

Blearily, she peered into the mirror on the wall. Her cropped brown hair was still stiff with flour, her wide-set brown eyes sticky with sleep. Chiara had a face that laughed easily. It was open, guileless even. Freckles dusted skin that quickly baked to caramel in the sun but right now was kitchen-worker pale. She knew she could still look OK if she gave herself half an hour and a decent supply of hair products and make-up, but this morning she couldn't be bothered. This was her bread-free day and she was going to make the most of every second. She pulled on a plain black sweater and jeans, attempted to run her fingers through her impossible hair and was ready.

She found a sleepy Salty stretched out along the full length of the carpeted hallway. He raised his head when he heard her footsteps and his tail thumped the floor hopefully.

'Do you want to go for a walk?' The tail thumped faster and louder. 'Well, get up then, you lazy dog.'

London could be beautiful at this hour, especially at weekends. Piccadilly Circus was almost deserted and Chiara walked briskly down past Fortnum & Mason and the Ritz, feeling as though the West End belonged to her and her alone.

Spring was pushing daffodils through the soil in Green Park. There were other early morning walkers there, some with dogs, and Chiara let Salty off the leash for a few moments to play with a boisterous standard poodle called Fergus, before snapping him back on and continuing her walk down past the Palace and along the lakeside path in St James's Park.

As she walked, she tried to work out why she didn't feel an awful lot happier. She had everything going for her after all. She was fit, healthy, the author of a fabulously successful cookbook and not all that bad-looking in a decent light. She had good friends and good luck. Her life was rich. So why did she feel so . . . insulated with sadness. It was as if the happiness she wanted was right there but she was too numb to feel it.

Salty's great, shaggy, grey head tilted up at her and he panted contentedly. Dogs had the right idea, Chiara thought. Give them food, somewhere to sleep, a bit of love and a walk every day and they were happy. Salty never seemed to suffer from random depression like she did.

By now they'd almost come full circle back to Soho. Chiara was more than ready for a cup of strong coffee, so she headed to Bar Italia where she grabbed an outside table and called for a cappuccino. She tied Salty to the leg of her chair so she'd have both hands free to wrap round her cup for warmth. It may have been spring but there was a stiff breeze blowing down Frith Street.

Salty spotted Harriet before she did. He practically towed her chair out into the middle of the road in excitement. Harriet smiled and waved at them. She cut a glamorous figure walking through Soho, even dressed down in old jeans and a fringed, red poncho. Men always turned and stared as she strode past but she rarely bothered to notice them. Harriet liked men but she liked them on her own terms. She took a lover every now and then and was as greedy for sex as she was for martini. But Chiara had only actually heard her say the words 'I love you, darling' to herself and Salty. She had no time for falling hopelessly in love or having her heart broken. As the years passed, and she suffered her own disappointments, Chiara often wished she could be the same.

'What are you doing out on the street at this hour?' she called out to Harriet. 'Did the flat burn down or something?'

'No, darling, I woke up and realized you were gone and I thought I'd better track you down fast before you gave in to the urge to eat the wheat-based product that dare not speak its name.'

'I was just flirting with the idea of ordering a couple of bits of toast and Marmite actually.'

Harriet glared at her.

'But then I remembered it was a bread-free day,' she added.

'Shush, don't speak of it. Don't think of it.' Harriet flopped into a chair and allowed Salty to rest his huge head in her lap. 'Make the nice man bring me coffee,' she pleaded.

The Italian waiter was handsome, his accent was strong and his English broken. 'Here is your cappuccino, beautiful lady,' he said, dimpling madly at Harriet. Since she'd long ago got used to being the uglier friend, Chiara didn't mind being ignored by the entire male sex whenever Harriet was around but there were limits.

'Oi, that's my cappuccino actually. You can bring another one for her,' she said.

He gave her a wilting look then shrugged theatrically at

Harriet. 'I will have your coffee here for you in mere seconds,' he told her crisply.

Harriet laughed. 'A moody one,' she noted, as he strutted back into the café. 'Perhaps you'd have had more luck with him if you'd spoken to him in Italian.'

'Yes, well, I'll add learning Italian to my long list of things to do if you think it will improve my standing with the local waiters.'

'You must speak a smidgeon though, darling.'

'Why must I?'

'You have an Italian name, Italian blood.'

'You look more Italian than I do.' She'd always been slightly envious of Harriet's jet-black hair and olive skin.

'I know, I know, but with me it's only skin-deep. You're the genuine article.' Harriet leaned back in her chair and appraised her. 'You know, I've always found that slightly strange about you.'

'What?'

'Well, you must have family in Italy right? And yet you've never made the tiniest effort to find them. Why is that?'

'I don't know. I suppose it's always been out of loyalty to my mum. She never encouraged questions about the Italian side of things. And that's putting it mildly. She didn't even cook Italian food, you know. I don't remember a single meal that wasn't English.'

Harriet wrinkled her nose. 'How odd,' she mused. 'Still, if it was me I'd want to know. It's your personal history, isn't it? Where you come from is a part of what you are. And, since you don't entirely know where you come from, how can you ever truly understand what you are?'

'So deep and meaningful, and you haven't even had any coffee yet,' Chiara teased.

'Yes, where is that moody boy with my cappuccino?'

Finally, with enough caffeine in their bloodstreams to keep them buzzing until bedtime, the pair left Bar Italia and walked slowly down the streets full of restaurants and brasseries that were beginning to wake up and ready themselves for the day's trade.

'So many types of food,' Chiara said wanly, as they passed Thai, Vietnamese, French and Hungarian restaurants. She peered at their menus – odes to lemongrass, poems to paprika – in something close to despair.

'There's no call for it really,' Harriet agreed. 'A decent lump of cheese and a ripe pear would do me.'

'So do we really need them? The cookbooks, the food magazines, the recipe websites?'

'It's not a matter of needing, is it?' Harriet pointed out. 'It's a matter of wanting. And people must want recipe books because they keep on buying them even if they never cook a single meal from them.'

'And that has to be the most depressing thought,' responded Chiara. 'Copies of *Queen of the British Kitchen* sitting untouched on bookshelves all over the country. Not a splodge of Granny's Gorgeous Gravy or a drop of Princely Parsley Sauce sullying their pristine pages.'

Harriet laughed. 'Don't think I don't know what you're up to,' she said. 'You're trying to talk yourself out of doing another book, aren't you? Well, it simply won't do.'

'Do I *have* to write a cookbook, Harriet? Can't I just produce a guide to ordering takeaways?'

'Good idea. You could call it *Duchess of the Drive Thru*. Janey will have you dressed up as a cheeseburger for the cover picture.'

Chiara laughed and glanced down at her watch. 'Come on, I'll help you get the club ready for lunchtime. Just keep me away from the yeasty thing of shame, OK?'

But it was the thought of Italy, not bread, that kept playing on Chiara's mind all day. What if she *did* have aunties, uncles and cousins there, maybe even a half-sister or half-brother? What if her real father were there? How difficult would it be to find them? And, if she did manage to track them down, what sort of reception would she get? The germ of an idea began to form.

As the afternoon wore on, Harriet eased the cork out a bottle of Barolo. 'Fancy a lively Italian, darling?' she asked.

'I certainly do.' Chiara pushed an empty glass forward. She took a sip and held it in her mouth for a moment to savour the fullness of the flavour. 'Mmm, that's divine.'

'It is good, isn't it?' Harriet agreed.

'I could drink bottles and bottles of it.'

'I already have.'

Chiara laughed. Thank God she had Harriet. There was no one else like her. 'So,' she began tentatively, 'I've had an idea. Do you want to hear it?'

'Go on,' encouraged Harriet.

'Well, the bread book is a non-starter, I think that's obvious. Every time I so much as consider baking I want to put my head in my hands and bawl.'

'What will you do instead?'

'What you suggested. I'll go away and find out who I am.'

Harriet looked confused. 'I don't understand.'

'Neither do I. Not completely,' Chiara admitted. 'It's probably a crazy idea but I thought . . . well, that I'd take a few weeks off to do some detective work and see if I can track down my Italian family. I don't know . . . maybe if I can discover where I come from it'll help me work out where I'm going.'

Harriet nodded slowly. 'Which region in Italy are they from?' she asked.

'I don't know. That's what I mean – it's a half-formed idea at best. Probably I should just forget about it and go upstairs to do some baking.'

'Stay right where you are,' Harriet ordered, topping up her glass. 'I think this is worthy of further consideration. If you *were* trying to trace your family, where would you start?'

'Well, let me see. I guess I'd go home to Merseyside for a few days. See if I can find any clues there first.'

'So all you're investing is the price of a train ticket,' remarked Harriet. 'I think it's worth a punt, don't you?'

3

Running an hour late, and with no buffet carriage, the train carved its way north through the English landscape. Chiara held a magazine up in front of her eyes but her gaze kept straying to the green fields and canals interspersed with Homebase superstores and carparks. At this rate, England was going to run out of countryside soon. One day a thin film of concrete would cover the entire land like an eggshell.

London often made Chiara feel claustrophobic. It was as if there were so many people in so small a space that there wasn't enough room left for her. In the old days that feeling would lift as the train left London behind. But the green spaces between the cities seemed to be growing smaller and, this time, as the train began to rattle through the dark tunnels that led to Lime Street Station, she realized she still felt as claustrophobic as ever.

Chiara hadn't telephoned ahead to say she was coming so the people waiting at the gate to greet passengers weren't there for her. She stood alone on the concourse for a moment, trying to decide how best to get home. Catching the bus through the Mersey tunnel was the quickest option but she dismissed the idea. Hadn't she always preferred the ferry? The service wasn't so frequent these days – in fact, the whole thing was becoming more of a tourist operation – but she'd walk down to the Pier Head anyway and if she was particularly lucky there would be a ferry there waiting to take her home.

Swinging her small case from her hand, she trekked down

through the tatty, proud city towards the river, her ears listening out for the familiar lilting accent that always let her know she was home. This was the place she came from. Much of it was dirty and rundown, litter choked the roadsides, but still, for some reason, she loved it. She wondered if there were a town in Italy she'd love as much, a place where she'd feel instantly at home as she did in Liverpool.

She'd asked her mother about Italy, of course she had. But Maria Domenica had always changed the subject or grown impatient with her. 'Listen to you trying to get me talking when your room is such a mess and I have a pile of laundry to do. Get away with you, girl,' she'd say with a flick of her long hair and then she'd turn on her heel and walk away. In the end it seemed easier not to bother her with questions.

She'd tried gently probing Alex for information but he wasn't any more forthcoming. His voice would echo out from the depths of whichever car engine he was tinkering with: 'Italy, never been there, love,' he'd say. 'Can't help you.'

Even though her name was Chiara Fox, she'd always known Alex wasn't her real dad – they'd told her that much. 'He went away and he can't be found,' was all Maria Domenica would say if Chiara asked about her birth father. 'I looked for him for years and never found a trace of him so it's pointless you trying, love. Just be thankful you've got a wonderful man like Alex to be your dad and stop worrying about what might have been.'

In the end she just stopped thinking about it. She shifted the whole business to the back of her mind and concentrated on the real, the here and now – like netball, schoolwork and, eventually, boys, Chiara had always imagined that one day, when she was ready, her mother would sit her down and tell her everything. On that day she'd learn her father's name, what had become of him and why he hadn't wanted to have anything to do with her.

Perhaps Maria Domenica had intended to tell her all those

things in her own good time but she'd been robbed of the chance. First came the crippling headaches that sent her rushing round the house pulling down blinds and drawing curtains and saw her curled up on the sofa for hours with her eyes closed tight. Then came the trips to the doctors and specialists for tests and scans and, finally, the diagnosis. Maria Domenica had a brain tumour.

'No one survives a tumour like this,' the neurosurgeon had told them. 'The best we can hope for is to buy you some time and a little more quality of life.'

Maria Domenica's speech had been the first thing to go and then her ability to read and write, as the tumour slowly shut her body down. Whatever secrets she'd had left to tell were trapped inside her then. Her eyes alone spoke of her frustration and terror. Chiara and Alex had taken turns to sit with her – reading, playing music or simply stroking her hand – until she'd slipped into the coma sleep from which she never woke.

She'd been buried beneath English earth and there had been no talk of Italy then. Chiara had left Alex alone in the tall house by the river and returned to London and the hot, frantic kitchens where she earned her living. It had taken her a long time before she could dial her home phone number and not expect to hear her mother's voice, all flat Liverpool vowel sounds and rich, rolling rrrrs. She supposed Alex would expect her to visit the grave while she was home. She hated being there, hated the thought that her mother was down there, suffocated by the layers of damp earth.

She could smell the salty tang of the river and hear the screams of seagulls now. Looming in front of her were the vast buildings that she remembered as black shadows from her childhood. Since those days they'd been sandblasted till they looked like new. There was the Liver Bird Building crowned with its two stork-like creatures and, right next door, the graceful Cunard Building. To her left was the restored Albert Docks with its shops, museum and art gallery, showing how good Liverpool could look when it made an effort. To her right, miles of worn-out docklands were still begging for a makeover.

She had to run the last few yards down the landing stage to the ferry and leap aboard as it tooted frantically. A belch of smoke came from the funnel and they were off, bobbing over the choppy grey waves. Despite the cold wind, Chiara sat on the top deck in the open air. This was where she'd sat with her mother so many years ago. They'd spent entire days on this ferry, crossing and re-crossing the river. She'd found it endlessly entertaining and her mother had never complained. She'd been content to sit with her, the breeze tangling her long black hair, until it was time to go home and put on Alex's dinner.

Chiara had been a much-indulged only child. Although her mother and Alex had tried for years to have another baby, it had never happened. There was talk of medical treatment but Alex dug his toes in, refusing to bother with doctors and their new-fangled ideas. 'Chiara's my daughter and she's the only one I need,' he'd repeat stubbornly. And as for Maria Domenica, whenever Chiara begged for a little sister to play with, she merely shrugged and said lightly, 'Not everyone gets on with their sister, you know.'

Chiara squinted at the terrace of tall Victorian houses that lined Egremont Promenade and picked out the one where she'd grown up. It must be so strange for Alex now, all alone, his wife and father gone. She'd have been happy if he'd found someone else but he'd blanched at the idea when she'd raised it. 'I was bloody lucky when I met your mum,' he'd told her. 'No one gets that lucky twice.'

It would have been polite to have telephoned and let him know she was coming, she realized now. Alex had never liked surprises. But it was too late. She was on her way.

As it turned out, Alex was relieved to see her. 'Been going

out of my mind the last few weeks to be honest,' he told her. 'Everything I do, everywhere I go, it reminds me of your mother.'

Chiara touched his shoulder gently. 'Dad, you can't go on like this.'

'I don't see that I've got much choice.'

'You could go for grief counselling,' she suggested. 'You could sell the house and move somewhere that doesn't hold so many memories.'

His jaw set stubbornly. 'No, I don't think so. I'm happy enough here. No point in change for change's sake, hey, love?'

Chiara noticed how thin he'd become. All the years her mother was alive, cooking huge, rich meals for him, he'd been in danger of tipping over into corpulence. Now he looked all rigid and ribby. She resolved to set to work in the kitchen while she was here and fill the freezer for him.

'Nice surprise, anyway, to have you home,' he grinned at her, his skin growing pink with happiness. 'I was planning to meet Bob and Tony in the Farmers' Arms for a pint or two later. You should come. They'd love to see you.'

'No,' she laughed. 'I'm not going to crash your lads' night out. And anyway, I've got stuff I need to do here.'

'What stuff?'

'Ah now, that's what I need to tell you about. Sit down and I'll put the kettle on.'

But she had difficulty coming to the point. She explained her lack of inspiration for book number two and how the baking idea hadn't really worked out. She made him laugh as she described her bread-free day and how she'd racked her brains to come up with something she felt truly passionate about.

'So what did you decide on then?' he asked impatiently.

'Well, the thing is, I'm not sure I can pull it off.'

'Why?'

'It's kind of complicated.'

'Because?'

'Because it involves other people besides myself and I'm not sure I'll be able to find those people.'

'Chiara love, what are you on about?' Alex took a sip of his tea and raised his eyebrows.

'Ah, is that not clear?'

'Not clear at all, no.'

Chiara puffed up her cheeks and blew out a stream of warm air. She tugged nervously on her short brown hair.

'Is this difficult?' Alex asked.

'It is a bit, yes,' she replied.

'I'd like to think there is nothing you can't say to me. I am your dad after all.'

Chiara sucked in a breath and prepared to puff up her cheeks and blow the air out again.

'Love?' Alex prompted.

'Yes, you are my dad and you've been fantastic,' she began. 'I couldn't have asked for better. But the thing is that somewhere out there I have another dad and maybe cousins and aunties and stuff, and I'd like to go to Italy and find them. If it's all right by you.'

Alex looked rueful. 'We weren't very fair to you, were we, your mum and I?'

'What do you mean?'

'All those questions and you never got any answers.'

Chiara looked at him. She didn't trust herself to speak.

'The trouble is I don't have the answers for you,' he admitted. 'Your mum would never talk about it to me either. I pressed her once or twice but she wasn't having any of it.'

'How could you have let her have this whole vast portion of her life that you didn't know anything about?' Chiara was almost angry for him.

'What you need to know is that I was a bit of a loser when I met your mum. No job, going nowhere and I didn't much care. She took me on when most girls would have given me a wide berth. And I was . . . well, I was grateful. I didn't want to rock the boat. Anything she desired, she could have, so far as I was concerned and that included me respecting her privacy about her past.'

'So you don't know anything?' Chiara couldn't believe it. 'No names, no places.'

'Nothing.'

'I might as well give up then. Go back to my sodding baking.'

Alex looked thoughtful. 'You know, there are things belonging to your mum upstairs. A couple of boxes full of drawings that I haven't been able to bring myself to open up. She kept them to herself while she was alive and it seemed wrong for me to intrude now. But you're her daughter so it's different for you. And you have all these questions, all these unanswered questions. Maybe there's something in those boxes to answer one or two of them.'

'Maybe.' Chiara sipped her tea and wished it was a lively Italian Barolo. 'I'll have a look through them later, shall I, when you're at the pub?'

'That's a good idea.'

Chiara put her mug down on the mantelpiece. 'In the meantime, why don't you see if there's a bottle of wine somewhere you can open and I'll shake the fridge and come up with something for dinner.'

4

The boxes were high on the very top floor of the house in the room Maria Domenica had always kept as her own. The armchair was still there, where she'd left it, pointed towards the window so she could look down on the sweeping view over the river towards Liverpool. She'd loved that view. She'd even loved the hideous, great concrete tower that had once housed a revolving restaurant and still dominated the skyline with its stark ugliness. 'Sometimes there is beauty in ugliness,' Maria Domenica had told her. 'In factories and smoke stacks, in buildings that should have been demolished decades ago or never even built. There's beauty there. You just have to know where to look for it.'

As she stood in the room that almost still smelled of her mother, Chiara remembered how she'd sit there for hours staring at the view, her long black hair falling down the chair back. She'd loved the view best when the weather was wild, when the rain lashed at the windows and the Irish Sea sent its best waves powering up the river. 'It reminds me of my wedding day,' she'd sometimes remark. And often, Chiara remembered, she did have a sketchpad on her knee and a pencil in her hand, although the drawings always disappeared somewhere before anyone had the chance to get a proper look at them.

The boxes, Chiara realized. They'd be in the boxes. She found them stacked on a high shelf at the top of the wardrobe. Wobbling on a stool, she took them down one by one and put them on the floor beside the armchair. They were just plain brown supermarket boxes stamped with names like Heinz Baked Beans and Kleenex Toilet Tissue, but on the top of each carton, in black marker pen, her mother had put her initials 'MF' and a date. Chiara opened the most recent box first and found what she'd expected – pencil drawings of the views Maria Domenica had preferred and two-minute sketches of the people she'd loved. There was one of Alex peering over the bonnet of a car and another that she recognized as herself playing on the promenade on her first bike. Her mother had possessed a real talent, she realized. The work was rough but she'd captured Alex's lazy, genial smile and her own fierce concentration as she tried not to topple off the bike.

But the cityscapes were best – great slabs of buildings brooding over the River Mersey. The cityscapes were wonderful. Chiara couldn't believe they'd flowed from her mother's pencil.

The second box yielded more artworks. Maria Domenica hadn't confined herself to working in pencil. She'd also tried her hand at watercolours and dabbled in charcoal. One or two of the pictures in this box were cruder and less well observed. Looking down, Chiara found Alex's initials in the corner. Clearly it hadn't taken him very long to realize he had no flair. As she neared the bottom of the box, she found only her mother's work once more.

The final box was her last chance. If there wasn't anything in that to lead her to Italy then she would give up, she decided, and return to her rolling pin.

The first few sketchpads held familiar scenes – Mrs Leary serving up sandwiches in the café, children dive-bombing into the pool. New Brighton Baths was long gone now, demolished when the council decided it was too expensive to maintain. Chiara felt an ache of nostalgia as she found a drawing of herself standing proudly at the top of the high slide and another where she was smothering her face in candyfloss.

Then, halfway down the box, the drawings changed. These scenes weren't cityscapes, they were pastoral. A crooked house surrounded by dusty fields and trees. A buffalo grazing by a lake. A dark man with a pixie face and silver spectacles putting on a white starched apron as he stood beside an old-fashioned coffee machine. They looked Italian. Had her mother drawn these from memory? Chiara wondered. If so, then they were startlingly well observed.

Right at the very bottom was an envelope addressed in her mother's writing and another envelope, left unsealed, but so slim that it might not contain anything at all. She slid her fingers into that one first and pulled out a creased, faded, black-and-white photograph. It showed a dark man with a large belly and laughing eyes, and a woman, also of generous proportions. They were in their best clothes and the picture had an air of formality. Chiara thought it was probably a wedding photograph, taken a long time ago. Excited now, she shook the envelope and peered inside but the photo was all it contained.

That left the letter. Chiara knew she was invading her mother's privacy and that she'd never have approved. She hesitated for a moment while she deciphered the name and address on the front of the envelope. It read: 'Erminio & Pepina Carrozza, Fattoria di Carrozza, San Giulio-in-Campania, Italy.

Oh, what the hell, Chiara thought, and, carefully, she tore open the envelope. The letter inside was three pages long and all in Italian. She recognized only the words at the top: '*Cara Mamma e Papa*'.

Chiara froze. She had a sense that at last she was beginning to untangle the mystery. Staring at the letter, she tried to understand more. She picked out her own name and the word Liverpool but everything else was unintelligible. Harriet had been right, she decided, she should have learned Italian. But one thing was clear, Maria Domenica had written to her mother and father in Italy and never bothered to post the letter. Why? What had stopped her? Chiara now had more questions than ever.

In the end, she packed everything back into the boxes, setting to one side just three things – the photograph, the letter and the pencil sketch of herself on the high slide at New Brighton Baths.

She yawned and stretched. There was nothing more she could do until she found someone who spoke Italian well enough to translate the letter. But she was feeling more confident now. With the address, the photograph and the words her mother had written but not sent home, she had enough to begin a search. Tomorrow morning she'd ring around for cheap flights, she decided, and then go into town to buy herself one of those Teach Yourself Italian tapes. It would help to have at least a few basics of the language before she went over there, although she was sure most people would speak English. Didn't everyone these days?

Taking her clues and her drawing, Chiara went back downstairs. She needed a drink. She rooted round in the kitchen cupboards until she found a bottle of bad French table wine. It tasted slightly corked but she didn't care. It was the hit of alcohol she was after, not a pleasant taste.

She took the glass and the bottle to the big front room that overlooked the river, and collapsed on the sofa. By the time Alex got home from the pub, she was down to the dregs of the bottle.

'Drinking alone?' he remarked. 'First sign of alcoholism.'

'Oh, I'm way past the first sign,' Chiara laughed. 'I live with Harriet, remember? Drinking is a matter of survival.'

'And you're a chef,' he remarked. 'They're notorious for hitting the bottle.'

'That's right. What's more, it may be in my genes. I may come from a family of hardened drinkers. And it looks like I'm about to find out.'

'What was in the boxes?' Alex asked quickly.

'Drawings and paintings, heaps and heaps of them, some very good. And these.' She showed him the photo and the letter. 'They are my only clues, but at least I have something to go on now.'

Alex took a good look at the couple in the picture and the address on the envelope. 'Sorry, I don't recognize anything.'

'I didn't think you would.'

Frowning now, he sat down beside her on the sofa. His breath smelled pleasantly beery but his thin body was just as tense and stiff as it had been earlier. 'I feel like I'm letting you down,' he told her. 'I should be able to come up with something.'

'You probably do know some useful stuff, you're just not aware of it. If you talked to me about Mum for a bit, perhaps that might help.'

'Well, if you like. But what sort of thing do you want me to talk about?'

Chiara paused and thought for a while. 'Cast your mind back to when she first moved into the house, when I was really little. What puzzled you about her? Did she do anything you thought was strange?'

'She walked,' Alex said without hesitating. 'Perhaps you remember those walks? Day after day, whenever she had any free time, she'd be off, dragging you all over town. She must have walked down every single street more than once.'

'She was looking for someone?'

'Yes, I think so, but she never found him.'

Alex stood up and went over to the cabinet in the corner. He pulled out a bottle of Australian Shiraz. 'For future reference, this is where the decent stuff is kept these days,' he told her as he uncorked it and poured himself a glass. He offered her the bottle.

'Oh, go on. I'm going to have a vile red wine hangover in the morning anyway so I may as well carry on,' she told him.

He sat down beside her again and sipped thoughtfully. 'She was funny about her drawing. Even though I gave her every encouragement – signed her up for art classes, bought art supplies, even had a go at it myself – she was reluctant to let me see her work. Of course, it may have just been shyness or a lack of confidence, but to me it seemed like something else.'

'What?'

'I don't know, like she was ashamed maybe, or frightened. She didn't even like me to watch her drawing.'

'But there are lots of pictures of you and me. You must have seen her doing those?'

'No, never, I guess she did them from memory.' He sculled his wine and refilled his glass. 'There's one more thing that may be significant.'

'Yes?'

'She was weird about our wedding. In those days people always used to send a wedding photo to the local newspaper so they could publish it; Maria wouldn't let me do that. She wouldn't even allow me to put a notice in the births, deaths and marriages column. And when I proposed to her she refused me at first. But she didn't say she didn't love me or fancy me. What she said was: "I can't marry you. It's just not possible". I've never forgotten that.'

'So what do you think it meant?'

'I don't know. I guess that I never wanted to know. But I've got a feeling you're going to find out.' He glanced down at the photo of the well-fed couple. 'And if these two people are still alive, you're going to track them down.'

Chiara smiled. 'I'm in with a chance, I suppose. And the first step is to find someone who'll translate this letter.'

5

It was one of those rare days when Soho seemed empty. Even Bar Italia was deserted. Chiara didn't think she'd ever seen so many free stools beside the long counter, and the coffee machine lay silent. The waiter she was looking for was standing outside doing calf stretches from the edge of the kerb, holding his round, silver tray in front of him like a steering wheel.

She fluffed up her brown hair. Flirtation might be required for the coming task, or charm at the very least. Feeling slightly ridiculous, she'd purposely picked clingy clothes from her rail this morning instead of the baggy track pants or sloppy jeans that usually disguised her slim figure.

'Hi.' She smiled winningly at the waiter. 'Remember me?'

He shook his dark head and scowled.

Chiara ploughed on. 'I was here with my friend Harriet – you know, the beautiful one – the other day. We were drinking cappuccino out on the pavement.'

'You and a thousand others.'

'Yes, but we had a very large dog with us.'

He shrugged and scowled again. 'You want a cappuccino now?' he asked grudgingly.

She pulled her mother's letter out of her pocket. 'No, actually I wondered if I could ask you for a favour? I have this letter. It's in Italian and I can't understand a word of it. I thought you might be able to translate it for me?' She was so desperate to know what the letter said, she was almost bursting with impatience, but she resisted the urge to thrust it into his hands.

Lemon-lipped, he eyed the letter dubiously. 'Is it from a boyfriend?' he asked finally.

'No, no, it's much more important than that. It's from my mother and—'

'Look,' he interrupted, 'I don't have time, I'm working.'

Chiara gestured towards the row of empty stools, 'Yes, but you're not terribly busy right now and I'm sure it would only take you a few minutes to translate it. Please? I'd be ever so grateful.'

He bristled. 'I'm working.'

'Well, will you have time later? I wouldn't be asking if it weren't really important.'

Reluctantly he took the letter from her hand. His shift ended at six, he told her, and he'd try to have it translated by then but he wasn't making any promises. Chiara looked at her watch. It was still so early. How was she going to fill up all that time?

On her way home she ducked into the supermarket and picked up a bag of cleaning products: a bottle of Jif, another of bleach, things to spray, things to wipe. She attacked the apartment from the front door inwards, coaxing flour out of crevices, washing the floor and walls, even cleaning the underside of the toilet and the deepest reaches of the shower cavity. But it was only a small apartment and it didn't take nearly long enough to clean from top to bottom. Picking up her bottle of Jif and a cloth, Chiara made her way down to the club. There was plenty more to clean there. She was scrubbing at surfaces, removing layers of dust, when Harriet stopped her with a dark look.

'I'm down to the dinosaur age,' Chiara told her. 'You want to watch out. Archaeologists might well insist on roping off the area and finger-searching the dust for fossils.'

'That's not dust you're stripping off, that's atmosphere. Leave it alone.'

'Oh please, just let me do these shelves and the mantelpiece. And maybe the far wall. Go on.'

'What the hell is the matter with you?'

'I'm restless, I can't settle. I've got to hang on until this evening for that waiter to translate my letter and it's bloody killing me.'

Harriet rolled her eyes.

'Yes, I know, I know. I should have let you take it to him. You'd have got results.'

Harriet prised the Jif out of her fingers. 'Why don't you do something useful? Go upstairs and listen to that Italian tape again. See if you can't pick up a few words. And don't worry, I'll come with you to Bar Italia this evening to make sure he really has translated your letter.'

'Thank you.' Chiara handed over the cloth as well. 'You're a true friend.'

But as it turned out, Harriet's powers weren't needed. Chiara fell through the door of Bar Italia at six on the dot and the waiter's eyes filmed with tears at the mere sight of her.

'Such a beautiful letter, such a sad letter.' He waved it at her and she could tell he was loving the drama of the moment.

'What does it say?' Chiara squeaked like an over-excited poodle. 'Read it to us.'

He shook his head. 'Not here. We need to sit down somewhere quiet. These aren't words to be read in a noisy place like this.'

'Let's go back to the flat,' Harriet suggested.

'Are you kidding?' Chiara was beside herself. 'That's five streets away.'

'Well, we'll walk up the road to Soho Square then, but hurry up.'

The grass was newly mown and the little square smelled as fresh as anything so close to Oxford Street could smell. They sat down on a bench, the waiter between them, and waited impatiently while he pulled the letter from his pocket.

He cleared his throat and paused dramatically. 'Are you ready?' he asked.

'Yes,' they chorused. Chiara wondered if Harriet wanted to strangle him almost as much as she did.

'This is what it says: "Dear Mamma and Papa, I hope this letter finds you well. I can't begin to tell you how sorry I am for running away in the night. I promised you both I would stay in San Giulio and I meant it, I really, really meant it." '

He broke off. 'Bits of the letter are smudged,' he remarked. 'I think she was crying.'

Chiara nodded, her throat tight.

He bent his head and continued to read: ' "Running away seemed like the right thing to do at the time. The only thing I could do. Marco is a bad man. He's vain and weak and jealous. He hurt me and I was afraid he'd hurt Chiara next. I know you thought you were doing the right thing, Mamma, when you turned me away that night and told me to go back to my husband. But you were wrong. A woman's place isn't always with her husband. Sometimes she's a million times better off without him.

' "I need you to know that I've found some happiness now. I'm in England, in a place near the city of Liverpool where I have people who love me and love Chiara too. No one has raised a hand to me here or threatened my daughter. We live in a nice house and we want for nothing. We've both been very lucky.

' "There's nothing left to say except that I love you both so much. When I think that I may never see you again it breaks my heart. I want to sit in the kitchen with you, Mamma, and help you bake bread. Or dig the vegetable patch and choose a rabbit for Papa's dinner. It's cold here. I want to feel the heat of the sun that always seems to shine on Italy. I want to eat decent pasta, drink Mamma's red wine and speak the language I grew up with. I want to steal some moments to lie beneath the peach trees. And more than anything I want to be an Italian again. But I'm afraid to come back. I think it is impossible now."'

The waiter raised his head. 'That's where it stops. She couldn't carry on.' There was silence for a moment and then he spoke again. 'Are you the Chiara she writes about?'

'Yes.'

'Has she never been back to Italy?'

'No.'

'She must go. If this is how she feels, she must go back. You should book a flight for her today.'

'No, it's not possible.'

'Well, if money's the problem, get a loan,' he cried.

Chiara almost couldn't bear to say the words. 'My mother's dead,' she managed.

He looked stricken. 'That's terrible.'

She nodded. 'Yes, it is. It's terrible.'

Harriet reached over and took her hand. 'Darling, I'm sorry that your letter is so sad.'

'Please don't be nice to me. I'll cry and I won't be able to stop.'

'What do you want me to do then?'

'Can we just sit here for a while?'

Harriet squeezed her hand. 'Yes, of course.'

So they sat on the bench, the three of them, as the light faded and they watched the late-night shoppers hurry past the square's high railings clutching their carrier bags. No one bothered to glance over at them. They were moving too fast and were too intent on getting to their tube station or the pub or on heading to Chinatown for a cheap meal.

Chiara stared at the funny little mock Tudor hut in the centre of Soho Square and wondered, as she always did, why someone had gone to so much trouble to build what could only be an implement shed. It didn't make sense.

'All those years she was so unhappy,' she said at last. 'And I never knew. She was just my mum doing the regular mum things. I never bothered to think about her feelings. And all that time she was desperately sad.'

'No, that's not what she's saying in her letter,' Harriet argued. 'That's not it at all.'

'What do you mean?'

'She was certainly sad when she wrote the letter. But she's telling them that she's found happiness and people who love her. She wants them to know that you're both safe.'

'She says her heart is breaking.'

'And she says she's very lucky.'

Grief turned to anger for Chiara as it so often did. 'Lucky? Stubborn more like,' she said bitterly. 'Too stubborn to go home to Italy and say she was sorry. Stubborn to the very last, she was. She wouldn't let Alex put up extra handrails for her round the house or let us move her bed down to the living room when she got very sick. No, we had to haul her up and down those bloody stairs day after day. She didn't want a nurse, no strangers in the house, she didn't want to go to hospital – and what Mum wanted, Mum got.'

'Chiara, you're not being fair.'

'I know, but I wish I'd never found this letter. Now I'm the one who feels bad. She left Italy because of me – she says she was frightened I'd get hurt – and she was miserable for the rest of her life. And it's my fault.'

The waiter was still sitting silently between them. He looked confused, as though he was having trouble keeping up. 'She never sent this letter to her family?' he asked when at last there was a break in their conversation.

'No, she must have had second thoughts.'

'So why don't you deliver it for her?' He looked at the address on the envelope. 'San Giulio, I know it. It's near Naples, not too far from the sea. It's not a tiny place, but it's not so huge either. And Carrozza is a fairly unusual name. It shouldn't be too difficult to find them.'

Harriet looked thoughtful. She took the envelope from the waiter's hand and stared at it for a while. 'I agree with . . . God, what's your name? We don't even know your name.'

'Eduardo.'

'I agree with Eduardo. You ought to deliver the letter. It's the right thing to do. But I think you need to prepare yourself for a few harsh truths.'

Chiara thought she might have a fair idea what those harsh truths could be but she wanted to hear Harriet voice them so she said, 'What do you mean?'

There was an awkward silence for a moment. 'Well,' Harriet began, 'what I mean is . . . Eduardo, why don't you read the letter through again and we'll have another good listen.'

So he did, managing to imbue his second reading with all the drama and pathos he'd lent to the first. Chiara thought he might even have pushed out a tear.

Harriet squeezed her hand again. 'The word that really leapt out at me that time was "husband". I think you need to prepare yourself for the idea that your mother may still have had a husband in Italy when she married Alex.'

'God.'

'Quite.'

'And I suppose this husband, this Marco character she says was a bad man, must be my father?'

'That seems most likely,' Harriet agreed.

Darkness had fallen like a theatre curtain. There was no moon and no stars and even the city lights seemed feeble. They could hear the hum of traffic from Oxford Street and Charing Cross Road, but in the centre of the square all was silent. Chiara was aware that probably they shouldn't still be sitting there. Someone would be along shortly to lock the gates. But she couldn't face moving. The thought of standing up and walking down the few streets that led home paralysed her. Eduardo had put an arm around her shoulder and

Harriet was still holding her hand. They seemed to be in stasis too.

She watched a young homeless boy setting down his sleeping bag for the night in a doorway opposite. Life was crap, she thought. The world was a grim, ugly place and she couldn't face it any more.

'My mother was a bigamist and my father was a basher,' she said quietly. 'Great.'

Eduardo smelled nice. Some cologne that he'd probably doused himself in this morning had faded to an acceptable level. She leaned into him, seeking some level of comfort.

'Darling, I'm freezing,' Harriet said then. 'Shall we go back to my lovely warm club and talk about this some more?' Sliding off the bench, she held out her hand to Chiara and hauled her to her feet. 'Come on, baby.'

'I'm not going to Italy, Harriet,' she said almost aggressively. 'Not now, not ever.'

Harriet's voice was soothing. 'You don't have to go if you don't want to.'

'That's right, I don't have to do anything I don't want to do.' She dropped Harriet's hand and, without a backward glance at Eduardo, stalked off, tears stinging at her eyes.

6

Chiara was wearing too many clothes. Sweltering in a long-sleeved T-shirt and thick jeans was no way to see Italy. Still, despite everything, she was glad she'd come. Rome was a beautiful city and the people here seemed somehow more alive than the Londoners she'd left behind. They dressed better, they walked better and they certainly ate better. Every meal-time was a joy. So this was how pasta was supposed to taste, she thought, as she sat at a pavement *caffe* in Piazza Navona and twirled spaghetti round her fork. She savoured the intense flavour of fresh tomato, fragrant basil and good olive oil. An idea for a book on simple Italian peasant food was even spinning around in her mind already.

As she ate, she watched two young children splashing each other with water from the fountain at the centre of the square. It was very different from the plain, square fountain in New Brighton Baths where she'd played as a child. This one was huge and impressive – all heroic figures and bravura. Simple food and complicated architecture was the Italian way, mused Chiara. She ran a crust of bread round her bowl to mop up the last of the delicious sauce.

'*E buono*?' The waiter, an older man, twinkled at her as he removed her wiped-clean plate.

'*Molto buono, grazie*,' she said with all the confidence of someone who had spent a fortnight listening to a Teach Yourself Italian tape.

'*Ah, brava, brava! Parla Italiano*,' he cried, his brown eyes crinkling as his smile stretched to its limits.

Chiara smiled back at him. The men here were amazing. They seemed to think it was their responsibility to admire every woman who passed by. Whenever she stepped on the street, she was greeted with appreciative whistles and a '*ciao, bella*' or two, although no one had dared to pinch her bottom yet.

It was tempting to stay in Rome, whiling away the coming days criss-crossing the city from the Coliseum to the Spanish Steps. But this wasn't a sightseeing holiday, she kept reminding herself. Tucked away in her suitcase, among the socks and underwear, was a letter, decades old and yellowing, she was going to deliver to a family in San Giulio. Her family.

Every time she thought about it she felt sick. She couldn't visualize that first meeting. Would they hug her or shut the door in her face? At night she lay awake in her hotel bed worrying about it.

Harriet had ordered her to stop panicking. 'Just focus on finding them and everything else will look after itself,' was her advice. Easy for her to say, thought Chiara bitterly. She was safely behind the bar of The Office, fortified by Barolo.

It was Harriet who had talked her into coming to Italy in the first place. Her insistence was matched by Eduardo's passion and the pair of them had first worn her down and then all but pushed her on to the plane. She was grateful to them now, she wouldn't have missed Rome for the world, but as the days went by she'd put off making the trip south.

She couldn't delay it any longer. Superstitiously, she'd packed just a few of her things in a backpack and left the rest at the hotel. All she needed was a couple of changes of clothes, a brush for her unruly hair, her laptop for recipes, a camera and, of course, the letter and photo. She didn't want to tempt fate by assuming she'd be in San Giulio for any longer than a couple of days.

The backpack was at her feet now, and once she'd finished

the tiramisu and coffee the waiter was about to bring, she'd make her way to the station to catch the train to Naples. From there, her guidebook told her, it was a bus ride to the piazza at San Giulio. She imagined it as a pretty village, with old stone buildings and interesting peasant types. And the food, she couldn't wait to taste the food. It would be the true *cucina povera*, less refined than the meals she'd eaten in Rome but no less flavoursome, she expected. Even if she never found her family, she was sure there would be so much to enjoy about this trip.

She was in no hurry to get to Stazione Termini. She could tell from her street map it was a long walk from Piazza Navona and she resolved to take it at a leisurely pace, savouring the sweet smell of frying onions that seeped from the open doors of restaurants and peering into shop windows at wildly embellished clothes she'd never dare wear herself.

Just observing the local populace was entertainment in itself. They drove like madmen or as if they were fleeing from a disaster, one hand on the horn, foot firmly down on the accelerator, as they took the narrow, clogged streets at speed. Chiara was frankly amazed that the roadsides weren't littered with car wrecks and dying pedestrians, and she was certain it would be all too easy for a tourist like herself, distracted by an unexpected piece of classical architecture or a beautiful fountain, to be mown down by someone driving from home to office in record time.

Even when they weren't encased in their cars, the Romans seemed on the brink of being out of control, talking with their hands as much as their voices, tipping from laughter to anger and back again with alarming speed and no warning. And God, were they loud. As she walked the back streets Chiara noticed more than one black-clad old lady standing in the street, holding a long, high-decibel conversation with someone on a balcony six floors above. Too logical for one of them to take the lift and join the other, too colourless and dull, too unItalian.

Suddenly Chiara felt terribly prim, like a character from a Jane Austen novel, all lovely manners and china teacups. She'd never thought of herself as unemotional before, but in comparison to the volatile people she was getting to know, her upper lip was the very epitome of stiffness. She'd had an Italian mother and, she presumed, an Italian father so she couldn't imagine how she'd turned out this way. English chilliness must have soaked into her from the icy winds that rolled off the Irish Sea, up the River Mersey and rattled the windows of the tall terraced house on the promenade.

There was a small fracas when finally she arrived at the station. The problem was that no one seemed able to agree on where she should queue to buy the specific type of ticket she needed to travel from Rome to Naples.

'You have to buy a ticket for the Rapido. I can't sell you one of those. You'll have to go to that booth over there,' snapped one ticket-seller in quickfire Italian.

So she waited in another queue at another booth only to be told, 'You need to buy a ticket for the Rapido. I can't sell you one of those,' and was sent back to the booth she'd just come from.

Chiara was hot, confused and sick of queuing. She opened her mouth and began to yell at him in English. 'I'm bloody sick of this. One of you tells me one thing, someone else tells me another. I just want to buy a bloody ticket to Naples and I'm not moving until someone sells me one.' She was behaving like an Italian, she realized, astonished.

The ticket-seller couldn't possibly have understood a word she'd said but he recognized the way she said it. Calmly he accepted her money and pushed a ticket over the counter, waving her away imperiously. Chiara felt exhausted by the effort of getting herself so worked up. She couldn't imagine what it must be like to operate on this highly charged emotional level all day, every day, and yet the people around her smiled and laughed more than their buttoned-up London counterparts. Perhaps it was healthier in the long run to live with your emotions on the surface.

It was a relief to sink into a window seat in the remarkably cool, ordered train that pulled smoothly out of the station at the exact moment the timetable had claimed it would. While it was a mystery to Chiara how such a chaotic race could have a rail system that worked, she was grateful they'd managed it.

She got off the train in Naples and stepped straight back into the real Italy – hot, confused and absolutely foreign. Taxi drivers straddled the bonnets of their cars, playing noisy, ferocious card games with each other; a fat woman with a very thin child, wearing only a long, grubby man's vest, begged for spare coins; and everyone seemed to be talking at once in a dialect that sounded both clipped and guttural to an ear accustomed to Roman tones. The people were shorter, darker and louder here, their faces harder and more cunning. Chiara was used to noise and crowds, but still she felt almost threatened as she walked across the station concourse, a lonely figure clutching a small backpack. It took all her self-control not to make a mad dash back to the train that would carry her safely away in comfort. This must be how you could tell you were finally a grown-up, she decided. When you really didn't want to do something but you did it anyway because you knew you had to.

Chiara boarded the bus that would take her closer to the family she was dreading meeting. It was hot and stuffy, but the windows were down as far as they would go and, once they started moving, a cool breeze fanned her face. Mothers and children were crammed into most of the seats. The mothers had tired faces and several extra kilos wobbling from their arms and chins, but the children were charming. Their eyes were like raisins and they peeped curiously over the seatbacks at the skinny, pale lady with the short spiky hair. Chiara tried to focus on the children rather than the road. No good could come out of watching the way Italian drivers behaved on the long, straight stretches of the *autostrada*, she was sure of that.

The countryside was brown, flat and barren. This wasn't the Italy of postcards or her imagination. She checked her watch, it couldn't be too far now. Sure enough, the bus began to cut a path through streets full of apartment blocks that looked as if they had been hastily thrown up in the seventies. Here and there she saw a tree, but otherwise there were no green spaces. Every building was stabbed a hundred times with TV aerials and laundry was drying from washing lines strung from balconies. Chiara imagined the sound of barking dogs and wailing babies that probably accompanied daily life in these grim boxes.

She waited to see charming peasant dwellings and quaint old churches, but there were none. The sad apartment blocks were faithful until the end of the bus route.

The piazza where she disembarked was the closest she'd come to picturesque. Tall palm trees marched across the old cobbled square towards a squat church, white plaster flaking from its walls. There were cars parked end to end, wedged wherever there was a space, and all around her Vespa scooters buzzed like mosquitoes, bearing pretty, bareheaded girls with flowing hair and muscular young boys in tight T-shirts. There were more young people gathered around the dry fountain in the centre of the square and on the benches beneath the palm trees. Laughing and chatting, they seemed carefree and, to Chiara, far more beautiful than their surroundings.

She stood, backpack over her shoulder, and surveyed the scene, trying to decide on her next move. In one corner of the piazza she spotted a little, old-fashioned *caffe*. From this distance she could just read the words curling in gold letters on the heavy glass door – Il Caffe dei Fratelli Angeli. She'd take a walk, she decided, and stretch her legs, which felt cramped after the bus journey. And once she'd worked up a thirst she'd come back and find a table in the little *caffe*. She wouldn't mention the name Carrozza yet. First she wanted to get a feel for the place where her mother must have spent her youth.

It was bound to have changed a lot since Maria Domenica's day. Most of the modern apartments wouldn't have been here then and the town surely hadn't stretched quite so far out into the barren countryside.

She walked in the shade of the palm trees and up some worn stone steps to the church. For a moment she considered ducking inside and taking a look but she was too intimidated. What if the priest wanted to speak to her? What if he wanted to know what she was doing there? So she kept on walking past a little market stall garlanded with strings of fresh lemons. The bent old lady whose wrinkled face peered out from behind the waxy yellow fruit called out to her, an invitation of some sort. But Chiara only smiled and walked on.

She walked past the shops: the bakery, the butcher's and the dairy, where six or seven old women with baskets over their arms queued for the day's fresh buffalo mozzarella. Chiara's mouth watered at the thought of the soft, yielding cheese melting on her tongue and she resolved to try a slice or two very soon.

Then the shops petered out into more cheerless apartment buildings and Chiara felt too discouraged by their ugliness to continue. She turned and retraced her steps back to the *caffe* she'd spotted earlier.

The heavy glass door of Caffe Angeli opened with a ching and she stopped stock still in amazement. Never in all her life had she seen a place as outrageous as this. Every wall was covered with frescos. Cupids climbed above the red leather banquettes and Venus stepped prettily from her half shell just behind the jukebox. An Italian love song was playing; she didn't understand the words but the vibrato in the singer's voice spoke of a broken heart.

Standing behind a long stainless steel counter, polishing a huge, old-fashioned Gaggia coffee machine with a clean cloth, was a good-looking man whose dark hair was tipped with silver. Laughter lines sat comfortably on a rugged face and he had the lean, fit frame of a worker who was on his feet all day. Chiara put him at perhaps four or five years younger than her mother and wondered if they'd known each other. It was an idea that made her shiver partly in excitement, part dread.

'*Buongiorno*.' The man looked up from his polishing and smiled at her invitingly. Fine grains of coffee dusted his big, square hands and dirtied the starched white apron wrapped around his waist.

'Oh, hello,' she replied, still thrown by the sheer extravagance of what she'd taken to be an unpretentious neighbourhood *caffe*.

The man treated her to his generous smile again. His teeth were white against his dark skin. '*Inglese* or *americana*?' he asked.

'*Inglese*. I'm English. Sorry, I speak a little bit of Italian but not much.'

'A little bit is better than none at all,' he replied. His English was good, his accent purer than that of many a waiter in Bar Italia. 'Would you like a coffee and perhaps a bite to eat?'

'Yes, please.' She slid onto one of the tall, leather stools beside the counter. A '*caffe con latte* and a panini would be great.'

He frowned slightly. 'I have some of today's fresh mozzarella with tomatoes and some home-baked bread. I think you would prefer that,' he told her. 'And it is too late for such milky coffee. It's bad for the digestion. I will give you an espresso and a glass of *acqua minerale*.'

His tone was polite but it didn't bear arguing with. Chiara nodded in quiet agreement. 'Thanks,' she said.

He busied himself with her food and drink. 'My name is Giovanni Angeli,' he told her, long-lashed, brown eyes peering over the top of the Gaggia.

'My name is Chiara.'

He paused, coffee in hand. 'Chiara, that's quite an unusual name. What's your surname?'

'Fox,' she replied, and he shrugged and put the coffee down on the counter in front of her. She took a sip. It was hot and strong, the caffeine made her nerve-endings sing. This was her chance and if she didn't move soon it would slip from her grasp.

'My name is Fox but my mother's name was Carrozza – Maria Domenica Carrozza.'

The name seemed to echo round the walls and bounce off the paintings. Even the Cupids seemed to freeze in mid-flight. Giovanni Angeli's jaw dropped and, without saying a word to her, he turned and pushed his way through the dusty red velvet curtain behind the counter. '*Papa, Papa, vieni qua subito*!' he cried.

An old man with a kind face and a straight spine emerged, complaining in a low muttering voice. He looked as though he had just been woken from a snooze. Giovanni was yammering away too quickly for her to understand what he was saying but she picked out her own name and her mother's – Maria Domenica Carrozza.

The old man fell silent, his rheumy eyes widened behind his silver-framed spectacles and he stared at her in disbelief. He walked around the counter and took her by the hand. '*Venga, venga*,' he said, tugging her towards a Madonna and child painting in the centre of the crowded wall. The face of the Madonna seemed familiar. She had long, straight hair, a beaky nose and deep-set eyes. The old man reached out and touched the face reverently, 'Maria Domenica,' he said in a croaky voice, then his wrinkled hand reached down to stroke the downy hair of the baby on the Madonna's knee. 'Chiara,' he added.

Chiara was confused. 'I'm sorry, I don't understand,' she said, turning to Giovanni. There were tears rolling down his face, running in rivers down his laughter lines and streaking his cheeks. He made no attempt to wipe them away. And when she turned back to the old man, he was crying too. He took her shoulders and pulled her towards him in a hug. Chiara felt his body trembling. She hugged him back, she didn't know why.

Finally Giovanni took her by the arm. His hand felt warm and reassuring. Pushing her gently, he made her sit down at the table next to the Madonna and child painting.

'Your name is Chiara and your mother is Maria Domenica Carrozza and she came from this town?' he asked gently, and she nodded in reply.

He pointed at the painting. 'Let me explain what my father Franco was trying to tell you. Here, on the wall, this Madonna was painted in the image of your mother and the baby's features were copied from your own.'

The world had gone crazy, Chiara thought. These bizarre Italians were talking nonsense and behaving like madmen. 'I don't understand,' she repeated.

'There is nothing much to understand,' Giovanni promised and his tone was calm and measured. She trusted him. 'Your mother worked here for my father and he was very fond of her. She left town all those years ago and we always hoped we'd hear from her but we never did. Now you are here in Caffe Angeli and it's wonderful. It seems like a miracle that you have found us again.'

He was crying freely again and Chiara began to dread the question she knew would surely come.

'How is your mother? How is Maria Domenica?' Giovanni asked, as she had known he would.

She sat back in her chair and studied them both in silence for a moment – the old man like a wizened elf, the younger whose eyes still danced with life. Expectation lit their faces. She didn't quite know what to tell them. These men had loved her mother, she was sure of that. She tried to find a gentle way of breaking the news that Maria Domenica was gone now.

'First you should tell your father that my mother made a happy life for herself in England,' she began. 'She found people who loved her and a comfortable home. I think she always missed Italy but England was a good second-best.'

'And now?' asked Giovanni in the voice of a man who was beginning to suspect the answer to his question. Both men cried again when she told them about her mother's slow, silent death and her own subsequent quest to find her Italian family and, hopefully, her real father.

'Perhaps you can help me?' she finished.

'Well, we can tell you where your family are easily enough,' Giovanni told her, wiping his tears away now with the corner of his starched apron and staining his face with coffee dust. 'They're where they've always been, on their small farm just outside town. I can drive you there, if you'd like.'

'No, I think I'd rather arrive alone,' she replied without hesitation.

'Well, in that case I'll point you in the right direction and you can walk there in twenty minutes. It's not the most pleasant walk – along the main highway – but it's flat and easy enough. Your mother did it many times in the old days, often pushing you in your pram.'

'Did she bring me here when I was a baby?'

'Of course she did. While she worked, you slept in your crib in my father's little sitting room behind the curtain. I remember how well behaved you were.' Giovanni smiled and she smiled back in return. 'My father was afraid you might cry all day and drive away the customers, but the only time we heard a peep out of you was when you were hungry or needed your nappy changing.'

Giovanni and his father were a storehouse of old memories and she longed to dust them off and hear more about her mother's life in Italy. But a more urgent question was pressing on her mind. 'My father, Marco, is he at the farm too?' she asked.

Giovanni grimaced a little just like he had when she had ordered her coffee with milk too late in the day. 'Your father?' He paused then said briskly, 'No, Marco isn't there. He left town ages ago. But the others are there and if you want to see them I think you should start walking soon. Come back tomorrow though, will you? My father and I would like to talk to you some more. We have lots of questions, just as I'm sure you do.'

Giovanni drew a map so she would not get lost and the two men hugged and kissed her as they said goodbye. Franco held her hand until the last moment as if he couldn't bear to let her go and he mumbled something in his strange, slurred old man's Italian.

'What did he say?' she asked Giovanni.

'He said you must come back tomorrow. He will make you his special pizza. It was your mother's favourite.'

As she turned her back on the two men she felt as if she had friends here in Italy at last. If things went badly with her family, she could come back here. Franco and Giovanni would look after her, she was certain of that.

Guilt was written large on Giovanni's face as he watched Chiara's strong, slim back disappearing out of the door of Caffe Angeli. When he was sure she had gone he turned to his father and asked, 'Should we have told her more?'

'What more did you want to tell her?'

'That I'm certain Marco isn't her real father, that Rosaria is a bitch and will give her a cold welcome, that her mother had good reasons for running away when she did.'

Franco grunted. His face was mapped in wrinkles now and the hairs on his head precious and few, but he'd lost none of his spirit. 'I think you've interfered enough in that family's affairs, don't you?' he said crisply. 'It's time to let things take their natural course. Whatever will be, will be.'

Giovanni went back to his polishing. His father had never forgiven him completely for what he'd done late that night all those years ago. It wasn't the money he'd objected to – he'd have given Maria Domenica his last coin – but the fact she'd been allowed to melt away into the grey morning light without a word. Giovanni still remembered his father's anger, his blistering tongue when he'd realized that she had disappeared completely, that no one knew where to find her.

It had seemed like the right thing to do at the time, he'd argued, but Franco was deaf to his excuses. Perhaps he had been wrong, he often thought later, but he had been so young and her face had been so bruised and battered that it had frightened him. He remembered trying to act brave and wanting to protect her, but in truth he'd feared that Erminio Carrozza and Gino Manzoni would land on their doorstep with a shotgun if they suspected his involvement. He had done what he thought he had to do. Was that so wrong?

He scrubbed harder at the Gaggia. No matter how well he cleaned it, the very next day it would be covered in a crust of dry, hard coffee dust again and so would his clothes, his hair and his skin. Everything would smell roasted and bitter. He had to tie up his work clothes tightly in plastic bags until he had time to wash them or the stink would taint every room in the house. At least Maria Domenica had escaped this town, he thought, and the dull predictability of life here, the bitter, harsh smells. She hadn't let family loyalty or duty hold her back. But now, against all the odds, her daughter had come back. Who knew what she would find here?

7

Giovanni had been right about the walk; it was easy but ugly. The road looked as though it had been widened recently into a two-lane highway. There had been no time for landscaping and mounds of hard earth blocked her path at intervals as she walked. At last the apartment buildings gave up their stranglehold on the landscape and Chiara found herself trekking past two-storey houses on larger sections. They were painted brightly in pinks, oranges or yellows, almost as if their owners, depressed by their outlook, had tried to lift their spirits with colour.

She was impatient to get there now. The feeling of dread had lifted at last and her legs couldn't carry her forward as fast as she wanted to go.

She saw the peach trees first and behind them a haphazard little house. She paused at the start of the driveway and considered for the first time how best to introduce herself. No point in beating about the bush, she decided, she might as well be upfront. She would tell them exactly who she was and why she was there from the word go.

As she walked up the driveway, a lumpy, brown dog, with long hair matted into dreadlocks, strained at its thick chain and barked at her hysterically. A family of dirty chickens scattered in front of her and raised a cloud of dust. A vegetable patch beside the kitchen door presented her with its weeds, towering basil and unruly tomato plants. The place looked unloved and empty.

Chiara propelled herself across the dusty courtyard and

rapped on the big wooden door with a heavy hand before she had time to change her mind. To her surprise it opened straight away and momentarily she was struck dumb. The tall, slender man standing in the doorway had to be the most beautiful human being she had ever seen. His eyes weren't brown but they weren't really green, and they were framed by eyelashes so long and lush they didn't look real. His olive skin was so smooth and clear it could drive a woman to Botox and his hair was as sleek as a blackbird's wing. She couldn't help noticing his long fingers that held the door open. Even his fingernails looked as though they had been buffed and filed.

'*Signora*?' he said quizzically, raising a faultless eyebrow.

She gathered her wits about her for long enough to stammer out, 'Hi,' then she reverted to staring at him, struggling to pick out a flaw.

'Are you lost?' he asked in hesitant English.

'No,' she gulped, and shook her head.

'How can I help you then?' he asked.

She got over being tongue-tied by his beauty and suddenly it all came out at once – who she was, what she was doing there, why she'd picked this time to come – a barrage of words that must have been difficult to follow. Somehow he managed.

'I think you had better come in,' he told her when she'd finished.

He held open the door a little wider and she stepped straight into a big kitchen that was rustic to say the least. A scrubbed pine table and old ripped vinyl chairs dominated the centre of the room. Hugging one wall was an aged dresser, its top shelves groaning with hard, round loaves of bread. The kitchen cupboards were mismatched and the old butler's sink cracked. There was no sign of modern conveniences like a microwave or dishwasher, she noticed, but on the ancient stove a huge pot was bubbling and, judging by the fresh splatter pattern on the wall, it was filled with a tomato-based sauce. She longed to lift the lid, to smell and taste, ask questions and take notes, but clearly this wasn't the right time for that.

'Sit down,' the Adonis said, pulling out the least damaged chair. 'Would you like a drink of water?'

'Yes, please, that would be lovely.'

He filled a grubby glass from the tap and she remembered all the warnings she'd had about sticking to bottled water. Her fingertips touched his briefly as she took the glass from his hand. She shivered and he smiled like a man who knew exactly how much power he wielded when it came to the opposite sex.

'My name is Paolo,' he told her.

'Are you . . . er . . . are we related at all?'

He shrugged. He seemed absolutely unfazed by her appearance on his doorstep. 'Cousins, I think,' he replied. 'Stay there and I will call Mamma. She is your aunt, I suppose.' He smiled again just as effectively as the first time. 'Her name is Rosaria. She is taking a nap right now, but I think she will want to be woken to meet you.'

Chiara waited five minutes, then ten, then fifteen. She thought she might have heard the sound of raised voices but couldn't be sure. Finally a door opened and a sour-looking creature filled the doorway. Perhaps she had been pretty once before her curves had lost their elastic and her mouth the energy to push itself out of a frown, but now it was impossible to believe she was any relation at all to slim, graceful Maria Domenica.

Her arms were big and lumpy, like two badly packed bags of laundry, her eyes two shrivelled raisins in a doughy bun of a face, her swollen body a burden to her. She lumbered into the kitchen like someone whose knees had grown accustomed to aching.

'Rosaria?' Chiara asked hesitantly.

She was rewarded by a stream of Italian that sounded more like invective than a warm welcome.

'I'm sorry, I don't understand.'

Smoothly Paolo stepped in. 'Don't worry. Mamma isn't properly awake yet and your coming here has been a bit of a shock for her.'

'Look, I can go. I could come back tomorrow or some other time if that would be better.'

'No, stay where you are. Mamma is always hungry when she wakes. I will find some food for her and her mood will improve. She does speak a little English – I taught her myself – and once her stomach is full she will probably remember some of it.'

Paolo lined up platters of bread, cheese, olives, strips of aubergine pickled in balsamic vinegar, salami and *prosciutto crudo*. Sure enough, as she chewed, Rosaria seemed to mellow. She didn't offer Chiara so much as a taste from one of her plates but, since she'd spotted the flies buzzing around the food and the chickens roosting beneath the table, she was grateful. She was far from anal about hygiene in her own kitchen but this was too much.

At last Rosaria stopped chewing, wiped some grease from her chin with her hand and said very slowly, breaking up each word into separate syllables, 'Maria Domenica.'

'Yes, Maria Domenica,' Chiara replied. '*Mia mamma*.'

'She ran away.'

'Yes, I know.'

'And now you're here.'

'Yes.'

'What do you want from us?'

'Actually I have something for you – a letter that my mother wrote to her parents Pepina and Erminio. I think this may be them in this photo.'

She pulled the creased black-and-white wedding picture out of her bag and pushed it across the table. Rosaria's surly expression didn't change. Perhaps she was too late, thought Chiara, and the old couple were dead.

Paolo turned and treated her to another flash of his charm. 'Pepina and Erminio? This time of day they usually take a walk through the orchard, holding hands like a pair of young lovers. I'll go and find them. They'll come as fast as their old legs will carry them as soon as they hear about you and your letter.'

When he left the room, Chiara sagged slightly and she realized she'd been holding an artificial posture – belly in, boobs out – to make the best impression. She'd even caught herself wishing she'd invested a few extra minutes in proper make-up instead of just waving the mascara wand at her eyelashes and dabbing on a bit of concealer here and there. He was gorgeous and he didn't seem to have a wife anywhere around the place, which perhaps wasn't so surprising when you considered the mother-in-law she'd have to cope with.

Chiara didn't have to wait too long before she heard the excited cries and gasps of two breathless old people. A round, white-haired lady fell through the door, followed by a rounder older man. They landed upon her, hugging, kissing, pinching her cheeks. 'Chiara, Chiara, *bella* Chiara,' they chorused. Then the old lady sat heavily on a chair, threw her apron over her head and began to bawl into the floral fabric. Rosaria rolled her eyes and shook her head, but the old man moved to his wife's side and stroked her arm. Chiara didn't understand the words he muttered but she could tell they were soothing. She pulled the letter out of her backpack, unfolded it and placed it carefully on the pine table. Rosaria's lips became pinched as she saw the shape of the handwriting on the yellowing paper.

When Pepina's sobs subsided, Chiara held the letter out to her. 'From Maria Domenica,' she said simply.

It was Paolo who took the paper from her hand. 'I'll read it.

Their eyesight isn't so great these days and they'll never be able to track down their glasses. They're always where you'd least expect to find them.'

He began to read the now familiar words in a beautiful voice that matched his beautiful face. As he spoke, Pepina held Erminio's hand tightly, her knuckles growing white. '*Mia figlia, mia figlia*,' she cried when he'd finished, followed by another stream of Italian.

Paolo translated. 'She wants to know where her daughter is.'

Chiara thanked God this was the last time she would have to break this news to people who had loved her mother. She repeated much the same words she'd used with the two old men in the *caffe* but nothing could soften the blow. Once again Pepina disappeared beneath her apron and Erminio mourned too, sobbing more freely than Chiara had ever seen a man cry before.

'She was happy,' Chiara repeated desperately. 'She had a happy life. She met another man, called Alex, who loved her very much and was like a father to me.'

Rosaria heaved herself onto her feet and went to stir the sauce bubbling on the stove. Chiara stole a glance at Paolo. He was re-reading the letter with a frown that barely creased his smooth face.

'So sad,' he said, looking up at her. 'Your mamma never came home yet all those years Pepina and Erminio were here waiting for her. Why didn't she come?'

'I don't know,' Chiara replied. 'I think maybe it was because she was afraid of my father.'

'Your father?'

'Yes, my father, Marco.'

'No.' He shook his head. 'Marco isn't your father, he's mine.'

'But I thought from the letter that my mother was married to him?'

Rosaria stopped her stirring and let loose a cackle. 'Married?' Her grasp of English had suddenly returned. 'Oh yes, she was married to him but that doesn't mean you were his daughter. We're talking about Maria Domenica here . . . *puttana*!'

Chiara felt dizzy. The situation was slipping beyond her grasp. It seemed they were talking about two separate people. She knew the meaning of the word *puttana* and it didn't describe her mother. She wasn't a whore. She'd never been anything but wholly faithful to Alex, Chiara was certain of that. For a moment she experienced a childish desire to thrust her fingers in her ears and refuse to hear any more, but curiosity got the better of it. 'So if Marco wasn't my father, who was?'

Rosaria's face was spiteful and her voice near hysterical. 'It could have been anyone,' she keened in Italian. 'That artist who painted the heathen pictures on the walls of Caffe Angeli or some man she met in Rome. It could even have been Franco Angeli or his son Giovanni. They were close, too close, and anything could have been going on behind that red curtain at the back of the *caffe*. She probably slept with them all.'

'I don't believe it.' Chiara's voice rang out, as Paolo translated. Pepina and Erminio looked up in alarm. They began their kissing and hugging and cheek-pinching again. '*Bella, bella*,' they repeated over and over.

The harshness of Rosaria's voice broke in. She was speaking angry Italian again – but this time Chiara had no problems translating her tone. She wasn't welcome here – that much was obvious.

She reached down to the floor and picked up her backpack, ready to make her excuses and leave. But the tiny movement and its intent didn't escape Erminio and he placed a gentle yet restraining hand on her shoulder.

As he turned to Rosaria she saw a look in his eyes that gave her a glimpse of the man he had been. He spoke briefly and calmly, and yet Chiara could sense the anger behind his words. He brooked no argument and, when he'd finished, Rosaria dropped the wooden spoon she'd been holding and stalked out of the room.

Chiara looked at Paolo for some sort of interpretation. To her relief, he seemed unconcerned by the exchange and merely smiled again. 'My grandparents want you to stay here. They say we will make up the room next door for you. It's where your mamma used to sleep.'

'But I can't, Paolo. Your mother doesn't want me here, that's quite clear.'

'Don't worry about her. She can be moody. And anyway, she doesn't own the house, it belongs to my grandparents and they won't hear of you staying anywhere else.'

'Won't it be a little awkward?'

'Possibly, but it will be even more awkward if you try to leave. You'll break their hearts all over again. And look at them. You don't want to hurt them, do you?'

Chiara gazed at the old couple with their wrinkled, nut-brown faces, faded clothes and stocky bodies. They were smiling at her hopefully, although Pepina still had tears in her eyes. If only she'd tried a little harder to learn Italian she might have been able to communicate with them. As it was she could only smile until her jaw ached and repeat the words, '*Grazie, grazie*.'

That evening, as it grew dark, Paolo shooed the chickens out of the kitchen and Pepina lit candles down the length of the pine table. They brought out their most delectable treats for her to taste: *prosciutto crudo* that Pepina had cured herself, a heavy wedge of *parmigiano* cheese for her to cut slices off with a sharp knife, a dish of feathery steamed broccoli tossed in a skillet with olive oil, a little garlic and some piquant red chilli pepper, a bowl of baby courgettes sliced and dried outside in the sun, then browned in olive oil and pickled in vinegar, garlic and torn mint leaves. And then the freshest melt-in-the-mouth mozzarella with the biggest basket of home-baked bread so hard and coarse that Chiara feared she might break her feeble English teeth on them.

Each time Chiara thought the eating was over, Pepina would return to her stove and bring more plates to the table. Balls of rice stuffed with cheese and deep-fried, tender vine leaves quickly sizzled in a pan with yet more garlic, strange yellow beans that Paolo told her were lupins. Chiara felt she would burst but she couldn't say no to anything.

The food had called Rosaria back into the kitchen, but she ate in silence and avoided Chiara's eyes. She emanated bad feeling, although no one else seemed to register there was anything wrong. Chiara took her lead from the rest of them and got on with the serious business of sampling a healthy portion from each dish.

Erminio watched approvingly as she ate. '*Manga*, *manga*,' he said, rubbing his rounded belly.

'My grandfather likes to see a woman with an appetite,' Paolo explained.

Chiara had him act as an interpreter once again so she could tell her grandparents exactly why the food she was tasting was so important to her. They nodded and smiled proudly when they learned she'd made her living as a chef and was now becoming famous as a writer of cookery books.

'My grandmother has always been a wonderful cook, the best in the neighbourhood,' Paolo told her. 'You must have inherited your talent from her.'

'I suppose I must have,' replied Chiara, nearly dazed with wonder. She was related to these people, she took after them. Just the thought of it made her feel happier.

Then she had a thought. She asked Paolo to translate one more thing for her. 'Would she teach me? Will you ask if she would show me how to make the traditional family food my mother grew up eating? The food that's been cooked by generations of Carrozza women? You see, I'm looking for inspiration for my second book. And I'm wondering if, maybe, I might find it here.'

So Paolo asked and the old lady seemed so excited by his words she sprang to her feet and turned to her pans on the stovetop as if to make a start straight away.

Erminio made her sit back down again. Then he spoke again with that same flavour of authority in his voice and Paolo nodded back at him. 'My grandfather says that early tomorrow morning Rosaria will stay here to clean up the kitchen, which apparently she has allowed to slide into a disgusting state, and we will take you into town to shop for fresh ingredients. Then, once we've had a little rest, we'll begin to cook.'

'That sounds great.'

'You should go to bed early,' he advised. 'You've had a big day and my grandparents will expect you to be awake at first light. No one but my mamma sleeps in late around here.'

Lying in the narrow bed where her mother had once slept, Chiara sniffed the sheets and pillow and imagined she could smell the scent of her long black hair. What dreams had she had while she was lying here? she wondered. What had she hoped and prayed for?

Seeing Maria Domenica through the eyes of her family was like standing and looking at a favourite view from a different point. Everything was familiar on the landscape but nothing was where it should be. She was beginning to think she had never really known her mother at all. And, as for her father, she was no nearer to solving that mystery. In fact, thanks to Rosaria, she had more candidates than ever before.

When she finally slept she dreamed of the kitchen next door. But in her dream there was a slender, young, dark-eyed woman who looked like her mother stirring the bubbling sauces on the stovetop and kneading the dough for bread. Her movements were quick, she was full of life and quiet plans for the future.

Chiara slept deeply. She wasn't woken by the murmur of voices speaking in Italian even if once or twice they were raised. She slept on and dreamed someone else's dreams.

Paolo and Rosaria were sitting together on the kitchen doorstep in their habitual pose, Paolo's head lolling on his mother's shoulders, her hand gently smoothing his already impossibly smooth hair.

'Mamma,' he wheedled. 'You have to behave, you have to be nice.'

'Why do I have to be nice?' Her voice was hard and too loud.

'Shh, you'll wake her and I need to talk to you alone.' He sank a little further into Rosaria's softness and she dropped a light kiss on his forehead.

'My Paolo, my Paolo, I love you so much I'd do anything for you,' she groaned. 'But please, don't ask me to be nice to that bastard girl. She has no right to be here. She'll ruin everything, ruin our lives. You heard how Papa spoke to me earlier? That's just the beginning of it, my baby. Like mother, like daughter, I say. Maria Domenica was bad news. She had everything her way from beginning to end.'

'Yes, but Mamma, now it's our turn. All we have to do is play along with her. We can help her gather recipes for her next book. And then, if we're patient, we'll have our chance to make some serious money.'

Rosaria wriggled a bit and shifted Paolo's head onto her

chest. She smiled as she felt the weight of him pressing down on her. 'I don't understand,' she murmured. 'How will we make money out of her?'

'Trust me, we will.'

'No, tell me how. Explain!'

Paolo lifted his head impatiently. 'You listened to her. Work it out.'

Her eyes widened and her lips drooped. 'Don't speak to me like that. First Papa and now you. Talk to me nicely.'

He returned his head to her breast and his voice resumed its wheedling tone. 'Think about it, Mamma. Her last book sold thousands and thousands of copies. She told me she's quite famous in England with her face in the newspapers and on television. If she writes another book and it's successful we will be famous too. Everyone will know she learned her Italian recipes from us and that's how we'll make our money.'

'I still don't understand.'

'Tourism, Mamma. We will get tourists here. Make them pay to stay on a typical peasant farm and learn to cook the authentic food of the region, the food they've read about in Chiara's book. They will pay dearly to learn the secrets of Mamma Pepina's kitchen. Trust me, I've read about this. Food tourism is all the rage. Rich people are happy to pay out for the privilege of travelling halfway round the world and preparing meals in someone else's kitchen.'

'But look at this place. Papa has let it get so rundown. Who would pay to stay here?'

Paolo shrugged. 'Yes sure, it needs a lick of paint and a tidy, but it's important for it to be rustic. That's what people are paying for – the ambience.'

Rosaria cackled. 'Oh yes, we've got plenty of that – ambience! Really, Paolo, I don't see why the tourists would want to come here to San Giulio. Don't they prefer to go to places like Amalfi and Positano, the pretty villages by the sea? You'll never get them to come here instead.'

'No, Mamma, I think it will work. We'll have to invest some time and perhaps a little money, print brochures, borrow a computer from someone, get trained up, create a website. But if my plan works, Chiara will do most of the publicity for us. She will bring the tourists to San Giulio.'

Rosaria should have felt happy – Paolo was close to her and her belly was full of food. And yet her only son's words had left her with the cold, empty sensation she felt every time she sensed his interest had been piqued by yet another woman.

'You like the girl?' she asked sharply.

'She seems all right.'

'She's like all the other ones before her,' she warned. 'Dazzled by your looks, my Paolo. But she'll never love you like I do. No woman will ever love you as much as your mamma does.'

He pressed his face into her soft body. 'Mamma, don't worry. I'm not going to leave you. I plan to use the girl, surely you can see that? You and I have to make some money. We can't sit around here waiting for the old people to die for very much longer. Anyway, like I'm always saying, there's no guarantee they'll leave us a thing. Uncle Salvatore will probably get the lot.'

'We're not that desperate for money, *figlio*. Your father sends us a cheque every now and then. He's always been very good like that.'

'If my plan works, Mamma, we can tear his cheque up into a hundred tiny pieces and send it right back to him. We'll be rolling in cash of our own. Trust me. You can do your bit by helping Chiara with her recipes, making her feel welcome.'

Rosaria sighed. She remembered herself, so pretty in her favourite blue dress, driving perilously in Mamma's car to the Manzoni farm. Where had the years gone? How had it all gone so wrong? For a moment the very thought of Paolo's plan, cunning as it was, exhausted her. She had no energy to step forward into the future with him.

'Mamma?' His head was resting on her belly now.

'If I must, Paolo, but only if I must.'

8

The sun was shining when Chiara opened her eyes. Hard and bright, it lit up the dustiest corners of the room, the yellowing walls, scarred where posters had once been tacked up, and the piles of odds and ends, old shoes and worn-out clothes, that had been stored here since this had become a spare room. Like everywhere else in the house, Maria Domenica's old bedroom spoke to Chiara of neglect. The place was falling into disrepair. Pepina and Erminio were getting too old to care about keeping up standards and Rosaria didn't have the inclination. If there were other children, thought Chiara, they must have moved away and had families of their own, for she'd seen no sign of them here.

From next door she heard the sound of someone moving around, someone old and slow whose movements suggested well-practised routine. Chiara heard a creaking from the pine kitchen table as if pressure was being exerted on it. Curious, she eased herself out of the narrow bed, pulled on jeans and a T-shirt, and went to investigate.

Pepina looked up and smiled as she walked into the kitchen. The sun was on her face, mercilessly spotlighting her wrinkled skin. The old lady looked tired, Chiara thought, and yet her arms were still quite muscular and her hands seemed strong as she kneaded dough rhythmically on the kitchen table.

'*Il pane*,' Pepina explained, and moved aside to let Chiara take a turn at kneading. The old wooden dresser still boasted a shelf groaning with loaves, but clearly her grandmother expected to need more because she'd poured another mound of coarse flour onto the table and had made a well in the middle to pour in yeast and warm water.

Peacefully, they worked together side by side, kneading the dough until Pepina was satisfied with its consistency. Chiara knew, without having to be told, that her mother had once stood in this exact spot beside Pepina, helping her to make the day's bread. Suddenly she felt very close to Maria Domenica, closer even than they'd been when she was alive. She was beginning to understand her mother, to get a glimpse of what had shaped her. Last night she had half regretted coming here but this morning she knew it had been the right thing to do.

Erminio and Paolo didn't wake until the smell of baking bread reached their rooms. There was no sign of Rosaria at all. It took Erminio's booming voice to bring her scurrying down the corridor, greying hair loose about her shoulders, face puffy with sleep.

She shot a sly look at Chiara and her sullen lips stretched into a half-smile. 'Good morning, I hope you slept well,' she said quickly.

They were the most affable words she'd spoken so far. Chiara was surprised but grateful. Perhaps she was over her initial shock and willing to make her niece feel welcome after all.

'Your mother seemed happier to see me today,' she said to Paolo later as he drove her into town, with Pepina and Erminio squashed together on the back seat.

'Ah, I told you, Mamma can be moody. Last night you saw her at her worst but I'm sure she'll be better from now on. She's pleased you're here, I can tell.'

The two old people insisted he took a longer route so they could drive through the older parts of town, past tall buildings the colour of washed sand with shaded courtyards hidden behind high walls like a secret.

'My grandparents say this is what most of the village looked like when your mother was a girl. There weren't so many apartment buildings then. San Giulio was a little village surrounded by fields of buffalo.'

'It seems a shame it had to change,' Chiara said wistfully.

'Oh, change isn't such a bad thing,' said Paolo lightly. 'There was a lot of poverty in those days and many people who lived in terrible conditions. My grandfather tells of families so poor that for dinner they shared just one bowl of spaghetti in the middle of the table. It's better now, I think.'

They managed to find a parking space in a corner of the piazza and, with her basket over one arm, Pepina led the shopping expedition. It was market day and stalls selling fresh vegetables, meat and cheese were lined up along the main street. Vendors called out as they passed, boasting of their smooth-skinned aubergines, sweet courgettes and big buds of artichokes. Pepina was a careful shopper, prodding and squeezing the produce before she'd deign to buy it, haggling if she thought she'd get away with it. She seemed to know everyone and their progress down the street was slow as they stopped off every few metres so Chiara could be introduced to yet another old family friend who remembered her mother.

Some of the old people became quite emotional when they learned who she was, hugging and kissing her, plying her with little offerings. Politely she drank a glass of cloudy, bitter liquid pressed on her by the old lady behind the lemon stand. A perfect plum was pushed into her hands by a fruit-seller, an entire salami by another stallholder. Both Pepina and Erminio seemed extraordinarily proud of her. 'Our granddaughter,' they told everyone who passed by. 'Meet our beautiful granddaughter, Chiara, home at last after so many years.'

As they turned back towards the piazza, Chiara remembered the two men in Caffe Angeli. They must be wondering what had become of her.

'Paolo, do you think we could stop in at the *caffe* before we go back to the farm? I ought to have a word with Franco and Giovanni.'

Paolo looked awkward. 'My grandparents don't go to Caffe Angeli,' he explained. 'They haven't been there since your mamma ran away. I think somehow they blamed Franco and Giovanni for what happened although I'm not sure why. And then they heard about that Madonna and child painting on the wall and it was the last straw.'

She frowned. 'That's a bit tricky then, isn't it?'

'A little bit,' he agreed. 'But we could sit on a bench in the shade for a while and give the old people a rest. That would give you a chance for a quick word.'

'I won't be very long,' she promised.

Caffe Angeli was packed. The hum of conversation rose above the squeal of the Gaggia and customers emptied their espresso cups faster than Giovanni could fill them. Busy as he was, he still had time to look up from his work and wink at her. 'I'd better tell Papa you're here so he can make that pizza he promised you.'

There was no space at the counter so she pushed her way round almost as far as the serving area. 'I can't stop for long because my grandparents and Paolo are waiting outside, but I just wanted to let you know that everything's fine.'

He raised his eyebrows. 'That's good.'

'I do want to talk to you though. I've got some questions.'

He looked at the queue forming in front of him and shook his head. 'You're right, now is not a good time, but come in this evening around five-thirty. It'll be quiet then and we can talk for as long as you like.'

The clock's hands seemed to have been pushed round by some extra force that afternoon. It was a shock to Chiara when she realized she and Pepina had been frying, baking, chopping and stirring for five whole hours. First they'd made a sauce with tomatoes, garlic, capers, olives and anchovies, then simmered thin slivers of veal in it until they were just cooked through. Next there were pizzas with a wafer-thin base and nothing on the top but tomato, good olive oil and scented basil from the garden.

With bits and pieces from her fridge, Pepina concocted a thick, luscious minestrone soup. And finally her grandmother showed her how to fry. Chiara had thought this was a skill she'd mastered years ago but Pepina's frying took things to another level.

She filled a black, cast-iron pan with sunflower oil and heated it to the exact temperature; not so hot so that the outside of the food burned before the inside was cooked, nor so cool that the food absorbed oil and became greasy. With one hand she rolled her delicious morsels in flour, or dipped them in batter or breadcrumbs, with the other she nursed along the food already sizzling in the pan, checking and turning and then removing at the right moment.

The family gathered round to taste her *fritti* while they were still piping hot. There was baby squid, cuttlefish rings and scampi tails, fried until they were crisp and sharpened with a squeeze or two of lemon juice. They melted in the mouth.

Then there were fritters of deep-fried dough flavoured with salt cod, olives, capers, pine nuts and raisins. Groaning with fullness, Chiara tasted batter-dipped fried artichokes reeking with *parmigiano* and she collapsed at the table to nibble on asparagus spears that her grandmother had wrapped in *prosciutto*, dipped in flour, egg and breadcrumbs and fried a few at a time.

Pepina didn't sit down to eat. She nibbled as she cooked, leaning over the sink. '*Friggendo mangiando*,' she said to Chiara, who turned to Paolo for translation.

'The cook can't afford to sit down when she is making *fritti*,' he explained. 'The oil is hot and dangerous. It demands attention.'

The food they'd produced was ladled into dishes and bowls and Paolo, a heavy, old camera round his neck, laid it all out on the table and shot pictures of it from every possible angle.

'I didn't know you were into photography, Paolo,' Chiara had said when he'd first produced the ancient camera.

'I've done a bit,' he'd replied, looking down at his camera and laughing. 'I know my equipment's not up to much but I've got a good eye. What I thought I'd do is shoot some pictures of you and Pepina cooking together – some black and white, some colour – and, you never know, one day you might want to put them in one of your cookery books!'

She had been touched by his enthusiasm. 'That's a great idea, Paolo. If ever they were used in a book I'd make sure you were paid a fee for them.'

He'd held up his hand. 'No, no, there's no need for that. I'm happy to help. I like spending my time with you, Chiara.' His eyes had met hers then and she'd felt a little shiver ripple down her body and had wondered what it would be like to kiss him.

She felt that extra bit alive all afternoon. Somehow, the fact that he was out of bounds made Paolo all the more desirable. And now, as she watched him bending down and stepping back to get the angle right, squinting his eyes and tutting at the long shadows cast in the late afternoon sunlight, Chiara couldn't damp down what she recognized was pure lust. She had to get a grip on herself. For all she knew, Paolo was her half-brother and the last person in the world she should be feeling this way about despite his and Rosaria's conviction that Marco wasn't her father. She was a disgrace. And yet she was certain the attraction was mutual. There was something in the way he touched her elbow and moved her body to the correct angle for his camera. He seemed to seize every chance to brush against her or lock eyes with her. Once, when he'd bent over to give her advice on the notes she was taking, she'd felt the warmth of his breath on the back of her neck and she'd almost moaned out loud.

The clock, still on high speed, had clicked round another ten minutes and Chiara knew she was going to be late for Giovanni.

'Could I ask you a favour, Paolo?' she said, pulling off her apron. 'Would you drive me into town? I promised Giovanni I'd be there by half past five.'

He smiled lazily at her. 'You might want to tidy yourself up a bit first. I can wait, and so, I'm sure, can Giovanni.'

Chiara was horrified when she saw herself in the mirror. There was food splattered on her face and caught up in her hair, her nose was red and shiny, and the little mascara she'd been wearing clearly hadn't coped well with the five minutes she'd spent chopping onions. Quickly she washed her face, brushed the unidentifiable gloop out of her hair and then peered into her make-up bag. What few cosmetics she owned had been rolling around in there for years. She rarely bothered to apply any make-up and, the few times she did, it seemed to slide straight off her face the minute she hit the heat of a kitchen. Today though, she made an extra effort to smear on as many layers as it took to look good – to even out her skin tones, widen her eyes, plump up her lips. She was very aware, although trying hard not to be, that she and Paolo were going to be alone in the car for at least five minutes.

He drove slowly, his eyes on her face as much as the road. 'You're very beautiful, Chiara,' he told her. 'Was your mamma half as beautiful as you?'

She laughed nervously. 'Oh, much more beautiful, I'm sure.'

'But you do look like her, don't you?'

'Well, no, not really. She was darker than me and much slimmer, and she had sleek, silky hair.' Chiara tugged at her own coarse spikes ruefully.

He grinned. 'I'm pleased. That means you must look like your father.'

'Not Marco?'

'No, you look nothing like Marco at all, believe me. I think you must take after the painter in the *caffe* that Mamma spoke of, or the stranger in Rome, or whoever was your real father.' He pulled up outside Caffe Angeli but left the engine running. 'I don't think you're my half-sister, Chiara. I think you're my cousin and that makes me very happy.'

Paolo leaned over and touched her lips with his. She didn't move. He kissed her, tentatively at first and then with more confidence. Then he leaned back and released her seatbelt for her. 'You're late, you'd better go,' he said gruffly. 'Call me if you want to be picked up.'

Her lips felt like they'd been scorched and her hands were shaking as she pushed open the door of Caffe Angeli. She couldn't believe she'd allowed Paolo to kiss her. He might be certain they didn't share a father but she still wasn't so sure. And yet there had been a moment just then when she'd have allowed him to do anything to her.

Giovanni seemed to sense there was something wrong. He was wiping clean the Gaggia, just as he had been yesterday, but he dropped his cloth the instant she walked in.

'Come and sit over here,' he said, leading her to the worn red leather banquette. 'Are you all right? You look as if you might have had a bad shock.'

'No, no.' Chiara drew her hand over her burning lips. 'I'm fine, really. Everything is fine.'

He glanced out through the big glass door at the street beyond. 'Was that Paolo who dropped you off?' he asked. 'Has he been upsetting you?'

'No, quite the opposite. He's been charming,' she promised, realizing she liked the fact that this rather handsome older man seemed so protective of her.

Giovanni sat down beside her and leaned his elbows on the

table. He looked wearier than he had yesterday, the lines around his eyes deeper, the silver tipping his hair more pronounced. 'Phew, what a day,' he groaned. 'I haven't stopped. We could do with a hard worker like your mother here, let me tell you.'

'Did she work hard?'

'She was perpetual motion. She made me look like a snail,' he joked. Then he grew serious. 'My father loved her like a daughter, you know. He hasn't spoken of her in years but last night, after you left, I couldn't shut him up. Today he's exhausted. I've had to send him home.'

'Oh, that's a pity. I had so many questions and I hoped he might be able to help me answer them.'

'Why not try asking me? I'll tell you anything I can. I knew your mother and I liked her a lot. We talked sometimes and she confided in me a little.'

She came straight out with it. 'Am I Marco's daughter?'

He shook his head. 'She always said you weren't and my father believed her. She only married him because she was forced to. In those days there were no such things as single mothers. A woman who fell before she was married was ruined . . . like Rosaria.'

'Rosaria was ruined?'

'That's right. A few months after Maria Domenica disappeared, everyone noticed that Rosaria was growing very stout indeed, then she too disappeared. Pepina tried to pass off the baby as her own but the whole town knew Paolo was Rosaria's child and that Marco was his father. In other circumstances she might have been made to marry him but she couldn't, of course, for he was still married to your mother.'

'Couldn't they have had that marriage annulled?'

Giovanni shook his head. 'After what had happened with Maria Domenica, I think Erminio would have rather died of shame than allowed another of his daughters to marry

Marco. No, Rosaria was kept at home. She had to watch while her brother and sisters each had their turn to marry, but no man would touch her.'

'God, no wonder she's such a cow.'

Giovanni laughed and the years fell away from him again. 'She's had her share of disappointments,' he agreed. 'But if I remember rightly she was a cow from the very beginning.'

Things were beginning to fall into place now for Chiara but still she had so many questions. What had happened to Marco, for instance?

Giovanni fetched a glass of Campari and soda and sat down to finish his story. He was a man who loved to talk to women and she liked that about him.

'Marco's parents were killed in a car accident,' he told her. 'They'd been drinking and they drove off the road in the dark. Marco inherited the farm and he sold it almost immediately for a good price to a developer who wanted to build apartments and houses. He used the cash to set himself up in Rome and the last I heard he was running a nightclub. If you really want to find him, it shouldn't be too difficult. And, after all, he's the only person alive who *truly* knows whether he is your father.'

Chiara took a sip of her Campari and nodded. It wasn't such a bad idea. But weren't there other men who might have fathered her?

Giovanni snorted with laughter when she asked him about the artist Rosaria had spoken of. 'You must mean Vincenzo? He painted a lot of the frescos in here, including the one of your mother. But there's no way he's your father, no way. You were already born by the time Maria Domenica met him. No, to me the most likely scenario is that your mother fell in love with someone during the year she spent in Rome.'

They talked their way through a couple more glasses of Campari, Giovanni dredging his mind for all he could remember about the old days. It didn't matter how trivial his stories seemed, Chiara drank them in gratefully.

'Is there anyone else you think I should talk to?' she finished. 'Anyone who knew my mother well enough to shed some light on who my father is?'

He considered her question carefully. 'There is Lucia, Pepina's sister, but she's so senile I'm not sure how much sense you'd get out of her. She lives in one of the older apartment blocks on the other side of the square. She has daughters, but they are both silly women and your mother never had much to do with them anyway.'

'I may go and see Lucia,' Chiara mused. 'But it sounds like Marco would be the best person for me to talk to. I suppose I'll have to try to track him down.'

'Cleopatra, that was the name of the nightclub,' Giovanni said triumphantly. 'I couldn't put my finger on it before. Flashy place, I expect, if Marco had anything to do with the decor.'

9

The days flew by. All were spent between the four walls of Pepina's kitchen and yet they offered infinite variety. The old lady taught her everything she knew and each evening, once they'd finished and washed up their pots and pans, they feasted on the dishes they'd created. Some days the earthy taste of a simple *pasta e fagioli* seemed to Chiara like perfection, other days a bowl of cabbage, arborio rice, pancetta and garlic simmered in dense chicken stock was all she wanted to eat for the rest of her life. The food was robust and flavoursome. It made the most of the vegetables each season offered, for the Carrozza family, like most others in the neighbourhood, had once been too poor to afford much meat.

In the morning Pepina would take her out to the vegetable patch to see what was ready to be harvested. As they moved between the untidy rows their legs would brush the straggling basil plants, filling the air with their pungent perfume.

Pepina showed her how to pick the tall, spiky artichokes before they turned to seed and later she stuffed roughly chopped garlic, parsley and salt between their tight, green leaves and steamed them in a little water and olive oil. Chiara couldn't wait to eat them. Greedily she dipped leaf after leaf in the oily juices and pulled them between her teeth.

They also plucked shiny red peppers from the vines and fried them in olive oil with a little onion, then simmered them in tomatoes. When she thought Chiara's back was turned, Pepina tried to sneak a pinch or two of a secret ingredient into the pan.

'What was that?' Chiara demanded.

'Nothing,' her grandmother promised, her eyes too wide and her smile too stretched for true innocence.

Finally, after some cajoling, she relented. 'Sugar,' she confessed. 'Just a little bit of sugar to sweeten my *peperonata*.'

Chiara was disappointed. She'd imagined some special herb that only her grandmother knew about. But in truth there were no secret ingredients. Only a pinch or two of sugar to lift the dish above the ordinary.

In Pepina's unruly little vegetable plot, tangled among the artichokes, peppers and basil, there were glossy plum tomatoes ripening in the sun. The earth they grew in looked hard and dry and yet mysteriously they were more like a tomato than anything Chiara had ever tasted before. As she bit into their skin, they exploded with juicy sweetness. The watery, pulpy balls they sold at the supermarket didn't deserve the name tomato, she decided, as her hands grew green from picking them and her tongue red from the eating.

On the hotter afternoons when Pepina grew tired, Paolo would put down his camera and help out. Together they made *polpette di carne*, succulent meatballs simmered in a tomato sauce. Paolo mixed an egg yolk with the ground pork, churning a little garlic, onion, stale bread, flatleaf parsley and seasoning into the pink gooey mess. And then together they shaped the sticky balls with their hands. 'Mmm, my favourites,' he declared. Pepina supervised him shallow-frying the meatballs to seal in the flavour before slipping them into the bubbling sauce to cook to perfection.

Some dishes, Chiara knew, would never find their way back to England or into the pages of a book. One day, for instance, Pepina produced a pasta pan full of fresh water and squirming live eels with slick black skins. She smoked them over her wood-fired barbecue and they tasted fantastic but Chiara didn't bother taking notes. Eels were unlikely ever to be on the menu in Islington, Notting Hill and the Home

Counties, and it was people in places like those who bought her cookbooks.

Some days Pepina made her rise extra early. No bread was made on those mornings for this was the time her grandmother had set aside to devote to celebration food, the more elaborate dishes enjoyed all over Campania on *festa* days and saint days. First they made a *ragu*, the queen of all tomato sauces, rich with chunks of pork and veal and studded with rolls of beef filled with garlic and pine nuts. They cooked it slowly on the lowest of heats for six hours, stirring frequently and adding water until the meat leached its colour into the tomatoes and the dark sauce developed an intense, penetrating flavour.

Then they made a *sartu*, a moulded case of rice filled with layers of delicacies: porcini mushrooms, tiny meatballs, spicy sausages and much, much more. The smell as the giant rice cake browned in the oven was exquisite and Chiara almost drooled when the time came to cut off a wedge, drizzle it with the *ragu* and take her first taste.

Pepina saved the best until last. Her *timballo di maccheroni* was a stunning creation – a pastry drum filled with pasta, flavoured with *ragu* and *parmigiano*, and layered with salami, peas, fried aubergines, creamy ricotta and diced mozzarella.

Rosaria's eyes grew as big as dinner-plates when she saw it enthroned on the kitchen table. 'A *timballo*,' she sighed. 'Mamma, you haven't made one of those for years and years.'

Chiara's aunt couldn't resist showing off how much she knew about the food of Campania. 'We hardly ever use garlic and onion in the same dish,' she'd say airily as she watched the two women chopping, peeling and slicing. 'It overpowers all the other flavours. You don't have to be greedy and fill your food with a hundred different things, you know, Chiara. Sometimes one ingredient is enough. See how Mamma makes her ravioli? All she stuffs it with is a little ricotta cheese. There's not even a speck of parsley in the filling. Oh, and another thing, there's no need to drown your pasta in sauce. All you need is enough to provide a coating.'

Sometimes Pepina told stories about the old days and Rosaria did what she could to translate them. 'Mamma says that in Naples they used to hang the *maccheroni* on washing lines to dry. No matter how poor you were, there was always pasta to sustain you. Meat, now that was a different story. Some families couldn't afford it at all. We always had it here though,' she added proudly. 'Papa kept cages of rabbits at the back of the house and once or twice a week he'd kill one for the pot. In this house there was always good food to fill our bellies.'

As Rosaria looked on, the two women spent hours at a stretch working side by side. At first Chiara worried that the effort would be too much for the old lady but, as the days passed, Pepina seemed not tired but younger and stronger. Erminio would sidle past once or twice a day, dipping his fingers in the food, tasting, savouring and stealing whatever he could. Laughing, Pepina always shooed him out of the kitchen with a tea towel the way she did the chickens.

At night Chiara put her laptop on the old pine kitchen table to type up notes about the dishes they'd created together. The words flowed from her brain so fast her clumsy fingers could hardly keep up. All her passion for food, quite lost when she was working on the bread book, had been recaptured at last and she didn't want to forget anything – not a single ingredient, not the taste of the first forkful of each new dish and, most especially, not the look of quiet joy on her grandmother's face as she shared all her knowledge.

Paolo always seemed somewhere about the place. If he had any sort of a job, it couldn't be taking up much of his time. He was mysterious when she asked him exactly what he did for a living. 'Business,' he said in a tone that didn't invite further questions. He took to hanging round the kitchen during the day and sitting beside Chiara at night as she wrote, topping up her glass from time to time with rough red wine. He hadn't kissed her again but he hadn't had a chance for they were never alone. Chiara made sure of that, she simply didn't trust herself.

Pepina may have been old but she wasn't stupid. Her wily eye was always trained on Paolo and Chiara when they were together and, if she could, she'd send Paolo out on errands that involved driving to town and back, four or five times a day. It was clear her grandmother had an unshakeable belief that Marco had fathered them both, decided Chiara. As for herself, while it now seemed unlikely, she wasn't prepared to take the risk.

One evening she felt so desperately confused, she waited until Paolo had driven into town and then reversed the charges to Harriet at The Office. An Italian male voice answered the phone and for a moment Chiara thought she had the wrong number.

'No, no, it's Eduardo here,' the voice said, as she automatically began to apologize.

'Eduardo, what are you doing there?'

'I'm working behind the bar. Harriet, she poached me from Bar Italia.'

He sounded smug, decided Chiara, which probably meant that by now he and Harriet were lovers.

When her friend finally took the phone she seemed a million miles away, her voice strange, her accent unfamiliar. 'God, what a mess you're in,' she said finally when Chiara had finished explaining the situation.

'I know I'm in a mess, dammit, but what am I going to do?'

'Well, do you really like this Paolo chap?'

'Like? Like? No, I don't bloody like him, Harriet, I'm crazy about him. Every time I look at him I . . .' Words failed her and she stammered to a halt.

'You've said that before about other men, you know, Chiara.'

'But this time it's different,' she wailed.

Harriet said nothing. All Chiara could hear was the steady hum of conversation and the gentle clinking of glasses. Although it was still early there must quite a crowd building up in The Office and for a moment she wished she were there too, hogging the best seat at the end of the bar and spending recklessly on good champagne. With the phone still glued to her ear, she looked around at the yellowing kitchen walls that had become the boundary of her world in the past days and longed to escape back to her real life.

'Harriet? Harriet, are you there?'

'Um, yes, sorry. I've got a bit of a queue building up here. The people of Soho are thirsty today.'

'I think I might come home,' Chiara told her, only half meaning it.

'But aren't you enjoying the time you're spending with your grandparents?'

'Yes but—'

'No, look, Chiara,' Harriet was exasperated, 'You're not letting this man come between you and your family, do you hear? Tell me, why do you always have to do this?'

'What do you mean? Do what?' Chiara was indignant.

There was the muffled popping of a cork and the hiss of Champagne foaming in a glass, then Harriet spoke again. The volume of her voice rose to compete with the noise of fifty people drinking as she launched into a lecture. 'Why do you always have to lose the plot like this when it comes to men? You're so sensible in every other area of your life. Can't you just play it cool?'

'I suppose so . . .' Chiara tailed off miserably.

'Your mother ran away from San Giulio,' Harriet finished. 'I can't believe you're going to do the same thing.'

Suitably chastened, Chiara put down the phone and plugged in her laptop. By the time she heard Paolo's car outside she was halfway through typing up the day's notes.

Paolo had gone into town quite late clutching a long shopping list, scrawled in Pepina's barely legible hand. He returned weighed down with parcels and supermarket carrier bags full of food, essentials for the next day's cooking. Empty-handed, Rosaria trailed into the kitchen behind him. When she set eyes on Chiara, she didn't linger. With a nod in her direction, she was off to her own room at the back of the rambling house.

Erminio and Pepina had gone too. Exhausted by the day's cooking and eating, they'd needed to lie down, and so, for the first time since the day he'd kissed her, she and Paolo were alone.

He sat beside her at the table and read the words on her screen over her shoulder. 'How's it going?' he asked finally.

Chiara loved the sound of his voice. It was low and sexy, as rich as warm chocolate and, while sometimes he struggled to shape the unfamiliar English words, the mispronunciations only added to his charm.

'It's going fine,' she told him, looking up from the screen and seeing his smooth-skinned, long-lashed face far too close to her own.

Her body craved him even if her mind knew it was wrong and now it betrayed her by responding to his proximity with a little hum of desire. As he reached over and touched her upper arm, the hum became a song despite her best efforts to silence it.

'Paolo, please don't,' she chided, snatching her arm away.

'I don't understand.'

'Yes, you do.'

His eyes flashed green with petulance as he slammed down his hand on the table and swore beneath his breath in Italian. 'What do I have to do to convince you? Is the word of Rosaria not enough? You heard her say that we are not brother and sister. We don't look alike, we don't sound alike, we are different in every way. And I promise you, if it were unnatural or wrong, I wouldn't feel this unbearable desire for you.' He looked at her for a moment and then repeated in his melting chocolate voice, 'I feel desire for you, Chiara.'

This time she gave herself up to the kiss completely. She let his arms encircle her and the hot musky smell of him wash over her. His lips worked urgently and his tongue pressed hard against her lips until she surrendered.

One hand had reached round to her breast and he was kneading it as firmly as his grandmother kneaded her dough when, from behind them, Chiara heard the whine of a door being pushed open and the shuffling of an old woman's feet across the flagstones. Paolo sprang back but it was too late, Pepina had seen them together. The words that spilled from her lips were furious and Paolo flushed and drew back even further as she spat out sentence after excoriating sentence of angry Italian. Chiara felt shame wash over her, but the old woman's anger didn't touch her, it was reserved for her grandson.

Finally Pepina turned her back on them and noisily began to unpack the shopping bags Paolo had left carelessly scattered over the table and floor. He looked at Chiara, as the old woman banged and slammed her cupboard doors. 'When you go back to England, I want to come with you,' he told her.

'I don't think that's a good idea.'

'I knew you'd say that but I don't care. It's a free country. Even if you are too rude to invite me, I'll come all the same.'

'Paolo, what good would that do?'

Chiara realized that London was the last place she wanted Paolo to be. Somehow he seemed too bright, too dazzling for the greyness of the city. She couldn't bear to see him in her world, he'd hurt her eyes. She tried to imagine him in The Office, clutching a glass of champagne and conversing with the strange mix of broadsheet journalists, minor aristocrats and would-be artists who frequented the place. She was certain it would never sit right. Even if Paolo did turn out to be only a cousin after all, how would they ever make a relationship work?

He was looking moody now and for the first time Chiara saw in his face some resemblance to his mother. It was in the way his mouth turned down and his beautiful face turned to stone. She longed to see the scowl disappear and for him to return to perfection.

'Paolo,' she wheedled, 'don't be cross. I'm not going to disappear for ever. I have to go back to London at some stage to see my publisher but I don't have to stay for all that long.'

He smiled and, risking Pepina's wrath, leaned over to quickly pinch her cheek. 'I just don't want you to disappear the way your mother did,' he told her. 'It would destroy us all.'

10

Chiara couldn't concentrate on food any longer. Her mind drifted as she watched Pepina stewing octopus in its own juices. She forgot to stir a sauce and it caught. She left the pork chops and fennel roasting in the oven until they began to burn. She let the pasta boil too long and had to throw it out and start again. Her mind was full of Paolo, the kiss they'd shared and the rush of shame and desire that had washed over her afterwards.

She felt confused and angry. Why had her mother been so secretive? Couldn't she have confided in at least one person when she found she'd fallen pregnant? It was all very well for Paolo to say they didn't share a father but there didn't seem to be anyone in San Giulio who could tell her for sure.

Then Chiara remembered that Giovanni had mentioned someone it might be worth looking up – Pepina's sister Lucia. He'd said she was senile and didn't make much sense, but still it seemed worth paying a visit.

Lucia lived in one of the original apartment buildings. With marble floors and high ceilings, it was more gracious than the squat boxes surrounding it. And it was just off the main piazza, round the corner from Caffe Angeli, which meant it wasn't too much trouble for Giovanni to pull off his apron and take a half-hour break to come and act as her translator.

The old lady's Italian was slurred and confused. Chiara wouldn't have understood a word she'd said even if she had spent more time listening to her language tapes.

Lucia had bleached blonde hair, remarkably smooth skin

and she wore a chunky gold charm bracelet around her wrist and a profusion of chains about her neck. She might have looked entirely normal except that she couldn't sit still for a second. As Giovanni tried to talk to her, she moved about her kitchen, wiping down cupboard doors and polishing handles with an obsessive energy. In the corners of the ceiling, though, Chiara could see cobwebs looping and the floor was dotted with dustballs.

When she heard her mother's name repeated once or twice, Chiara asked impatiently, 'What's she saying?'

'I'm not sure. I asked her about your mother and whether she confided in her when she got back from Rome and all she keeps saying is, "She loved him too much, she loved him too much." '

'Who did she love too much?' Chiara demanded. 'Marco?'

The old lady stopped her polishing and turned to her. '*No, no, non Marco*,' she said sounding sane and certain. '*Tuo papa*.'

'Yes, but who was her father?' Giovanni pressed the confused old lady.

But Lucia had gone back to her cleaning and babbling again and Giovanni could only shrug when she asked him to translate. 'There's no point. None of it is making any sense to me.'

They had drunk the tall glasses of flat lemonade she'd offered and were just about to take their leave when the old woman had another moment of clarity. She took Chiara's face gently in her hands and spoke directly to her before kissing her goodbye. Giovanni stifled a smile and waited until they were outside the front door before he translated her words.

'Lucia said that if only they'd given her a picture or two, some ornaments, maybe a decent piece of furniture to brighten up that miserable place, Maria Domenica might never have run away. And then she said that those Manzoni wives were always a stingy lot.'

Despite herself, Chiara giggled. 'Oh it's not funny really. The poor, confused old thing,' she said, her hand over her mouth.

Giovanni laughed too. 'For a moment there I really thought she was going to tell you something important. But, if she ever knew anything, it's well gone now.' He led her to one of the benches that lay in the shade of a tall palm. 'Let's sit here for a little while. I don't have to go back to the *caffe* just yet.'

'Have you always worked there?' Chiara asked him. He nodded. 'Yes, ever since I was a boy and I used to get into your mother's way and mix up all the orders.'

'Did you never want to do anything else?'

'Of course.' Giovanni held his hands, palms open, before her. 'I meant to do so many things. I was going to study and travel. I learned English because I thought one day I'd go to live in America and make my fortune. But in the end something stopped me leaving San Giulio. My father maybe? I knew he'd be so lonely once I was gone. And then there was always the hope that your mother would come back one day. We thought she might.'

'So you waited for her?'

'I suppose.'

'Were you perhaps a little bit in love with her?' she teased.

Giovanni tucked his hands between his knees and squeezed them tight. 'Love? Well, I don't know, I was just a boy after all,' he said, sounding serious. 'Certainly I had a big crush on her. She was pretty, clever and funny after all. But love . . . I don't know.'

'And you've never married?' Chiara wondered out loud.

Giovanni stood up awkwardly and she realized she had pried too far. Whatever this man had felt for her mother was locked inside him just as securely as poor Lucia's secrets were hidden inside her.

11

Chiara left San Giulio with far more than she'd had when she arrived. The little backpack had been supplemented with a suitcase packed with lighter clothes she'd had to buy to take her through the hot days she'd spent bent over Pepina's stove, simmering, stirring and tasting. And her laptop was full of notes and ideas.

At last she had made up her mind what she was going to do next. She *would* write a book. But not just an ordinary volume of recipes. It would be a book full of sadness, joy and, most importantly, passion. She would tell the story of how her mother had fled San Giulio and how she had rediscovered it. And she would share the secrets she had learned within the four flaking walls of Pepina's kitchen.

When she'd shared her plans with her grandmother, the old lady had reached out and squeezed her hand. Paolo seemed elated too. Even as he kissed Chiara goodbye he had still worn a smile on his face.

Ahead of her lay more weeks of cooking, testing and refining the recipes in her own kitchen until she was certain they were completely foolproof. At that stage Janey would call in the photographer and food stylist and Chiara would have to trust her recipes to someone else.

Before she left town Chiara had spent an entire day in Caffe Angeli. With endless patience Giovanni had taught her how to use the temperamental Gaggia and she'd helped him serve up coffee and shell-shaped *sfogliatelle* pastries rich with ricotta all morning. At lunchtime Franco had baked the long-promised pizza and she'd eaten it sitting on the red leather banquette beneath the Madonna with her mother's face. She'd even helped them clean and sweep up at the end of the day, stacking chairs on tables and talking nonsense with Giovanni just as Maria Domenica must have done all those years ago.

She could imagine her mother slotting easily into the simple rhythm of life in the *caffe*. Sustained by strong coffee and good gossip, she could have worked hard all the days of her life side by side with Franco and Giovanni. Her existence outside these walls must have been unbearable to have driven Maria Domenica away from this easy happiness, Chiara realized.

The two men hadn't wanted to say goodbye and Franco had clutched her in a long, tight embrace. Then Giovanni had hugged her against his strong, spare body and held her there for a heartbeat or two longer than she'd expected. At least they hadn't wept like Pepina and Erminio. Despite all her promises that she'd return very soon, her grandparents had been inconsolable.

Rosaria had emerged at the last minute to give her two quick, dry kisses on the cheeks and although Chiara was sure she'd be glad to see the back of her, her face had worn a benign smile.

Paolo stayed with her until she boarded the bus. As they said goodbye he kissed her long and hard, right there in the middle of the piazza, not caring who saw. In his pocket he had a piece of paper with her phone number and address in London neatly printed on it. 'I'll call you every night,' he promised. 'And if you don't come back soon I'll come over to get you.'

She hugged him and breathed in his musky smell one last time. 'I'll miss you,' she told him, fighting not to cry.

And then, just as she was climbing on board the bus, with one foot on the first step of the platform and the other still on the cobbles of San Giulio, he said the words she'd both dreaded and longed for: 'I love you, Chiara.'

The driver tooted his horn to speed them up and there was only time to squeeze Paolo's hand before the doors slid shut and the bus lurched off down the corridor of ugly apartment buildings.

Chiara's mind was full of Paolo for most of the trip back to Rome. It was crazy even to think about having a relationship with him and yet, with each day that passed, she was more determined to try. Yes, there were cultural differences, but people coped with those all the time. All she had to do was sort out once and for all the messy business of who had fathered her, and any other problems that cropped up after that could surely be handled.

Rome seemed so gracious and proud after the ugly dustiness of San Giulio. She took a taxi from right outside Stazione Termini telling the driver, 'I want to go to a nightclub called Cleopatra.'

'I know it but it won't be open yet, it's far too early,' he replied. 'And if you don't mind me saying so, it's probably not your sort of place. Only the kids go there.'

'That's fine. I'm not planning to stay and party,' she told him, feeling faintly depressed that even the taxi drivers considered her too ancient to go nightclubbing these days.

The club looked fairly impressive from the street. A huge sphinx head stared down from above a set of intricate bronze doors. They were firmly closed and locked and she had to hammer on them for a full five minutes before anyone responded. The man who finally opened the doors was in his early fifties with greasy hennaed hair falling down his back and thick gold hoop earrings in each ear. 'What do you want? We're closed,' he barked at her.

'Are you Marco Manzoni?' she asked hesitantly, and felt some relief when he shook his head in reply. 'Well, is he here?'

'Who wants to know?'

For a moment Chiara considered saying, 'His daughter,' but thought better of it. The bronze door was likely to be slammed shut in her face far more quickly than it had been opened, she suspected.

'I'm just an old family friend he hasn't seen in a very long while,' she said in the end.

He pulled open the door a little wider and Chiara caught sight of pyramids and more sphinxes looming out of the darkness behind him. 'You'd better come on in then. I'm sure Marco will be pleased to see you. I've never known him not be pleased to see a pretty girl.'

He sent her down an unlit corridor towards the bar. A man was sitting there alone on one of the barstools, languidly eating olives out of a martini glass.

'Are you Marco Manzoni?' she asked. He turned round slowly. She knew the answer to her question as soon as she took her first look at his face. Long lashes brushed cheeks that were as smooth as a girl's. His lips were full and soft, his hands manicured, his clothes beautifully tailored. Still chewing his olive, he nodded and waited for her to say more.

'My name is Chiara,' she told him.

He smiled at her and for a moment she thought he must know who she was.

'Chiara, that's a pretty name,' he said, brushing his hand quickly over his neat, short hair. 'But darling, I'm sorry, I don't remember you. In my business you tend to meet a lot of pretty girls, you know, so it can't be helped if one or two of them slip your mind.' He smiled at her once more. 'I'd be very happy to get to know you all over again though,' he told her in his half Italian, half fake-American accent. 'And I'm sure I won't forget you a second time.'

He was flirting with her, she realized to her horror, and she was thankful his son Paolo had inherited only his looks and not his phoney charm and lascivious old-man chat-up lines.

'Look, it's hardly surprising you don't remember me,' she told him briskly, 'because I was very young the last time we met. But I'm sure you'll remember my mother. Her name was Maria Domenica Carrozza.'

She'd expected him to be shocked or at least surprised, but he only raised an eyebrow and replied, 'Ah, my lovely wife. And how is she?'

'Dead actually.'

He shrugged and said without feeling, 'I'm sorry for your loss.'

'Really? I don't imagine for one second that you are.' Her voice was hostile now. She'd taken a strong dislike to him and couldn't be bothered disguising it.

'Look, I don't know what your mother told you about me—' he began.

'Nothing,' she interrupted. 'She never said a word about you to me.'

Now he looked surprised. His vanity didn't allow for the idea he'd been forgotten. He took a slug of the martini and tilted the glass towards her. 'I'm having breakfast. Care to join me?'

'Bit early for me.'

'I'm a little surprised she never mentioned me, you know. She could have told you that I did my best by you, by both of you. It wasn't easy being saddled with a wife and baby when I was still pretty much a child myself. But, I'm pleased to see you've grown up into a beautiful woman. Why don't you come and sit with me, have a glass of mineral water and talk about the old days?'

He was *still* flirting with her. Now he'd shifted into a pool of light and she could see the puffiness beneath his eyes and the red broken veins in his cheeks and around his nose. His hair was a flat, matt black that betrayed the cheap hair dye he'd been using.

'I only came for one reason,' she told him, 'and that was to ask you a question.'

'Yes?'

'Are you my father?'

He threw his head back and laughed heartily, his gold-filled teeth glinting in his open mouth. 'Me? Oh no, I don't think so.'

'You don't think so or you're sure?'

'I'm sure, I'm sure. I probably do have a few daughters littered around the country but you're not one of them, darling. Definitely not.'

'How can you be so certain?'

'Because I didn't sleep with your mother until after you were born. I married her because I was young and stupid and I allowed myself to be forced into it by our parents. But I'm not your father.'

'So who is?'

He drained his glass, ate his final olive and considered her question for a moment. 'Now if you'd asked me that back when Maria Domenica ran away the second time I'd have pointed my finger directly at Vincenzo, the artist who painted those ridiculous pictures in Caffe Angeli. You've seen the one of your mother, I take it?'

She nodded.

'I only got a glimpse of it. Franco banned me from the place after Maria Domenica disappeared. Must have blamed me for some reason, I suppose.'

'So this Vincenzo character. You think he was my father?'

He lit a cigarette and sucked on it greedily, blowing the smoke into Chiara's face. 'No. I did back then but not any more. After she went he didn't seem to care and he certainly never made any attempt to follow her. I still see him from time to time around Rome. He paints tourists' portraits at the Spanish Steps, the Coliseum or in the Via Veneto.'

Chiara was growing impatient. 'So if not him, then who?' she demanded.

'Good question. I don't know the answer, I'm afraid. It's

true that we were in Rome at the same time, me and your mother, but I never saw her. She was working in some *caffe* by the Spanish Steps and I was working crazy hours in a butcher's shop in Trastevere. Our paths hardly ever crossed. You're some man's daughter but not mine.'

Chiara wanted to believe him but there was nothing about Marco that made her think he could be trusted. He was a liar and a cheat. He'd abandoned Paolo and Rosaria.

'You do have a son though, in San Giulio,' she put in.

'Handsome young Paolo.' He flicked his ash into the empty martini glass on the bar. 'He has nothing to complain about. He cashes the very generous cheque I send every month and I'm happy to say I never hear a word from him.'

Someone had switched on all the house lights and in the brightness the pyramids were shown up as badly painted polystyrene and the sphinxes yellow with nicotine.

'I have to go,' she told Marco.

'Come back later when the place is pumping,' he invited. 'I'll shout you a few drinks.'

She didn't bother to reply, just turned and walked down the corridor past tacky fake papyrus pictures of Egyptian stick figures. The club smelled stale and she was happy to find herself out on the street again, the bronze doors clanging shut behind her.

If Marco was telling the truth then there was now nothing standing in the way of her relationship with Paolo. She ought to have felt pleased but there was only numbness where happiness was meant to be.

12

People kept shoving Chiara off pavements. Office workers running late for work elbowed her out of their way and straight into the path of motorbike couriers going the wrong direction up a one-way street in the rush to deliver a parcel. Tourists with their eyes on maps blundered into her as she walked and black cab drivers drove straight past when she waved an arm in the air to flag them down. She'd lost her London-proofing, she realized. The weeks in sleepy San Giulio had left her rusty on the rules of the city.

It hadn't felt like coming home at all. She'd stepped off the Heathrow Express train in Paddington Station and London's dense sprawl of streets had closed in around her like a trap. She'd only just arrived and was already working out how soon she could leave again.

There had been no one at the station to meet her for the simple reason that she hadn't let anyone know she was coming. As she'd struggled to drag her bags out of the train and fought for a luggage trolley, she'd been aware of the hugging and kissing and greeting going on around her and had thought of Paolo then and how far away from him she was now.

She'd sat in the traffic, breathing in diesel fumes from the old Routemaster bus in front, watching the meter click round in the cab. The driver had tried to strike up a conversation with her. 'Been on holiday then, love?' he'd asked. But she'd been monosyllabic enough for him to become quickly discouraged.

Harriet hadn't been expecting her and the apartment was a mess. There seemed to be a little of Eduardo in every room – his grooming products in the bathroom, a pair of his shoes left on the kitchen floor, his denim jacket on the chair in the hallway.

Chiara had been right, he and Harriet were sharing a bed. But their love life was too exuberant to be confined to one room and, in the days that followed, she never quite knew when she might stumble on the pair of them hot and half-dressed in the kitchen, or locked together frantically in the steamy bathroom. She started feeling like an intruder in the small apartment and, although Harriet hadn't so much as dropped a hint, took to buying the *Evening Standard* each day and turning first to the Property for Sale and Flats for Rent columns. They made depressing reading and Chiara quickly realized that even a small place at the far end of a tube line was going to suck up a big chunk of what was left of the money she'd made from *Queen of the British Kitchen*. The royalties were still trickling in but sales had slowed right down. Chiara couldn't avoid it any longer. It was time to go and see her publisher Janey and explain what had happened to the promised book on baking.

The phone call was made and an appointment set up. This meeting wasn't going to be an informal chat over a restaurant table. Instead Janey would receive her, she was told, in the shiny executive boardroom of her large, successful publishing company.

Chiara made an effort to spruce herself up. She had her hair, which had grown wild lately, tamed by an expensive hairdresser and she bought new clothes, a matching pale blue skirt and jacket from some new designer line she'd found at Harvey Nichols.

'My God, you're wearing a suit,' Harriet exclaimed, when she popped into The Office for a fortifying half-glass before the meeting.

'If I'm going to take on Janey I need to look like I'm the type of person who speaks her language,' she explained gloomily. 'I'm going to have to talk marketing strategies and leveraging opportunities and product endorsements.'

Harriet shuddered and filled her glass right up to the brim. 'Please don't get all grown up on me.'

'Look, don't worry, if Janey goes for my book idea the suit will be straight off and I'll be locked away in the kitchen wearing my old stained apron for the foreseeable future.'

As Chiara had feared it might, the meeting got off to a very bad start. Janey's face fell when she heard of the death of the baking book. 'But I thought . . . I thought it was all agreed. I'd imagined that's what you'd been working on all this time.'

'I know, I'm sorry.' Chiara didn't know what else to say.

Janey blinked and swallowed hard. 'The marketing department had product tie-ins set up for the bread book,' she continued in a tight little voice. 'There was interest in a TV series and I'm pretty sure you'd have got sponsorship for it. You might have told me you'd changed your mind before we put in all this groundwork.'

Chiara perched on the edge of her chair and leaned a blue-suited elbow on the glass boardroom table. 'I know, I'm sorry,' she repeated. 'But what I've got instead is a million times better than the baking thing. Let me explain the whole idea.'

Janey stared at her for a moment. Her blonde hair was pulled back from her face so tightly it was practically creating a mini-facelift, her black cashmere cardigan was buttoned up to her neck. She didn't seem to trust herself to speak. She was clearly cross.

Chiara pulled a bundle of pictures out of her briefcase. They were the photos Paolo had taken but on the top of the pile was a shot of Paolo himself, laughing at whoever had been wielding the camera, as he tasted tomato sauce from a wooden spoon.

'See this man here?' Chiara turned the photo round to face her publisher. 'Well, I'm in love with him. Only I'm not a hundred per cent sure we'll ever be together because there's still a tiny chance he may be my brother.'

Janey's eyes had widened and her eyebrows were raised.

Chiara slid over a shot of Pepina rolling out gnocchi on the worn pine table. 'See this woman? She's my grandmother and because of her my mother became a bigamist.'

She'd captured Janey's attention now so she went on to explain the whole story. 'And that's what my book will be about,' she said at the end. 'It'll be about my search for the truth about my Italian family and the amazing cuisine I discovered along the way.'

'My God,' said Janey, awed. 'It's like Jerry Springer with food.'

'No,' Chiara corrected. 'It's like Jerry Springer with sensational food.'

'This guy.' Janey waved Paolo's picture in the air. 'Does he cook?'

'No, the old lady is the cook.'

Janey stared at the photo again. 'God, he's gorgeous though, isn't he? And you say he might be your brother?'

Her pique forgotten, she began to sift with increasing excitement through the pictures of Chiara bent over Pepina's old stove and of the aged pine table groaning beneath platters of food.

'Some of these are nice,' she remarked. 'But most of the food we'd have to re-shoot and style properly or it'll wind up looking like cat food.'

'That's OK,' Chiara nodded.

'And this business of your father. Who is *he* exactly?' Janey was glowing pink and she'd undone the top button of her cardigan.

'Well, that's the whole point, I don't know. I'm hoping the publicity from the book may jog someone's memory, bring someone out of the woodwork. The thing is, until I find my real father, I can't begin to consider starting a relationship with Paolo.'

'Well there's DNA testing,' Janey suggested. 'This Marco bloke, can't you get a strand of his hair or something?'

'I'd considered that, of course.' Feeling more relaxed, Chiara leaned into the comfort of the high-backed chair. 'But just ruling out Marco isn't enough. No, I have to find my father. I won't be completely satisfied otherwise. I need what the Americans call closure.'

Janey glanced at her watch. 'It's getting late,' she noted. 'Why don't we get out of this place and go and have a glass of Chardonnay round the corner. I want us to have a good, long chat about Italian food.'

Half a bottle of Chardonnay later, Janey had forgotten all about baking. Chiara could tell there were ideas bubbling away in the back of her mind, a saucepan or two of clever concepts that Janey would simmer down into money-making plans. But she didn't care about all that. She just wanted to get away, to start testing and refining the recipes, checking the necessary ingredients were widely enough available and begin writing. She needed the time and space to write the story of Maria Domenica's life.

Deep down, Chiara didn't truly believe she would ever find the man her mother had fallen in love with that year in Rome, the man whose genes she carried. But the idea seemed to have gripped Janey. The sheer human interest married to hearty, robust peasant food smelled like a winning combination to her.

'How long?' Janey asked. 'How long will it take you to write it?'

Chiara was honest. 'I don't know. There's lots of work to do. Plus I have to get up to Liverpool to see my dad Alex at some point and I want to go back to Italy to finish the book there.'

'I want it fast,' said Janey crisply. 'Do I have a deal?'

Spilling back onto the pavement, her head muzzy from afternoon drinking, Chiara felt a moment of elation followed by a feeling of rising panic at the amount of work she had to do. She was the hardest working lazy person she knew. Given half a chance she'd cook for pleasure and spend the rest of her time reading or taking Harriet's dog for long walks. Now every hour of every day was going to be crammed full of hard work.

Harriet and Eduardo were waiting for her in The Office, a bottle of champagne on ice and Salty panting at their feet.

'How did you know we'd be celebrating?' Chiara asked.

'One of us has got to have some confidence in you,' Harriet replied.

'I don't know.' Chiara watched her friend fill three glasses. 'I've got so much to do. I should get myself upstairs straight away and make a start.'

'No, no, no.' Harriet pushed a full glass towards her. 'You're allowed to spend a night celebrating before you get all grown up and serious again. You can shoot upstairs quickly though if you like and change out of that awful suit. I think people might be staring at you.'

Eduardo seemed to have one hand resting on Harriet at all times, Chiara noticed. To her it suggested ownership but Harriet didn't appear to mind. She was thriving on the intimacy, her beauty shining several watts brighter. She seemed to have gained softer curves to round out her angular frame.

The champagne was enjoyed, the bottle drained. Salty at her heels, Chiara climbed the creaking wooden stairs, eager for her bed. There was a message from Paolo on the answerphone. 'I miss you, darling,' he told her, his voice rich and buttery. 'When are you coming home to San Giulio?'

She'd go soon, decided Chiara. She couldn't stay away too long.

13

Paolo was standing in the exact spot Chiara had last seen him, beside the bus stop in the main piazza of San Giulio. To her eyes the town seemed different, more vibrant and colourful than before. The heat of late summer had stripped the layers of clothes from people's bodies and turned their bare limbs golden brown. Wearing high heels and short skirts, bags slung casually over their shoulders, the girls looked like they'd sped on their Vespas straight off the pages of Italian *Vogue*. And there waiting, head and shoulders above everyone else, was the most perfect man she'd ever seen, who somehow, and she couldn't imagine how, was managing to look more beautiful than ever.

Perhaps he'd been sunning himself on the beach, thought Chiara, as Paolo caught sight of her staring at him through the window and began to wave excitedly with both hands and bob up and down on the spot. Perhaps he'd changed his hairstyle or lost weight, she didn't really care. She just wanted to be off this bus, with her feet beside his on the cobbled piazza of San Giulio.

'*Bella*, *bella*,' he was mouthing at her through the glass.

When at last she allowed him to kiss her his lips were warm. The skin on his face smelled of suntan oil and his body of fresh sweat. 'I'm so relieved I made it here in time,' he told her between kisses. 'I was so busy working on the farm, I almost left it too late to drive into town.'

'What work have you been so busy with?' she asked.

He laughed in reply. 'You'll see,' he told her.

As Paolo drove, Chiara sneaked little glances at his profile. She never failed to be astounded by his perfection – the smoothness of his skin, his even tan, the faultless engineering of his bone structure. Harriet was right, she really had lost the plot. She'd been like this all her dating life, falling in love far too easily and then craving the men she fell for like some women crave milk chocolate. But this time she'd outdone herself. Paolo was the most unsuitable man yet. Even though she was now almost convinced they didn't share a father, he was still her cousin. And while Chiara was pretty sure marriage between cousins was allowed, it seemed wrong to feel this way about him.

Brother or cousin, they had the same blood in their veins. The thought kept coming back to Chiara, nagging at her. At times she allowed herself to worry about it, turning the situation over and over in her mind and wondering what she should do about it. Cling to this chance for love? Or let it go and perhaps never come across another one? There was no easy answer.

Chiara didn't want to think about all that now. Here she was at last, sitting beside Paolo and heading towards the old farmhouse where her grandparents were waiting to greet her. She didn't want to worry about anything. She only wanted to feel happy.

Something was different, she realized, as they drove up the dusty driveway.

The place still looked very much like the haphazard little house surrounded by peach trees that she'd seen for the first time in her mother's drawings, but something had shifted.

A fresh coat of paint, blue to match the sky, a rustic, long wooden table and a row of chairs beneath the lemon tree beside the kitchen door. The vegetable patch had been freshly hoed, planted and weeded. Even the dog and chickens looked like they'd had a bath. And out the back, between the rows of peach trees in the orchard, some kind of building work was going on.

Paolo looked sideways at her and smiled. 'We've been making a few improvements,' he told her.

'So I see,' she replied, and was about to say more when the door opened and two ecstatic old people spilled out and fought to be the first to greet her.

As she hugged her grandmother and grandfather, Chiara felt she was back where she belonged. Then she caught sight of Rosaria hovering in the doorway, staring at her. She looked quite different too, sort of deflated. Her hips and belly weren't spreading as far as they used to, the puffiness around her face was gone and finally Chiara could see how once she might have been a pretty girl. She looked back at her for a moment, calmly meeting her gaze, then her aunt nodded half a greeting and nervously wiped her hands on the apron she wore around her thick waist.

'Mamma, come and say hello to Chiara,' Paolo encouraged. 'Back from London at last.'

'Oh, London.' Chiara shuddered. 'I can't tell you how glad I am to be away from that place.'

'We're glad you're not there any more as well,' Paolo told her. 'It's good to have you home.'

The smell of cooking hit her as she stepped through the door. Pepina had been busy in her kitchen preparing all the food she knew her granddaughter loved best. A *spaghetti con le vongole*, freshened with a big bunch of flat-leafed parsley, to be followed by red peppers, fried in olive oil with onion, anchovies and coarse bread, a platter of artichokes steamed with more olive oil and garlic, and a dish of thin fillets of veal coated in breadcrumbs and fried quickly in Pepina's wide, black, cast-iron pan.

They ate beneath the lemon tree, with a green tablecloth spread over the new outdoor table and linen napkins beside huge, white china plates.

'This is yummy,' Chiara told them, wiping artichoke-infused oil from her plate with a hunk of hard, golden bread. 'The best I've ever tasted.'

The old people had hardly touched their own food. They seemed content to sit back and watch Chiara enjoy hers.

'*Manga*, *manga*,' she exhorted Erminio in her stilted Italian and, laughing, he picked up his fork.

Yet again, Paolo acted as translator. 'Our grandfather says you learned to cook on your last visit, this time you must learn to speak Italian properly.'

'I will,' Chiara promised. 'I'd love to be able to talk to them without you always having to be the go-between.'

Rosaria reached over and took hold of the serving spoon, ready to scoop up another glistening pile of red peppers, but Paolo shook his head and clicked his tongue against his teeth. Dropping the spoon, she stared disconsolately at her empty plate.

'Mamma is on a diet,' he explained to Chiara.

'Yes, I thought she'd lost weight,' she replied. Turning to Rosaria she added, 'You're looking great. You've lost a lot already.'

Rosaria merely nodded. For a moment there was an awkward silence until Chiara broke it by saying brightly, 'So tell me about the improvements. What's been going on?'

'Why does anything have to be going on?' Rosaria asked. 'We can tidy the place up a bit if we want.'

Paolo patted his mother's arm. 'We'd been so busy with other things that we'd let the property get run down, hadn't we, Mamma?' he said placidly. 'But things are looking a lot better now.'

'Well, the new paint job looks great,' agreed Chiara. 'And I like the outdoor furniture. But exactly what are you building in the orchard?'

'Cabins. What did you think?' Rosaria said scornfully.

'Cabins?'

'Yes, that's right.' Paolo looked cheerful. 'It's going to be a little project for you, isn't it, Mamma? We're planning to try to attract tourists here. We thought they could come and be part of a real Italian family and learn to cook the authentic food of the region just like you did.'

Chiara thought it was a great idea. Her book, when it was published, could only help them, she realized. The publicity it brought with it would be priceless. 'Oh, I see. The tourists will stay in the cabins,' she smiled. 'I'm impressed with your business brain, Paolo. I'd never have thought of that.'

He grinned and spooned the pile of peppers Rosaria had coveted onto Chiara's plate. 'Have a little more,' he told her. 'It's so delicious.'

Guiltily she tasted a strip of pepper, savouring the saltiness of the anchovies and feeling the olive oil ooze from the softened bread onto her tongue as she chewed. Rosaria watched like a hungry dog but said nothing.

'So will Pepina teach the tourists to cook?' Chiara asked.

Paolo made a slightly dismissive gesture with his long, tanned fingers. 'We haven't really talked to her about the finer details yet. There's no point in getting her all stressed out until we know for sure it's going to work.'

'But the cabins in the orchard, don't Pepina and Erminio mind?' Chiara persisted. 'They love to walk there in the evenings, don't they?'

'They can still walk there,' Paolo promised. 'The cabins won't stop them.'

The meal was finished and, despite her protests, Rosaria was sent to bend over the sink and wash the pile of dishes. No one would allow Chiara to do anything but sit, drink red wine and talk long into the night. The moon cast longer shadows and the stars looked brighter here, she thought. She imagined tourists sitting in a row down the long table, napkins in laps, rubbing full bellies, and yet again was impressed by Paolo's business acumen.

His voice broke in on her thoughts: 'Ah, I nearly forgot,' he said. 'Franco and Giovanni Angeli have been asking about you. Perhaps you should drop in and see them in the morning.'

Chiara was surprised. 'I didn't think you ever spoke to them?'

Paolo shrugged. He'd bumped into Giovanni once or twice in the piazza, he explained, they'd talked and now he was thinking that maybe it was time to let bygones be bygones. 'So many things have changed,' he explained. 'Franco, Giovanni, my grandparents, they had their reasons for falling out but that's in the past. You're here now and perhaps that's all that was needed to bring us together.'

She was glad some good had come out of her being in San Giulio. It felt as if she was giving them something back in thanks for all those recipes. There had been so many of them that sifting through, picking out the most appealing and then going through the testing process had been more difficult than she'd thought. But at last the final step of having each dish styled and photographed had been completed and now all that was left was for her to write the words. She'd been procrastinating about this, partly because she hadn't known quite where to start but also from fear of failure. Chiara had never attempted any real writing before. Her last book, *Queen of the British Kitchen*, had only required a four-line blurb before each recipe and after that it was purely ingredients and method.

Franco and Giovanni were all the excuse she needed not to start writing first thing the next morning. It would be rude not to go and say hello to them, after all.

'Perhaps I'll get up early tomorrow and have coffee and a pastry at Caffe Angeli,' she told Paolo. 'A big, sweet pastry and a hit of caffeine should give me all the energy I need to get going on chapter one.'

He dug his teeth into the yellow flesh of a ripe peach. 'Mmm, good idea,' he said, as a thin trickle of peach juice dribbled down his chin. 'They'll be pleased to see you, I'm sure.'

'Will you come with me?'

He wiped the peach juice from his chin with his fingers and then licked them clean. 'No, I have too much work to do here,' he told her. 'You mustn't tempt me to start slacking, Chiara, otherwise it will never be finished.'

Some of her clothes were still hanging in the wardrobe of her mother's old bedroom. Already it felt less like a neglected spare room and more like her own space. Chiara heaved her suitcase onto the single bed and proceeded to unpack and arrange more of her things. Her laptop fitted neatly on the table in the corner. On the chair beside the bed she placed a bottle of perfume, some moisturizer and her make-up. Above her bed an old print of a Madonna and child gazed down on her benignly. This was to be her room for the next month, she thought, warmed with happiness. She could pause here for a while.

Outside in the orchard, flashlight in hand, Rosaria was pacing between the half-built cabins. As well as half-starving her, Paolo had insisted she take daily exercise.

'When the tourists come,' he had told her, 'it will be up to you to greet them, make them feel at home. Your image is important.'

She had rolled her eyes heavenwards but he'd persisted. 'It doesn't matter if you're a little chubby, Mamma, you'll just look like you enjoy your food. But right now, I'm sorry to say, you look like a greedy pig.'

That had hurt and so she'd made an effort. Paolo had started supervising her portions at mealtimes and every day she walked back and forth through the orchard. Sometimes

Paolo came out too and encouraged her to pick up her pace. 'You're looking better already,' he kept telling her. 'You just have to keep it up.'

Rosaria hoped he'd come out tonight – not because she wanted to be pushed into walking faster, she didn't, but she had things she needed to say to him before it was too late. She looked for his long, dark shadow among the trees but it never appeared. So she stayed out longer than usual, half an hour in all, in the hope he would worry and come to find her.

'I might have had a heart attack and be lying dead in the dust and who would care?' she mumbled bitterly. At long last there he was, calling, 'Mamma, where are you?' into the night.

'I'm here, you idiot,' she snapped, wiping a film of sweat from her brow with the back of her sleeve.

'What are you doing? It's late. Come inside.'

'No, you come here,' she called.

She was a little breathless from all the pacing but she had puff enough to say what was important. 'Can you please stop fawning over that girl?' she hissed at him. 'You've got what you wanted, haven't you? The cabins are being built, she's going to help us pull in the tourists, so you can turn off the charm now, eh?'

Paolo put an arm round her broad shoulders. 'Don't worry, I know what I'm doing.'

'If you break her heart, she's not going to help us.'

Her son said nothing. His arm slipped from her shoulders and he tilted his face away from her so she couldn't see his expression in the torchlight. Rosaria felt a little jolt of fear.

'You can't really be interested in her, the plain little thing,' she said, alarmed.

'Oh, I don't know.' She thought his voice had the ring of a taunt about it but she couldn't be sure. 'She's a bit different to all the girls round here. Not a beauty for sure but she has money and prospects – what's not to like?'

A hard look came over Rosaria's face.

'But you're quite right,' he said soothingly. 'I don't want to break her heart. We have to keep her sweet until we get our business well and truly off the ground and then we won't need her any more.'

As he took his mother's hand and towed her back towards the house, he turned to her and her flashlight caught his smile. 'Chiara tells me they're going to use some of my photos in her book,' he said proudly. 'It could be the beginning of a whole new career for me.'

14

The two men in Caffe Angeli were more than just pleased to see Chiara. Franco hugged and kissed her while customers kicked their heels waiting for their espresso. Giovanni's smile couldn't have been any wider if he'd discovered he had a winning lottery ticket.

She kissed their cheeks, the one so wrinkled and old, the other still firm and rough with the stubble of half a day's growth.

When she'd been thoroughly greeted she took her usual seat, beneath the Masaccio Madonna with her mother's face, sipped strong coffee and struggled to make sense of the local newspaper.

'What's this article about?' she asked Giovanni when finally he had time to take off his apron and join her for a few moments.

He collapsed into the chair opposite and treated her to another helping of his infectious grin. 'Oh, just the usual scandal about buildings that don't meet council standards being put up without the official permits.'

'Did you know that Paolo is building cabins on his property? Do you think he got a permit?'

Giovanni laughed. 'Not likely. But he'll have slipped some money to the right person and there won't be any problems.'

'Is it really so corrupt here? Is that what everyone does?'

Giovanni shrugged and laughed again. 'That's what some people do, yes.'

She grimaced. 'Yes, but not Paolo. Why would he behave like that?'

Giovanni studied her for a moment. He began to say something and then stopped himself.

'What?' she prompted.

'Nothing,' he replied.

'You were going to say something?'

'Yes, but it doesn't matter. Let me get you a delicious cornetto. I have one that is filled with *crema* and covered in almonds.'

He sat with her quietly while she ate the pastry. When she'd finished and had mopped up the shavings of almonds and icing sugar with her fingertips, he spoke again hesitantly. 'You like Paolo, don't you?'

'Yes, I like him a lot.'

'Perhaps you should be a little careful. He might not be exactly the person you think he is.'

'What do you mean? Is this about the feud between your family and his? I thought that was all forgotten now.'

'Not forgotten, I'm sure, but yes, it's in the past.'

Loyalty lent an edge of anger to Chiara's voice now. 'So why are you so down on Paolo then?' she asked.

Giovanni glanced quickly at his father. 'It's not for me to interfere,' he said. 'I'm sorry I said anything.'

'No, I think you should explain.'

He scratched his ear evasively.

'Giovanni?' she urged.

'Oh look, it's nothing really, just a feeling I have. He's the son of Rosaria and Marco, so he has their genes. Since they are two of the most sly, dishonest, self-serving people I've ever come across, I don't see how Paolo can have escaped inheriting some of that.'

'No, no.' Chiara shook her head. 'He's been nothing but generous and kind to me. He's given me so much help with my research. He took these amazing photos of me learning to cook with Pepina. Without those shots I'd never have talked my publisher into accepting my book idea.'

'I'm pleased he's being kind to you, Chiara. I'm just asking you to be careful. I watched Marco nearly destroy your mother. I don't want to see his son do the same to you.'

Chiara leaned over and kissed his cheek. It felt warm beneath her lips. A shaft of sunlight shifted and caught the silver tips of his hair and briefly she had the urge to reach out and stroke his head affectionately. He was only looking out for her like a father might, she thought, and she let herself run for a moment with that idea, losing herself in the fantasy. He had almost admitted that one time to loving her mother. Wouldn't that be the ideal scenario, if sweet, kind, generous Giovanni turned out to be her father? She liked him so much.

It was the sight of a large, black shape looming on the other side of the glass door that brought Chiara back to reality. What was Rosaria doing here? she wondered.

She was even more surprised when, plate loaded with pastries, slopping *caffe con latte* from her cup, Rosaria made her way over to join her.

'*Ciao*, *ciao*, everybody,' she said.

Giovanni pulled out a chair for her.

She ate with quiet determination. Chiara didn't dare mention the diet. Finally, when there were only crumbs left, Rosaria stifled a burp and smiled. 'Beautiful day,' she remarked sanguinely.

'Yes, isn't it,' Chiara replied.

'Bit of a queue building up over there, Giovanni.' Rosaria nodded at the counter. 'Your poor old papa is having a struggle.'

With a guilty start, Giovanni jumped to his feet. 'Excuse me, Chiara, but Rosaria is right. Papa is too old nowadays to be coping alone.'

'Bring me one more little pastry, will you, when you get a chance?' Rosaria called after him and then she turned back to

Chiara. 'So, you're glad to be home in San Giulio,' she said, her voice laced with icing sugar and almonds.

Chiara nodded uncertainly. She wasn't sure she was ready for the new, friendly Rosaria.

'I'm glad you're back too,' Rosaria continued, sounding almost like she meant it. 'All these years I've felt so bad about Maria Domenica and the way she left without saying goodbye. We all hoped she'd phone or write but she didn't and I'm sure she had her reasons. But now you're back and it's made my parents so happy. It's wonderful that you've brought them so much joy at this stage in their lives.'

Chiara covered Rosaria's hand with her own and her eyes reddened with tears. 'Thank you,' was all she managed to say.

'And Paolo is all fired up about this tourism business. It's given him something to focus on,' Rosaria continued. 'We're all thrilled that you'll be using some of his photos in your book.'

It seemed too good to be true, thought Chiara. Her Aunt Rosaria was at last prepared fully to welcome her as part of the family.

And then, like a bottle of corked wine that looks so good from the outside, Rosaria opened up and Chiara smelled the first whiff of rot. 'But Paolo and you,' she said in a low voice, 'you know it can never happen?'

'What? Why?' Chiara was confused.

'Stay away from him, that's all I'm saying.'

Chiara's voice rose, despite herself. 'I saw Marco in Rome. He promised me that he isn't my father,' she said.

Giovanni slid another plate of pastries onto the table, but Rosaria was too distracted to notice. 'You saw Marco?' she said quickly. 'Did he ask about me?'

Chiara decided it was a wise time to depart from the truth. 'Yes, of course he did. I told him that you and Paolo were doing well.'

Rosaria's hand drifted automatically to the cornetto and settled around it comfortably. 'How did he look?' she asked.

'Oh, fine, I suppose.' Chiara didn't know what else to say.

'Sometimes I think about going there, to his nightclub, and seeing him myself.'

'Well, maybe you should,' Chiara said carefully.

Rosaria loosened her grip on the cornetto. Once she was slimmer, and had cash in her pockets from the tourists, that would be the time to go to Rome.

'Yes, maybe,' she mused. 'But in the meantime, be careful with Paolo. It's by no means certain you're not brother and sister, no matter what Marco might have told you. Once I get to Rome, I'll get to the bottom of the whole business for you, I promise. Until then, best you stay away from my son, hey?' Rosaria's tone was like a perfume, thought Chiara. Beneath the layers of friendliness was a base-note of menace. She was a difficult woman to like and Chiara wondered how her mother had handled her. Was it better to fight her or surrender?

'Marco seemed pretty certain he's not my father and I believed him,' she tried and, as she saw the scowl forming on Rosaria's face, added hastily, 'But Paolo and I won't rush into anything, I promise. We'll wait until we're certain. You must realize how special he is to me though. He's been so wonderful.'

Rosaria looked thoughtful and something about her face changed. All the hardness seemed to fall away from it. 'My Paolo is wonderful,' she said softly, 'He's all I've got.'

Over by the Gaggia machine, there was a small argument raging. Franco had been watching his son talking to Chiara and thought she seemed upset.

'What were you saying to that girl?' he barked at Giovanni above the whine of grinding coffee beans.

'Nothing, Papa.'

'We agreed we weren't going to interfere with that family, didn't we? That we were going to let things take their natural course.'

'Yes, Papa, we agreed,' conceded Giovanni. 'But there has been so much trouble, so much hurt. I don't want there to be any more.'

Franco gazed over at the spiky-haired girl with the honest face who was deep in conversation with Rosaria. 'Your interference didn't help Maria Domenica, did it? You just sent her far, far away and we never saw her again. Leave her daughter alone, will you? She seems a clever girl. She'll sort things out.'

15

The windows in Chiara's room were wide open and the breeze was welcome. She was sitting, bent over her laptop, trying to concentrate, to bring to mind exactly how she'd felt when she embarked on her search for her family and for good food. Her screen remained blank, her fingers still, for she wanted the words, when she found them, to be exactly the right ones.

At long last she stirred and began to type:

> Just outside the little Italian town of San Giulio, in a grove of peach trees, is a house. And in that house is a kitchen. It doesn't look like much – no microwave, no mod cons – just pans bubbling on the stove and an old lady kneading dough on a scrubbed pine table. This is the story of how I found that house and unlocked the secrets of its kitchen. But it's also a tale of betrayal, infidelity and loss, of family feuds and doomed love. And at the very heart of my story is a quest that's still far from finished . . .'

Once Chiara had managed that first paragraph it was as if the floodgates had opened. Words poured from her brain and flowed through her fingers. The outside world blurred and what she saw on her screen was all that mattered.

Bare-chested, sweat trickling between his shoulder blades, Paolo was up a ladder hammering nails urgently into the frame of yet another wooden tourist cabin. Giacomo Salerni was beside him working at half the speed, his mind on other things.

'Giacomo, wake up,' Paolo snapped, exasperated.

'I'm working as fast as I can,' Giacomo replied in his flat monotone.

'I'll be interested to see how fast you work when the time comes to write up your bill,' Paolo couldn't resist saying.

Giacomo dropped his hammer and threw his hands in the air dramatically. 'If you don't want me here, I'll go, Paolo. There are more apartments going up in town. I won't have any trouble getting work on them.'

Paolo climbed down, picked the hammer out of the dust and handed it back to Giacomo.

'Just shut up, OK, and get on with it,' he said shortly and went back to his own work, beating in nails with haste and passion.

Unnoticed by her son, Rosaria paced between the peach trees. The heat of the midday sun had sent a beaded curtain of sweat falling down her forehead, but still she kept on with her pacing.

She could hear Paolo's wild hammering and, whenever he paused, the sound of Chiara's fingernails tapping on the keyboard of her laptop. Everybody was busy.

Shapeless black skirt flapping round her legs, she picked up a little more speed. 'Oh why did I eat all those pastries?' she cursed beneath her breath as she turned at the boundary fence and made her way back towards the house.

She could see her parents now, resting in their twin cane chairs in the shade of the grapevine that grew over the trellis outside their bedroom door. They were shrivelling, the pair of them, like autumn leaves. Erminio's voice no longer boomed from his barrel chest as it used to. Pepina shuffled around the kitchen rather than walked. Their excitement at Chiara's arrival seemed to have leeched their last reserves of energy from them.

Rosaria turned and walked down the shady path along the

back of the house. The wide tops of her legs were rubbing together and she knew they must look red and sore. She wiped the sweat from her brow with her handkerchief and sighed wearily. One more circuit, she decided, and then it would be time for lunch.

Erminio and Pepina sat in silence, side by side, watching with only semi-interest the activity in their orchard. Their old bodies were wedged into their cane chairs with cushions, newspapers lay unread in their laps and a carafe of ice-cold homemade lemonade sat on the low table between them. Every now and then, when Paolo's hammering grew too loud, Pepina winced and cupped her hands over her ears, but mostly she simply stared into space, daydreaming.

Erminio gazed at her, too deaf to be disturbed by the noise of the building work, too tired to care what his grandson was doing. It was a relief to hand over the responsibility of the farm to another man and step back from being the head of the household. He'd be happy if he had some good years left to sit in his cane chair, eat his wife's good food and enjoy the granddaughter fate had brought home long after he had lost hope of ever seeing her again.

In Caffe Angeli, Giovanni was staring at the newspaper. It was hot today and, other than the odd child running in for an ice cream, the place had been quiet. He'd been crouched over the front page of his newspaper re-reading the same two paragraphs for at least twenty minutes now. Beside him a cup of milky coffee lay untouched, a skin forming over it as it cooled.

Resting his chin on his hand, Giovanni sighed and said out loud to nobody but himself, 'It's impossible.'

He'd been unsettled since the girl had arrived in San Giulio. Pretty Chiara with her laughing, honest face and earnest heart was still unaware of the havoc she was causing. Since she'd waltzed in here with a backpack over her shoulder, things had changed for Giovanni. The past had washed up on the present for a moment and he was now picking through the driftwood left behind.

He liked her, no . . . he loved her. He was painfully aware she looked on him as a brother, worse still perhaps as a father figure. Giovanni was vain enough to believe he didn't look his age but there was still no denying he was a man in his late forties, just a few years younger than her mother would have been. Chiara was only halfway through her thirties. She'd want a younger, stronger man than him.

'It's impossible,' he announced again and then, hating the hollow echo of his voice through the empty *caffe*, stood up and strode over to the jukebox to fill the place with noise.

As the old songs played, he sat back and gazed around him. The paintings Vincenzo had worked so hard on were looking old and tired and the Gaggia coffee machine with its sleek body and worn wooden handles was officially an antique but his father refused to replace it with one of the efficient new push-button models.

'The coffee would never taste the same,' he complained whenever Giovanni suggested it was time for a change.

Perhaps when he reached Franco's age he'd be like him, unwilling to alter anything about the business in which he'd worked his whole life. The thought depressed him.

Giovanni's mind drifted to Chiara again and how, with a word or two, he might be able to change the courses of both their lives for ever. Brave in thought, timid in life, he knew in his heart he would stay silent.

16

The launch of Chiara's book was a glamorous affair. It was the sort of party she always longed to be invited to and never was.

She pushed her way through the crowd of unfamiliar faces, searching for a friend. All around her glasses were being drained to the last drop by elegantly pissed people and she shuddered to think how many cases of decent Italian wine they were getting through.

Harriet had offered to let her throw the party in The Office, but Janey had shaken her glossy blonde head at the sight of shelves full of dusty books and the jumble of old leather sofas and mismatched dining chairs. 'You know I think it's lovely, darling,' she'd said finally, 'but this isn't the right space for your book launch at all.'

They'd ended up in a Soho art gallery, run by a friend of Janey's, that happened to be showing a series of works inspired by Italian food. The place was long and tunnel-like, about the width of a London Underground Station, and the canvases on the white walls were covered in lurid, oversized bowls of spaghetti and bulbous orange mussels on the half-shell. They were quite revolting, thought Chiara, but fortunately there was such a press of people that most of them were blocked from view.

Janey had got her own way about more than just the launch party. She'd maintained an unflagging enthusiasm and a firm control over the book through the long slog of the editing process, calling in lawyers to make absolutely sure they weren't defaming anyone and checking and re-checking page proofs long after Chiara's heart had begun sinking at the very sight of them.

'I love this book so much,' she kept telling Chiara, 'it's got to be absolutely perfect.'

Almost predictably, Chiara found herself posing for the cover photo in a crown made of plum tomatoes, wearing a necklace of basil leaves and balancing a bulb of garlic in each open palm. On the book's jacket, the words above her head read: *Chiara Fox is Queen of the Italian Kitchen.*

With the proofs all signed off, Chiara had been left with nothing to do but mooch around London, drinking too much red wine in The Office and restlessly walking Salty four or five times a day until the exhausted dog began to hide under Harriet's bed every time he saw her approaching with the leash.

And then, just when she'd thought she'd been completely forgotten by the entire publishing world, Janey had called with the exciting news. Her team had managed to pull off a TV deal. The whole series was to be shot in Pepina's kitchen and Paolo was going to be her co-star. He was beside himself with excitement. Chiara could see him now in the centre of the party, standing out in a crowd of beautiful people, swirling his wine round in a glass, deep in conversation with a stranger.

She tugged at his sleeve. 'Paolo, there you are. I've been looking for you everywhere.'

'Ah, Chiara.' Paolo reached down and kissed her cheek. 'Come and meet Roger. He's a TV director and he's got some great ideas for our series.'

Since he'd arrived in London, Paolo's life had been one big whirl of meetings. He'd lunched with travel consultants, breakfasted with food writers. There had been meetings with agents, TV producers and publishers. He was flexing his entrepreneurial muscles for all he was worth and barely had enough time to pat Chiara on the head or peck her on the cheek.

How could she have feared he would never fit into her world? she wondered as she watched him moving off into the crowd, charming each person he encountered. Everyone here seemed to love him. In fact, this felt more like Paolo's book launch than her own.

Roger the TV director glanced over her shoulder, found someone more famous and moved on. For a moment Chiara was alone, drowning in a pool of strangers. Then, on the other side of the tunnel she spotted Harriet, with Eduardo on one arm and Alex on the other. Thank God for Harriet, she thought. Alex might have been lost and lonely at the party, but her best friend had sought him out and made him feel welcome.

'Darling, you look wonderful.' Harriet wrapped her in her arms. Once she'd let go, Eduardo and Alex took their turn.

'Your mother would be so proud of you,' said Alex, holding her at arm's length to get a proper view. 'Although,' he added with a wide grin, 'she might have sent you home to change that frock you're wearing for something more substantial.'

Chiara's little black dress was shorter at the bottom and lower at the top than she would normally risk. But with its usual alchemy the sun had turned her skin to gold and she'd thought she might be able to get away with it. Not that Paolo had noticed. The expanse of smooth, tanned leg and clavicle had been lost on him, so busy was he with business.

Harriet raised her glass and toasted her. 'To you, darling. To your success as queen of all manner of kitchens.'

She nodded her thanks and then took a second look at the drink Harriet had raised in the air. It wasn't her usual wine or champagne. Instead she was drinking something long and cool that might possibly be gin, but was more likely lime and soda.

'Would you like a glass of wine, Harriet?' Chiara asked, testing the waters.

'No, darling, I'm fine,' she replied and took a tiny sip of her colourless fizz.

Chiara's eyes raked her friend's body. Harriet's bones were disappearing beneath a layer of flesh, her waist had thickened and her tiny buds of breasts had swelled.

'Harriet, you're pregnant,' she gasped.

Eduardo smiled proudly and his hand snaked round Harriet's waist until it rested on her swelling stomach. Harriet herself looked horrified and Alex, trying to take his cue from those around him, simply looked confused.

'I hadn't meant you to find out like this,' Harriet told her.

'How pregnant are you?'

'Nearly four months.'

'Well, when were you going to tell me, Harriet? When the child started school?'

'Oh God, I'm sorry.' Her friend seemed to sag a little. 'I couldn't tell you, Chiara, I felt like I was letting you down.'

'What?'

Harriet took a determined slug of her impotent cocktail. 'It was always going to be you and me, wasn't it? In our flat above The Office, having a good time, not falling into the old husband and baby trap like all the others. We weren't worried about the fact we'd hit our thirties because we were always going to have each other. And now I've ruined everything.'

'No, Harriet, don't be so crazy, you can't . . .' Chiara trailed off. It was the wrong time for this conversation. Plus Janey was at her elbow busting to introduce her to someone and she wasn't going to be ignored. 'We'll talk about this properly later, OK?' Chiara promised as she turned to shake the stranger's hand. He was a slightly ramshackle figure in an old-fashioned grey greatcoat, with a schoolboy's rucksack thrown over his shoulder. His brown hair was thinning, his front teeth stained yellow with nicotine and he gave off the acrid smell of a two pack-a-day man. He wasn't Janey's speed at all, thought Chiara, and she couldn't imagine why her publisher seemed so keen on him.

'This is Pete Farrell from the *Sunday Post*,' Janey said, her usual smooth tone ragged with excitement. 'Pete, this is Chiara Fox, the Queen of the Italian Kitchen.'

Pete Farrell. For a moment Chiara couldn't quite place where she'd heard his name before. Then she remembered hearing a group of journalists discussing him one night in The Office. He was the *Sunday Post* reporter who got all the big exclusives. He had a reputation for being pushy and on the wrong side of the tabloid/broadsheet divide, despite his paper forever trumpeting itself as a quality title. The boys in The Office hadn't liked Pete Farrell much and, now that she'd met him, Chiara wasn't sure that she did either.

'Fantastic book, love,' he told her, his twitching fingers holding an invisible cigarette to his lips. 'I mean the recipes are great obviously but the story, that's tremendous.'

'Thanks,' she said lightly.

Pressing one hand into the small of her back and taking her arm with the other, he steered her over to the corner of the room. 'Let's get out of this crush, shall we, so we can have a quiet word. Need another drink? No? You sure? That's better, isn't it?'

He'd sat her down on a red leather sofa that was clearly part of the artist's installation. There were bowls of lasagne glued onto its arms and, where there should have been buttons, there were now dried pasta shapes. One was poking itself uncomfortably into Chiara's barely clad upper thigh and she was forced to shuffle closer to Pete to escape it.

'Right then, your story,' he said leaning closer to talk confidentially. 'The bigamous mother, the search for your real dad, the boyfriend who might be your brother – it's great stuff. Janey's publicity people say I can have the newspaper exclusive and I reckon it could be our front-page splash this Sunday, barring a royal death or a terrorist bomb.'

He talked quickly, out of the corner of his mouth and Chiara noticed he'd already pulled out a notebook and pen from his rucksack.

'Look, I don't know. I'm going to have to think about it,' she told him.

'No time for that, love, I'm on deadline.'

'Well, in that case, the answer's no.'

'Come on, love,' he wheedled. She noticed he was jiggling one leg up and down nervously. 'Think of the publicity for the book. Front page of the *Sunday Post*? You couldn't ask for much more.'

'Yes, I'm sure it would be wonderful publicity but there are other people whose feelings need to be considered, like my stepfather Alex,' she pointed out. 'He's having to come to terms with the idea that my mother married him bigamously and I don't think it's going to help him if it's splashed all over the newspapers. It's bad enough that I put it all down in the book.' She noticed Pete was jotting down notes as she spoke and quickly added, 'Hey, you're not to quote me on this.'

He dropped his pen reluctantly. 'It's not as if the whole story isn't going to be out there anyway, is it? It's in your book so it will all be a matter of public record. One little article's not going to make much difference to anyone.'

She said nothing and so he pressed on. 'Look, I wouldn't usually do this but in your case I might be able to get my boss to offer some financial incentive. Would a nice, fat cheque make any difference to you?'

Chiara caught sight of Paolo pushing his way through the crowd of people and mouthed, 'Help,' at him. When she'd written her book she hadn't considered any of this. Perhaps she'd been naive, but she hadn't realized her life would be opened up and spread out for people like Pete Farrell to pick over, or that her every last secret might be blasted into newsprint.

Pete was now pitching his story idea to Paolo and he didn't seem to think it was such a bad idea. 'Have you got a photographer here tonight?' he was asking the reporter. 'You could get a shot of me and Chiara together if you want.'

'Yeah, great, great.' Pete was nodding.

'No, wait, not so great,' Chiara argued.

Paolo tried to balance on the arm of the chair but was thwarted by a bowl of lasagne. So he perched beside her on the dried pasta shapes and put an arm round her shoulders. 'Don't be crazy, this is fantastic,' he insisted. 'This man Pete is offering to let millions of people all over the country know about our book. Be nice to him, Chiara, before he changes his mind. Let's give him a really good story for his readers.'

Reluctantly, she agreed to answer Pete's questions. She watched nervously as he filled the lined pages of his notebook with his unruly shorthand. She couldn't help noticing that Paolo did nearly as much of the talking as she did, colourfully describing their first meeting. 'Yeah, yeah, great stuff,' Pete kept muttering as he scribbled on.

Once he'd finished, a photographer made them pose in front of one of the lurid spaghetti paintings with their arms wrapped round each other. 'Heads together, come on, heads together,' he cried.

'Do we have to stand so close?' Chiara asked, pulling away a little, but Paolo shot her a hurt look and she relented. She could already imagine the feeling of sick dread she would have this Sunday when she nipped across the road to buy the papers. All those *Sunday Post*s with her and Paolo's faces staring out. Chiara began to pray for a royal death but felt smitten with guilt almost immediately.

The party's volume had been turned up several notches and people were mouthing at each other now rather than speaking. Chiara decided to stop resisting the urge to escape. She pulled at Paolo's sleeve. 'Let's get out of here,' she said. 'I'll grab Alex, Harriet and Eduardo. We can all go and get some dinner.'

He looked distracted. 'You go ahead,' he told her. 'There's an agent over there I want to say hello to. Just let me know where you're going and I'll catch you up later.'

She left him deep in conversation with an intense, black-clad girl in dark-framed glasses. Their heads and bodies were close together. The *Sunday Post* photographer would love *that* pose, thought Chiara, as she followed Harriet out of the front door.

17

When she saw the headline of the *Sunday Post*, Chiara was a million times more horrified than she'd thought she'd be: 'BIGAMY, INCEST, BULIMIA: CHIARA FOX TRIUMPHS OVER TRAGEDY.'

The newsagent didn't say a word when he sold her the paper, just stared at her like she was some sort of weird museum exhibit, a shrunken head or a duck-billed platypus.

She couldn't get back into the apartment fast enough. But then, once inside, she couldn't bring herself to look at the newspaper.

'Harriet,' she wailed. 'Help.'

She heard a tired, defeated voice calling, 'Hang on, I'm coming,' and after a few minutes a wan face appeared around the bedroom door. 'This is worse than any hangover,' Harriet groaned. 'Don't believe anyone who tries to tell you otherwise.'

'Aren't you supposed to be over the trimester where you get morning sickness?' Chiara asked and was given a withering look in reply.

'You asked for help,' said Harriet tersely. 'What with?'

Silently Chiara proffered the *Sunday Post*. 'Can you please read this and tell me what it says? I can't bear to look at it.'

'Oh gawd,' said Harriet, taking the newspaper from her and scanning the first few lines.

Chiara waited, miserably, for the verdict. 'Well,' Harriet began, 'it's all reasonably close to the truth if a little breathless. The only bit I really don't get is this stuff about you being a bulimic. Did you regurgitate a prawn into your napkin at the book launch?'

'Well, yes, but it was off,' replied Chiara, outraged.

Harriet began to laugh. 'Well, according to Pete Farrell, you're bravely battling bulimia.'

'The bastard. I could sue him for that.'

Harriet was still laughing. 'There's an absolutely huge picture of the book cover and a whole blurb about how Paolo's going to be your co-star in the TV series. It's priceless publicity.'

'The bloody prawn was off,' she repeated to Harriet's back, as her pregnant friend made another dash to the bathroom.

Retreat seemed Chiara's only option. The outside world was full of people having morning coffee and scanning the newspapers for gossip and the small, safe zone beneath her duvet was the only sensible place to be. The phone rang repeatedly as the day wore on, but nobody in the flat bothered to pick it up. Alex was probably trying to get hold of her, thought Chiara, and Janey too. And maybe Paolo had rung once or twice – Paolo who had thought it wiser to rent a room in a cheap hotel off Russell Square than stay with her in Soho. His excuse had been that there was no space in the flat, but Chiara was sure there was more to it. She could sense a pulling back, a withdrawal of intimacy. Paolo hadn't said anything, he hadn't done anything. Nevertheless, her instinct told her there had been a subtle shift in their relationship.

She must have dozed off for when she opened her eyes, the light had changed. She squinted into the afternoon sun and, still groggy with sleep, struggled to raise her head from the pillow. Her stomach was empty, her mouth dry and the safe zone beneath her duvet was now unpleasantly limp with sweat.

Ignoring the frantic flashing of the message light on the answering machine, Chiara picked up the phone and tapped out the number of the mobile Paolo had rented for the duration of his London visit.

He answered after just a couple of rings. '*Pronto*,' he said, his voice still honey and chocolate.

'Paolo, it's me. Have you been trying to call?'

'No, baby, not me.'

'Well, have you seen the damn newspaper?'

'Of course. I've bought ten copies to send home. It's a great picture of me, I think, but you look a bit stiff and uncomfortable.'

'Did you actually *read* the article, Paolo?' Chiara demanded.

'*Si, cara*, of course. I didn't know about the bulimia. Why didn't you tell me?'

She stifled the urge to scream but still there was a rising note of irritation in her voice as she said, 'I need to see you. Will you have lunch with me . . . if I promise not to throw it up afterwards?'

Soho always seemed like a deserted lover on a Sunday, she thought, as she walked to meet Paolo. There was no market-day buzz in Berwick Street, just a few squashed cauliflower leaves and tomatoes in the gutter. Most of the cafés were closed, the litter bins overflowed with detritus from last night's partying and the pavements were sticky with beer and other, less savoury, fluids. Only the sex shops up the side streets hummed steadily with customers and, as ever, Chiara steered clear of those.

Paolo was twenty minutes late to meet her at Pizza Pizza. By then she'd given in to garlic bread even though she'd never really liked it much. Pepina would think she'd gone mad stuffing down bread, butter and practically raw garlic but, in light of the amount she'd had to drink last night, stodge liberally basted with grease didn't seem such a bad idea.

He kissed her lightly on both cheeks when he finally arrived and took a seat opposite rather than next to her. He frowned at the menu, at the pizza, at the waitress; nothing seemed to please him.

Chiara waited until the waitress served their coffee – which he condemned as too weak – before broaching the subject that had been on her mind. 'I've been thinking about something Janey suggested a while ago,' she explained, as he took tiny, pained sips from his cup. 'DNA testing – what do you think? We should be able to establish pretty conclusively whether Marco is my father and if, as we all believe, he isn't, then there'll be nothing standing in our way.'

He nodded dubiously. 'I suppose so,' he said. 'But you know, I wouldn't rush into anything if I were you. The book's out there now and it wouldn't surprise me if it brought your real father out of the woodwork. Then there'll be no need to bother with Marco or expensive scientific tests.'

'So you think we should just bide our time?'

'Exactly,' he agreed.

She wanted to ask more, to find out if his feelings towards her were changing, but she was almost too afraid to know the answer.

'Paolo,' she began, 'is everything all right?'

'Yes, yes, of course. Everything is fantastic.'

She pulled on a tuft of hair nervously. 'I love you,' she risked.

He only nodded, took another sip of coffee and scowled.

'Do you still love me?' she pushed.

He slid his cup onto the saucer. 'I'll always care for you, Chiara, you know that.'

'But do you still *love* me?' she persisted.

He took her hand in his. 'Let me be honest,' he said softly and smoothly. 'For a while when we were in Italy and you were there every day cooking in my grandmother's kitchen, perhaps I thought I was falling in love with you. But now we're going to have a working relationship and I think it would be wiser if we kept a little distance.'

She was furious. 'I can't believe you've got the cheek to say that to me,' she said, pulling her hand away. 'You led me on. It was you who kept saying that you loved me. I even put it in my book. And now you think you're going to drop me just like that?'

'I'm not dropping you.' His anger flared too. 'Let me refresh your memory, Chiara. Nothing ever happened between us beyond a kiss or two. Things might have gone further but, despite everything I said, you were too hung up on the idea that Marco was your father. Now the moment has passed. I have a business to run, I have a career now. I don't have the time or the energy to deal with scenes like this. Why can't we just keep things professional?'

'Fine, if that's what you want.' Angry and upset, Chiara pressed her lips together, too proud to say any more. She'd been dumped enough times to know that creating a fuss never changed things. Slipping on her jacket, she paid the bill.

As they were leaving the restaurant, a girl called out to them, 'Hold on, hold on.' She was tall, with long, curly red hair and she was clutching a copy of the *Sunday Post*. Chiara's heart sank as Paolo's hand reached out to take the pen the girl was offering. 'I'm so embarrassed, I don't usually do things like this,' she promised, as Paolo signed his name next to the photo on the front page, 'but if I don't get your autographs, my friends will never believe I've met you.'

Reluctantly, Chiara signed her name next to his. Paolo seemed not to notice her discomfort. He watched the girl turn her back on them, her rear end swinging flirtatiously in tight hipster jeans, and then began to giggle like a schoolboy. 'My God, if it's like this now, imagine what it will be like when the TV show screens,' he said. 'We're going to be famous. Isn't that fantastic?' Then he looked Chiara up and down, as if he'd only just seen her, and the grin slipped from his face. 'What on earth are you wearing?' he asked suddenly.

She looked down at her baggy track pants and her ratty old black sweater. 'It's Sunday. Everyone dresses casually on a Sunday.'

'You've got your image to think about now,' Paolo replied coldly. 'You should get yourself some decent clothes and grow your hair a bit. If you looked after yourself properly you could be quite a pretty girl, you know, Chiara.'

As she trudged home alone, Chiara felt very like she imagined movie stars must feel the morning after Oscar night when they had to return the cases of fabulous jewels they'd only had on loan. She was sad to be losing Paolo but she wasn't surprised. She'd never expected she'd be allowed to keep him for long.

18

In a few short days Chiara had gone from being fatherless to having a surfeit of them. It seemed as if men all over the country wanted to claim her as their daughter. Janey had received a pile of faxes and e-mails and Pete Farrell forwarded over a whole lot more.

'Cranks most of them,' Janey told her over an evening bottle of wine in The Office. 'But there are some I think are worth following up. Pete Farrell says the *Sunday Post* will pay for a private detective to do the legwork so long as it gets the exclusive on your first meeting with your real father.'

'No thanks.'

'Well, at least think about it.'

'No,' Chiara was adamant.

'Look, I know he's a bit sleazy, but he's a bloody good journalist and that story of his gave *Queen of the Italian Kitchen* the push it needed. The book is a phenomenon. The reps didn't have to sell it into the shops, it walked in by itself and now it's flying straight out again.'

The idea that the book was selling well because the recipes were fabulous didn't seem to have occurred to anyone, thought Chiara bitterly. She eyed the level of wine in the bottle and realized that, even if she started sculling it, she'd still have to sit here talking to Janey for at least fifteen minutes before it would be polite to slip away. And then what if she suggested another bottle?

Chiara longed to go upstairs and work her way through the messages from would-be fathers, a pot of Earl Grey tea at her elbow. She trusted her own instincts enough to know that when she saw the fax, e-mail or letter that her birth father had sent she would recognize it instantly. Despite herself, excitement filled her as she imagined meeting him face to face.

'So Chiara?' Janey's voice broke in on her thoughts. 'What will I tell Pete Farrell?'

She swallowed down a generous mouthful of wine and then grinned as she replied. 'Tell him . . . tell him if it hadn't been for that business about the prawn in the first article I'd have gone with him for sure. Tell him he blew it and that I'm going to give the exclusive to *Hello!*'

The comforting smell of hot Earl Grey scented her small room. Chiara closed the curtains, turned on the bedside lamp and lay on her bed across a pile of pillows. She began with the letters first, envelopes full of old men's spidery handwriting, many complete with a passport-sized photo. There were bald men, grey-haired men, ridiculously young men, hilariously old men. Some wrote of how they'd loved her mother, some described one-night-stands with strangers who might have been her mother and still others claimed to have been secretly watching and following Chiara for years.

Creepiest of all was the letter, in beautiful copperplate handwriting, that quickly turned into a graphic description of the extraordinary sex life this man claimed he'd had with her mother. Chiara crumpled that one up and flung it at the bin with extra force. The faxes and e-mail printouts ended up going the same way and, after an hour of solid reading, she was left with just two 'maybes'. One was a man from Scotland who said he had been in Rome at the same time as her mother. He had slept with a waitress, he never knew her name, it was a one-night-stand. 'There is a tiny chance I could be your father,' he wrote, 'so tiny that I'm in two minds whether to post this letter at all.'

The other was an e-mail from an Italian man, now living

in Brighton. He seemed the right age, he'd been born and brought up in Rome, and said he'd been there throughout the sixties. He'd slept with hundreds of women, he boasted, and Maria Domenica could easily have been one among them.

She put both messages in the top drawer of her bedside table. Neither one had made her spine tingle, but she couldn't bring herself to throw them away. Perhaps later, when she'd finished shooting the TV series in Italy, she'd take a train to Brighton or Scotland and check these men out. She wasn't in any hurry though. It could wait.

From downstairs she heard the door of the club open. It sounded busy down there tonight. Then she heard a cellphone ringing and realized Harriet – who hated the things – had ejected a member who'd insisted on answering a call. He came halfway up the stairs towards the apartment to talk to his caller well away from the unmistakable sound of bar-room buzz. 'No, darling,' he was saying loudly. 'I won't be home for a while. I'm working late at The Office.'

Chiara smiled. That old chestnut. She couldn't believe men were still getting away with it. While she knew she ought to have an early night she was sorely tempted to work a little late at The Office herself. She could help Harriet behind the bar for a bit, make her sit down and take her pregnant weight off her feet. And she could have that conversation with her. The one about how now might be a good time for both of them to stop travelling light. And how choosing a conventional life with a husband and baby perhaps wasn't such a disgraceful thing after all.

19

Chiara and Harriet were standing together in the doorway of a place they'd never imagined they would need to visit. Before them, lined up like soldiers on parade waiting for inspection, were racks and racks of miniature clothes – some pastel pink, some palest blue, but most of them in violent primary colours that clashed shamelessly.

Shops like this were a total assault on the senses, thought Chiara as she peered into the Baby Factory. The air smelled different, somehow sweeter, and it was filled with the cries of tiny human beings.

Reflexively, Harriet sucked in her growing belly as an assistant looked up and caught her eye. 'Can I help you?' she asked with a polite smile.

'I need . . . I need . . . oh, you know . . . baby things,' Harriet replied.

The smile didn't falter. 'What sort of things in particular?'

'Well, everything really,' Harriet admitted. 'But perhaps we should begin with clothes. Have you got anything in black? A simple shift dress or a gypsy shawl perhaps?'

'No, black would be the one colour we don't stock, I'm afraid,' she replied gravely.

'Oh, I see. Well, what else do I need do you think?'

By the time Harriet had a comprehensive list of all the equipment her unborn child would require, she looked ashen. 'Changing tables, cots, pushchairs, special this, that and the other,' she repeated in horror. 'Disposable nappies and car seats . . . and I don't even have a car. I'm sure we didn't have all that stuff when I was a child. It's ridiculous. I can't cope with this right now.'

'Well, you've got months to go, so there's no need to buy it all at once,' pointed out Chiara reasonably. 'Let's just get one item today.'

'OK,' Harriet agreed. 'I'll have a pair of booties, in plain white, and then I want to go and sit in a bar and look at the alcohol.'

The booties, in their cheery Baby Factory bag, were thrust to the very bottom of Harriet's handbag. Once she'd wedged herself behind a low table in the corner of the pub it was difficult to tell she was pregnant at all.

'I'll have a double whiskey with a Pernod chaser,' she told Chiara. 'And three bags of cheese and onion crisps.'

Chiara returned from the bar with two glasses of Perrier water, depressingly decorated with aged slices of lemon, and a bag of unsalted nuts. 'They're all out of whiskey and Pernod so I got you this instead,' she said.

Harriet nodded glumly. 'Good idea.'

They sipped in silence for a while, listening to the annoying squeaks and jingles from the general knowledge quiz machine that someone was playing in the far corner.

'Fancy a game of pool?' Chiara said at last.

'Go on then,' Harriet replied.

Both as useless as each other, they spent ages fumbling around chalking their cues and arranging the balls in a neat triangle. Chiara made the first break and sent balls spinning all over the table but none of them so much as flirted with the idea of sinking into a pocket.

'I'm worried about you,' she told Harriet.

'No, I'm worried about you,' her friend replied, leaning over the table and taking a clumsy shot at the white ball.

'That was terrible,' Chiara said. 'You missed it completely.'

'I know. Can I have another go?'

This time she managed to send the white ball rolling feebly down the table and, as if by divine intervention, it seemed to bend slightly and knock a red ball into the pocket.

Harriet waved her cue into the air. 'Yes! I did it,' she announced to the almost empty pub and bent down to take her next shot. 'I'm going to be all right, you know, Chiara,' she said, bashing the white ball more forcefully this time. 'I was in a bad way after I realized I was pregnant. It took me a while to make the decision to keep the baby, that's why I couldn't tell you before now. But now I'm certain I'm going to be all right. It's you that I'm worried about.'

'Why?'

'You're on your own. The thing with Paolo seems to be fizzling and you still don't know who your father is. I feel guilty. You would never have started this whole Italy business if I hadn't nagged you into it.'

Chiara put her cue down on the table and pulled her friend into a comforting hug. 'Don't feel bad, Harriet. I'm going to be all right too. I found my grandparents in Italy and I've made new friends there. I don't regret going. I don't even regret my stupid crush on Paolo because it was fun while it lasted.'

'Yes, but I know what my future is.' Harriet stroked her belly. 'Do you know yours?'

'I've got a TV show to make. That's as much of a future as I can handle at the moment.'

20

Pepina's kitchen had been taken over completely. There were camera men trampling dust all over the floor, there were girls wearing headphones, rushing round and rattling out instructions, there were mountains of equipment being ferried in from trucks that were lined up in the driveway. Paolo was at the centre of things as usual while Pepina sat on a smart, new kitchen stool, fanning herself and trying to look as though none of this chaos was fazing her in the least.

Chiara paused in the doorway. 'My God,' she said. 'This is ridiculous.'

A clipboard-toting girl whistled over. 'Deliveries at the back door, please,' she said crisply, looking down at Chiara's luggage.

'I'm not delivering anything . . . well, except myself. I'm Chiara Fox.'

The girl blushed. 'Sorry, I didn't recognize you,' she apologized. 'You look really different without your tomato crown and your basil necklace. And Paolo said he wasn't sure what time you were due to arrive.' She flushed even deeper when she said his name and hurriedly looked down at her clipboard and began ticking away officiously.

Just then, Pepina looked up and spotted her. She dropped her fan and pushed her way through the crowd and past the camera gear in her rush to embrace her granddaughter. '*Ciao, bella*,' she said and kissed her on both cheeks.

Summoning up her shreds of Italian, Chiara launched into an apology. 'I'm so sorry about all this. I had no idea—'

'Don't worry. It's no problem,' Pepina reassured her and reaching over, gently pinched her cheek. 'You beautiful girl,' she said in her heavily accented Italian. She looked older and smaller. The weight had dropped off her and the colour washed from her face.

Erminio was hiding out round the side of the house, dozing in his cane chair, beneath the grapevine. Rosaria was sitting beside him, writing in a big book she had balanced on her knee. A cordless phone was on the arm of her chair and she was wearing spectacles that kept slipping down her shiny nose. She looked slightly thinner than she had the last time they'd met, thought Chiara, but also more harried.

'Paolo has double-booked us,' she complained, treating Chiara to an accusing stare. 'Unless Giacomo Salerni can build another two cabins by the time we open next month, we're completely sunk.'

'What are you opening next month?' Chiara asked, confused for a moment.

'This tourist business my Paolo is so keen on. The diary is filling up with bookings so fast.' She patted the huge volume on her knee. 'Since your cookbook came out everyone is calling me wanting to come and learn the secrets of Mamma Pepina's kitchen. God knows what it will be like once my Paolo has been on the television. I'm not sure I can cope.'

'What about Pepina, how will she cope?' demanded Chiara, angrily. 'She's old, she can't be expected to stand up and teach people to cook day after day.'

Rosaria shrugged. 'Oh, I'll help and so will Paolo. Mamma only has to chop the odd onion and look decorative.'

'And how about Erminio? Doesn't he mind his house being overrun with strangers?'

Her grandfather heard his name being spoken and opened his eyes. Focusing on Chiara, he smiled broadly. 'How's my beautiful girl?' he asked, then launched into a volley of Italian so fast and excitable she couldn't hope to keep up.

'What's he saying?' she asked Rosaria.

'Oh, it's fine for him, he doesn't have any of the work to do,' was all the reply she got.

'Yes, but what did he say?' she insisted.

Rosaria explained that the shockwaves of excitement caused by the book and TV show had reached beyond San Giulio, all the way to Milan where Salvatore, her only brother, lived with his family. He was coming home to be part of the thrill of the shoot and so were her younger sisters, Sandra, Giovanna and Claudia.

'For years they've been too busy with their work and their children to bother coming back to see the old people. Now they're all coming at once and I'm the one who'll have to find somewhere for them to sleep and put food on their plates. The old man is thrilled, of course, especially about Salvatore, he was always the favourite. But it's all right for him,' Rosaria repeated wearily. 'He doesn't have any of the work to do.'

The house was so full that Chiara couldn't stay in her usual room. There were boxes of food and gear stacked up in there now and, once they were removed, the room would be needed for her uncle or one of her aunts.

'I'm sorry, I just assumed I'd be able to stay here,' said Chiara, slightly put out. 'I told the production manager there was no need to book a hotel room for me but I should have checked with you first.'

'Call Caffe Angeli,' suggested the harassed Rosaria, waving the cordless phone at her. 'Perhaps you can go and stay at Giovanni and Franco's place.'

Before she could make the call, the girl with the clipboard caught up with her. 'I'm really sorry,' she began. 'You didn't think we were going to be shooting with you today, did you? Only all we have scheduled is food shots for the opening credits and we're running late with that.'

'I can stay to watch though, can't I?'

'Yes, of course you can, although I can't imagine it will be terribly exciting. All the really clever stuff will be done in post-production.'

Roger, the director, had come up with a concept for the opening credits that involved using time-lapse photography to make it look as though piles of Chiara's food were being eaten away and plates were being licked clean by some invisible ravenous force.

As she watched them setting up for the first shot, Chiara fought a feeling of regret. She'd spoiled the peace of this place with her book. She'd changed everybody's lives and she wasn't sure it was for the better. Only Paolo seemed truly happy.

She'd missed him today when her bus pulled into the piazza. She'd peered out the window, half expecting him to be standing there in his usual spot, waving and blowing kisses, but he was far too busy these days to waste time standing at a bus stop.

'Your brother Paolo, he's totally gorgeous,' the clipboard girl rattled away enthusiastically beside her. 'Is he single? All the girls on the crew are crazy about him, you know. They're having a challenge to see which one can get to kiss him first.'

'He's not my brother, he's my cousin . . . and he was sort of my boyfriend,' said Chiara.

'Oh really? I'm sorry, I hadn't realized.' The girl giggled nervously. 'Well, I wouldn't let him out of your sight in that case. You've got a lot of competition out there.'

By now the crew was almost ready to begin shooting. The cameraman was slugging back the dregs of his coffee and polishing off a wedge of *calzone* stuffed with thinly sliced *prosciutto* that Pepina had made for the crew. A food stylist had baked a flat, round loaf that was sitting proudly on the pine kitchen table as she fussily dredged flour over it. There was just one hold-up. Roger was standing in the middle of the kitchen having a tantrum. 'No, no, no,' he was yelling. 'It's not right at all.'

'What don't you like? Is the loaf the wrong shape?' said the poor food stylist, looking horrified.

'No, that's not it,' he snapped in reply.

'Is it the range of crockery we're using? You approved it when we were in England.'

'No, the crockery's fine,' he said, glancing down at the blue-and-yellow hand-painted plates on the worn old pine table. Then he struck his forehead with his right hand like a bad pantomime actor. 'That's it, it's the damn table. It's not rustic enough. It has to go. It's not the right look at all. To me, it just doesn't say Italian kitchen. Get me something that's more distressed.'

Nervously, the girl in headphones looked down at her call sheet. 'This is going to put us behind schedule, Roger,' she warned. 'And if we're behind schedule, we'll go over-budget.'

'I can't work with this table,' he insisted and stormed out of the room, calling over his shoulder. 'I'll give you an hour to find another one.'

Chiara watched Paolo. He looked so handsome and seemed utterly relaxed, standing there surrounded by the cameras and crew. She was almost glad about the delay, for it would give her a chance to talk to him again. Despite everything he'd said to her that day in Pizza Pizza she was still struggling to believe he'd turned cold on her so fast.

'Ah, *bella*.' He noticed her at last and smiled a lukewarm welcome. 'This Roger, he is amazing, eh? He notices every detail. I think our show is in good hands with him.'

Chiara wondered when exactly her TV series had become 'our show'. She caught sight of Paolo's handsome face looking out at her from a monitor in the corner and realized the viewers would love him.

'If you have a moment,' she hissed. 'Perhaps we could go outside and talk?'

'Of course, of course,' he replied and followed her out of

the door and into the orchard. Once outside, away from the TV crew, he took her hands and brushed her cheeks with his. 'What's wrong, *cara*?' he asked solicitously. 'You don't seem so happy today?'

'It's not "our show" Paolo, it's mine,' she snapped.

'I know that, I'm sorry. It's hard work for me, you know.' He smiled at her ruefully. 'I'm juggling so much right now and it's exhausting. I have more than the TV series and my tourism business to think about. My photography might be taking off too. I've had amazing feedback about those pictures of mine that appeared in your book and there may be opportunities for more work.'

Something was slowly dawning on Chiara. Had Paolo been stringing her along the whole time? Was Giovanni right about him after all?

'So many opportunities . . .' she mused. 'And none of them would have happened without me and my books, would they? The business, the cabins, your fifteen minutes of fame?'

'That's right and it's insane. It's all happening at once and I have to make the most of it, don't I? And I'm a little frightened, Chiara, to tell you the truth.'

'Frightened of what?' she asked briskly.

'Mamma keeps telling me I've bitten off more than I can chew. And you know, maybe she's right. When all these tourists arrive and fill the place up, will our family be able to cope? I'm not sure we will. Perhaps I've made a big mistake investing so much in these cabins.'

He seemed seriously concerned and despite herself, Chiara softened. 'I can stay around once filming has finished, you know. There's no reason for me to go rushing back to London. Perhaps I can help out.'

Paolo grinned. 'Would you? That would be great. And maybe, once everything is under control, we'll have a little more time to spend together. We're still the best of friends, eh?'

Paolo gave her a squeeze and Chiara felt her stomach flip-flop in reply. She still wasn't completely immune to him, no matter how much she wanted to be. Then she noticed he seemed distracted. He was gazing over her shoulder at Giacomo Salerni, who was leaning back on one of the half-built cabins, dozing in a pool of warm sunlight.

Paolo cursed vigorously in Italian and, letting her loose, strode over to give his builder a rude awakening.

21

It was late and the light was fading by the time Chiara made it into San Giulio. A group of teenagers was outside Caffe Angeli, propped up on scooters, chirping like excited birds as they admired each other's clothes and jewellery.

Inside, Giovanni was at his post behind the stainless steel counter while Franco, at the corner table, was playing cards with his cronies.

The welcome she got was as warm as ever, but Giovanni held up his hand before she could enquire about her chances of staying in his spare room. 'Before you say a word,' he began, 'we said no when Paolo asked us and our answer is going to be the same for you.'

Chiara felt terrible. 'Look, don't worry. I can find a hotel or *pensione* or something. I don't want to impose on anyone and really I could just—'

With another wave of his hand, Giovanni stopped her mid-sentence. 'Wait a moment, I think we're talking about two different things. I assumed you were going to ask me if you could shoot part of your TV show in Caffe Angeli. That's what Paolo wanted.'

She was horrified. 'Oh God, no. Don't let them come and shoot here. They're a nightmare.'

Giovanni laughed. 'Don't worry, even if I'd entertained the idea, Franco wouldn't hear of it. But you wanted something different? You need a place to stay?'

She nodded. 'Yes, but it was really cheeky of me to ask and honestly I'll find a hotel or—'

'Chiara, Chiara, of course, you are welcome to stay with us for as long as you like. Franco will be thrilled . . . so long as you don't bring any of your cameramen home with you, that is.' He smiled over at his father. 'Papa won't even watch television, he says it's all rubbish. In our house we listen to a little opera and the radio news.'

'That sounds perfect to me. Honestly, they only managed about half a day of filming and already I'm completely over the whole thing. Paolo loves it though. I think he's more cut out for it than I am.'

'Yes, he seems very excited,' agreed Giovanni. 'He was in here the other day and spoke of very little else. Also he seemed to think we might want to get involved in his tourism business, but Papa wouldn't hear of that either. He says that at Caffe Angeli we're happy with things the way they are.'

Chiara slipped on an apron and helped serve the trickle of evening customers. It was a quiet night and there was time to chat to Giovanni and catch up on the local gossip. He seemed to know everything of interest that had happened in the town.

'They've put Pepina's sister Lucia in an old folk's home,' he told her. 'Poor thing, she loved that apartment of hers and no one thought they'd ever budge her, but she was becoming so senile it wasn't safe to leave her there alone.

'And what else? Oh, Gina Rossi has closed the lemonade stand she used to have in the corner of the piazza. God knows how old she is, a hundred maybe. She says she doesn't have the strength any more to squeeze lemons all day and none of the young people are interested in taking it over.

'And did you hear about Giacomo Salerni?' Giovanni's eyes twinkled. 'He's been going round town complaining to everyone about what a terrible payer Paolo is. Apparently he insists on using the cheapest materials and he never gets Giacomo's wages to him on time.'

'You're just saying that because you don't like Paolo,' teased Chiara.

'Me? It's nothing to do with me,' said Giovanni, all innocence. 'I'm only passing on what Giacomo's been saying. But Papa reckons those cabins are likely to fall down on the heads of Paolo's tourists they're so badly built.'

'So he did put them up without planning permission then?'

'Don't ask me. I know nothing, I know nothing,' laughed Giovanni.

The days settled into a pleasant routine. The insanity of life in front of the cameras was balanced each evening with the soothing time she shared with Giovanni and Franco. Some nights she was too dazed to do more than take a bath and have an early night. Other times she helped out in the *caffe* for a couple of hours and entertained the two men with stories about her day.

She felt so close to both of them. Even though her grasp of Italian remained frankly pathetic, she and Franco made themselves understood with a mixture of sign language and smiles. Warmth and affection radiated from him.

And Giovanni, well, he was special. No matter how tired she was, her day didn't seem complete unless she spent a few minutes talking with him before bath and bedtime. His conversation soothed her. It worked at the knots in her back and the cricks in her neck as cleverly as a masseur might. Each day she looked forward to the moment when she could sit down and refresh herself with a slice of watermelon and Giovanni's company.

Roger, the TV director, had been relentless. He'd shot scenes of her and Paolo digging in the vegetable patch, charring fish over Pepina's wood fire and shopping in the market for fresh supplies. He had footage of them feeding forkfuls of food to each other, he'd captured Erminio sneaking into the kitchen to pinch little treats and he was planning a big final scene showing the extended family enjoying a long, Italian lunch at the table beneath the lemon tree. But, no matter how many tantrums he threw, there was one shot he couldn't get. Franco wouldn't be persuaded to allow a single camera inside Caffe Angeli.

'Crazy old man,' Roger complained. 'He's got all those amazing paintings over the walls. You'd think he'd want to show them off. Paolo, Chiara, you must be able to do something? Talk to him, offer him more money.'

'We've tried, we've tried,' Paolo promised. 'You've asked him, haven't you, Chiara?'

'Yes,' she lied. 'But he won't do it for me either.'

Another envelope had arrived for Chiara this morning, from Janey. 'More fathers for you,' she'd printed neatly on the front. There hadn't been time to open it yet, but as soon as they'd finished the day's shooting she was going to go straight back to Franco's house to find out what was inside.

Franco lived around the corner from Caffe Angeli in one of the few old-style buildings left standing in the town. Built round a tiny courtyard it was just ramshackle enough to be charming. Inside it was filled with big, old-fashioned pieces of furniture, dressers and carved chairs, all wedding presents given to Franco and his wife years ago. The place was guarded by a scruffy brown dog called Bruno, a stray that he had started feeding and now couldn't get rid of.

Strictly speaking, Bruno wasn't supposed to be inside the house but, when Chiara got home, the two men were still at work, so she coaxed the dog indoors and pulled him onto her bed to curl up beside her.

'If you don't tell, I won't,' she whispered in the dog's ear and snuggled so close she could feel the strength of his heartbeat. She tore open the envelope and pulled out Janey's letter:

'More cranks, I expect, but you never know, do you? Pete Farrell from the *Sunday Post* says to tell you his offer about the private detective still stands. Let me know if you change your mind.

Book still selling well. Have ordered a reprint to tie in with the start of the TV show. Can't wait to see it.

J xxxx

There were only a few faxes and e-mail printouts this time and Chiara quickly scanned through and dismissed them. She saved the sole letter until last, squeezing and prodding it like an excited child with a Christmas present. It felt fat enough to contain a photo and a couple of sheets of decent quality notepaper.

As she tried to open it she felt a trembling. At first she thought it was the dog, still pressed against her, that was shaking but he was in a blissful sleep and it was she, Chiara, who was quivering with excitement. Impatiently, she tore at the envelope and tipped it upside down. A black and white photo fell out. It was a typical tourist shot, taken in front of the Trevi Fountain and it showed a slender, dark-haired girl with deep-set eyes and a strong nose standing close to a handsome, fair-haired boy. They were both smiling at the camera and squinting in the bright sunlight. They seemed terribly young.

The letter was on plain, white notepaper and the handwriting neat and clear. Chiara almost couldn't bear to start reading it. She put the letter down on the bed for a moment, took a few deep breaths, then picked it up again and let her eyes focus on the writing:

My dear

The photo you have in your hand is of me, William Smith, and the girl I was in love with whose name was Maria Domenica Carrozza. I met her one day when I was drinking coffee in a *caffe* beside the Spanish Steps. I was in Rome studying art and had been feeling lonely. She noticed me and was kind. First she gave me her friendship, then her love. We'd only been together a few months when she told me she was pregnant. I panicked and fled home to

England. By the time I'd come to my senses and gone back to Rome to find her, she'd disappeared. No one knew where she was, she seemed to have left without a trace. I realized then how little I knew about her. In those months we'd been together, I'd done all the talking. Even the name of her home town was a mystery to me. I feel so ashamed and sad that all these years I've had a daughter and not known her. Sad too that Maria Domenica and I never found each other again.

Chiara put the letter down and allowed the tears that had filled her eyes to spill at last. She cried for Maria Domenica and for this stranger William but most of all she cried for herself. The brown dog licked the salty tears from her cheeks and, when her eyes cleared, she read the final few lines.

I'm not a writer like you. I'm not used to putting my thoughts and feelings down on paper so I fear this letter is woefully inadequate. I would love to talk to you, to see you. I'd happily come, if you say the word. But I think the ball must be in your court, my dear. You must decide how far we take this. After all these years it may be too late for me to be father to you. Although I hope not.

Yours,
William Smith.

Chiara rested her head on the dog's woolly back and took comfort in the even rhythm of his breathing and the warmth of his fat, little body. She held the letter tightly in one hand and the photo in the other. She tried to imagine this man, this William Smith, and what he might look like now. He wanted to meet her but she wasn't sure about that. She imagined embarrassment, awkward silences and pulling away from his attempts at fatherly embraces.

When Giovanni and Franco arrived home, exhausted from the day's work, she was still lying on her bed, Bruno sleeping at her side. He woke at the sound of a key in the lock and sat up and barked, but he was far too lazy to jump down and investigate.

Giovanni pushed open her bedroom door and peeped round it. 'What's that animal doing in the house? Bruno, get down right now,' he said, shocked by the sight of the little dog caught up contentedly in the sheets and pillows.

'Sorry, my fault,' Chiara mumbled.

The dog rolled its eyes and slunk off the bed and out of the room, but Giovanni didn't seem to notice. He was staring at Chiara, curled up in the foetal position on her bed. 'What's wrong?' he asked, concerned.

She unfolded her body and held out the letter and photograph in reply. Giovanni sat gingerly on a corner of her bed and examined them. 'Well, this is good, isn't it?' he said when he'd finished reading. 'Finally you've found your real father.'

'I know. I thought I'd feel so fantastic if I found him but I don't. I'm in such a mess over what I should do next.'

'Go and meet him.'

'It's not that simple.'

'Yes, it is.'

Chiara tried to explain how she felt but, as she spoke, her words seemed pathetic even to her. She was frightened, she realized, scared to take this next step in case things didn't work out perfectly. 'What would you do if you were me?' she asked.

Giovanni looked thoughtful. He eased himself more comfortably onto the bed and propped himself up with one of Chiara's pillows.

'Never mind me, think about your mother,' he began. 'She may have been headstrong and stubborn and taken a few wrong turns in her life, but she was brave. She was never afraid to step out into the unknown. If she were in your place now I don't believe she'd think twice. She'd go to meet this man.'

Chiara looked at him and chewed her bottom lip. 'Do you think?'

Giovanni lay back into the pillow and curled his legs up on the bed beside him. He held William's letter out to her. 'Yes,' he insisted. 'On paper he sounds good. And this is certainly your mother beside the Trevi Fountain with him. To be honest, Chiara, you don't have a choice. If you don't go to find him you'll regret it for the rest of your life. You've come this far, you found me and Franco and your family, now you just have to go one final step further.'

He was right, she knew that. As soon as the TV show was in the can, she'd go and meet this stranger who owned a little bit of her.

Giovanni was curled up now in the same spot Bruno's stout, hairy little body had occupied a short while earlier. If she shifted slightly she could warm herself next to him like she had with the dog. Perhaps he'd put his arms around her and take her weight against him and her nostrils would fill with the bitter smell of roasted coffee beans mixed with the soapy scent of the baby shampoo he used on his silver-tipped hair.

But then they heard Franco's voice echoing down the corridor and Giovanni jerked himself up. 'Papa will kill me,' he whispered, perching awkwardly on the edge of the bed again. 'He blames me for letting Maria Domenica slip out of our lives and now here I am sending you away.'

'I'm not running away though, Giovanni. You'll always know where I am, I'll make sure of that.'

He looked at her sadly and then blurted, 'If I were only ten years younger, I wouldn't let you go. I'd make you stay right here with me for ever.'

He got up quickly then and was out of the door and gone before she could reply.

Chiara was stunned. How could she not have noticed

Giovanni was falling in love with her? And if she had noticed, what would she have done?

It was too much to think about. Chiara could only cope with one emotional crisis at a time and for now it was William Smith, her real father, who was patiently awaiting her reply. She'd write the letter this evening and post it tomorrow, she decided.

22

A plastic cup of weak coffee was jiggling on the table in front of her, a giant chocolate chip cookie posing beside it. Chiara couldn't stomach the thought of tasting either. She wished she were anywhere but here on this train, streaking up the spine of England, taking her closer to a stranger called William Smith.

Chiara had read and re-read the words of her father's letter before she'd noticed the most important things of all, the postmark and the return address. She'd stared at them in shock for a while and then cried. William Smith was in Liverpool, just across the water from the house where she'd grown up. Had he been there all along?

She sipped her drink and scowled at its bland, bitter flavour. Desperate to keep herself occupied, she pulled a clear plastic folder out of her handbag and sorted through the contents for about the hundredth time. Inside was the pencil drawing her mother had made of her giggling nervously as she stood at the top of the high slide at New Brighton Baths; the old wedding shot of Pepina and Erminio before time and sadness had stripped the youth from their faces; and the shot William had sent of himself and Maria Domenica posing together by the Trevi Fountain. She had stared at that one for so long she could shut her eyes and still see every detail – the sunflowers on her mother's dress, the ugly hat on the head of the tourist sitting on a bench beside her, the glorious fountain behind them. Maria Domenica was smiling but on closer inspection her eyes seemed wary as they squinted into the sunlight. Had she distrusted or disliked whoever was behind the camera? Or, more likely, by the time this shot was taken, had she already begun to suspect she'd fallen pregnant?

Chiara imagined how lost and alone her mother must have felt for all those years, her story locked up inside her, never feeling free to confide in anyone. She felt angry with herself and disloyal. How could she have put that most intensely private of stories into cold hard print for strangers to read?

If it hadn't been for her obsession about finding her father, *Queen of the Italian Kitchen* could have been a simple book of recipes and it wouldn't have been any the worse for it. People would still have bought it to drool over the photos and sworn that one day they'd remember to buy the ingredients for a *pasta e fagioli* before slipping it on the shelf with all their other cookbooks.

But Chiara hadn't been content with that. Spilling her mother's secrets, she'd managed to succeed where Maria Domenica had failed. She'd found the man who had stood so proudly next to her beside the Trevi Fountain all those years ago. She was on the brink of meeting him. Unless . . . unless.

Chiara tried for a moment to imagine what her mother might have done in her place. Not an easy thing, for Maria Domenica had been a very different person – more restrained, sometimes slow to give of herself, often solemn. Despite what Giovanni had said, would she have gone through with this meeting with William? Or would she have decided that their lives had progressed so far that it was hardly safe or desirable for their paths to cross at this point?

Somehow she could imagine her mother, satisfied merely by knowing her William was alive and well, carrying on with her life without ever seeing him.

Lost in indecision, Chiara stared out of the window. There was a canal winding its way parallel to the railway line with brightly coloured narrow boats and little hump-backed bridges. It was pretty but it was soon left far behind as the train rushed onwards.

She had made this trip so many times when her mother was alive. Snatching a day or two from whichever hot restaurant kitchen had claimed her time, she'd sat on the train and counted the landmarks to home: first Watford Junction, then the sprawl of the Midlands rolling to the north and suddenly the Runcorn Bridge and she was nearly there.

Alex liked to meet her at Lime Street Station, driving her home through the Wallasey tunnel in whichever of his clanking, unreliable cars was on the road. When they got there her mother would always be waiting in the kitchen and often there was some favourite treat like shortbread biscuits baking in the oven, filling the narrow room with a sweet, buttery heat.

When it was time to leave again for London a day or two later, Maria Domenica would stand at the gate waving until the very last minute. 'Last chance for a goodbye to your mum,' Alex liked to say as he steered round the corner and when Chiara looked back, her mother was always there, always waving.

Homecomings would never be that way again. Death had swept away the warm, safe world her mother always pulled Chiara into. Remembering that it had disappeared for good was the loneliest, saddest feeling.

She unwrapped her chocolate chip cookie and took a comforting bite. Staring out of the window again, it slowly dawned on Chiara that there was only one track for her to take. She really had no choice. Like the train from London Euston to Liverpool Lime Street she had to keep moving forwards.

Things had changed in the tall house by the river. Alex had the property pages spread all over the place and was madly circling ads for comfortable retirement bungalows and one-bedroom units. 'You're thinking of moving on,' Chiara said in shock. She dropped her holdall on the floor and shed her jacket.

'Property market's gone crazy,' he told her. 'This place is worth an absolute fortune. I'm planning to sell up, buy something cheaper and spend the difference on a little boat so me, Bob and Tony can go fishing together.'

Chiara nodded towards the choppy sludge of the Irish Sea. 'What sort of fish are you going to catch in that?' she asked. 'Radioactive ones?'

He laughed at her. 'It's not about catching fish, Chiara, is it? That's not the point at all.'

And then he sat beside her and took her hand, serious now. 'You didn't say why you were coming home, Chiara my love. Is everything all right?'

Unexpectedly muted by unspent tears, she plucked William Smith's letter from her bag and handed it over. 'My father,' she managed to mutter.

Alex didn't rip into the envelope blindly as she had, but weighed the letter in his hand and considered it for a moment. 'It's got a Liverpool postmark,' he remarked matter-of-factly then pulled out the sheets of notepaper.

Chiara saw how his pink skin faded to pale as he read William Smith's words. 'I'm sorry, Dad,' she told him. 'This is upsetting you.'

He shook his head and now it was his turn to struggle with silence. At last he cleared his throat and managed to say, 'I'm not upset, only a bit shocked.'

'Shocked? What by?'

'Here.' He pointed to the return address at the top of the letter. 'See what it says here.'

'William Smith, Liverpool Art Supplies, Bold Street, Liverpool,' Chiara read. 'What's so shocking about that?'

'Well, the thing is,' Alex said slowly, 'Liverpool Art Supplies is where I used to go to buy your mother's drawing paper and pencils.'

Chiara considered his words for a moment. 'Oh,' she said faintly.

'It's probably changed hands ten times since then though,' Alex added hurriedly. 'I mean, what shop is run by the same bloke for over thirty years in this day and age?'

'No, you're right,' agreed Chiara, but there was a heavy feeling in the pit of her stomach that hadn't been there before. She rubbed her belly nervously.

'Are you OK?' Alex asked.

'Giant chocolate chip cookie on the train,' she replied. 'Can't have agreed with me.'

Alex wasn't really listening. His expression was dazed and the pink hue still hadn't returned to his cheeks. 'She went there once, on her own, your mother,' he offered.

'To Liverpool Art Supplies?'

'That's right. She said she wanted to see exactly what sort of stuff they had there. Maybe she wanted to try her hand at some different techniques or something, I don't know.'

'And?'

'She only went the once. Came back empty-handed and said she preferred it when I went over and bought things for her. Said it was like getting a present every time.'

Chiara couldn't believe her mother had managed to hide a secret this big from her for so long. 'So do you think . . . ?' she began.

'I don't know, Chiara. Maybe.'

'So what was he like?' she pressed him. 'You must remember the man who served you. What was he like?'

'I don't know, Chiara.' There was a look of hopelessness about Alex. 'To be honest, he never made much of an impression on me. He was just a bloke. Why don't you go over there to Liverpool Art Supplies? Then you can see for yourself.'

23

He hadn't tried to kiss her yet or even touch her and she was thankful. Chiara wasn't ready for William Smith to be her father.

She had decided to come to Liverpool Art Supplies without telling him, to catch him by surprise. This was the last piece of the puzzle, the final unwritten chapter of her book, and her step had slowed as she walked down Bold Street and neared the racks of arty postcards grouped around the doorway of the shop.

She stared through the window. William's shop was a cramped, disorganized place. Shelves stacked with tubes of paint and drawing paper rose to the high ceiling and every inch of floor space was cluttered with wooden easels and yet more racks of artists' tools – slabs of pastels, tins of acrylics, brushes and inks. Behind the counter, immersed in serving a customer, was a tall, slim man with a strong face.

Mentally, Chiara compared him to the photo she was still carrying in her handbag. Perhaps his hair, now thinned to a downy layer, had once been lush and fair; and his cheeks, now cobwebbed with wrinkles, had once been smooth. Maybe in his youth he had looked like the man who had posed in front of the Trevi Fountain with his arm around her mother. She couldn't be sure.

She'd stood by that window staring in as customers came and went. Although she wanted to walk through the door, somehow her feet wouldn't carry her forward.

Stranded out on the pavement, she watched and waited

until the last customers left, the door was shut behind them and the yellowing closed sign hung up on it. Then, feeling weak and stupid, she'd sloped off home like a coward to Alex and he'd made her tea and lavished her with sympathy and understanding, but then, at long last, just as she was about to climb the stairs to her old bedroom at the very top of the house, a sterner note had crept into his voice and he'd told her, 'You've got to go back there tomorrow, you know, love. You've come this far, don't go giving up on things now.'

So she slept on it and when she woke in the morning the fear had mostly gone and what had replaced it felt more like anger. She took the bus through the Mersey tunnel to Liverpool once again and this time moved briskly up Bold Street and didn't let her pace falter as she approached Liverpool Art Supplies. Trying to look inconspicuous, Chiara slipped into the shop and, half-hidden by an easel, pretended to be absorbed in some jars of paint. When she thought it was safe, she sneaked a closer look at the man behind the counter and thought she caught some similarities to herself there – in his wide eyes and generous mouth when he smiled goodbye to a customer, in the broad fingers that tapped out numbers on the till.

He looked up and met her gaze. 'Good morning. Having a good day?'

She flushed, nodded a yes and, her nerve failing her, scuttled out of the shop as soon as it seemed decent.

Over a coffee at a café across the road, she scorned herself for cowardice and contemplated her next move. Should she march back in there bold as brass and introduce herself? Or should she run home to the safety of Alex again? Chiara was draining the last of her coffee when she heard someone nearby clearing his throat.

'Excuse me,' a deep male voice said.

She looked up. William Smith was hesitating in the doorway. 'You're Chiara, aren't you?' he asked.

'How did you know?' she said in a voice suddenly strangled by shyness.

He smiled. 'I saw your picture in the *Sunday Post*. I recognized you from that.'

They stared at each other for a moment and then Chiara remembered her manners. 'Would you like to sit down and have a coffee?' she asked. She'd wondered about this man for so long and now here he was, standing right there before her.

Her father had tired eyes and fine hair that seemed to stand out from his head in little tufts just like hers always had. As he tugged anxiously at a wisp of it, she recognized her own nervous habit. She saw herself in the line of his jaw, the openness of his face, the easiness of his smile. It was wonderful but strange. She hardly knew what to feel.

'I've only got fifteen minutes,' he said, choosing the seat opposite her. 'A friend is minding my shop but she can't fill in for long.'

There was an awkward silence. Chiara smiled at him but she couldn't find the right words.

'My mother looked for you,' she blurted at last. 'She walked around New Brighton for years hoping she'd see your face.'

He looked away from her and flushed. 'I know. I read your book. I'm sorry.'

'She tried so hard to find you before she married Alex.'

'I know that,' he said, still struggling to meet her eyes.

'Did you ever think about her? Or me?' Chiara was growing angrier now.

'Yes, of course I thought of you. I was stupid and irresponsible but I wasn't a monster. I'm not unfeeling.' He paused for a moment and lowered his voice. 'To be honest, after a while, I tried not to think of you. I grew older, got married, had two sons and life seemed to pass by at an extraordinary pace.'

'I have brothers?' Overwhelmed, Chiara felt herself softening towards him.

'Yes, David and Mark. My marriage broke up but I still see them. They know about you now.'

'Do they look like me?'

He smiled. 'Your eyes, your hair.'

'Do they want to meet me?' She was eager now.

Slowly, he shook his head. 'It's a difficult situation. They haven't forgiven me for leaving their own mother yet. They're not ready to accept that I had a child with another woman before they were even born.'

'You keep leaving women,' she said numbly.

'No.' He glanced down at his cooling coffee but didn't take a sip. 'It's not like that at all. I've made mistakes. I never should have left your mother. I never should have married my wife.' He held out his hands, palms upwards. 'Everyone makes mistakes, don't they?' He waited in silence for her reply.

Chiara thought carefully. Whatever words she chose to say next were the important ones. She formed the sentence carefully in her mind as if she were speaking a foreign language.

'I do understand,' she said at last. 'But I can't forgive you. Not just like that.'

When William's fifteen minutes were up, Chiara agreed to come back and meet him later, once he'd closed up the shop. He suggested they could return to the café for an early supper.

'I think you'll like the food,' he told her, clearly relieved to find refuge in safe pleasantries.

Saying goodbye to William Smith was almost as awkward as saying hello had been. Chiara hoped they could do something about the tension that lay between them. She wanted so desperately to like her father. But, more importantly, she needed there to be a reason, a really good reason, why he'd never tried to find the woman he'd abandoned and the child he surely knew she would be raising.

Of all the meals she'd ever eaten, this dinner was the

strangest. Not the food, that was fine. How could she complain about a wide bowl filled with a soup of braised leeks, broccoli, bacon, pine nuts and broken spaghetti. There was a salad of rocket with generous shards of Parmesan and a basket of bread to mop up the soup's salty juices.

To Chiara's relief, the conversation flowed. She told William all about her childhood growing up in the tall house on Egremont Promenade, about her life in London and her experiences in San Giulio.

But the stuff she wasn't saying was more important. This was the first time she had ever sat down to eat with her father and she could feel the evening speeding by – the pasta plates were cleared away, the pudding bowls were brought – without ever feeling like they were getting to the little nuggets of things they truly needed to speak about.

Time after time he tried to divert the conversation away from Maria Domenica. He listened uncomfortably to Chiara's description of how her mother's life had turned out after he'd left her. He fidgeted with his cup and the sugar bowl as she recalled their ferry trips across the River Mersey and described the café in New Brighton Baths where her mother had worked for the Learys long after she really needed the money. He looked thoughtful while she told him of the strength of Alex's love for them both and he rubbed a broad finger beneath moist eyes when she spared no detail of her mother's final months.

'How sad it all is,' he said when she'd finished. 'Whoever would have thought things would turn out like this. Your mother never knew what a success you've turned out to be.'

Then, with a little coaxing, he told Chiara the story she didn't know – of how he first met Maria Domenica in the *caffe* beside the Spanish Steps. He had been a student, newly arrived in Rome from Florence where he'd been studying Renaissance art and architecture. He didn't know anyone in the city or have much money.

'Every day I'd treat myself to a drink at her *caffe*, standing up at the counter because I couldn't afford the table prices. I think your mother realized how lonely I was. She always found time to stop and exchange a few words with me.'

'What did you talk about?'

'Usually I'd been out sketching buildings or people's faces and Maria Domenica liked to look at my sketchpad to see what I'd been working on. She was a pretty girl and I'd already half lost my heart to her. So when she mentioned that on her days off she liked to explore the galleries or the Vatican Museum, I offered to go with her. Then she asked me to help her with her English and that gave us the chance to get closer. I didn't seduce her though. The truth is I was just as inexperienced as she was. I guess that's why she got pregnant so quickly. Neither of us really knew what we were doing.'

'And what happened when you realized she was pregnant?' This was the crux of things. This was what she needed to know.

He said nothing for a moment. He looked at her and then looked away. 'It's not a story I'm proud of,' he said softly.

'Tell me,' she urged.

'Maria Domenica broke the news to me one evening,' he began tentatively. 'We'd been for a walk and were sitting beside the Trevi Fountain watching the tourists toss in their coins. She'd seemed quiet, distracted, and finally she blurted it out. She was pregnant. She was sure of it. And then she cried and I held her, muttering I don't know what – something comforting, I suppose – but inside I felt pure panic. That night she smuggled me up to her room above the *caffe* and we stayed awake for hours, talking and making love. The next morning she rose early for work and I stayed in her room until the coast was clear and I could sneak out without anyone seeing me. I went back to my *pensione*, packed my sketchpads and clothes into a suitcase and left. I ran away. I don't remember what was in my head that day beyond fear and panic. Only that I thought I was too young to be a father and wanted to put as much distance as possible between myself and the mess I'd made.'

There were tears in Chiara's eyes and she let them fall for she didn't have the strength to brush them away. 'Imagine how she must have felt. Can you imagine it?' she asked him, when she trusted herself to speak again. 'She'd have waited all day for you to come in for your drink. For days she'd have wondered where you'd gone. Perhaps she wandered round Rome looking for you in the galleries and museums. I wonder how long it took before she realized you weren't coming back.'

William looked agonized and said nothing.

She tried not to hate him, tried to understand him. 'Do you think you ever really loved her?' she asked.

'Yes, I loved her,' he replied in a low voice.

Chiara only had one question left. She was reluctant to ask it. She'd wanted to give William every chance to tell her freely. But she was down to the last dregs of her hot chocolate now and he was showing no signs of coming to the point.

'So you were here all along?' she asked at last.

He nodded miserably.

'All the time my mother and I were pacing the streets of New Brighton, you were here just across the water?' she repeated numbly.

'I was here,' he agreed. 'I was right across the road in the art shop. It was my uncle's place and he gave me a job when I got back from Italy. Then, when he retired, I bought him out. And I've been here ever since.'

She waited a heartbeat or two, knowing her next words might destroy what little friendship they'd forged. 'My stepfather used to come here, you know, to buy stuff for my mother,' she said at last.

He hesitated, seeming taken aback. 'Is that right?'

'Yes, he came here a lot.'

'That's strange, isn't it? What a coincidence.'

'Yes, and you know what's even stranger? My mother came here once too.' Her tone was accusing. 'She must have seen you.'

He sighed and looked upset.

'She did see you, didn't she?'

He nodded slowly.

'And so? You knew she was here. You must have known about me?'

William tried to calm her. 'Don't blame me, Chiara,' he said in a low voice, moving his head closer to hers. 'It wasn't all my fault.'

She jerked away from him, pulling back her chair so hard its legs made a complaining shriek on the polished concrete floor and the waitress looked up in surprise.

'*Why* wasn't it your fault?' she asked angrily. 'Who else's fault could it have been?'

'Look,' he started to say but right then the waitress came over toting the bill. William pressed his credit card onto her and waved her away. 'Look, she did come here that one time, you're right. It was awful. I don't know who was the most shocked, your mother or me.'

'And so?' Chiara prompted.

'She told me about you, of course she did. She showed me the wedding ring on her finger and told me she'd found you a wonderful father. She was fierce and angry. She hardly gave me a chance to speak. And she certainly didn't want me to be part of her life . . . of either of your lives. She turned on her heel and stalked out of my shop and I never saw her again.'

'And you didn't run after her? Or try to find her?'

'Chiara, I was stunned. Seeing her again was the last thing I'd expected. And I had a wife and two small children. None of them knew about you. Surely you can see how difficult it was for me?'

'All that time,' Chiara said unsteadily, 'you were on one

side of the river and my mother was on the other. Both of you, keeping your secrets. Neither of you giving any thought to what was best for *me*.'

The waitress was back. William signed his name on the chit without bothering to look at it properly. 'That's not fair,' he said, his attention Chiara's again. 'It's not fair to me or your mother. She told me you were both happy without me and I didn't want to ruin that. Would it have made things better for you if you'd known I was here?'

Chiara shrugged. Her face was closed, her mouth a thin line, her eyes stones. 'I think you must be a very weak man,' was all she said.

'Weak? Maybe I am. I've done a lot of things I've regretted. But I don't regret not following Maria Domenica the day she came here. It was too late for us by then. We'd both married other people, we'd both made other lives.'

'And what about me?'

'Yes, I know, I'm sorry. But we have our chance now, don't we? Stay here in Liverpool for a while and let's get to know each other properly. Let's give it a try. I think it's worth it. Don't you?'

Chiara wanted to try. She wanted to fall into his arms and give herself up to him as completely as she had to every other man in her life. But something was holding her back. Perhaps it was loyalty to her mother. Or maybe it was simply that she wasn't sure William Smith could ever be the father she wanted, the one she'd dreamed of and wondered about all those years while she was growing up on the other side of the river.

She shook her head. 'It's not going to be that easy,' she said with some sadness. 'You've known about me for years and done nothing. You can't expect me to be a daughter to you now simply on a whim.'

'Not a whim . . .' he began, but the waitress had brought their jackets and there was no reason for them to stay sitting at their table any longer. Standing up, they let themselves be moved towards the door and said an awkward, chilly goodbye on the street.

'Will I see you again?' William asked almost desperately.

'Yes, but I don't know when,' Chiara replied truthfully, taking a step or two back from his attempt at an encircling arm.

'Don't walk away from me like this,' her father pleaded.

Chiara nearly surrendered. Then she pictured her mother running down Bold Street knowing she'd finally found her William but that it was too late. She hardened towards the tall, tired-looking man standing before her.

'Please don't expect too much of me.' She nodded towards the darkened windows of Liverpool Art Supplies. 'I know where you are now. I'll be in touch, I'll see you again . . . just give me some time.'

As she left him and walked down the busy city streets in search of a taxi, Chiara felt exhausted, sad and still a little angry, but mostly she felt lonely. Somehow she'd imagined meeting William Smith would feed the part of her that had been empty since her mother had died, that finding him would fill her up. Now the promise of him had gone and she felt emptier than ever.

She wanted to run away from Liverpool, leave the city and this stranger who was her father far behind her. For a second or two she thought she was going to cry. Then her mind seemed to clear and she realized there was only one place she truly longed to be. A place where she knew in her heart she could expect nothing less than the warm, safe feeling of a proper homecoming.

24

With a wide-brimmed straw hat covering her dark hair, Harriet looked perfectly at ease sitting at the long table beneath the lemon tree. There was a fat baby boy on her knee and a wine glass in her hand and perhaps there were some tired lines in the corners of her eyes that hadn't been there a few months before.

'Come on, Chiara, I'm starving to death here. Hurry up,' she called into the kitchen.

Erminio, understanding the sense of what she'd said if not the words, laughed with her approvingly and patted his round belly.

There was going to be a wedding. All the most important people in her life would be there and today Chiara was making a long, late lunch for them in her grandmother's kitchen.

A seafood soup to start, stained with squid ink and tomatoes and swimming with shellfish and tentacles. Alex looked dubious at the sight of it but Franco encouraged him to spoon a little into his mouth and then he said he didn't mind it too much at all.

There was going to be a wedding and everyone seemed happy.

It was only just springtime but Chiara had insisted it was warm enough to eat outside. She'd spread a red-and-white checked cloth over the wooden table and covered it with baskets of Pepina's golden bread and jugs of her nearly black wine.

Her grandmother had refused to let her cook alone and shadowed her in the kitchen, nudging her with an old cook's deft hand if she thought Chiara was pouring too little oil into the frying pan or being too sparing with the salt.

This was how Chiara loved to cook, carelessly with a pinch of this and a drizzle of that. Who cared if these dishes never tasted exactly the same way again? This was food for now, for the people out there gathered in the dusty courtyard, the only people she truly cared about.

Harriet had come alone to San Giulio. 'Eduardo's looking after The Office,' she'd declared. Chiara had thought she'd detected a tiny note of disenchantment in her voice but not pushed her any further.

As for Alex, he had been overcome to be here, in the home Maria Domenica had kept hidden from him, meeting the family he'd always wondered about. He was stiff with shyness but, sensing his discomfort, Franco hovered by his side, offering friendship and kindness in equal measure.

Chiara had considered sending an invitation to William Smith, but in the end it hadn't been posted and she didn't regret it. William didn't belong here. Maybe one day she'd be ready to let him join the others at her table but not yet. He still felt like a stranger and this was about family.

'Here we go, eat, eat,' she told Harriet as she put a bowl in front of her. 'But don't eat too much of that bread. Remember we have lots more food to come. There are tender, young broad beans with warmed goat's cheese and a dish of broccoli smothered with hot chilli and garlic. There are artichokes braised with tiny new potatoes and there is chicken stewed with white wine, lemon juice and sage leaves. And then we'll take a little rest and maybe a stroll in the orchard before we finish our lunch with a bittersweet chocolate and almond tart and, to help you digest, perhaps a glass or two of my grandmother's homemade *limoncello*, which will be *bellissimo*.'

She kissed the tips of her fingers as she had seen her

grandfather do so many times and smiled at the sight of her guests lining the table and breathing the scented steam of her seafood soup.

Before she returned to the heat of the kitchen to fetch more food, Chiara couldn't resist pausing and leaning down to kiss the back of a smooth male neck, breathing in a now familiar bitter, roasted smell and brushing silver-tipped hair with her cheek as she pulled away.

Giovanni turned and looked up at her. '*Bella*, do you need any help in there?' he asked, the corners of his mouth crinkling in a smile.

'No, no, you stay there. I'm cooking this meal.'

'At least let me help you carry the heavy things from the kitchen.' He caught Chiara's hand and pulled her back towards him for another kiss.

There was going to be a wedding. She and Giovanni would stand together and say their vows in the crumbling white church in the piazza and then afterwards they'd eat their wedding breakfast in Caffe Angeli.

It was there that friendship had turned to love for them one afternoon as they sat on the red banquette beneath the watchful eyes of the Madonna with her mother's face. They'd eaten ice cream, drunk the inevitable coffee and talked for hours. And Chiara had realized that passion didn't always come first. Sometimes, just as her kitchen worker white arms had been turned slowly to caramel by a summer's worth of sunshine, love could deepen gradually.

And it could fade too, as fast as a summer tan, when the clouds came.

Protective of the fragile new feelings that lay between them, Chiara had offered to slip on a starched white apron and find her future behind the ageing Gaggia and the worn, stainless steel counter. Her fingers would work the levers Maria Domenica's hands had once touched and, at the end of the day, she'd wipe down the tables, stack the chairs and sweep the floor, as she and Giovanni exchanged nuggets of the day's gossip.

'But what about your career?' he had argued. 'You've worked so hard to become a success, you can't give it up now.'

'I could still cook,' she'd pointed out. 'And I suppose I could still write books. Maybe I won't be so famous any more, but I was never in it for the fame anyway, only the food.'

Giovanni had doubted her. Glancing over at his father pottering behind the counter, he had offered with only half his heart to follow her to London. 'Surely I'd find a job in some restaurant or *caffe*? We could make it work.'

They'd talked about it for days, trying to find a future that could work for both of them, until late one sun-warmed winter afternoon when they'd hung the closed sign on the door of Caffe Angeli and escaped to her grandparents' farm to sit beneath the peach trees.

The farm had already begun its slow, steady slide back to disrepair. Some of Paolo's cabins had started to lean at crazy angles very early on and Erminio had declared them unsafe for human habitation. Paolo had tried to argue but before he knew it, Pepina's chickens had commandeered one of the cabins and a cock crowed lustily from its crooked windows all day, reminding everyone of Giacomo Salerni's shortcomings as a builder.

When Pepina took to storing the overflow of her jars of pickles and preserves in some of the other cabins, Paolo hadn't put up much of a fight. The stream of tourists had slowed to a trickle by then and Chiara suspected that as her fame faded it might dry up altogether. There were so many other cooking schools, smarter and better run in much more beautiful locations, surely people would prefer to go to them. The cabins would topple over eventually and the peach trees would spread their branches over the ruins and life would continue in its slow steady way. Rosaria would eat her way fat again, Pepina and Erminio would take shaky steps through their old age, and only Paolo's sulky dissatisfaction would sour their days.

As she lay on her back, gazing at the patches of blue sky through the lace of branches, Chiara realized this was where she wanted to be.

'I want to stay here,' she told Giovanni, 'not just for you but for my grandparents and for Franco too. And yes, for myself as well, I suppose. I'm closer to my mother here. I feel like I know her at last.'

Still Giovanni asked her every day, 'Are you sure this is where you want to be?'

And every day she said to him with still more certainty, 'Yes, I'm sure.'

Now, as she darted in and out of Pepina's kitchen, serving up platters of spring vegetables, she watched Giovanni eat. His head was bent over his plate as he dipped a hunk of bread into his soup, swirled it around and took a bite with relish. He caught her stare. 'It's delicious,' he told her, fishing a clam shell from the soup and tipping its meat and liquid into his mouth with greedy pleasure. 'Everything is completely delicious.' And her heart filled with a fierce love for him.

The music of eating rose up from the table – a percussion of cutlery on plates, a chorus of appreciative murmurs. Chiara took her seat, picked up her spoon and looked around her.

She longed to photograph the scene or make a drawing of it as her mother might have, so she could remember this time for ever: Pepina scolding greedy Erminio for stealing food from her plate; Franco and Alex, faces flushed, clinking red wine glasses; Harriet kissing the top of her baby's head.

Paolo and Rosaria were seated at the far end of the table, wearing their best faces. When they thought no one was paying attention they bickered quietly between themselves. Chiara had come to see her aunt and cousin through Giovanni's eyes at last and knew them for what they were: greedy, self-serving, not to be trusted. And yet they were still family and she was soft-hearted enough to think they deserved a place at her table among the others.

Chiara's eyes swept the scene once more as she raised her spoon to her mouth. 'All of my happiness is here,' she startled herself by saying out loud.

Giovanni glanced over, raised an eyebrow and smiled.

'Well, it is,' she said indignantly, as he ruffled her spiky hair with a gentle hand, 'and I don't see that there's anything wrong with that.'

In the distance she could see storm clouds gathering and there was a faint rumble of thunder, but above their heads the sky was still clear and blue. It would be dark by the time the storm hit them, and she and Giovanni would be safely inside their rented cottage, warming each other's bodies in bed, as they listened to the drumming rhythm of torrents of rain, washing clean the terracotta-tiled roof.